Déjà Vu
All Over Again

Déjà Vu
All Over Again

Bil Holton

Liberty Publishing Group
Durham, North Carolina

This book is a work of fiction. Names, characters, places, and incidents are the product of the author's imagination or are used fictitiously. Any resemblance to actual events, locales, or persons, living or dead, is coincidental.

Requests for permission, as well as to schedule Bil Holton for speaking engagements, may be addressed to:

Liberty Publishing Group
Attn: Author, Bil Holton
1405 Autumn Ridge Drive
Durham, NC 27712

ISBN: 978-1-893095-96-0
Library of Congress Control Number: 2017914342

*Dedicated to strong women everywhere, who have the
courage to follow their passion and stand up
for what they believe, regardless of the odds . . .
and to my amazing wife, Cher, the love of my life
and the strongest, most incredibly resourceful, and
forward-thinking woman I know!*

Preface

This book, while it stands on its own, is the sequel to my previous book entitled *Silent Echoes*. (Warning: This Preface is a spoiler alert for those who haven't read *Silent Echoes*.) I want to give you enough 'catch-up' information in this Preface to add the needed clarity to enjoy this sequel—without revealing too much prequel plotting and intrigue for those who want to read it later. For those who have read *Silent Echoes*, however, you will discover delightful nuances throughout this sequel that will be especially meaningful to you.

Silent Echoes describes Monica Pitt's extraordinary discovery that she is the clone of a young woman named Monica Proxmire. Her quest to fully understand her horrible predicament and expose the highly organized and well-monied malefactors who are operating cloning factories all over the world to provide body parts for the rich and affluent puts her life and those close to her in danger—and in some cases result in tragic deaths. Her search for truth leads her to the highest levels of America's government.

What she finds shocks her and eventually sends her into hiding to save her life—and the lives of those she loves. What she discovers in *Silent Echoes* serves as the incredible backdrop for this follow-up suspense novel. Monica has fled to Paris, changed her name to Gabby Garceau, and gone off the grid. But she is still haunted by the evil actions of the corrupt Life Extension Institute, and she feels driven to bring them down, once and for all!

You will find many plot twists in this novel that keep you guessing, as her highly probable story comes to such an unexpected dramatic conclusion you will find yourself wondering—is this really fiction or is it fact?

Cast of Characters
(including the name changes created to protect identities)

Monica Pitt (aka Gabby Garceau, aka Alexa Rousseau) – The young woman we first met in *Silent Echoes*, who discovers she is a clone. Her search for truth leads her to a global conspiracy created to clone people for body parts, with ties to the highest levels of government. As those closest to her begin dying, Monica runs for her life to Paris, France, taking on a new identity as Gabby Garceau. But the horror continues to haunt her, and with the help of a handsome Parisian counterintelligence officer, she decides to bring down the Life Extension Institute of Geneva.

Andre Bordeaux (aka Andre Rousseau) – The well-connected counterintelligence operative who leads a crack team of highly competent, covert operatives across two continents to bring a mammoth corporation to its knees.

Agent Brian Cramer – The CIA special ops agent who pursues Monica Pitt and then has a crisis of conscience which puts him at odds with the very government that sponsored his covert operation.

Agent Sergio Rodriguez (aka Warren Schmidt) – A rogue CIA agent who mutates into a monstrous hit man, and takes way too much pleasure in his kills.

Eleanor Franklin (aka Lisa Archibald) – The aristocratic Deputy Assistant Secretary of Health and Human Services who gets caught up in the corrupt human cloning drama and finds that her elite status has been compromised.

Frank Marino – One of Andre's dedicated teammates who provides a safe haven for the human xerography-busters.

Rita, Jack, and Hank – Three of Andre's crack team of under-cover agents, who willingly volunteered to put their lives at risk for their friend and colleague.

Michael Marino – Frank's father, a retired Colonel now fortuitously working as Director of Emergency Services at New York-Presbyterian Hospital.

Paul Marino – Frank's brother and gourmet chef, who keeps everyone well fed at Zeus' Den while they fight for justice.

Caleb Latourelle – a courageous reporter with *The New York Times*, who bit off more than he could chew with this story.

Marge Henry (aka Marge Proxmire) – Monica Pitt's devoted mother, who suffers a near-fatal car crash which saves her life.

Sandra Henry (aka Simone Bardot) – Widow of Senator Carlton Henry (whom we met in *Silent Echoes*), who discovers her daughter is also a clone. She risks her life to protect her daughter, Peaches, and the other victims of this travesty.

Monica (Peaches) Henry (aka Sophie Bardot) – Sandra's daughter, (also a clone of Monica Proxmire) and the young woman who helps hold the protected witnesses together.

Emma Cody (aka Emma Carlyle) – The mother of deceased Monica Proxmire, who knows what it's like to lose a daughter and find her again in the person of Monica Pitt. She finds herself in the middle of a dangerous covert operation.

POTUS – The self-aggrandizing Chief Executive of the United States who takes his maniacal aim at Monica Pitt to new lows to eliminate her as a threat. He vows to end her mission for good, and is willing to use all the resources of the Federal Government to do it.

Chapter One

Are you sure that's her?" barked the President of the United States, his frustration level clearly at its limit.

"We think so. Well, we're almost sure!" came the agent's hurried reply.

"What do you mean almost?"

"Sir, we're waiting on Agent Brian Cramer. He's been the senior agent since we've begun this initiative and he's the one who saw her three years ago in Baltimore before she vanished. He was assigned to clean up the Senator Henry problem. Remember?" Agent Rodriguez answered mechanically.

I'm not believing you forgot it was Agent Cramer who found the subject's tape player by Senator Henry's phone and the note she left you about your role in the human xerography affair, Agent Rodriguez said to himself.

"Yes, yes. I remember," POTUS raised his voice agitatedly. "What's his ETA?"

"We're expecting him any moment."

"Good. This has been drawn out much too long! I can't believe she's outwitted the most powerful security agency in the world."

Agent Rodriguez's silence punctuated their mutual agitation.

"Rodriguez, are you there?"

"Yes, sir."

"I can't express to you how important her capture is to the security of this country. So, for Christ's sake, it's got to happen today!" the President huffed his frustration, filling the phone connection with an air of sanctimonious combustibility.

POTUS remembered the difficulties his covert team had experienced this past three years locating the pesky woman who discovered his role in the illegal human cloning enterprise. His special ops teams had managed to keep a lid on her discovery, but now everyone recognized the need to eliminate the source of the leak.

Agent Rodriguez remained calm and professional as he fielded POTUS's vocal ballistics.

"You've made sure the CIA and FBI aren't aware of this," the President confirmed rhetorically, as he moved through his mental checklist.

"Yes, sir. Absolutely. They aren't aware of our covert activities. As you know, those two agencies have always been inept. We have remained—and will remain—invisible as always," Agent Rodriguez answered from his secure line.

I'm amazed myself at how a woman untrained in espionage tactics and counter-intelligence could have dodged our worldwide net, Agent Rodriguez thought, sharply conscious of their inability to silence her.

"Good. Good. I'm counting on that!" POTUS replied softly. "Where are you?"

"We're at the Walgreens on Peachtree Road, Northeast in Atlanta. We haven't taken our eyes off her for a minute."

"Is she alone?"

"No, sir. She's with an older woman. It looks like they're picking up prescriptions."

"Does the older woman look familiar?" the President asked with quiet vehemence.

"Yes, sir. I believe she's Carlton Henry's widow, Sandra Henry. The younger woman looks older than Mrs. Henry's daughter, Monica Henry, so I don't think she's her daughter. And the young woman's hair color's different. She's a blonde now and not a brunette," Agent Rodriguez volleyed his assumption.

Agent Rodriguez was on the team who found Senator Henry slumped in his chair in his home office after committing suicide over his culpability in the human cloning project was discovered.

They had pitched his suicide as his highly emotional reaction to an incurable terminal illness diagnosis, so the public could sympathize with his decision to spare his family months of home hospice care-giving as they watched him die.

"So, we may be looking at the long lost Monica Pitt!" POTUS presumed, cracking an automatic smile the agent couldn't see over the phone.

"Could very well be, sir. We'll know when Cramer gets here," he chorused, alluding to his earlier statement.

"Let me know when she's in custody. I'll be expecting your call back momentarily."

"Roger that, sir."

"Oh, ah. If that shouldn't be her, I want you to take the two of them to the bunker for questioning. They've got to know where Pitt is, assuming that's not Pitt with her. I'm all out of patience when it comes to this Pitt woman. Do you get my drift?" the President spoke emphatically, as a roguish smile creased his drawn face.

"Yes, sir."

"Oh, and one more thing. It's time we changed our tactics with Mrs. Henry. The only reason she hasn't had a convenient accident is because I believe she's in constant contact with Pitt. It's time we got a little unpleasant, don't you think? If the young woman isn't Pitt, she's probably the senator's daughter. Use her daughter's continued welfare as leverage to get the mother to talk. When we terminate Pitt, we'll silence those two as well. If it is Pitt, you're no doubt familiar with the project's complete termination plan."

"You mean *Déjà vu Down*, sir?" the agent verified.

"That's the one," POTUS confirmed sarcastically.

"I've been fully briefed, sir; look forward to carrying it out,"

"Call me when Agent Cramer identifies Pitt and then call me again when you've convinced Mrs. Henry it's in her best interests to insure her daughter's safety."

"I serve at the pleasure of the President."

* * * * * *

Their sportive tussle with provisional foreplay complete, the soft collision of their flesh heightened their desire for one another.

Gabby's hands, automatically solicitous, left imprints of her long fingernails on his back and arms. She moved restlessly under him, welcoming his caresses and kisses that bathed her body with a mixture of gentleness and passion.

His passion mirrored her constant stirring and her self-absorbed groaning was unabated, calling for him to complete what they had started.

"I love you," she cooed, "I love you so much!"

Andre hungrily reciprocated by ravaging her mouth passionately, almost savagely, knowing she would not want him to stop.

She moved her eager hands up to his shoulders and increased her grip around his neck, pulling him closer to her, so he could not stop.

"I love … how … you love me," Gabby whispered breathily, enjoying the rhythm they'd established.

"You're so beautiful, Babe," Andre said softly, as he upped the intensity of their encounter.

She adored the teasing punishment he so freely and expertly gave, and submitted willingly to his sensual inquisition. She surrendered to the drug of the rapturous desire they had created as a loving couple.

"Yes, yes … Yes! Yes! Oh, yes … yesssss," she trailed, realizing that their mutual bliss had completely engulfed her. Her mouth eased open in unuttered confirmation of absolute elation. The intoxication of ecstasy had found her.

Andre released a deep breath, recognizing their timing had been perfect.

"I love making love to you," he confessed joyfully. "We are so good together."

Gabby smiled her agreement, pulling his face down to hers for another kiss that had been temporarily deferred.

"Let's stay here forever," came her kittenish petition, as she impulsively let out a lengthy sigh of satisfaction.

Andre nodded his agreement and gave her thighs a playful squeeze, a little squeeze, the pressure of complicity, before he repositioned himself beside her so that his arm was extended under the pillow that cushioned her neck.

"Wherever we are, whatever we're doing will have a foreverness to it," he consented, as she turned on her side toward him and caressed his chiseled stomach and chest before waltzing her fingers along his neck and cheeks.

"I believe that too," she whispered softly, "It's as if we've always been together."

He kissed her forehead through her bangs and held his lips there to emphasize his affection before caressing her shoulder with his free hand.

Gabby's hand moved across his chest to the scars on his abdomen that retailed the three bullet wounds he had received in Afghanistan when he was in special forces. The scars were inches apart and formed a triangle. They had healed nicely but showed the permanent marks that bullet wounds do to flesh as reminders of the effects of the life and death nature of combat.

"I'm glad these didn't take you before I met you," Gabby admitted tenderly, as her index finger traced each bullet scar.

"Me, too," he agreed, enjoying her soft, methodical, long-nailed patronage.

"You could have been killed," she pouted, as the words fell out of her mouth before she realized where she had gone with the afterplay.

"It was the nature of my business then—and now," he reported almost mechanically as he reached down to caress her hand before he brought her fingers to his mouth to kiss them. "Besides that was six years ago and the last year of my tour of duty."

"And now you're with the French National Police," Gabby stated the obvious, purposefully updating the conversation.

"Yes, and I love my consultant role," he admitted, thinking to himself, *I need to tell her about my Directorate connection, but not now!* "But I'm not expecting to be on the business end of hostile fire these days," he interjected as he used his index finger to playfully poke Gabby in her ribs to mimic bullet wounds.

"Stop. Stop," Gabby mimicked counterfeit protests, as she tried to keep his teasing fingers from her tickle zone. All she could do now was laugh her protests as he accelerated his playful probes.

"You know I'm really ticklish there ... you heathen ... I ... you ...," she testified joyfully, grabbing his finger to prevent another laughing spree.

"You mean here?" Andre teased, pushing his finger toward her ribs. "And here?" he repeated. "And there!"

Gabby squealed her delight and at the same time tried her best to censor his tickle attack.

"Stop ... Stop. I mean it now," she said breathily. "You're so bad. Don't you have a flight to catch?"

Andre allowed her to place his hand on her cheek.

"Why, Gabby Garceau. It sounds like you want to redirect my energies," he said, raising his eyebrows.

He leaned down toward her and kissed her softly on her nose and then on her lips.

"I'd rather keep my poking energies intact," he mused, faking another assault on her tickle zone.

"Don't you dare," Gabby howled. "I'm all poked out, and if you'd poked your head at the clock on the nightstand, you'd have seen you've got to get ready for your four o'clock flight."

He smiled his corroboration.

"Yes, I know, Babe," he surrendered as he sat up on the bed.

"I don't want you to go," Gabby pouted.

"I don't like leaving you either."

She eased herself up and used her pillows to cushion her against the headboard without pulling the sheets up to cover her slim, well-proportioned body. The swell of her breasts and the playfulness in her emerald eyes retailed what he would miss when he left for Germany.

* * * * * * *

After she had dropped him off at the Charles De Gaulle Airport, Gabby decided to go to the Louvre Mall to get a take-out order from Jean-Francois Rouquette on 5 Rue de la Paix. It was one of her favorite restaurants next to the Meltem and LeComptoir du Louvre at the Carrousel du Louvre Mall, and had the best burnt eggplant, spring onions and souffléed potatoes in Paris.

"I think we've still got some Riesling at the apartment," she schooled herself. "If not, I'm sure there's a couple of bottles of Chardonnay on the wine rack."

She had developed a taste for wines, but Andre was a connoisseur. In one of their earlier conversations about wines he had described his wine interests and connoisseurship as like graduating from rainbow-colored sprinkled doughnuts to plain croissants. *As your 'pastry palate' develops,* he would muse, *you no longer require confectioner sprinkles to satisfy the palate.*

As she turned her 2016 Citroen SUV into the garage she reminded herself that she would not have to go through the same wine tasting motions as Andre. He would always take the serving temperature seriously and fuss over the proper glassware. And he would sh-sh-sh-swish the wine in his mouth and gurgle and gulp his way to test the wine's virtue.

The only gulping I'm going to do is enjoy each swallow of a completely full glass, she speculated to herself.

Gabby was glad she had chauffeured Andre to the airport in her t-shirt and the jeans with the holes in the knees she had rescued from the flea market. She wouldn't have to change back into them for the rest of the evening. And wearing them now meant there wouldn't be a delay in getting dinner on the TV tray.

She smiled as she found the Riesling in the frig.

"Now, that's what I'm talkin' about," she rejoiced, carefully plucking the chilled bottle out from behind a quart of milk on the top shelf.

She sat on the throw pillow she had placed on the couch to heighten her seating and pulled the TV tray in front of her. Instead of turning on the TV she elected to recruit Alexa, their electronic Echo device to play music.

"Alexa, play *Imagine* by John Lennon."

'*Imagine*, remastered in 2010, by John Lennon.'

As the music played, Gabby thought of her harrowing escape from America to avoid capture by the human xerography traffickers supported by the President and financed by greedy corporations and scores of millionaires and billionaires.

She thought about her name change from Monica Pitt to Gabby Garceau in order to help guarantee her invisibility.

"So many people lost their lives for me," she mourned out loud. "Sarge, Betty, Naomi, the young police officer, two newspaper investigative reporters!" she pined, as the words to the remaster struck her: '*Nothing to kill or die for ... and no religion, too!*'

All of these heinous acts were perpetrated by people who donate to charities and go to church, she retched silently. *I know most people who go to church are good, law abiding people, but these President's men dress for church on Sunday and kill people on Monday, Tuesday ... Wednesday ... everyday!*

"They kill people for a living," she raised her voice. "They've got to be stopped!"

She frowned at her dinner which had been untouched.

"Growing cold, huh!" she fretted the obvious.

The lyric '*No need for greed or hunger*' prompted her to cut a piece of eggplant and stuff it in her mouth. She followed that up with a sip of wine as the lyric '*You may say I'm a dreamer, But I'm not the only one...*' punctuated her melancholy.

"There are good people," she reminded herself.

There's my ex-husband, Jonathan—well, he's sort of good— and Mrs. Cody, and Mrs. Carlton Henry and her daughter, Peaches, who is a clone like me, and my mother, and Dr. Genomé, and Andre, and millions of other people who've never hurt anyone, she reassured herself thoughtfully.

She speared a souffléed potato and did a proper job on it before she migrated to the onions and eggplant again.

The more her thoughts raced, the slower her fork worked: *There are people like Andre who believe this world can be a better place. He's an anti-terrorist consultant. He's in Germany right now as a member of a special counterterrorism task force to share intelligence on how to stop the proliferation of terrorist acts around the world.*

"This world's a crazy place," she said aloud thinking of her own dilemma. "I've got to tell Andre who I really am. That my real name is Monica Pitt. That I'm divorced. That I'm on the run! That he might be in danger."

She took a sip of courage from the almost full wine glass.

"I thought I was hungry," she announced to herself out loud.

A guttural whisper escaped from her lips, "I can't eat and think about those wonderful people who gave their lives for me—for those of us who've been Xeroxed."

She let out a deep breath.

"For those who are being cloned, and those who will be cloned for body parts for the rich."

She picked up the remote for the TV and pointed it at the cable box.

"It's time for the news. I may as well watch France 24," she addressed herself, as she punched the 'ON' button on the remote and closed the lid over the take-out order.

Her trip to the refrigerator to put the food away was interrupted by news of the U.S. President's trip to London to discuss the implications of the latest Internet hacks and data breaches which involved U.S. and UK military systems.

"Oh, I loathe that man," she fumed to herself, sending her disgust at him more ominously than if she had screamed at him face-to-face.

You sanctimonious hypocrite, she thought as she glared at his image on the TV screen before she closed the refrigerator door. Then she stumbled over several angry thoughts before she found one she could use: *How could you have mindlessly killed all of those people?*

"I can't let you do this. When you had that *New York Times* reporter killed, I went into hiding. I thought I wasn't going to be able to do anything to stop you," she said aloud as she inched toward the TV.

The steel in her eyes spoke volumes. Every wrathful curve of her perfectly-formed eyebrows expressed the anger she felt. She leaned next to the screen and poked her index finger at his image.

"I'm not going to run like a scared little girl anymore. I'm coming for you! And this time I'm not going to stop until I expose you and all of the other corrupt policy holders!"

She stood back a half step as the segment ended, but kept her eyes glued to the TV.

"I backed off because I didn't want you to hurt anyone else," she explained, not caring that a commercial had replaced the news.

Then her over-all awareness caught up to her spontaneous tirade and prompted her to turn off the TV.

She thought to herself, *Sometimes, if you're not careful, the inhuman stuff that goes on in the world can get you really depressed.* She looked at the multi-colored koosh ball lying on the couch. It was the one Andre and she had used to take turns tossing into one of his boots the week before. They had placed the boot in the middle of the living room floor and had taken turns tossing the koosh like a mini basketball. Surprisingly, she was the one who made the 'boot basket' first, to Andre's consternation and delight. *I don't want to adult today! I'd rather let my inner child out!*

She tossed the remote on her napkin on the coffee table and walked over to Andre's sport shirt he had laid over the arm of the couch.

"When you get back from Germany on Friday, I'm going to tell you everything," she declared. "And I hope you'll still love me once you know the real me!"

* * * * * * *

"Good afternoon, sir," Agent Cramer said evenly. "It wasn't the Pitt woman. It was Henry's wife and daughter."

"You're wrong about that," POTUS responded dryly.

"Sir?"

"It's not a good afternoon."

"No, sir. It's not!" Agent Cramer confirmed, catching his drift. "Anyway, we're headed toward the bunker," he announced. "I can assure you we'll put the necessary pressure on Carlton's widow, so she'll want to keep her daughter safe."

"Good. Let me know the results. Oh, and I'm also giving you the green light on the other two women and Pitt's husband."

"The other two women. Sir?"

"Yes. The Cody woman and Pitt's mother. I think it's about time we get tough with all of them," POTUS trumpeted, speaking so the agitation was clearly evident in his voice.

"Copy that, sir."

"Pitt's been silent for three years and I don't believe she's going to let this go," POTUS interjected solemnly. "She's got something planned, and that's what's worrying me."

"Sir, our worldwide net is tightening. It may look like she's vanished on the surface, but our operatives are everywhere and have ears in key places and in key organizations. She's made mistakes and they'll come back to haunt her. I can assure you," Agent Cramer's tone expressed his desire to put the President at ease.

"As long as her mistakes haunt her and not us," POTUS hissed.

"I'll stake my reputation on it, sir. We'll neutralize her before she even becomes a blip on the radar."

"I'm holding you to that Agent Cramer, and Agent Rodriguez as well. You're supposed to be the best. So, I think it's time you proved it. Show me how good you are at finding a needle in a global haystack."

"I serve at the pleasure of the President, sir!" came Agent Cramer's quick reply.

He was used to orders from obnoxious superiors and had enough military and covert ops experience to see threats like this as harmless as flies. It was important for him to succeed in any mission assigned to him, but he knew he'd land on his feet regardless of the obstacles he faced. He was from a multi-generational military family and knew he had built-in survival instincts in his DNA.

"You'll apprise me of your 'chat' with Carlton's widow?"

"Yes, sir. As soon as we're done."

"Good."

Agent Cramer heard the click which signaled the end of the phone connection and smiled to himself.

The old boy is becoming unglued, he mused to himself and then shifted his train of thought. *However he is the President and it's my duty to serve him regardless of how I feel about him.*

His thoughts were interrupted by Agent Rodriguez who had just entered the field office.

"She's ready. Her daughter's in interrogation room #2."

Agent Cramer looked up and motioned for Rodriguez to close the door.

"Sergio, the President's getting really antsy and wants this thing to end. I'm concerned that he will make mistakes that will compromise our ability to help him."

Agent Rodriguez lowered his eyebrows and moved his head slightly to his left, in anticipation for what Agent Cramer was going to say next.

"You're as focused on this Pitt thing as I am, so I know you want resolution sooner than later too," Agent Cramer continued. "And I can't blame POTUS. I'm surprised we haven't found her yet."

"She's the luckiest woman I've ever seen," agreed Agent Rodriguez.

"Well, we've got to see that her luck runs out. And if it is luck, it *will* run out! When we agreed to take this assignment, we both joined the network of policy holders so we could ensure that our families would have perfect donors for body parts if they needed them. It's as much in our interests as it is POTUS's to put an end to the Pitt threat."

Agent Rodriguez tightened his lips and nodded in agreement.

"And it sounded really good at the time," he said as he followed up on his nod. "I wanted to protect my family, and I still do! I didn't think it would turn out like this, but I'm not ready to surrender the best whole life health insurance policy my family's ever had—or ever will have!"

"I know. I know," Agent Cramer repeated. "I feel the same way. And I'm sure the other team members do too."

His colleague nodded his agreement again.

"So, we've got to close the lid on this and close it for good!" Agent Cramer noted anxiously, feeling his way around his collusion.

"So POTUS has given us the green light?" Agent Rodriguez surmised.

"Yes, and it appears we can do anything we want to do to terminate the Pitt threat."

"I'm all for that," Agent Rodriguez responded, knowing they'd done more already than the covert ops team they replaced eighteen months ago.

A slippery smile formed on Agent Cramer's face as he extended his arm and gave Rodriguez a pat on the shoulder.

"Let's see how much fear his widow can take. We'll even add a little pain to make sure we have her attention."

Both men smiled at each other as they started down the hallway toward the interrogation room.

Chapter Two

"Hi, Mother. You're calling me a little earlier this month. Is everything all right?"

"Well, I'm not sure, Monica. Oh, I still can't get used to calling you without knowing where you are," Marge replied fretfully.

Gabby smiled her understanding, but the geography of her face changed quickly. She hadn't told anyone about her name change for their protection as well as her own.

"Mother, you're calling me on your burner phone, aren't you?"

"Yes, Dear. I know how important that is! And I make sure I'm at the hair salon so I can call you. Sharon lets me keep my vanity pack in her locker so it's there when I'm here. She doesn't know I have a phone in it. I go into the restroom to call you. That's where I'm calling from now."

"Good. You mustn't ever forget. Okay? Your life depends on it!"

Oh. mom. I worry so much about you doing this, and yet I want to know how you're doing, Gabby thought to herself, fully understanding the implications of a slip-up.

"I know, Honey," her mother assured her, "I'm calling because I haven't heard from Sandra or her Monica this week. We chit chat every week just to touch base and make sure each other's okay. I'm a little worried."

"I'm sure she's okay, Mother. Monica's minoring in the performing arts and she's the lead in a play, so Mrs. Henry's probably busy with costumes and trips back and forth to school."

"I know. I know. I thought about that, but it's not like her not to call. She's a stickler for detail and punctuality. Honey, I'm worried. I wouldn't have called you if I didn't think it was important," Marge elaborated, not sure what Monica could do about it, because she didn't know where Monica was.

Her voice sounded weak and unsteady, almost raspy as apprehension pinched her throat.

Conscious of her mother's tension, Gabby hoped to diffuse it by remaining calm herself.

"Mom, why don't you give it a couple more days and see... No, wait. Why don't you call her. The phone works both ways you know!"

"I did call her, Honey. I've called her twice today. I'm telling you it's not like her not to call back!"

"Okay. Look. Let's assume you two will connect sometime today and you'll discover that everything's all right. Okay?"

When her mother didn't respond, Gabby repeated her question.

"Okay?"

"Okaaay," Marge replied pensively. "But I won't feel settled until I hear from her."

"I understand, mom. Now let's talk about you for a bit. Okay?"

She took her mother's silence as confirmation that it was okay to change the subject.

"Besides being concerned for Mrs. Henry and Peaches, how have you been?"

"Well, Honey, I've been fine. As you know, on the 20th I'll be celebrating three years of sobriety."

"I know, mom. And that's absolutely wonderful. I'm so proud of you!"

"I'm proud of me, too!"

"It takes considerable courage and determination to be able to put that kind of addiction behind you."

"Yep! It takes more willpower than won't power!" Marge triumphed.

"And it takes a classy lady to be able to do that!" Gabby celebrated, knowing how her mother had struggled for years to beat alcoholism.

"Well, I don't know about classy. You're the only one whose ever called me classy. But I like the sound of it! Thank you, Honey."

"You deserve that status, Mother. I love you."

"I love you, too!"

Gabby was going to say something about her renewed intentions to follow through on closing down the human xerography affair, but decided to wait for a better time since her mother was worried about Sandra and Peaches.

"Mother."

"Yes, Dear."

"Even though you've called me a little early, I still want you to call at our regularly scheduled time this month, so we can stay on schedule. Okay?"

"Of course, Dear. I was hoping you'd say that. I'd like to call when I hear from Sandra. Is that Okay?"

"Absolutely! And if she calls me before she calls you, I'll ask her to call you. How 'bout that?"

"Thank you. I'd like that very much."

"Oh, Honey. Have you heard from Emma?"

"Yes. Just like clockwork. She's fine and tells me she enjoys talking with you, too. She's just started taking a water color class and loves it."

"Oh, good for her. She hasn't told me about it yet."

"She just started it," Gabby repeated. "I'm sure she'll tell you all about it."

"That woman keeps real busy. She's always doing something," Marge said admiringly.

"That's something you might try," Gabby offered, hoping her mother would not take offense at her suggestion.

"Aw, no, Honey. I don't have an artistic bone in my body."

"Of course you do. Everybody does. It just looks like it's something you may not be interested in," Gabby spoke softly, wanting to communicate the polite acceptance of her mother's hesitation to try something new.

"But I am still interested in you know what! And so are the others. Monica. We all want to know where you are and what kind of life you have. Are you working? Of course, you're working," she corrected herself. "Are you happy? Do you have someone special? You are divorced, you know. Will we ever see you again? Can you let us know if you're close? Can we send you birthday gifts and 'just because' cards?" Marge petitioned, knowing what her daughter's answer would be.

"Oh, Mother. I wish I could tell you—all of you—where I am and what I'm doing. We've talked about this how many times before? I can't tell you for your own safety. What you don't know, you can't tell! I'm doing it for your own protection! Someday, when this is all over, we'll be back together again!"

"I know, Honey. But I just had to ask. It's so hard not seeing you, and holding you, and being more a part of your life, and ..." Marge missed the next couple of words, letting her emotions over-take her.

"I'm sorry, Mother. It's got to be this way for a little longer," Gabby answered in a level voice.

"How much longer?" her mother agonized.

"I don't know. Don't ask me to put a date on it. But soon! I promise you it will be soon!" Gabby assured her, trying her best to sound confident and assured.

She heard her mother breathe heavily through her end of the connection.

"I promise you, Mother. Okay?"

"Okay."

"Let's not end our call like this," Gabby announced, wanting to resuscitate their conversation.

"I agree, Honey."

"Mother. I love you and look forward to the day when we can be together without a care in the world."

"I love you, too, Monica. And that day can't come soon enough."

"Call me when you know something."
"I will, Honey. Be careful."
"I'm always careful. Bye!"
"Bye, Honey."

* * * * * * *

"Sir, we're convinced she's telling the truth," Agent Cramer explained, speaking professionally and unperturbed.

The President huffed his disappointment.

"You're absolutely sure about that?" he asked resolutely.

"Yes, sir. We've grilled her for over five hours. She didn't show any of the tells she would have shown if she were holding out on us. Believe me, we would know!"

"I'm going to ask again. You are convinced without a doubt that she hasn't heard from Pitt?" POTUS echoed, with a marked undercurrent of capitulated irritation.

"Absolutely. We broke her and put the fear of God in her. We made it very clear that her daughter's life depended on what she told us today. We even brought her daughter into her mother's interrogation room and threatened to cut off her daughter's finger if we felt she was lying. And believe me, we would have if we had a half ounce of doubt."

The agent's cold objectivity and reputation as a top notch interrogator softened the President's sullen disposition.

"And, sir," Agent Cramer continued, "Her house, phones, computer and car have been taped for years. Her mail is continually under surveillance. There is no indication she's communicated with Pitt at any time. And neither has her daughter. We've had constant surveillance on the others too. Everything they do is recorded."

"What do you suggest we do?" POTUS asked, realizing Agent Cramer would modify established protocols if he deemed it necessary.

"Sir, we're going to chat with the other two as well. Once they know we've stepped up our eavesdropping one or more of them will make a mistake. Our leverage is they'll want to ensure each other's safety without risking their own safety. And quite frankly, we do have a couple of 'expendable cards' to play to tighten the squeeze," Agent Cramer volunteered mechanically.

"What do you mean?" POTUS quizzed, sounding very interested.

"Pitt's ex-husband and the Cody woman are expendable. There's nothing in the wire taps in their places that suggest they've been in communication with Pitt, but we could do without each of them and use their sudden deaths as a warning to the others. Their departures would also reduce our over-all 'loose end' liability without jeopardizing the leverage we have over the others."

"Just a minute. Let me think about what you're suggesting," the President's levity was unmistakable. "I like the way you think Agent Cramer. You not only have my approval. You have my blessing. That should bring Pitt out of the hole she's crawled into."

"We'll move on that right away, sir."

"Good. Keep me appraised."

* * * * * * *

"Babe, I could have picked you up," Gabby pouted good-naturedly.

"We got back earlier than expected and Pete brought me home," Andre replied, dropping his gear inside the doorway and pulling Gabby toward him.

Each of them were acutely aware of the other's eagerness as they sealed their longing embrace with a lengthy kiss.

She was dressed in her favorite jeans, the ones with the holes in the knees, and her low cut blouse showed she was braless as usual. Her perfume complimented her over-all sexuality and her body warmth was all he needed to feel at home.

"I'm so glad your trip went so well," Gabby congratulated Andre, as she pulled back a little to allow him to take his jacket off.

"Yes, it did. It actually went very well. There were agents from seventeen countries, as I mentioned yesterday on the phone, and we had one of the most meaningful discussions we've ever had on counterterrorist surveillance tactics. We've got a long way to go, of course, but there seems to be a concerted effort to improve intra-agency and intra-governmental cooperation," he explained, as he freed his tired feet from his boots.

"It would be nice if their cooperation extended to freezing financial assets and putting more boots on the ground," Gabby added, trying to sound official.

Andre raised his eyebrows and nodded his agreement.

"Yes, we're making some headway in the terrorist-occupied territories. The airstrikes aren't the complete answer, but we're beginning to cripple them militarily and financially. It's the soft targets we worry about. They're the ones the homegrown lone wolves and small groups of radicalized insurgents target," he elaborated, realizing they had had this conversation before.

"My trip went well," he repeated. "How about your root canal recovery?" he queried, knowing how much she hated going to dentists, let alone endodontists.

"Okay, actually. It was a bit unnerving, but it was the best experience I've had at repairing my teeth."

"You know, Babe, that's the whole purpose of going to an endodontist. It's meant to be an *unnerving* experience!" he teased, showing his patented levity.

Gabby laughed, "You know, you're exactly right. It was an unnerving experience. You're so clever."

"Just wanting to keep the memory of your experience a good one."

"It definitely was. How 'bout a glass of Chardonnay?" Gabby changed the subject, wanting to move their conversation from 'war talk' and root canals.

"Sounds wonderful, Babe. Give me a minute to get out of these clothes and take a quick shower to wash the trip off. And then I'll be ready for that wine … and an intimate evening with you," he alibied, giving her a quick kiss before heading for the master bedroom.

Abby followed him to the bedroom door. She would normally disrobe and follow him into the shower, but tonight she was trading their lovemaking for a more serious conversation. It would be a conversation that would either strengthen their relationship or end it.

"I got a phone call from Mother while you were gone," Gabby raised her voice to compensate for the distance between them, and to keep a conversation going by reporting news from the States.

"Oh, how is she?" he spoke with his back to her as he peeled himself out of his clothes.

"She's fine," Abby stalled, knowing she was going to explain her mother's call in more detail a little later. "She just wanted to touch base and catch up on what we're doing. She sends you her love."

"I'm sorry that my schedule has been such that we haven't been able to take a trip across the pond to see her," Andre retreated quickly into an excuse, hoping there wasn't a trip to America planned for the near future.

"I know, and that's okay. I've been busy, too, getting my WordPress website up and running. Messing with the themes, plugins and menus is not as much fun as I hoped it would be," Gabby substantiated their mutual busyness.

"I'd like to see her though, when the time is right. We've talked about spending a week or so in the States, so let's see if we can get something planned," he volunteered as he stepped into the bathroom.

"I'd like that," Gabby chorused, watching him open the shower door and start the shower water. She loved how he took care of his body. He had just the right amount of sinew to suggest discipline and invincibility, but not enough to label him as narcissistic. His height and good looks postured him as a man of presidential appearance, accented with an air of homespun wisdom and believability.

"Babe, I'll just be a minute. I'm tired and a hot shower will feel good. I'll be ready for that wine in a little bit. It's so nice to be home again … here … with you!"

Gabby smiled her delight as compassionate gaze met loving admiration.

"Take your time, Hon. The wine will be ready when you are."

"Oh, Babe. Would you throw my towel over the glass stall. I forgot to put it there?"

"Sure," Gabby exclaimed thoughtfully and then decided to be a bit more playful. "Suppose you come out and get the towel!"

"You mean you're going to make me step out of a warm shower and get cold?" he bantered.

"That would be an awful thing to experience. Especially after such a long trip," she goaded him good-naturedly.

"The towel, please!" he conspired cheerfully, planning on a reciprocal surprise.

"Okay. I need to let you shower in peace," she surrendered, as she started to fling the towel over the stall door.

He caught her totally by surprise as he opened the shower door and pulled her into the shower with him.

"Gotcha!" he triumphed joyfully, pulling her to him so that she was soaked from head to foot.

"Andre, I can't believe you did this," Gabby objected, too flabbergasted to be upset. "You heathen! My hair and clothes are drenched!"

"Aw, poor baby! Would you like a towel?" Andre mocked merrily, as he held her, wet blouse and all, next to him.

"You are so beautiful, Babe," he admitted affectionately, moving his gaze from her wet blouse which accentuated the curve of her breasts up to her angelic face that beamed with the joy that comes with being caught completely and endearingly off guard.

Gabby smiled her surrender, forgetting all about her unscheduled baptism as she readied herself for the passionate kiss she knew would personify the love they had for one another.

Andre thoughtfully extinguished the waterfall as they fed on each other, desire meeting desire, affection complementing affection.

After a few moments of mutual caresses, punctuated with kisses and affirmations of mutual devotion, Andre announced the obvious.

"Babe, let's get you out of those wet clothes."

Gabby threw him a suspicious look before consenting for his help in extricating her from her wet clothing.

"You behave now," she threatened, half seriously, half gleefully, before unbuttoning her jeans.

"I promise," he pledged, "Scout's honor," he adlibbed, holding up three fingers to signify the Scout's oath hand gesture.

But the lure of her exposed breasts was too much for him. He bent down and gently kissed them without any objection coming from Gabby.

"Suppose we dry each other off?" Andre proposed respectfully. Then he caught himself right away. "I'll get you your towel so you won't get cold."

Gabby smiled and nodded her consent.

Andre left the shower stall gracefully and retrieved Gabby's towel. He returned wearing his own smile and the two of them dried one another off making sure every area of their bodies was appropriately taken care of.

Andre volunteered to clean the shower stall while Gabby blow dried her hair. She stopped before the dryer completed its job because she wanted her hair to remain damp for a while.

"Hon, I've got something very important to talk to you about tonight," Gabby announced, turning toward Andre. "It's something I've been meaning to tell you for some time."

"Okay. Sure, Babe," he acquiesced, sensing her seriousness.

"I've kept it from you because I didn't want to lose you. I ..."

"Babe, you'll never lose me. I love you!" Andre interrupted.

"You may want to wait 'till you hear what I have to say before ..."

"It's not going to happen," he cut her off again. "I can't think of anything that could come between us."

Gabby took a deep breath.

"Okay. I'm going to hold you to it!" she ratified.

"So, let's get dressed and you can tell me all about it," Andre promised, wondering what had gotten Gabby so worried.

Both agreed to get dressed without interruption, so she could say what she felt she needed to say.

Andre got dressed first and headed toward the hallway just beyond the master bedroom door.

"I'll have our wine ready, Babe, by the time you're ready. Okay?"

"Yes. Thanks, Hon," came Gabby's quick reply, as she decided to slip into another pair of air-conditioned jeans.

In a few moments she joined Andre on the couch. And although she smiled when he handed her the wine glass, her face was a pallet of nervousness.

Conscious of her tenseness, he reached out and touched her cheek.

"Babe, what is it? I'm concerned because you think you should be concerned."

Gabby moved his hand to her mouth and kissed his palm. Then she placed her wine glass on the coffee table and faced him directly.

He focused on her face, especially on her eyes, which were staring directly into his.

"What I have to tell you is going to blow your mind!" she began, trying her best to steady herself.

She tried valiantly to still the shaking sensation that seized her, to control the involuntary twitching that pulsated at the corner of her left eye, a telltale sign of her growing distress.

"Babe. Just take a breath. Relax. And blow my mind," he encouraged, wanting to start with just the right amount of levity to show her that nothing she was about to say would damage their relationship.

Gabby took a slow, deep breath, paused slightly, and tightened her lips before she spoke.

"When we met at Starbucks in January, I was running for my life!" she began her story, feeling the blood thundering in her ears.

Andre's narrowed his eyes momentarily and caught himself before he spoke, wanting to give the love of his life free rein to share more of her personal history.

"My real name is Monica Pitt. I was a CPA and co-owned my own company. I used to live in Raleigh, North Carolina," she reported as fast as her lips could move. "I'm divorced. I was married to a minister. My mother still lives in Raleigh and she's a recovering alcoholic."

Andre leaned closer and took one of her hands in his.

"Wow! When you said you'd tell me more about yourself after we got to know each other better, I had no idea what you'd been going through."

Gabby offered him a weak smile which didn't completely form because she had much more to say.

"Is your ex the one you're running from?" Andre asked before Gabby had a chance to continue.

"No. No! Not at all. We divorced a year after I went into hiding. It was mutual, and amicable. As a matter of fact, he helped protect me from men who wanted to kill me," she admitted nervously. "Wait, I'm getting ahead of myself," she caught herself.

"Men wanted to kill you?" Andre verified, sensing his protective genes turning up a notch.

She forced herself to pause long enough to take a deep breath and placed her hand over Andre's.

"Yes. But it all started with a dream I had about a woman's husband being stabbed and the men who murdered him chasing her into their house. She ended up shooting two of them in my dream before Jonathan, that's my ex-husband, woke me up!"

"Wow, that's quite a dream, ah, nightmare," he responded, sipping his wine to gather his thoughts, which were beginning to be trumped by his emotions.

"It turned out not to be a dream, and that's what started my real life nightmare!" she continued, feeling a whirlpool of emotions tugging at her.

She told him of her visits to a Jungian dream interpretation specialist, a wholistic healer from her husband's church, and a reputable psychic who diagnosed her stigmata and its implications.

"Stigmata?" Andre questioned.

"Yes," she touched her neck with her free hand. "There were strangulation marks on my neck and bruises on my chest!"

"Babe, that's ... that's ..."

"Strange! I know," Gabby completed the sentence he couldn't.

She explained what stigmata was and how it was directly tied to her nightmare. When Gabby told him about the *déjà vu* experience and its relationship to her transpersonal memory and subconscious recall, Andre's eyes widened under his raised eyebrows and his mouth flung open.

"Because of Dr. Genomé, that's the psychic I'm talking about, I left Raleigh and went to Baltimore, Maryland to find out more about the couple in my nightmare. Their names were Richard and Monica Proxmire. Babe ...," she interrupted herself, "I found out that they really existed and that they were both murdered!"

Before Andre could speak, Gabby continued.

"Babe, Monica Proxmire died over thirty years ago and she looks just like me! And there's a good reason for that!" she paused and segued immediately into an invitation for Andre to take a sip of liquid courage. "You might want to take a drink before you hear what I'm about to say."

She watched as he took a sip and then followed that up with a mouthful of Chardonnay to buttress his amazement.

"Oh, Hon. I really hesitate to tell you this," Gabby agonized, as she sent Andre a dreadful look.

"No, go ahead," he countered. "You're earning a Ph. D in blowing my mind. In all of my years in counterintelligence, I've never—and I mean never—heard a story like this!"

"It's true!" Gabby insisted, raising her voice.

"Oh, Babe. I have no doubt it's true! I didn't mean it that way," he justified his previous outburst. "I have never seen you so serious! Believe me. I believe you!"

The emotional weight of the thoughts swimming around in his head prevented him from putting two syllables together, but he shook off his funk in time to voice his next question.

"Gabby, ah … Monica … ah … Gabby … What do you want me to call you?" he agonized.

"Babe!" she quipped, sending him a patented smirk. "Hon, please call me Gabby. I'll always be Gabby to you!"

Gabby raised her eyebrows, and grinned a grin that said 'Okay buddy, you asked for it. Here it comes!' Before she announced her bombshell, she invited him once again to have a sip of wine.

"I'm a clone! I'm Monica Proxmire's clone!"

Andre choked on the sip of wine he had just brought to his lips and then spilled what was left in the glass as he tried to wipe his mouth.

"A clone!" he parroted, voicing his amazement. "You're a … No! … That's … That's impossible!"

"No. It's not only possible," Gabby retaliated sharply. "I have proof! I have documentation. I have paper and electronic files — dozens of flash drives — and I have personal experience!" she blasted.

Andre's face was as much a mixture of bewilderment and discombobulation as his shirt was a fusion of wetness and dryness.

Struck by his cartoonish confusion, Gabby calmed herself down enough to enjoy his bafflement without putting a harsh judgment on it.

Before she spoke again, she got up and retrieved a damp hand towel from the kitchen so Andre could blot the wine stains off his shirt, realizing they would have to salt the stain, soak it in boiling water, and machine wash it later.

"Three years ago I was as mystified and disbelieving as you are tonight," Gabby spoke calmly and calculatedly. "But you've got to believe me when I say there is a global, clandestine organization, based in Switzerland, that is cloning human beings as we speak!"

Andre laid the damp hand towel next to his empty wine glass on the coffee table and scooted forward on the couch as if he were going to stand. If he had those intentions, he quickly aborted them when he looked at Gabby's over-all countenance.

"We found out that Senator Henry—he's deceased now, and so is his brother Cecil—were the masterminds behind the human xerography operation, that's what we call the cloning scandal," she continued, assessing where he was emotionally.

"We. You said 'we.' Who's the 'we' that helped you, Babe?"

"My ex, and Mrs. Sandra Henry, and Peaches, and … and my mother, and Mrs. Cody and Sarge and Betty Heller, and Sara Mae, and several others," she named her selfless supporters. "Some of them have been killed by the cloning syndicate," she added, catching herself tearing up as she remembered the ultimate sacrifices some of them had made.

She tearfully explained how she had confiscated Cecil Henry's xerography files, out-witted his henchmen, and out-maneuvered his brother. She elaborated on the contents of the files and on how she, her mother and Sandra had copied the files electronically and had hidden the stolen discs. She told him about the life-and-death scene near the airport and about how she had escaped the clutches of one of the most powerful men in the world.

"Babe, you're really scaring me now," Andre confessed as he stood facing her. "You're telling me that President Raymond Goodnight, the President of the United States of America, not only knows about the human cloning operation, but that he is helping to finance it through an off-shore entity called The Life Extension Institute of Geneva!"

Gabby nodded the President's complicity.

"Oh, my God." Andre half whispered, as he lowered himself back on the couch.

"Hon, I can show you the flash drives. You can see for yourself! I have the names of almost all of the policy holders and the people who are cloned from them up until three years ago— their names, birthdates, where they lived, their deaths when they became expendable to serve as body parts …" Gabby blunted her own explanation when she saw that Andre was struggling to keep up.

He buried his head in his hands and then held one hand up, his palm toward her, in a 'stop and decease' gesture.

Gabby understood the need for the awkward silence and waited for her macho counterintelligence consultant to regain his disciplined composure. She watched, her makeup streaked with tears, testament to the chilling nature of a story that had been repressed for much too long.

"Babe," he spoke from behind the cupped hands shielding his face, as he looked directly at the woman who had just totally rocked his world.

"Babe," he repeated. "I am so thankful you believe enough in us to have told me what you've just told me. And I know it took tremendous courage! I remember that shortly after we met and began to get serious about one another, you told me you felt it was important for me to know more about you," he eulogized, motioning for her to slide closer.

Gabby followed his warm prompt and held both of his hands in hers. His moist eyes mirrored her own as they breathed into each other's loving demeanor.

"That's not quite the personal history I expected," he confessed, allowing his lips to form into a smile.

Gabby offered her own smile and then extended it as Andre lifted her hands and kissed them.

"Now that I know the real you, all of you, the complete you, Gabby," he hesitated to reinforce his acceptance of who she was now. "I have a question for you."

Gabby took a quick breath and smiled her consent.

"There's probably more that you haven't told me ..." he hesitated, realizing Gabby's raised eyebrows indicated she had anticipated his observation. "And I know we're going to talk about that, if not tonight, then later ..." he paused again knowing she was one step ahead of him. "But my question is — why haven't you exposed the President for what he is and closed down his operation?"

"That's why I decided to tell you everything tonight!" Gabby spoke softly, being careful to measure her words. "If we're going to make a life together, I've got to expose him and his role in the Life Extension Institute of Geneva. And ..." she blunted her own explanation. "I've got to make it possible for some very special people to get their lives back too!"

Andre took a deep breath and decided not to say anything, because it was obvious that Gabby was going to speak.

"I'm going to ask you something, and you can think about it ... or say no. Would you ..."

Andre didn't let her finish.

"Absolutely, Babe! Of course, I'm going to help! I love you! I'd do anything for you!" he declared, cupping her face in his hands and kissing her to emphasize his promise.

He inched his face back from her face just enough to steel his gaze into her emerald eyes, which were glued to his.

"I'm going to have to process what you've said tonight. And I'm sure I'll have more questions, but I have a couple more questions. Do you mind?"

Gabby nodded to give her consent and then reclaimed the wine glass she had neglected earlier. She motioned for Andre to do the same, so he politely excused himself, opting to leave the spent wine glass on the coffee table and pouring his second serving into a clean wine glass.

When he returned he sat next to Gabby, who had repositioned herself with her back against the cushioned arm of one end of the couch. He gently lifted her legs and placed them over his lap so both of them were on the same end of the couch.

"Okay," Andre started. "You said you have the flash drives and other electronic records here," he paused to acknowledge her approval. "Then where are the paper files?"

"They're under lock and key in a storage unit in Marietta, Georgia. I've been renting the unit six months at a time using the business account of a friend in order to protect their whereabouts."

Andre smiled his praise. "You want to work for us?" he joked, referring to the French National Police.

Gabby laughed for the first time that night and then took a celebratory sip of wine.

"I tried to expose them before I left the States," Gabby volunteered soberly. "But I got two investigative reporters killed."

"What do you mean?" Andre asked, sounding like the counterintelligence officer he was.

"One worked for the *New York Times* and the other for *The Atlanta-Journal Constitution!*" she fretted, remembering how gallant they had been. "I don't know how the xerography goons found out, but they killed them both before they could get the news to their respective editors."

Andre threw Gabby a knowing nod.

"I freaked out, figuring if they could get to two seasoned reporters, they'd be able to get to me!"

"But, to your credit, you've out-smarted them, Babe. I'm so impressed!"

He squeezed one of her thighs and reached for her free hand, patting it to emphasize his admiration.

Then Andre gave Gabby a strange look that startled her, sending a cold chill up and down her spine.

"Hon, what is it?" Gabby asked, trying her best to shake off the chill that renewed its trip up her spine.

"You've got to contact the people who've helped you. The ones who are alive—your mother and the people you've mentioned tonight. I'll help you contact them. We've got to get them to safe houses before we launch our news feeds. Their lives will be in danger. Do you understand?"

"Andre, you're scaring me!" Gabby voiced her apprehension.

"Babe, you've been undercover for three years. The rogue Institute will eventually find you, so we've got to crush them first. The people who are helping you are in danger too! When is the last time you've contacted them?"

Gabby's nervousness got the best of her and she started to cry.

Andre leaned over and embraced her affectionately, cupping her face in his hands again.

"Babe?" he urged.

"Just the call with mother I told you about, and with Mrs. Cody. I talk to most of them once a month on feature-dumb burner phones that are flip-phones, except for my ex. I haven't spoken to him since our divorce. I ..." Gabby trailed off, realizing her head was spinning.

Suddenly, his ruggedly handsome face became a commercial of facial expressions as his compartmentalized counterintelligence instincts took over.

Gabby noticed his odd change in demeanor and was going to address it when he rose and gently pulled her up to his standing position.

"Hon, what are you doing? You look so serious!"

"You've been running from them for three years now. Right?"

Gabby nodded and sent him a puzzled look.

"Right. You already know that," she countered, wondering why he had brought that up again.

"Babe, the only way they wouldn't be able to know your whereabouts is that they aren't able to track you—or haven't tried since the senator's and his brother's death!" Andre said emphatically, expressing it in such a way that Gabby knew his observation was going to be followed up with another one.

"They would have arranged to track you from the very beginning—at your conception—they would have placed a GPS tracking device of some type to ..."

Gabby cut him off and laughed sweetly at his intuitive hunch.

"You're amazing, Hon, I love how you can think out-of-the-box! That's one of the things I admire about you," she admitted. "Yes, you're exactly right! They had put a tracking device in my clothing when I was small and then in my watch band when I was older. Carlton told mom it was necessary, because the children of politicians and diplomats were soft targets for kidnappers. When they divorced, Mother did a proper job on the device with a hammer." Gabby assured him, whipping her hands together in the usual gesture that signifies being done with something.

"Wow! Okay. Good," was all Andre could say.

"I told Mrs. Henry to do the same thing with her daughter, Monica—she goes by Peaches now— when I told them about Carlton's and Cecil's cloning operation."

Andre's raised eyebrows prompted her to continue.

"A couple of weeks later, Peaches told me they had discovered hidden tracking devices in her favorite clothing and in her ankle bracelet. Sandra, Mrs. Henry, told me she hadn't known about them before, and had confronted her husband after my visit by throwing the damaged devices at him. As far as I know, Monica ... I mean Peaches ... never wore the devices again."

"We're going to make this okay. And, Babe, you need to know that we've got to figure out someway to protect the other surrogates worldwide. There are other ways they can track the unsuspecting surrogates these days."

"Oh?" Gabby wondered, wanting him to explain.

"Microchip technology exists to implant microchips in humans."

"Oh, no!" she hugged his words to her, squeezing them tightly, so that she could comprehend what she had just heard.

"The implant device is called an RFID transponder. It's encased in silicate glass and implanted sub-derminally anywhere on the body. And it contains a unique 16 digit ID number that can be linked to information contained in one of the Institute's external databases. I'm sure they've got plenty of them. It holds information like personal identification, medical history, medications, allergies, and contact information."

"I can't believe it!" Gabby gasped. "No ... I can believe it. They're well-financed by the richest people in the world!"

"The implants could make it possible for unsuspecting surrogates to be physically located by latitude, longitude, altitude, speed, and direction of movement," Andre continued to elaborate, realizing he was upsetting Gabby, but wanting her to grasp the global implications of the good they were about to accomplish when they compromised the Institute's monstrous aims.

"The implantable device has been around since 2004 or 2005," Andre guessed. "Theoretically, the technology could lead to political control and repression as governments use implants to track and persecute human rights activists, labor activists, civil dissidents, and political opponents. What we're doing now would necessitate making sure that no one on our team had a sub-derminal implant."

"Hon, you're really scaring me!" Gabby confessed. "Self-aggrandizing people and corrupt governments will use this technology for their own vested interests and sacrifice as many people as they need for profit and power."

"I don't disagree. Listen ... I've got associates in the States. Give me your family and friends' contact information. We'll contact each of them within the next 24 hours," he assured her. "I know what I'm doing, Babe. Trust me!"

"Oh, Hon. I do. I'm glad I told you everything!"

"Me too!"

Chapter Three

Now remember, Gabby. Follow the phone protocols we've established. They're all going to want to know where you are and how they can get in touch with you," he cautioned her. "Do not under any circumstances divulge your whereabouts."

Gabby nodded and took a deep breath.

"Okay, Babe. They're ready for you. And remember ... to these folks you are still 'Monica.'" Andre spoke mechanically, as he handed the burner phone to Gabby. "Okay ... here's your ex. His phone is ringing."

Gabby put the phone to her ear, reminded herself not to hyperventilate, and waited for him to pick up.

"Hello."

Gabby took another deep breath.

"Jonathan. This is me, Monica," Gabby greeted him nervously.

"Who?" Jonathan inquired, squinting to recognize the sound of the caller's voice.

"It's me, Monica!"

"Oh, my God! It is you. Sorry I didn't recognize you at first. It's been over two years since we ... since we talked."

"I know. I ..." she trimmed what she was going to say because he interrupted her.

"You've dropped completely out of sight! I ... Oh, wait just a minute," he shortened his dialogue with her. "I'm sorry, I've got to tell Tracy where the extra hymnals are."

Gabby rolled her eyes at Andre and shook her head.

Jonathan covered the receiver and instructed the volunteer where to look for the extra hymnals.

"Sorry," he apologized in an official tone. "We're planning for the evangelist this week, praise the Lord, and so many volunteers have stepped up to help who aren't familiar with where things are."

Gabby frowned her frustration.

Looks like things haven't changed one iota, she reminisced. *He still puts the church above everything else.*

"Jonathan, I've got something very important to tell you. I ..."

"Monica. I'd like to catch up, but you've caught me at a very busy time," he interrupted. "Perhaps we could talk early next week."

Her irritation turned to resentment and into anger before she was able to compose herself.

"You may be dead before next week, Reverend!" Gabby lowered her voice.

"What?"

"You heard me. I'm calling to warn you of the danger you will be in if you don't listen to me!" she railed.

Her whole demeanor had changed, as she adopted a more caustic tone, one that was very familiar to her when it came to dealing with his religious fundamentalist orientation.

"I'm going to close my office door," he announced, as he made his way over to the door and pushed it shut. "All right ... You've got my undivided attention."

Gabby relaxed a little and got an approving wink from Andre.

"I know I haven't kept up with you since our divorce, but Mother and Emma have told me how you've been, so I've kept track of you. A lot has happened since I saw you. I know you haven't remarried and you're still the minister at the church,"

Having regained her composure, she took a deep breath and continued.

"Jonathan, I've decided to expose the President's role in the Life Extension Institute of Geneva and that's going to put you and the other's in jeopardy. You've already been shot over this and I don't want you to be hurt any more over this or killed."

She heard his sigh over the phone.

"I'm serious! I don't want you hurt. I…"

"I heard you," he huffed, as he glanced at Warner Sallman's famous painting of Jesus.

"Do you know if you're being watched or if you're under surveillance?" Gabby petitioned carefully, wanting the information, but not wanting to upset him further.

"They've been around two or three times, once at my church office and twice at the parsonage. And they call occasionally."

"Oh."

"They asked me if I knew where you were or if I had spoken to you," he frowned. "I told them I had written you out of my life after our divorce and that since my religion disapproves of divorce, it's been all I can do to save my ministry. I told them I didn't care if I ever saw you again. I thought that would stop their visits, but it hasn't."

"I'm so sorry Jonathan."

"It's not your fault, Monica. I know what you're up against. I don't blame you."

"Jonathan, you've got to get to a safe house for awhile."

"What?"

"There are two agents standing outside your office as we speak. We have sent them there to escort you to the safe house."

"You're kidding. They're out there right now?"

"Yes! They're part of a special ops team that that's going to help me bring the President and his clandestine Institute down," Gabby spoke authoritatively.

Jonathan got up from his desk and started toward his office door.

"You might want to invite them in. I want you to see that they're working with us so you can trust them."

"I'm walking to the door now," he said, holding the phone to his ear.

"Good," Gabby responded, wondering how Jonathan was going to handle all of the intrigue—and a major change in his life.

Jonathan's eyes turned to saucers when he opened the door. The two special ops agents were standing next to his office administrator's desk and being cordially entertained by Mrs. Watson, who had taken it upon herself to tell them all about the evangelist's up-coming visit.

"Do you see them?" Gabby queried, knowing they were stationed just outside his office.

"Yes. They're here," Jonathan acknowledged sheepishly. "They're here."

"Invite them into your office and ask your staff not to disturb you."

"I'm disturbed already," he admitted half timidly, half incredulously.

He motioned for the two agents to join him in his office.

"Okay, they're here," Jonathan announced weakly, coughing to clear his throat.

"Good. I'm going to have Andre, the agent in charge of the special ops unit assigned to help you, talk to you. You don't have much time so listen carefully to what he's going to tell you. Okay?" Gabby instructed.

"All right!" Jonathan begrudgingly obeyed.

Gabby handed the burner phone to Andre.

"Reverend Pitt," Andre began. "Hand your phone to the lady agent. I want to make sure the agents are who we think they are."

Jonathan did as he was told and held the phone out to the lady agent.

"Sir, this is the Curator of the Mordecai House," Rita announced.

"Pleased to meet you, Ms. Curator. You can give the phone back to the reverend," Andre corroborated.

The agent handed Jonathan the phone and gestured for him to let Andre know he was on the phone again.

"I'm here," Jonathan whispered. "I'm back."

"Reverend Pitt, it's extremely important that you accept the advice we're giving you today. Quite frankly, your life depends on it!"

Weak kneed, Jonathan migrated slowly over to the office chair behind his desk and plunked down into its black leather folds.

"I can't believe this is happening," he lamented sorrowfully, squinting at his impromptu visitors.

"I know this has completely caught you off guard, but ..."

"No kidding! You think?" Jonathan interrupted, trying to smile, but finding his smile muscles didn't work.

"When the President and his thugs discover we're coming for them, they're going to visit you and the others who helped Monica. They're going to lean on you, Reverend Pitt. They're not going to believe any of you are oblivious as to ... your ex-wife's whereabouts ..."

"But I don't know where she is ... I don't think the others do either," he interrupted Andre again.

"They're going to torture you, Reverend. And the others, if they get a chance. And believe me, you're not going to want to be on the business end of their harsh interrogation tactics."

Gabby grabbed Andre's arm and put her head on his shoulder, realizing the awful implications of her decision to stop the world-wide cloning operation.

"We're going to ask you to go with the gentleman and the lady to your house immediately. You'll have an opportunity to gather a few things and go to your bank before they take you to the safe house. Plan for a few months stay. We'll sit down with you later—when you're safe—to take care of your financial and work responsibilities."

"This is all happening so fast! Who's going to take care of the revival this week, and my church responsibilities, and ..."

"We'll take care of that. But first, we've got to take care of you," Andre insisted.

"I'm not going to do it!" Jonathan blasted. "I appreciate your concern, but I'm not going to abandon my flock!"

Gabby could tell by the change of tone in Andre's voice that he was running into a snag with Jonathan.

"Reverend Pitt!" Andre countered, sensing the good reverend was going to make his extraction difficult.

"No. That's it. I'm staying right here. Ask your people to leave my office!"

Andre sighed his disappointment and threw Gabby a look of supreme irritation.

"Staying is not in your best interests, Reverend. You don't know what danger you're putting yourself—and the others in!"

Gabby shook her head, realizing how difficult Jonathan could be. She gravitated in front of Andre and held her arms up in the surrender position.

"I don't believe they'll do anything to me. I've told you and I'll tell them again, I don't know where Monica is," he growled. "They might watch me. They might keep me under surveillance, but they're not going to hurt me!"

"I can appreciate your distress, Reverend Pitt. However ..."

"There is no however," Jonathan cut him off a second time. "God Almighty will protect me! When they see I don't know where she is, they'll leave me alone!"

Gabby motioned for Andre to hand her the phone. He hesitated for only a second and then acquiesced.

"Jonathan! This is me again."

"It's not going to work, Monica. My mind's made up!" he scowled.

"Okay. Okay!" she yielded blandly, wanting to calm him down. "We're not going to force you," she said evenly, glancing at Andre for his approval.

It came quickly, because Andre knew her ex couldn't hurt anyone but himself.

Gabby placed her hand over the receiver and addressed Andre, asking "Can I tell him about the others?"

He hesitated thoughtfully, then nodded his consent.

Gabby slid her hand off the receiver and took a deep breath.

"Jonathan," she began slowly. "We've decided you can stay there if you want. But here's the thing. We have approached all of the others at the same time we approached you this morning. We've already gotten word that all of them except my mother have agreed to go to a safe house. The only reason my mother hasn't yet is because they've been unable to reach her," Gabby confirmed confidently.

"That's nice," Jonathan responded sarcastically.

Gabby lifted her ear slightly from the phone, recoiling from his slight, but wanted to finish what she had to say.

"Mrs. Cody told us that she thinks Mother is shopping. I'm telling you this because, if you decide you'd rather trust the President's men—who you've already had run-ins with—instead of us, you won't have a support system, because they'll all be in safe houses."

"I'm already in a safe house," Jonathan boasted. "I'm in God's house and He is my Co-pilot!"

"Oh, Jonathan ..." Gabby shook her head slowly, as a tear made its way down her face.

Andre signaled for Gabby to give him back the phone.

Gabby bit her lips, knowing what a mistake Jonathan was making.

"Okay. Well, it looks like your mind is made up," Gabby said calmly, as Andre leaned closer to the phone so he could hear Jonathan.

"Yes it is. In all things Christ strengthens me!" he preached.

"The agent in charge wants to say something else to you and then we'll let you go."

"He's not going to try to talk me out of my decision, is he?"

Gabby looked at Andre, who shook his head.

"No. Here he is. Goodbye, Jonathan." She shook her head again as she handed the phone to Jonathan.

"Reverend Pitt, I'm not sure what shape you'll be in this time next month. But if you should change your mind, we'll do our best to help you."

"Thanks, but no thanks. I'm sure I'll be just fine. Is that all?"

"Yes. Let me tell the two agents with you that you're staying."

After Andre apprised Rita of the minister's decision, he thanked her for driving all the way down from Jersey and set up a phone chat later on to debrief. Then he instructed her to hand the phone back to the minister.

"Reverend Pitt, we wish you the best of luck ..."

Click.

* * * * * * *

"We can't get in to see her now," Sergio reported to Agent Cramer.

"What's her status?" came Agent Cramer's rote response.

"A severe head injury and collapsed lung as a result of the accident. And her pelvis is broken. That's all we know at present."

"Where are you?" Agent Cramer asked, retailing his disappointment in the harsh tone of his voice.

"UNC Rex Hospital in Raleigh."

"What's the status of the accident scene?" his senior agent asked.

"As planned. Everything, except her mother's death, went according to plan. Agent White ran the red light and drove the pickup into her car at 65 miles an hour at impact!"

"And that was tonight?"

"Yes, sir. He collided with her car in the middle of the intersection, sending her car across the intersection and down an embankment a couple of blocks from her house. And before you ask, there were no witnesses. He was able to drive away from the scene before anyone arrived. That's what happens when a reinforced, full-bodied pickup creams a Prius," Agent Rodriguez bragged, satisfied that they had pulled off a successful mission.

"And the truck?" Agent Cramer probed.

"It's already being taken care of. Nobody's going to find it!"

"Good! And Agent White?"

"Not a scratch. His days as a crash derby contestant paid off."

"Excellent."

"Sir, I'm going to stick around here until I find out the extent of her injuries. I may have to complete the job the accident didn't take care of," Sergio offered, sounding as ruthless as he was elated.

"Roger that. Let me know as soon as you hear anything."

"Understood, sir. Oh, sir. She's a tough old gal. We couldn't break her in the interrogation. Her response of choice was to spit in our faces."

"I figured you might run into her wrath. I've had personal experience with her myself. And that reminds me. Did you make sure her alcoholic content was over the legal limit?"

"Absolutely! We forced some cheap bourbon down her throat during our unpleasant 'chat' with her earlier this evening. After a few more threats and a couple of back hands, we left her quite disheveled sitting at her kitchen table, with a promise to give her a chance to think it over before we paid her another visit. We told her we didn't believe she hadn't been in contact with her daughter and that we were going to be a fixture in her life until she confessed."

"Did she take the bait?" Agent Cramer asked rhetorically.

"Yep! We followed her to her hair dresser's shop and asked ourselves why she would go there this late at night? As you know, we all suspected she's been going somewhere to contact Pitt since she's figured out her house is bugged. When she pulled up in front of the shop, we made our presence known by pulling up behind her. When she saw us she drove off predictably, and that's when we staged the accident."

"Have you found anything yet at the hair dresser's shop?"

"As a matter of fact we did! She's been using a burner phone she kept in one of the lockers at the shop. We're guessing all of them are using burner phones. We're on that as we speak. If they think using disposable phone numbers and twilio clouds is going to prevent us from finding out where Pitt is, they're in for quite a surprise!" Agent Rodriguez boasted, feeling proud of himself.

"Speaking of the others," Agent Cramer pressed, wanting to speed up his report. "Where do we stand on our chats with them?"

* * * * * * *

Gabby was beside herself as she anxiously paced the floor, trying her best not to hyperventilate.

"Babe, relax. The team knows what they're doing. And they're good at what they do. I know. I trained them," Andre assured her.

She sent him a disquieted look as she hugged herself in mid-stride to relieve the pressure.

"Seriously, Babe. We've acted on this very quickly. I was able to reach my team before they left D.C. and, as you know, Frank already knows what's going on. Four members of my team are long time associates, and were attending a reconnaissance symposium there and were in the right place at the right time to help," he reassured her.

"I'm sorry, Hon. I just want everything to go well. I love all of them so much!" she said tearfully.

Andre held out his arms in a welcoming gesture.

"Come here, Babe," he petitioned softly. "We're going to do our best to get everyone to safe houses."

Gabby sought the refuge of his embrace, but her adrenaline was on hyper-drive. She shivered her restlessness which caused Andre to rub her back and arms.

"Waiting is the hardest part," he reassured her and then kissed the side of her head just above her temple.

"Do you still think I'm doing the right thing?" Gabby backpedaled, sensing she didn't have to ask, yet wanting his validation.

"Without question!" came Andre's quick reply. "There's no way we could make a life together with that hanging over us. Sooner or later they would have caught up to us and would have been better prepared. You would have felt guilty for letting them by with it and worried about your friends' and family' safety. And I wouldn't have seen it coming in time to react intelligently to the threat," he assessed, cradling her face in his hands so their eyes met.

"So, yes," he continued. "You're absolutely doing the right thing and we're doing the right thing now in getting them protection."

"When do you think we'll hear something?" Gabby asked, realizing she was seeking an answer he couldn't give.

Andre gently pulled her face closer and smiled just before he kissed her.

"I expect we'll hear from my team sometime later tonight or early tomorrow morning," he guessed, smiling when he saw her frown. "There's a six hour time difference between us and the Eastern Time Zone in the States. So, we're in for a late night, Babe."

Gabby glanced around his right shoulder and looked at the time setting on the TV.

Before she could speak, Andre volunteered the obvious.

"It's 2030 hours here, Babe. Let's affirm my team's success and their collective ability to accomplish the mission. Okay?"

Gabby nodded her agreement and initiated another kiss.

"I'd like to suggest we continue packing," Andre proposed, sounding calculatedly official. "When the Institute's goons discover your friends and family are missing they'll renew their efforts to find you. They're obviously well-monied and that means their political and covert military reach will be something to be reckoned with."

Gabby shot him a worried face.

"Babe," Andre smiled his appreciation for her concern. "All that means is we've got to stay several chess moves ahead of them!"

She tightened her lips, but nodded her understanding of the predicament she had placed them in.

"It looks like we've found each other for more than a perfect relationship," Gabby proffered, referring to his military and counterintelligence training.

"Our finding one another, Ms. Gabby Garceau, is a result of soulmates finding their perfect soulmate by right of consciousness! We are meant to be together in this life! Our philosophies, education, interests, talents and even our professions, are the perfect ingredients that will bring us awesome happiness! Do you hear me?" he eulogized, bringing his arms over her head so he could give her a proper bear hug.

Gabby smiled her delight and braced herself for the strong hug she knew was coming.

"I love you so much," she cooed.

"I love you, too!" he chorused, as he pointed to the conglomeration of boxes, some taped shut and others either half full or empty, scattered across the living room.

Gabby smiled and acknowledged his well-timed entreaty with raised eyebrows.

"Okay, you old soulmate! I guess we'd better finish our packing!" she volunteered, as she retrieved the picture of her mother off the bookshelf in the living room to add it to the box marked 'framed pics.'

Chapter Four

"Sir, we've started our roundup of Pitt's sympathizers, and there are a few things you need to know," Agent Cramer began, sounding hesitant, yet decisive, although with a tinge of guardedness.

"Go on," the President said, appreciating the agent's official tone. *Things must not be going as he expected,* POTUS thought to himself, as he waved off one of his staff members who seemed to want an audience with him. POTUS held his hand over the receiver and whispered to the staffer, "I'll be with you in a moment." His staffer took the hint and quickly retreated toward the open Oval Office door and disappeared through the doorway.

"Last night and early this morning our agents positioned themselves for simultaneous sweeps of the Pitt sympathizers in Raleigh, Baltimore and Atlanta. I'm in Baltimore this morning. I'll report the status of the other units in just a moment."

This doesn't sound as if it's going well at all, POTUS thought to himself. *Cramer would have started our conversation entirely differently if he had good news to share.* However, the President decided he wanted to hear what Agent Cramer had to say in order to take any remedial actions, if necessary, to support tightening the net around the bothersome Pitt woman and her entourage.

"Okay. Let's hear it," POTUS spoke softly, not wanting to sound an alarm that may not be necessary.

"Last night Agent Rodriguez's unit interrogated Pitt's mother in Raleigh. As we suspected, she was totally uncooperative. They used all of the leverage they felt necessary to get the information we needed out of her—to no avail. They had no doubt she'd been in contact with her daughter, I'll explain that in just a moment. And we have little doubt Pitt's ex-husband is not a threat," Agent Cramer recounted, measuring each word he said.

POTUS's patient silence on the other end of the phone prompted Agent Cramer to continue uninterrupted.

"Pitt's mother relieved all doubt about the good reverend. It was obvious during her interrogation that she loathes him. She made it clear he was never a good son-in-law and that she could care less if she ever saw him again. They live in the same city and have not talked since the divorce."

"Agent Rodriguez is certain about that?" POTUS asked, wanting incontrovertible reassurance.

"Yes, sir. Absolutely! Agent Rodriguez is an excellent interrogator, sir. He's the best there is when it comes to interpreting tells and other nonverbal communication leakage."

Agent Cramer's impassioned appraisal of his colleague's consummate interrogation skills softened POTUS's doubt about Mrs. Henry's estranged relationship with her ex son-in-law.

"Before they finished with her they forced bourbon down her throat knowing she's got an alcohol problem. They baited her with threats, knowing that when they left her house she would try to get in touch with her daughter. And that's exactly what happened," he narrated optimistically.

Once again the President used silence to keep the agent divulging details.

"When she drove away from her house, two agents stayed behind and searched her house while a third agent followed her. She drove to her hair stylist's shop, which was a strange trip to make for that time of night, so we suspected that's where she's been communicating with her daughter. She discovered our tail and got back in her car without going into the shop and drove erratically down the street. The alcohol we poured down her throat had just about incapacitated her."

"As I'm listening to you, Agent Cramer, I'm getting that you have a point to make somewhere in your story," POTUS chimed in, growing impatient with the agent's lengthy account.

"Yes, sir. I figured you wanted to know the details. I ..."

"I do," the President agreed abruptly, cutting him off. "But could you move the details along a little faster?"

"Of course, sir. Yes, sir. We found her burner phone in a locker at the shop ..."

"That's good," POTUS punctuated, cutting into Agent Cramer's explanation again.

"Yes, sir. That's very good. We're tracing the burner phone now."

"Good work."

"Thank you, sir. We were able to stage a near fatal accident as she drove away from the shop ..."

"Near fatal?" the President questioned.

"Yes, sir. Unfortunately she was not killed!"

"What's her status now?"

"She's in critical condition, sir," Agent Cramer reported. "Rodriguez says the surgeons have placed a ventriculostomy drain to remove cerebrospinal fluid that's causing considerable swelling. It doesn't look good for her, sir. And she's in a coma, so she's not an immediate threat."

"And likely may not become a threat at all," POTUS inserted, liking the sound of what he had just heard.

"That's the way it looks, sir," agreed Agent Cramer.

"You're watching her?"

"Yes, sir. Agent Rodriguez's team is keeping an eye on her. If her condition changes, an agent will be there to make sure she will not pose a threat."

"Good. Excellent!" came POTUS's confirmation.

There was just a brief moment of silence before the President spoke again.

"You mentioned there are a few more things I need to know about Pitt's sympathizers!"

"Yes, sir, Mr. President. Rodriguez's team is camped outside of the good reverend's parsonage as we speak, waiting to help him gain clarity about what his life will look like should he feel a need to protect his ex-wife. But I've got to tell you, after discovering what seems to be an irreconcilable rift between Mrs. Henry and the disenfranchised reverend, we believe he's not necessarily expendable. We think we'll be able to use him to find Pitt. At least that's how we're thinking now. Time will tell, of course!"

"Where are you?" POTUS queried.

"I'm in Baltimore," Agent Cramer reminded POTUS from his parked car position just down the street from Mrs. Cody's house. The overcast Baltimore sky and early morning fog served as the perfect covers for their planned visit with the Cody woman.

One of the other agents, sitting in the backseat of the car, frantically motioned for Agent Cramer to take an incoming call.

"Sir, it looks like the Atlanta unit is calling me. Okay if I call you back?"

"Of course. However, I've got a staff meeting coming up, so call me after lunch."

"Roger that, sir."

As soon as the President terminated his end of the connection, Agent Cramer focused his attention on the incoming call. The agent who fielded the call announced it was Agent Lantz Cunningham calling from Atlanta.

"What's the story down there?" Agent Cramer demanded, still a little upset he hadn't been able to give better news to the President.

"Sir. They're not here!" came Agent Cunningham's frantic reply.

"What do you mean they're not there?"

"Mrs. Henry and her daughter aren't here! Her steward said they left late last night with who he believed were CIA agents. But our call to our CIA contacts confirmed that whoever picked them up were definitely not CIA agents."

"You've got to be kidding!" blasted Agent Cramer.

"No, sir. They took suitcases with them, and money out of the home safe. The steward said it's the first time he ever saw Mrs. Henry ever do anything like this. They didn't even touch dinner on the table," Agent Cunningham gushed anxiously, realizing that something was terribly amiss. "And we haven't been able to track the daughter's GPS coordinates. I'm thinking she's not wearing the devices."

"I'm not believing this!" railed Agent Cramer. "Okay! Find out what else the steward knows and talk to any of the other house staff. Look at her other properties. Contact her social network …"

"Already on it, sir," Agent Cunningham cut into Cramer's off-the-cuff damage control.

Suddenly, Agent Cramer looked toward the Cody residence, as he let the phone slip slightly from his ear.

"Shit! Shit! Shit!" he blurted, losing his composure.

He quickly re-established his phone connection with Agent Cunningham.

"Follow-up on anything that makes sense and get back to me asap," he ordered and tossed the phone to the agent in the back seat.

"Everybody out now," he screamed. "Cody may not be in her house! Everybody converge on the house NOW!"

* * * * * * *

"You're safe! Praise God! You're safe," Gabby celebrated joyfully.

"Yes we are, dear. Both Peaches and I are quite safe. But we are definitely wondering what in the world is going on," Sandra Henry voiced her concern and uncertainty.

"I promise I'm going to tell you everything, Sandra. But first let me revel in the fact that you two are safe and sound in a safe house," Gabby responded enthusiastically, jumping up and down like a school girl.

Andre smiled at her adolescent jubilation and signaled a "two thumbs up" to celebrate. Gabby stretched out one are and pulled Andre toward her in joy.

She thought to herself, *I am so glad I decided to share my secret with this amazing man! It's going to be okay!*

A comment from the other side of the phone call brought her attention back to the present moment.

"What? I'm sorry. I didn't hear what you just said," Gabby apologized.

"Hi. It's me," Peaches repeated. "I wanted to let you know I'm here too!"

"Oh. Hi, Peaches," Gabby cried joyfully. "I'm thrilled that you were both home so we could get you out safely."

"I know. I'm glad too. But like Mom said, 'What is going on?' The agents came late last night and ushered us out of the house as fast as they could. They said that we were in danger and that you would tell us what is going on."

"Can your mom hear me?" Gabby asked.

"Yes. We've got you on speaker phone."

Sandra scooted closer to her daughter on the loveseat in the sparsely furnished safe house.

"I promise I'll tell you everything, but we're expecting calls from the others. So, I can't talk long now. However, I've decided to bring the President's Life Extension Institute of Geneva down and I've got the resources to do it."

"Well, I can't say I'm surprised," Sandra admitted soberly, as she hugged Peaches tightly. "I knew you'd have to take this route someday."

"I'm so sorry I have to disrupt your lives like this," Gabby confessed, as she felt the tears coming.

Andre improved his position next to her and put his arm around her waist.

"That's okay,' Peaches consoled.

"This disruption will save our lives," Mrs. Henry conceded quickly. "Monica, dear, we've been living in fear for your safety for three years now—and for ours—waiting for the hammer to fall!"

Gabby realized that Andre's team had instructed her to use her old married name as her 'contact identity' in order to insure her anonymity and whereabouts until the Institute was extinguished.

"I know. I know," Gabby repeated. "Sandra, I need to ask you. Peaches isn't wearing any tracking devices, is she?"

"Oh, for heaven's sake no! She hasn't worn them for years, thanks to you. When you told us what they were really for, I destroyed them!"

"Good," Gabby replied, just wanting to cover all of the bases. "I'll be able to tell you more later, Okay?"

"We'll be patient, dear. Do you have any idea how long this is going to take?" Mrs. Henry ventured, knowing her question was probably premature.

Gabby shot Andre a quick glance, realizing he had heard Mrs. Henry. He tightened his lips and held five and then six fingers up. And then he held both hands, palms up, to indicate it could be longer.

'I'm sorry,' he mouthed the words.

"Listen, you two," Gabby began slowly. "It could take five or six months, or longer. I'm so sorry."

Although Mrs. Henry frowned and Peaches showed her begrudging acceptance, both mother and daughter realized it was for the best.

Peaches was the first to speak.

"Monica, I've always considered you my older sister. I told you that years ago. So, we sisters have to stick together. You don't have to apologize. No sacrifice is too great if it means we can all be back together again."

Gabby wiped the tears away with her fingers before Andre had a chance to offer her tissues.

"Peaches is right, Monica," came Sandra's motherly endorsement. "We'll do whatever it takes."

"Thank you both," Gabby graciously accepted their familial alliance, as her attention was diverted by Andre, who held up a second phone. He mouthed the words 'Mrs. Cody' as he pointed to the phone.

"Oh, you two. I've got to go. Emma's on the other line."

"Okay, dear," Mrs. Henry complied. "Tell her we said 'hi' and God speed."

"Okay ..."

"Wait, Monica. Wait, dear," Mrs. Henry interjected, blunting Gabby's reply. "I've got to tell you something else."

Gabby motioned for Andre to hang onto the other phone for a second.

"Okay."

"I found another set of papers in Carlton's office downstairs. They were Monica's, Monica Proxmire's health records."

Gabby automatically put her hand to her throat, remembering the red blotches on her neck produced by her nightmares a little over three years ago.

"I found them a couple of days ago and was able to take them with us when we were escorted out of my house last night."

"Wa ... Wow! That .. is fan ... fantastic!" Gabby fumbled for the words.

She thought they had found all of the human xerography records three years ago.

"It was serendipitous. I wasn't even looking for them," Mrs. Henry editorialized. "I haven't had a chance to read them yet, but if they're about Emma's Monica, they're about you and Peaches, too!"

Sandra's surprise announcement had Gabby's head spinning, but she regained her composure quickly.

"When I see you, the three of us can go over them," Gabby instructed. "Get the agents with you to flash drive them to me. Okay?

"Yes. Okay, dear."

"Okay, you two, I've got to say goodbye for now!"

"We love you," Peaches and Sandra took their leave.

Gabby raised her eyebrows and took a deep breath before bringing the phone Andre held out for her up to her ear.

'I love you, Babe,' he mouthed again, *'You can handle this.'*

"Hi, Emma. This is Monica."

"Thank God, you're safe. How are the others?" Mrs. Cody asked, as she accepted a glass of water from one of the agents called Frank.

"I'm fine, Emma. The bigger question is 'How are you?'"

"These gentlemen have taken very good care of me. I suppose my late night abduction means you're going ahead with your campaign to expose the President and his Life Extension Institute of Geneva?" she summarized, surprised it had taken Monica so long, and concerned she was doing something about it now.

"Yes, as you predicted. Thanks to your encouragement and belief in me, I've found the courage to do it!"

"Honey. Unfortunately, I've got some bad news to share with you."

Gabby swallowed hard before she could get the words out. "Oh! What is it?"

"I've asked these agents to allow me to tell you before they report the success of their mission to your agent friend."

"What is it, Emma. You sound heartbroken!" Gabby intuited, wondering what Mrs. Cody's news was.

"Oh, Honey. Your mother's been in an accident!"

"What!" Gabby wailed, almost dropping the phone.

"I'm so sorry to have to tell you this, but when they escorted me from my house and told me you had sent them, I asked about your mother and the others. They told me your mother was in a serious auto accident and that it was alcohol-related."

"What? Is she…"

"No, thank God, she's alive. She's seriously injured though!"

"I can't believe this!" Gabby balked. "Did you say it was alcohol-related? She'll be celebrating three years of sobriety this month. There's no way I believe she was drinking!"

"I thought that, too. Someone must have staged the accident, because the police said on Peaches' scanner that it appeared like the accident was intentional. It looks like the President's henchmen may have gotten to her first, and staged the accident!"

Gabby put her hand over her face and closed her moist eyes, allowing her seething anger to feed her tears.

"You said she's alive, though — right?"

"Yes," Mrs. Cody soothed. "But Monica, she's in a coma."

"So help me God, they're going to pay for this," Gabby sobbed, as Andre hugged her from behind.

"Your friend's agent, Mr. Marino, said the President's henchmen are still at the hospital, so he said Agent Jack's going to stick around in Raleigh. Frank said Jack and another agent are there to protect her, and if they have to, they'll extract her to keep her out of harm's way."

"Where is she? What hospital is she in?"

"UNC Rex!" Emma replied quickly.

"I've got to see her!" Gabby sobbed, speaking as much to Andre as she was to Mrs. Cody.

Andre nodded his agreement, as he mouthed his okay.

"Emma, I'm going to have to let you go now, but I'll see you and the others soon," Gabby promised. "Oh, Sandra and Peaches are fine. They're in a safe house in the Atlanta area and are being transferred to your location. So, that's three of you who are safe."

"How 'bout Jonathan?" Emma chanced, feeling she should inquire about him.

"He's refused our help, so he's on his own," came Gabby's immediate response.

"Oh, that's too bad."

"Yes, it is," said Gabby mechanically. "I'll call you as soon as we know anything about mother. You and the Henry's will be together very soon. Okay?"

"That's great! We're looking forward to that."

"Love you, and bye for now ... Oh, hand the phone to Frank," Gabby said, ending the call cordially, but abruptly.

"Bye. Love you, too."

Gabby put the phone on her lap and then remembered Andre needed it.

"Oh, here, Hon," she sent him a weak smile. "Looks like mom's safe, too, for now!" she added, as she handed the phone to Andre.

Andre sent her a puzzled look.

"The coma is her safe house for a while," she said sadly.

Andre tightened his lips and nodded to Gabby, agreeing with her quick assessment of her mother's immediate situation. Then he put the phone to his lips.

"Frank. We'll see you soon. Tell Paul 'hi' and tell the others I said 'great job'!"

* * * * * * *

"Longwood, you take the back of the house. Foster, you come with me through the front door," Agent Cramer barked, as the three of them headed toward Mrs. Cody's house.

It was a sprawling split-level house screened by dogwoods and bordered by azaleas, manicured hedges, and fine fescue grass that enclosed the variegated liriope which lined the walks.

A variety of drought-tolerant ground covers blanketed her property which showed she loved gardening. There were thyme, creeping sedums, old-fashioned hen-and-chicks, sweet woodruff and bishop's weed.

She seems like a really nice lady, Agent Cramer thought, as he admired her landscaping handiwork on his way to the front gate. *It's too bad she's caught up in this.*

The latch on the gate was stuck, so Allen had to finagle it for them to gain entry.

Always something to do for a homeowner, Agent Cramer mused to himself as they made their way up the sidewalk to the front door.

"It's dark inside," Agent Foster reported the obvious. "There's not a light on in the house except for the porch light."

"It must be on a timer," Agent Cramer guessed, as he cupped his hands against the window to the left of the front door. "You're right. I don't see a light on or any sign that anyone's up or possibly even home."

Agent Foster rang the doorbell and both hired malefactors waited.

Satisfied that no one was up and about, Agent Cramer nodded at Agent Foster which signaled him to pick the front door lock.

Once they had gained entry, Agent Foster disabled the alarm system and both men began their room-to-room search. In a few moments Agent Longwood entered through the backdoor and joined their search.

"Looks like she left in a hurry," Agent Foster noted, referring to the afghan thrown across the back of the couch and to a half empty, cold cup of tea on the coffee table.

"Yeah," echoed Agent Longwood. "The TV's still on and the cable box is off. She left in a hurry, all right."

"But in not too much of a hurry," countered Agent Cramer as he entered the living room from the kitchen, holding a slip of paper.

The comedic expression on Agent Cramer's face told them he had found something that had amused him.

He stopped a few steps in front of the framed painting of Mrs. Cody and her daughter, Monica Proxmire that hung on the living room wall behind him. He read the note out loud:

> *You poor, misled ruffians,*
> *You boys are like hungry wolves in a hen house!*
> *But this hen has got you all figured out—and so*
> *does MP. You have sworn your allegiance to a*
> *hooligan. And there will be a reckoning when*
> *the Chief Executive and his horrible Institute*
> *experiences déjà vu all over again!*
> *Shame on you! Shame on all of you!" EC*

The three of them exchanged looks that telegraphed their admiration for a feisty old lady who had given them, and the President of the United States, a smack on their collective hands.

Agent Cramer folded the note and stuffed it in his shirt pocket. Then he thought to himself, *How about that. I've placed her note next to my heart. Maybe I should pay attention to her moxie?*

"Okay, guys. Let's do a once over sweep before we leave. Maybe there's … something we can use," Agent Cramer proposed, still emotionally touched by the impact of Mrs. Cody's handwritten note.

* * * * * * *

"Reverend Pitt, there's a Mr. Schmidt waiting in the outer office to see you. He says it's very important," Mrs. Watson announced, looking a little sheepish.

Jonathan looked past her as she stood in the doorway to his office and saw a well-dressed man in an impeccably-cut business suit standing next to her desk. His hair was cut very short and framed a face that was stoic and chiseled.

"Show him in Mildred," Jonathan okayed, as he tidied up his sermon outline and stacked the reference materials that had been sprawled across his desk.

He rose from the seat behind his desk to greet the visitor who had just stepped through the office doorway.

Jonathan nodded for Mrs. Watson to close the office door, but she had already anticipated his preference for privacy and begun to close the door.

Jonathan extended his hand for a handshake and invited the visitor to seat himself just as the office door sounded its closure.

"Good morning, Mr. Schmidt," Jonathan greeted as they released their firm handshake and the visitor seated himself. "What can I do for you?"

"This visit is more about what I can do for you," came his emotionless reply, as he crossed his leg over his knee and looked squarely into Jonathan's puzzlement.

"I'm not sure I understand," Jonathan responded, sensing this early morning visit wasn't going to go well.

"I'm here to ensure your safety, Reverend," said Agent Rodriguez, posing as Schmidt.

The confusion on Jonathan's face allowed the visitor to continue uninterrupted.

"I represent the interests of the Life Extension Institute of Geneva ... and ... I can see by your reaction that you've heard of it!" he noted, smiling his enjoyment.

Jonathan felt as if the pounding of his heart was going to explode in his head as he realized the predicament he might be in.

"Yes, I know exactly what it is," he admitted, unsure of how much he should reveal.

"Then you know I'm here because of your past association with your ex wife.'

Jonathan lowered his head slightly and then nodded cautiously.

"You still maintain a past association with her, is that right?" the visitor postured, expecting it to be a rhetorical question.

"I haven't seen or heard from her in three years—and could care less if I ever hear from her. She's possessed by the Devil," Jonathan spewed, sounding more worried than defensive. "I told your agents how I felt about her two years ago, three years ago, and I'm telling you now—she's the Devil's demon!"

"You haven't seen or spoken to her in three years?"

Jonathan answered his question by giving him an incredulous look.

"She's a carbon copy without a soul!" he raised his voice to emphasize his distain for her. "I'm a pastor. Being married to an alien is not the kind of relationship that congregations understand."

"Do you have any idea where she is?" queried his visitor.

"Haven't seen her since we signed our divorce papers two years ago in my attorney's office."

"Your attorney's office?"

"Yes, we used my attorney. It was a simple, uncontested divorce. He is one of my church members."

"I'd like to speak to him," the visitor petitioned, reaching for his pad and pen.

"Sure, he's one of our trustees—Jack Wilson. His office is in downtown Raleigh. Let's see," he blunted his own sentence while he looked up the address on his phone, "it's at 331 Hillsborough Street."

"That's great. Thank you. Oh ... ah ... have you spoken to her mother lately?" the visitor probed discretely.

"For heaven's sake, no! I'm not exactly one of her favorite people. She and I have never gotten along," Jonathan spouted as if he were proud of their adversarial relationship.

The visitor narrowed his gaze, scrutinizing Jonathan's every move.

"Then you would have no trouble helping us find 'this soul-less devil' if you got wind of where she was?"

"Absolutely not," came Jonathan's speedy reply.

The well-dressed visitor seemed pleased with Jonathan's chumminess and agreed with his colleagues' prior assessment that this religious fundamentalist minister could be of value to them in the future. He would be terminated, of course, when they no longer needed him. But for now he felt certain they would all agree Reverend Pitt was salvageable.

"Reverend, I want to thank you for taking the time to see me this morning," his visitor spoke evenly, as he rose from the chair.

He pulled a business card out of his pocket and handed it to Jonathan. It had 'Mr. Warren Schmidt,' his alias, typed in bold letters centered on it and a phone number, which was a burner phone number, printed under it.

"My pleasure, Mr. Schmidt. If there's any way I can help, let me know," Jonathan volunteered as he stuck his hand out.

"We appreciate that, Reverend," he said, shaking Jonathan's hand. "I expect you'll be hearing from us from time to time. We take the sustainability and thriveability of the Life Extension Institute of Geneva very seriously, and are aware that there are some elements of our society that want to limit the good we can do."

Jonathan formed a partial smile which stuck to his face just long enough for him to give his visitor a corroborating head nod.

"I know what you mean. We are constantly defending our faith against the lunatic fringe elements in our society like the New Thought communities and the cults they represent."

"Then you know some of the challenges we face!" his visitor ratified, using Jonathan's religious extremism to fuel their collaboration.

"Yes, yes I do. I pray to God that we shall both prevail."

"Amen to that," chorused the visitor.

"God is good all the time," Jonathan concurred.

Chapter Five

"Sir, have I caught you at a good time?" Agent Cramer asked, as he shuffled through the various reports from his subordinates about the success or failure of their assignments.

"Yes, I've got a few moments," POTUS answered cautiously. "Wait just a moment while I initial this report, so Ned can be on his way."

Agent Cramer used the extra time to make sure he had the reports in the order he wanted to present them to the President. He put Marge Henry's hospitalization on top and readied himself for discussing it with POTUS.

"Thanks Ned," the President addressed his aide. "Please close the door on your way out."

The aide nodded and then retreated toward the Oval Office door, closing it as he exited.

"Okay. I'm back," came the President's clipped response.

"Sir, as I promised when we last talked, I've got some updates for you."

"Good. I hope you're the bearer of good news," POTUS ventured, as he got up and headed to the window next to his desk.

"I want to start with the update about the Pitt woman's mother, Marge Henry," Agent Cramer began cautiously.

Sensing quickly that the President wanted him to continue, Agent Cramer thought he should explain her current condition first and then elaborate if it became necessary.

"Sir, she's out of the operating room and on her way to ICU. She's still in a coma and they haven't stabilized the cerebral bleeding yet. They've attended to her other injuries, but her head injury and coma are their main concerns. The police are saying that alcohol was a factor. Her alcohol content, thanks to us, was off the chart."

Both he and POTUS smiled their satisfaction.

"She's still in critical condition. As soon as she gets to ICU we'll make our move to insure she's no longer a threat."

"Make sure you do," came the President's emotionless response. "Oh, how 'bout the burner phone trace?"

"We're still working on it. As soon as we get the results, we'll move quickly. I promise you that!"

As he stood by the window, the President saw his own son playing with their year old Airedale Terrier, Spartacus, on the White House lawn. The two were inseparable. His son's laughter reminded him that he hadn't laughed at anything at all these past several months.

"Good. Good," POTUS commented mechanically, trying to get back in sync with their conversation.

"Sir, we don't believe Reverend Pitt is going to be a problem. As a matter of fact, we all agree with Sergio, Reverend Pitt will be an asset when it comes to locating the Pitt woman. Pitt's mother detests him and he believes his wife is in league with the Devil. He has agreed to help us, and I believe he means it. Give us a little leverage, sir, and I believe he'll be a valuable asset. When he's served his purpose ..."

"We'll send him off to his Maker," POTUS cut into Agent Cramer's report.

"Yes, sir. Without a doubt, sir."

POTUS watched as his son played toss and retrieve with a tennis ball.

Pretty good arm there Nathan, the President said to himself, as his son launched another lob over Spartacus' head.

"Sir," Agent Cramer started cautiously. "We have not located Carlton's widow and her daughter, or the Cody woman!"

"What?" POTUS bellowed, turning from the window, irritated at having his vicarious 'quality time' with his son interrupted and annoyed at Pitt's sympathizers falling through the cracks.

"Sir, it appears there are people with competing interests synced with ours!"

"What do you mean?"

Agent Cramer took a quick breath before he spoke.

"Agent Cunningham said Carlton's widow and her daughter were taken from their home in Atlanta by a group of men claiming to be CIA agents. It wasn't true. We checked it out. Her house staff was surprised by the extraction which appeared to be well-planned and friendly. They don't think it was a kidnapping and there's been no ransom demands."

"When?"

"Late last night, sir."

"I don't like this!" POTUS whined, settling into his chair behind the desk.

"You're not going to like this either," Agent Cramer chanced, realizing he would experience the brunt of the President's anger.

"I'm not going to like what?"

"The Cody woman left us a note!"

"What? You've got to be kidding!" hissed the President, trying to keep his composure, but finding it more difficult to control.

"I think you ought to hear it, sir," Agent Cramer suggested. "She knew we were coming—and by 'we' she meant you and us!"

POTUS narrowed his eyes and his nervousness caused him to move his phone to his other ear.

"Okay. Let's hear it," he huffed, surrendering to something he knew would take his anger up a notch.

"Here it is, sir," Agent Cramer began, and then read Mrs. Cody's threatening note to him.

POTUS remembered another caustic note he had received three years ago. It was from Monica Pitt. She had left it in an envelop next to her recorded message on the phone, quoting from the second paragraph of the Declaration of Independence. She had called him out for his role in the human xerography operation.

"So, Pitt is renewing her promise to bring the Institute down," the President voiced stingingly, half talking to himself and half talking to Agent Cramer.

"If she's behind this, she may be one step ahead of us now, sir, but we'll catch up very fast," he boasted to reassure his employer.

"Yes. You're right, Agent Cramer. And since that's where we are—one step behind—I'm going to distance myself from the day-to-day covert logistics and have you report to the Deputy Assistant Secretary of Health and Human Services.

"Copy that sir."

"If this thing hits the news, my energies will be devoted to saving my political ass and Presidency," he scoffed, with no intention of extinguishing his rage.

Agent Cramer remained silent, thinking it was best to let POTUS vent.

"Effective immediately," the President fumed, "you are to report to the Deputy Assistant Secretary of Health and Human Services. I'll set the initial meeting so you can brief her and the senators and senior staff involved."

"Roger that."

"How fast can you get to D.C.?"

"I'm on my way, sir."

I can't believe this particular sitting president could become a two term president, Agent Cramer thought to himself. *He had no prior political or government experience, and won the primaries solely on his Washington outsider status.*

Agent Cramer made sure he had placed copies of the report notes he had just discussed with the President in his lapel pocket and gathered the documents he thought he'd need as he left the command post to head back to Washington, D.C.

Goodnight's whole campaign was based on the fears and anger of the American people who were ready for a change— any change—in government. His own party hadn't even endorsed him in the primaries, and his over-all popularity rating was one of the lowest in American history. He chuckled, remembering perhaps, the oddest primary the US had ever witnessed. *Yet he won the general election in November, because people were sick and tired of being sick and tired with public officials they didn't trust or respect—and the fact that the other party's candidate was less popular than him, had gained him the White House!*

He stopped his train of thought long enough to text Agent Rodriguez to tell him that he was headed to Capital Hill for a meeting with the Deputy Assistant Secretary of Health and Human Services and that he would rendezvous with the team as soon as he returned.

As he settled in the driver's seat in his black SUV, his thoughts took him back to his prior ruminations. *Always with more of a businessman's eye than a politician's wit, POTUS had waltzed his way into the Oval Office. I've seen firsthand some of the things he's done. And I'm not so sure how much longer I can flush my conscience down the toilet.*

Sitting there, in the privacy of his government-issued transportation, Agent Brian Cramer, a summa cum laude graduate from Harvard Law School and decorated Navy Seal, was beginning to feel guilty about his role as covert ops commander of a Chief Executive's cloaked, clandestine secret service unit.

He looked at his palms and thought to himself, *POTUS's human xerography fiasco was only one of the money-making schemes that has made him both dangerous and unfit for the presidency. I wish now I'd never gotten mixed up in any of his ungodly schemes.*

* * * * * * *

"Just to be safe, Babe, we're pitching your burner phone. If those goons confiscate your mother's burner phone or the phone of any of the others, they may be able to ping your location. Burner apps are fine, but I don't want us to take any chances," Andre assured her, as he put her phone in the blender and emulsified the phone into shards of its former nature.

"Well, it served its purpose," Gabby corroborated, taking its remains out of the blender to give them a proper burial.

"It certainly did, but we live in a different world now," Andre continued, "Technical surveillance of communication between cellphones and wireless cell towers or radio links that connect radio towers to networks worldwide is commonplace. So, we've got to be careful. I'm surprised you were able to keep in touch with your mother and friends for so long."

She showed her amateurish knowledge with digital communications by raising her eyebrows, which disappeared under her bangs.

"Hon, I'm so sorry you're going to lose your apartment. It has a perfect view of the Eiffel Tower from our balcony. I ..."

"Don't give it another thought! The view that means the most to me is the one I get every morning when I wake up with you beside me," he admitted affectionately.

Gabby interrupted packing the clothes she was going to store and walked provocatively over to Andre, who grinned his adulation.

"I've got to be the luckiest girl in the world," Gabby boasted, pulling him to her for a quick kiss.

"I'm the lucky one," Andre countered, kissing her nose and then her forehead through her bangs. "Besides I'm looking forward to my leave of absence."

Both of them turned around and canvased the living room. The items they were taking with them were in boxes near the front door. The ones they were storing were placed at the other end of the room next to the couch and loveseat.

"My team will take care of these," he assured her. "We've got ways to transport things out of the country without having to worry about customs. "

Gabby returned his arm hug with one of her own as they huddled in the middle of the living room.

"Except for the vintage Napoleon's chair, which my team will make sure comes with us, they'll distribute the rest of the furniture to the needy. My Nautilus equipment will be gifted to someone, too. And so will the treadmill."

Gabby rubbed his arm, migrating up to his biceps and powerful shoulders which were testimonies to his physical fitness.

"Oh, Hon. We're going to replace all of that equipment," Gabby promised, feeling guilty she had put him in that position.

"All of that can be replaced," he said quickly. "You and your mother and friends can't."

Gabby squeezed his waist and rotated her body so that both of them faced each other and buried her head in his chest.

Andre kissed the top of her head and gently released their embrace.

"Looks like we're about done here. The team will be here soon to move our things," he announced, taking her by the hand and leading her toward the double glass doors to the balcony. "They're airbussing our things to a secure location in the States on an A400M Atlas transport. We're, of course, flying JetBlue to JFK International."

"Let's get another 'Eiffel' of Paris before we leave," Gabby pined, knowing it would probably be a long time before they returned, if ever.

Both of them stepped out on the balcony and focused their attention on the 81-story tower, the most-visited pay-to-access monument in the world.

"It's beautiful," Gabby reveled.

Andre nodded and hugged Gabby around her neck.

"Did you know that the base pillars of the Eiffel Tower are oriented with the four points of the compass?" Andre announced. "And it was almost torn down and scrapped in 1909, because it was originally intended as a temporary exhibit," he elaborated to a surprised Eiffel admirer.

"Wow! No, I didn't know that!" Gabby responded, narrowing her eyes so she could get a clearer long distance look at the skylined structure.

"City officials opted to save it after recognizing its value as a radio-telegraph station. Years later, during World War I, the Eiffel Tower intercepted enemy radio communications and relayed zeppelin alerts. It was also used to dispatch emergency troop reinforcements," he continued, showing how proud he was to be a Parisian.

"You would know things like that," Gabby praised. "You're a military brat!"

"What?" Andre quizzed, surprised at the ease she fell into her American terminology.

Gabby turned her head and kissed him on the cheek.

"I just mean you're the product of a military family and would know military stuff about the Tower."

Andre kissed the top of her head through her hair, the fragrance of strawberries still lingering from her scented shampoo.

"Hitler ordered its demolition, but his command was never carried out," Andre continued. "Also, during the German occupation of our fair city, French resistance fighters cut the Eiffel's elevator cables, so the Nazis had to climb the stairs."

"How cool was that!" Gabby chorused, enjoying his history lesson. "You mentioned zeppelin alerts a while ago. Did that have something to do with those huge balloons I read about in European history?"

Andre laughed and playfully squeezed Gabby before he leaned forward and kissed her on her neck.

"Those balloons, as you call them, were huge airships that were capable of travelling at 85 mph and carrying up to two tons of bombs and dozens of incendiaries. We called the zeppelins 'baby killers' because the Germans bombed people's homes and killed men, women and children!"

"I didn't know that," Gabby confessed, feeling a smothering sensation wash over her. "How awful!"

Why do people—and governments—marginalize the value and worth of people? We are all expressions of the One Power and One Presence, she thought mournfully to herself. *Why can't we see that and take better care of each other?*

"Why don't we change the subject," Andre suggested, sensing her heavy sigh telegraphed a subject matter change.

Gabby squeezed his arms that enveloped her and breathed her agreement.

"As you know, we're going to miss the light show later on tonight. The Eiffel will be cloaked in multi-colored lights from hundreds of light projectors and strobe lights again tonight," Andre continued, pleased they had decided to lighten the conversation.

Gabby sighed her corroborative disappointment, realizing how much they both had enjoyed this view of the Tower.

"Your parents are really okay with your moving?" Gabby queried, knowing how difficult it was for him to leave France.

"As far as they know I'm on a special ops undercover mission for several months. It's best they're not in the loop yet for their own safety. I'm pretty sure they'll be okay. We should have this wrapped up in a couple, to three, to six months. I come from a multi-generational military family. So, they know the drill."

"I've contacted the reporter you suggested with the *New York Times,*" Gabby reported, knowing it wasn't news to Andre. "We meet him a week after we get to the States. And, like you so wisely suggested, I used my real name, Monica Pitt."

"So, the nitty gritty begins," Andre said softly, looking forward to perhaps one of the greatest adventures of their lives. "Caleb is thorough and tenacious. He was a diplomat's diplomat. He fought human trafficking in Africa and brought the heads of several African governments down. He knows what he's doing. He'll be a great help to us."

"I can't wait to meet him."

"I think you'll be impressed. He's your kind of people!" Andre badgered, winking at her.

Gabby threw him an amused look.

"What do you mean—my kind of people?" she quizzed, catching his mischievous smile.

"He's very suspicious of the existence of a human xerography operation. In his travels worldwide as a diplomat, he had the opportunity to research the Twin Strangers Project, which believes each of us has up to 6, and perhaps 7, look-alikes—doppelgangers—around the world. You've probably heard of that organization!"

"Well, yes, of course. But how does that make him my kind of people?" Gabby repeated, caught completely off guard.

"On one of his trips to South America, he ran into one of those twins! Caleb and he looked alike, and they discovered they had the same DNA! They also discovered they're not related in any way, yet they're identical twins."

Gabby sent him a weak smile.

"I can find out for sure when I check the files."

"He knows there has to be something crazy behind their identical twinship, but he hasn't found out who or what's behind it. When I told him about you, he wanted to see you immediately. To him, you're a Godsend!"

"If he already has an identical twin, I mean clone, his data is in my files," Gabby repeated herself.

Andre nodded his head.

"He believes he's been cloned like you!"

* * * * * * *

"Hi, I'm her minister. I just wanted to check in on her so I can let her family know I visited before I left the hospital today," said the well-dressed man who wore a plastic pastor's badge attached to his suit pocket.

The nurses at the ICU's central work station hardly looked up, but indicated their standard approval by letting him know his presence was known without making eye contact.

He waved at the huddle of nurses and quickly made his way past the nurses' station toward Marge Henry's room.

Standing-height computer workstations dotted the corridors and wall-mounted boom systems in each room were stacked with monitors that recorded each patient's vitals.

As he got closer to her room he passed an orderly pushing a small half empty trash cart filled with the usual hospital waste in plastic bags.

He had timed his visit between monitor checks so that he could spend a little 'quality time' with Mrs. Marge Henry.

Two quick peripheral looks to his right and left just before he entered her room told him his timing was perfect.

Her name was on the patient card next to the room number on the door. But when he entered the room he could see that there was a middle-aged man in the bed instead of Mrs. Henry.

"What the ...?" he questioned as he wheeled around so quickly he collided with a nurse.

"Oh, I'm so sorry," he apologized, using his most dignified tone. "I thought this was Mrs. Henry's room!"

The nurse looked at his clergy nameplate.

"I'm so sorry, Reverend Smith, Mrs. Henry was moved to a room in an undisclosed location. It all happened so fast that we haven't changed the name tags yet," she explained, trying her best to conceal the anxious tone in her voice.

"An undisclosed location?" he gave her a puzzled look. "Why would she be moved there?"

The nurse frowned her pretense at confusion and thought she'd better choose her words carefully.

"We just found out she was in the witness protection program and had to be moved. Because of her condition, moving her was difficult. You can check with the central nurses' station ..."

His quick departure blunted her need for an explanation as he headed for the stairwell exit a few feet away. In his business, the only thing worse than pretending to be something you're not was not completing your mission, and Agent White was in a foul mood.

Once he was in the stairwell, he screamed his dissatisfaction as he amped-up his private rage.

* * * * * * *

"Thanks for picking us up, Frank," Andre greeted his friend, as he placed Gabby's and his bags in the back of the SUV.

"Good to see you, Bro," Agent Marino responded, giving Andre a macho hug. "So, this is your main squeeze!" he added, tilting his head toward Gabby.

"Yes, very definitely. Gabby, this is Agent Frank Marino," Andre said, introducing her to the agent she had spoken to on the phone just a few hours ago.

"Frank's one of my old time basic training buddies and counterintelligence colleagues."

"Nice to meet you face-to-face," Gabby smiled as she extended her hand for a handshake.

Agent Marino dodged her handshake and reciprocated her greeting with a hug.

"He's a hugger," Andre explained, smiling at both of them as he motioned for the trio to board the SUV.

Andre ushered Gabby into the back seat, then joined Agent Marino in the front.

"How was the flight?" Agent Marino asked nonchalantly, knowing it was the proper thing to say.

"Okay. Fine. Long," Gabby responded.

"Uneventful," Andre followed. "Uneventful, on-time flights are nice."

"The USO Center is really nice," Gabby announced before either of them could speak.

"Yes. Yes, it is. It's only a couple of years old," Agent Marino announced to both of them. "Andre, that's why I told you to fly in here. They opened it in September of 2014. It makes military travel between countries much easier."

"Much appreciated," Andre replied, giving Gabby a quick wink.

"As you have already seen, it's equipped with a couple of TV's, iPads, self-serve coffee station, and dispensers for munchies," Agent Marino continued his update. "They've even got video and board games."

"Thanks for the tour, Frank," Andre teased. "Maybe next time we can enjoy more of their amenities. We're kinda in the middle of something right now."

"I think it's nice for servicemen—and servicewomen—to have a place to go to relax between flights," Gabby countered, disapproving of Andre's slight.

"Ms. Garceau, you may want to check what's in the bag on the seat next to you and the cooler on the floor," Agent Marino publicized jokingly, venturing a quick glance at Gabby in the mirror.

Gabby opened the bag first and pulled out a cream-filled doughnut.

"Now that's a nice touch," she cheered, blessing his thoughtfulness. "Look, Hon. Cream-filled doughnuts."

Andre looked at Frank and then at Gabby, who was offering him a doughnut.

"That'll take care of my sweat tooth," Andre hooted, accepting the high carb treat from Gabby.

Her trip to the cooler turned up a cache of bottled soft drinks

"How 'bout a Diet Dr. Pepper to go along with that?" she coaxed Andre, who had already reached for it.

"You want one, too, Bro?" Gabby offered, feeling comfortable enough with Agent Marino to push formalities aside.

"Yes. Thanks, Sis," came his immediate reply, which brought good-natured laughter from the three of them.

Gabby handed him the diet drink via Andre and settled back in her seat to down her own doughnut before Andre, who had his hand held out for another one, could consume all of them.

"Andre, thanks for including us in this special assignment," Agent Marino addressed him, wanting to get down to the business of their visit.

"I wouldn't want to do this with anyone else," Andre concurred. "You guys are family. I'm glad I was able to talk my superiors into detailing you. When we get to our Newark command center, Gabby and I will tell you what you've really signed up for."

Andre looked at Gabby, who had just finished her doughnut.

"What we're asking you to do will make the world a safer place for thousands of people who are unsuspecting victims of a crooked regime."

Gabby closed her eyes and thought to herself: *Oh, I hope so! What they're doing has to stop!*

"You know we'd follow you into hell," Agent Marino pledged. "Sis, you've won the heart of a man who has the guts, integrity and wisdom to make this world a better place. And because he believes in you, we'd follow you into hell, too!"

All Gabby could do was put her hands over her mouth and heart to keep herself from crying.

"You guys are the best," Andre vouched, giving Frank a pat on the shoulder. "We just might be taking you into hell!" he glanced at Gabby, who was trying her best to stop the tears from coming.

"We've got a forty-five to fifty-five minute drive, depending on traffic, before we get to Newark," Agent Marino announced. "Or it could be longer than that, depending on what we're going to do with what I report. I've got two things to report before we get there."

Both Gabby and Andre gave him their full attention. Gabby improved her position by inching up in her seat so that she could place her arms on the back of Andre's seat.

"We've moved the assets ..." Agent Marino stopped himself when he heard Andre's sigh. "We've relocated Sandra Henry and her daughter, and Mrs. Cody from their initial safe houses to our Newark, N. J. location ..."

"They're all there?" interrupted Gabby gleefully, smiling broadly at both of them.

Agent Marino nodded.

"Good," Andre affirmed. "I didn't realize you guys had time to do that.'

"And that's not all!" Agent Marino crowed. "Gabby, we've moved your mother closer, too! She's at New York-Presbyterian Hospital, just across the tunnels."

Gabby shot Andre a quick look.

"I want to see her!"

Andre's nod meant he wasn't going to hesitate giving his approval.

"Frank, it looks like we're heading to East 68th Street."

"I'm already headed there, Boss."

"I figured you'd catch that," Andre teased as he winked at Gabby.

"I didn't mean you," Agent Marino addressed Andre, giving Gabby one of his patented smiles in the mirror.

Chapter Six

He entered her plush home office which was just a few blocks from the White House. The upscale furnishings complemented her exquisite tastes as a woman who was used to luxury and money—and getting her way. The plush and cozy atmosphere featured a range of chocolaty shades, from mocha to bitter cocoa. Framed prints of her trips to the city landscapes of Paris, the savannahs of Africa, the outback of Australia, and the slopes of Mt. Everest which lined the walls were statement-making accents.

"Thank you for taking the time to brief us, Agent Cramer," Eleanor Franklin, the Deputy Assistant Secretary of Health and Human Services addressed him cordially.

Agent Cramer gave her the appropriate eye contact and stuck out his hand for the perfunctory handshake.

"Pleased to meet you Madame Deputy Assistant Secretary," he said politely, waiting for the across-the-board introductions of the others present.

They came in the order of each senator's seniority and senatorial role.

"Senator John Chapman, Democrat from the great state of California, and Chair of the Ways and Means Subcommittee on Health," she introduced the senator, who was standing next to her, according to customary protocols.

Agent Cramer and the senator, who was an intimidating, muscular 220 pounds, shook hands.

"Pleased to meet you, sir," Agent Cramer greeted him heartily.

"Senator Helen Schwartz, Democrat from the great state of Nevada, who Chairs the Subcommittee on Human Resources."

The senator from Nevada, who was standing a few feet away from Senator Chapman, stuck out her age-spotted, but elegantly ringed hand. She looked her age, but the years had been very kind to her.

"My pleasure, Senator Schwartz," Agent Cramer parroted amicably, making the necessary eye contact without over-doing it.

"Senator Jeb Boswell, from the great state of Maryland and Ranking Member on the House Committee on Homeland Security."

He was a stereotypically-dressed senator, wearing a dark blue business suit, white shirt and red tie, but his rotund figure gave him the appearance of a politician who could take care of himself in a dog fight.

"Pleased to meet you, sir. Read your very fine book on the Syrian crisis and its implications for our homeland security," Agent Cramer praised him, shaking his hand firmly.

"Thank you, Agent Cramer. I hope it helps you boys tighten your surveillance and ability to identify lone wolves who've been radicalized," the senator asserted, expecting a resounding positive response from the agent.

It came.

"Yes, sir. Absolutely, sir. Your research addresses one of our major concerns. I'm guessing everyone associated with homeland security has read it. I'm not kidding about that!"

The senator's smile telegraphed his appreciation and the twinkle in his eyes and a pat on his shoulder told Agent Cramer he had said the right thing.

"If everyone will be seated, we can get started," the Deputy Assistant Secretary spoke affably, extending her hand toward the cushioned chairs in her office.

A subtle nod from her told her administrative assistant to make sure her guests were offered coffee or tea.

Having accomplished that, her assistant took her leave and closed the door to the spacious office.

"I see you have come prepared, Agent Cramer," the Deputy Assistant Secretary spoke softly, but directly.

Agent Cramer looked down at his attaché case and coupled his tight smile with a head nod.

"Shall we begin," she directed in a tone that was all business.

Agent Cramer's slight hesitation before he distributed copies of his report to all of them was noticed immediately by the extremely observant Deputy Assistant Secretary.

"Agent Cramer, it's perfectly all right. These people are some of the chief advocates and principle donors of the Life Extension Institute of Geneva. You're among friends here!"

His sigh of relief told her she had relieved his concern.

Agent Cramer renewed his intention to distribute the documents, including his notes on Marge Henry's disappearance, which he placed at the end of his report. Having distributed them, with the first copy going to the Deputy Assistant Secretary, he began his cautious, and as it turned out, lengthy explanation of what had happened over the last year.

"I know I speak for all of us," the Deputy Assistant Secretary began, in a calculated, cool tone. "This competing covert organization has to be found and compromised."

Head nods came from around the room.

"They appear to be a few steps ahead of you and well-organized," she continued, showing how much she disdained saying it.

"Do you have any idea who or what they are?" echoed Senator Boswell, wanting to extend the discussion around the bothersome—and dangerous—entity that was a growing threat to their collective enterprise.

"Not yet, sir," Agent Cramer responded immediately. "However, as I mentioned earlier, Monica Pitt has evidently gained the support of a well-organized and well-monied renegade element that is hell-bent on destroying the good we can do!"

Good for whom? he thought to himself, realizing he had positioned what the Institute was doing as benevolent. *It certainly isn't good for the ones who are being used for body parts.*

"Well, you have the ear of the President, young man," chorused Senator Schwartz, showing her faith in him. "And now you have Eleanor's and our total support as well."

The group offered their simultaneous, aggregate smiles.

"We would invite you to stay for lunch," the Deputy Assistant Secretary proffered. "However, it's only ten-thirty and we have more to discuss without taking any more of your valuable time today. We're all looking forward to hearing from you again and believe you will relieve us, and those we serve, of the unfortunate threat to our fine Institute."

Agent Cramer managed a stiff smile and shook all of their hands again before he was escorted out by the Deputy Assistant Secretary. He glanced at the framed painting of the Eiffel Tower, which was larger than the other framed paintings displayed on the adjacent walls.

"I'll be right back," she informed the senators, as she walked confidently beside Agent Cramer.

She noticed his interest in the Eiffel painting as they made their way past it and stopped their advance.

"I see you like that artwork," she addressed the embarrassed agent, and retraced several steps so that they were standing in front of it.

Agent Cramer broke eye contact just for a moment and glanced at the painting again, before re-establishing eye contact with her.

"Yes, it's beautiful. I've never been there, but if I ever get a chance, I'm going!"

"Paris is one of my favorite places," she announced. "I lived there for three years and loved every minute of it. By the way did you know that when you're in the City of Lights, and are about to snap nighttime pictures of the Eiffel Tower, you could be fined?"

Agent Cramer lowered his eyebrows and shook his head, perfectly comfortable with acknowledging his ignorance of one of the most visited cities on the planet.

Eleanor smiled cordially.

"An obscure clause in EU law states that the tower's evening light display is a 'work of art'—and therefore copyrightable. The lighting is an artistic work separate from the structure itself. As such, the artistic lighting is not in the public domain and subject to author's rights as well as brand rights. Tourists can be fined for taking pictures of the Eiffel Tower at night and sharing them on Facebook, Twitter, or online," she elaborated.

"I had no idea," he admitted.

"Taking pics during daytime hours is okay," she continued, "because the tower is classified as public domain, so when the lights are off, picture taking and sharing is permitted."

"Thanks for the warning," he voiced his appreciation. "If I ever get there, I'll be sure to limit my pictures of the Tower to daytime hours—you know, to be legal."

She smiled her admiration for his good-natured joshing.

"Shall we?" she invited him to follow her.

"Yes, ma'am," he replied respectfully, as she escorted him to her front door.

"Agent Cramer," she spoke evenly. "I can't tell you how much we're depending on you and your team. And the 'we' I'm referring to is the 1,250,673 insurance holders and their families here and abroad, including your family and friends, whose safety and health and longevity require the assurance of rejection-free transplants if the need arises. We're counting on you. I'm counting on you. The President's counting on you. Over a million families are counting on you and your team!"

She shook his hand again.

"We're all counting on you," she trumpeted and then took her leave.

He left her elegant quarters with a distinct feeling of being used, of being a means to an end, a cog in the gigantic wheel of political self-interest machinery.

I'm hired to do a job, he reminded himself, *but am I doing the right job for the right people for the right reasons?*

As he took his leave, he couldn't help thinking about his ethical role in the human xerography operation. His whole family was on his policy. His wife, from whom he was separated, his son and daughter, and himself.

"I care about them all," he said out loud when he got to his SUV. "But so do the parents and families of the ones who have been cloned, unsuspectingly, for body parts!

* * * * * *

"How did you get her here?" Gabby wondered, knowing that critically ill patients must be transported safely by experienced and trained personnel using the appropriate equipment.

Frank turned his head slightly without taking his eyes off the road. Before he could respond to Gabby's question, Andre spoke, praising his colleague.

"No problem! Frank made the arrangements for the interhospital transfer," he announced jubilantly. "I didn't realize he'd gotten your mother here this fast or I would have told you we were making arrangements."

Gabby divided her curious looks between the two of them.

"My father is the emergency room director at New York-Presbyterian," Frank stated proudly. "He's a retired army colonel with twenty years experience in mobilizing mobile army surgical hospitals in the Mid-east."

"Wow!" was all Gabby could say as she tried to grasp the incredible synchronicity that was at play. "What about the transfer standards and regulations between the referring and receiving hospitals?" she continued, wondering how they were able to make the transfer work.

"No problem!" Frank dittoed. "Andre, you want to tell her?"

Andre put his arm over the back of the front seat and looked at Gabby, who had scooted toward the front seat.

"Frank's dad rode with the specialist retrieval team in the mobile intensive care ambulance from here to Raleigh. He had fake witness protection papers signed by a bogus FBI agent, courtesy of Frank," Andre elaborated humorously, "who pulled the release order out of thin air."

"What?" Gabby howled, amazed at their daring and flabbergasted that they would even attempt such a inter-hospital operation. A pink flush began to appear on her neck and cheeks.

"The fact that dad had accompanied the intensive care crew in such a well-equipped ambulance and had fake official-looking papers from a fictitious FBI division sold the need for a quick transfer. They were also careful to shield their identities from the overhead exterior cameras."

"Patient transfers are a bit tricky," added Andre.

"Yes they are, and that's why Dad's presence was so important," Frank caboosed Andre's statement. "Patients must be maximally stabilized prior to transfer. Meticulous pre-transfer checks and adherence to standard protocols during the transfer keeps the entire process smooth and unwanted events free. The transport team must be trained to anticipate and manage any possible contingencies, medical or technical, during the transfer. Coordination between the referring and receiving hospitals must facilitate the prompt transfer to the receiving facility to prevent additional injury or casualty. The benefits must outweigh the risks, if you know what I mean."

Gabby raised her hands in the prayer position and brought them to her lips.

"Thank you Agent Marino," she whispered gratefully.

"Dad made sure the MICU ... I'm sorry, the mobile intensive care unit—that's what the special ambulance is called, was equipped with the right equipment so they could provide continuous pulse oximetry, electrocardiography, non-invasive blood pressure and respiratory rates. And that meant being able to provide advanced airway management and intravenous therapy, identifying and treating arrhythmias, and being skilled in basic and advanced life support."

Gabby lifted her eyebrows admiringly.

"The MICU ambulance Dad used had fake tags and fake side striping and unit identifications. The hospital logos were fake, too!"

"And that brings us to the urgent reason which demanded your mother's immediate extraction, Babe," Andre added with his eyes steeled on Gabby, who was trying her best to manage her astonishment.

"ETA in five minutes," Frank announced, as he merged toward the lane that would lead them to the front entrance to the hospital.

Andre took ahold of Gabby's hand and looked her directly in the eyes.

"Babe, we had to get her out of there, because our team discovered that the President's goons were going to kill your mother!"

Gabby swallowed so hard she was unable to speak, but her wide eyes and nail marks in the top of his hand recorded both her horror and stupefaction at Andre's startling pronouncement.

"They were going to kill Mother?" she blurted out, raising her left hand to cover her mouth.

"Our team had been waiting at the hospital ever since your mother was admitted. They got there just after the goons did," Frank reported in his usual unflappable manner. "It was obvious what the goons were going to do as soon as they had a chance, so we forged your mom's transfer documents and notified my dad. He's a household name in the medical community, domestic and military, so his being part of the transfer operation raised no questions."

"And your brilliant witness protection ploy sold it!" Andre boasted, high-fiving Frank's left hand as he drove up to the hospital entrance.

As Frank came to a stop, Andre addressed Gabby, who had not taken off her stunned look yet.

"Well, Babe. Are you ready to see your mother?"

* * * * * * *

On his short drive to the unit's home base command center on Wisconsin Avenue in Bethesda, Maryland, Agent Cramer wondered what he was going to say to his team about the Deputy Assistant Secretary's abhorrent expectations for cleaning up the Pitt problem.

His personal debrief of his meeting with the cadre of government officials was beginning to haunt him.

I know many of my teammates are members, like me, of the Institute's policy holders program, he reminded himself as he glanced at his attaché case on the passenger's seat.

"It sounded so good at first," he mumbled aloud, as he pulled up to the intersection. "And it's good for us, for all of those who are guaranteed rejection-free organs in case of an accident or injury."

He watched a cyclist, sporting his stripped Novara or possibly Pearl Izumi tights and matching jersey ease his way across the intersection.

Perhaps you're one of the quarter of a million insureds, Agent Cramer addressed the biker. *If you suffer a mishap on Wisconsin Avenue or Connecticut or M Street or Massachusetts, and need an organ transplant, you'll be able to file a claim, or your family will, and voilà ... the perfect, rejection-free donor's replacement part will appear! Again and again. As many times as you need it!*

The light changed and the honking horn from an agitated motorist in the car behind him broke his train of thought.

He glanced in the rearview mirror at the annoyed motorist, but didn't say anything. Instead he just hesitated a while longer and then pulled slowly away as the light changed from green to red. A second glance in the mirror revealed that the upset motorist had not made the light and was making a hand gesture that registered his complaint.

"Get a life," Agent Cramer said aloud. *That's a first world problem,* he mused to himself, having to wait for a traffic light again. His self-reflection was diverted when he received a text on his secure line.

A quick glance at the message told him it was from Agent Rodriguez: *How'd your chat on Capital Hill go?*

He wasn't going to answer Rodriguez's summons, but then decided he would ask his colleague to meet him for lunch before he joined the team at home base. So, he pulled into a BP station to text his friend and stop for gas at the same time.

While he waited for his gas tank to fill, Agent Cramer texted: *How 'bout meeting me off site? We can taco 'bout lunch @ the Taco Bell on Democracy Blvd. Does that work 4 U?*

Just fine. You're talking about just U and me?

YES!

Copy that. I'll b there in 15.

Brian knew he could trust Sergio. They'd been military buddies for a long time. He knew Sergio would understand his consternation about the changing atmospherics surrounding the Institute's willingness to put millions of unsuspecting people at risk. His meeting forty-five minutes ago with the Deputy Assistant Secretary and her key human xerography allies had convinced him that helping them was the wrong thing to do.

He drove quickly to the Taco Bell, and was still sitting in the parking lot when Sergio pulled up. When the two agents made eye contact, Brian exited the SUV and waited for Sergio at the restaurant's glass door entrance.

Happy to put their "Agent" titles on a back burner for a while, the two friends gave each other the typical 'bro' handshake and entered together. And then in a stereotypically opposite sex fashion, they both headed for the restroom at the same time.

"Too much coffee this morning," Sergio confessed.

"Too much Capital Hill talk," Brian chorused.

When they both reached adjacent stalls, they initiated the proverbial stall-to-stall small talk.

"How'd it feel to talk to the big wigs?" Sergio quizzed politely.

"Awkward," came Brian's immediate reply. "Daunting. Chilling. Appalling."

"Tell me how you really feel about it," Sergio joked, as he made his way to the sink to wash his hands.

"No, seriously, Bro. Their whole consciousness of entitlement and privilege was disquieting, to say the least," Brian admitted, as he joined Sergio at a nearby sink.

Sergio gave him a puzzled look as he dried his hands on the air dryer next to him.

"We had this same conversation in Kuwait," he reminded his colleague.

Brian stood at the hand air dryer, but didn't set it in motion. He sent Sergio the most pitiful look.

"Yes, I know… Sergio… I'm feeling the same despondency and moral dilemma now that I felt then. You were there! You felt it, too!"

Just as Sergio was going to offer his friend a well-thought-out rejoinder, another customer with his two sons walked through the restroom door.

Both agents exchanged knowing looks and exited the restroom without saying another word.

Brian's going through another major guilt trip, Sergio reminded himself. *He's a good guy. He's my best friend,* his thoughts kept pace with their trip to the front counter. *But he's got to look at the world through counterintelligence eyes. The world's a nasty place! And it's going to take the survival of the fittest to stay the fittest and take care of the fittest. I'm beginning to wonder if he's one of the fittest!*

Chapter Seven

I'll call Frank when we're ready," Andre assured Gabby, as they made their way to ICU. "You can have as much time as they'll give you for this visit."

Gabby sighed as she nodded her agreement. *I don't want to leave,* she pined to herself. *It's been three years since I've seen Mother!*

"Frank's father is aware we're here and will run interference for us if we need it. Frank says his father will take care of everything," Andre continued.

All Gabby could muster was another nod and sigh combination as she grabbed Andre's hand.

"As far as they know, you're in the witness protection program, too!" He paused, and thought to himself: *Well, actually, you are! You've been a witness that's needed protection for over three years now!*

They mustered through the ICU security station without incident with the help of a special visitor's pass issued by Frank's father. Just past the security station was an orderly holding a visitor's sign which had Andre's name printed on it:

Special Agent Bordeaux
Security Pass Access
WPP

"That's us," Andre schooled Gabby, as they approached the orderly.

I'm guessing the WPP stands for witness protection program, Andre said to himself, figuring the hospital wanted to honor the secretive nature of Marge Henry's patient status.

Gabby focused her attention on the slightly over-weight orderly, who was dressed in lime green medical attire. His body seemed to be a high carb product of too many pizzas, doughnuts, and fried chicken. Or perhaps the accumulation of a lifetime of steaks and fries, laced with high calorie sauces, and most likely washed down with his beer or wine of choice.

I'll give him the benefit of a doubt, she reasoned, feeling a tad ashamed of her judgmentalness. *However, his body is a body devoid of hard angles and disciplined muscle,* she mused, as she loosened her hand clasp with Andre and moved her hand up to his sinewed bicep.

They shortened the distance between them and the orderly who was eyeing them with a quizzical expression.

As the pair waltzed up to the orderly, Andre presented his modified ID which retailed his position as: Special Agent Andre Bordeaux, FBI, Witness Protection Unit Assistant Chief, Northern Virginia Division.

The orderly nodded his acknowledgement and started to ask for Gabby's ID, but was pre-empted by Andre, who used his assumed authority as leverage.

"She's Mrs. Henry's daughter. I'm sure you were notified I was bringing her to reunite with her mother!"

The orderly bobbed his head slightly in response to Andre's forceful announcement.

"Yes, sir. Would you both follow me?" the orderly spoke softly, not wanting to upset an FBI agent.

"How is she? Do you know how she is?" Gabby petitioned the bald spot on the back of the orderly's head.

All she could think about was what she was going to do when they got to her mother's room. *Oh, Mother. I love you soooo much!*

The orderly turned his head somewhat to his left so they could hear him.

"I know you're concerned about your mother, but I'm going to have to defer to the charge nurse. She'll know how your mother is. Her doctor may even be here."

"Okay. Thank you," Gabby acknowledged, looking at Andre who gave her a conspiratory wink.

Both of them had had a cursory debrief by Frank's father when they saw him in the ER on their way to the ICU, so they knew she had been stabilized, but that she was still in a coma. Her asking the orderly about her mother was more perfunctory than informational.

He led them through the maze of corridors, lined with hospital equipment and critical care personnel.

"If you've seen one hospital you've seen them all," Gabby whispered to Andre, who nodded his agreement, at the same time visually memorizing their surroundings.

"Here we are," the orderly announced. "I'll get the charge nurse and see if the doctor's ..." he blunted his own sentence. "He's here," he put what he saw into words. "That's Doctor Ori."

Marge's doctor was just down the corridor from them, headed their way. He was thin and sported a high forehead with a slightly receding hairline. His stride was hurried, but confident. He had evidently seen them and guessed they were the ones Dr. Marino had described. Therefore, he wanted to apprise them of her mother's prognosis.

"I'm pleased to meet you," he greeted them warmly. "You must be her daughter, Monica," he assumed, holding out his hand for a handshake.

"Yes, I am," Gabby replied, taking his hand. She didn't want to seem rude, but her heart was beating so fast with anticipation that she thought she was going to burst if she didn't get to see her mother NOW!

"And you're with the FBI," he addressed Andre rhetorically, wanting to be polite as he accompanied them into her mother's room.

Andre dipped his head and flashed his official-looking FBI badge.

Gabby's eyes were pools of tears as she saw her mother covered with tubes, IVs, and bandages. The ventilator's appendage, the breathing tube, was stuck in her mouth and the sound of the ventilator unnerved Gabby, who brought both her hands up to her mouth.

"As you can see, she's still in a coma as a result of the accident. Dr. Marino may have told you that we had to insert another ventriculostomy drain to remove cerebrospinal fluid to relieve the pressure inside her skull," he began, realizing they probably already knew much of the information he was about to share.

Gabby made her way closer to her mother's bedside and tearfully touched her hand. She looked away momentarily and caught the doctor's gaze.

"She's not in any pain," Dr. Ori volunteered, realizing from the look on her face that that was going to be her question.

Gabby tightened her lips and leaked a weak smile, while turning her attention again on her mother. *Mother, I'm going to find out who did this to you. So help me God!* she promised herself.

"Are you sure you can handle this?" Andre asked Gabby, trying his best to sound more official than personal. He was standing beside the doctor, just inside the door to gatekeep the room.

"Yes, I want to hear whatever Dr. Ori has to say," Gabby responded, trying her best to keep herself composed whenever she heard the monitors blare their alarms. But the tears still came, streaking her make-up and filling her eyelashes with salty water.

"Her head swelling is going down, so next week we're hoping we can re-implant the bone piece we removed to allow her brain room to expand."

Gabby winced at his disclosure, and remembered it was the same reaction she had when Dr. Marino described the surgical procedures she had undergone.

"We have no 'miracle drug' to prevent nerve injury or improve brain function immediately after trauma" he continued, "but we can use medication to modify her blood pressure, optimize the delivery of oxygen to her brain, and prevent further brain swelling."

Gabby closed her eyes and braced herself against her mother's hospital bed.

It was all Andre could do to hold himself back from rushing over and holding Gabby.

Be patient, he told himself. *She's going to ... we're going to ... get through this together.*

"How long will she have to be on the ventilator?" Gabby asked the doctor.

"Until she can breath on her own," Dr. Ori stated reservedly, realizing her daughter was looking for the normal signs of recovery.

"How much brain damage do you think there is?" Gabby scrolled down to the next thought in her mental rolodex.

"It's hard to say. We were able to relieve the pressure and brain swelling early on, so we're hoping any brain damage, if any, is minimal. We're testing for brain stem compression and are confident that we're preventing any infection that may have been caused by debris from the accident. Her alcohol content contributed to the bleeding, but we're managing that with medica ..."

"She stopped drinking!" Gabby interrupted, glaring at the doctor. "We were going to celebrate her third year of sobriety on the 20th. We were in the witness protection program," she countered, playing along with the FBI sponsored protection hoax. "Somehow they found her ... us ... and staged this ridiculous accident," she blasted, finding it difficult to stop the tears from coming.

Andre stepped forward to add an official tone.

"You see, Dr. Ori, that's why we had to extract these two as soon as possible. We're in the process of establishing their new identities and making sure this doesn't happen again," Andre articulated, attempting to sell his official role as best as he could, hoping to maintain their cover.

"I understand," responded Dr. Ori, showing his gullibility by believing both of their stories.

Undeterred by Gabby's outburst, Dr. Ori stepped closer to the opposite side of her mother's hospital bed and addressed Gabby.

"You're mother's getting the best of care here, Ms. Henry. I'm sorry that both of you are having to go through this. Your lives are turned upside down enough with being placed in a witness protection program …" he glanced at Andre and then back at Gabby. "And now you're going through the trauma of dealing with your mother's injuries. But I assure you, we can help with this … the accident recovery aspect of your lives … and I'm sure the FBI will help get both of you resituated once your mother recovers."

"Thank you, Dr. Ori. I look forward to that," Gabby voiced her appreciation for his genuine sensitivity.

She looked at Andre, who signaled that they should leave by tilting his head toward the door.

"Normal visiting hours are from 10:00 A.M. to 8:30 PM." Dr. Ori announced. "But you are here under special circumstances, so the hours are open to you."

Gabby smiled for the first time.

"Thank you again, Dr. Ori," she replied gingerly, knowing that no matter how often she wanted to see her mother, she'd have to be very cautious, maybe even painfully economical, with her visits.

"Oh, how can I contact you if there's a change in your mother's status?" Dr. Ori asked sincerely, realizing there must be covert protocols that come into play.

"We'll contact you for obvious reasons," Andre snapped diplomatically. "You'll hear from us quite often, since we're working toward these two good people's relocation as soon as it's feasibly possible."

"Yes, of course. I'm not used to this sort of intrigue," Dr. Ori apologized amicably. "You can stay as long as you like," he proposed, as he took his leave.

Before Andre and Gabby could say anything, a nurse came in to check Marge's vitals. She was a dumpling of a woman, as horizontal as she was tall, like many healthcare professionals seem to be. Her pug nose was lodged between apple-rosy cheeks, and her short curly hair was fixed in a perfect permanent. Every hair was meticulously in place.

"Hi. Are you her daughter?" the nurse asked, as she checked the stack of monitors at the head of the bed.

Gabby nodded and used her forefinger to wipe a tear that had formed and started its salty trip down her cheek.

"We're going to take good care of her, dear. Don't you worry."

Gabby responded with a weak smile, then quietly waited until the nurse left, so she could spend a few more precious minutes with her mother.

Andre stood at the foot of the bed while Gabby kissed her mother's forehead and hand.

"I'm ready to go now," she pined, as she stepped back from the bed and started toward Andre.

"Frank. We're ready!" Andre phoned his patient colleague.

* * * * * * *

"How'd the meeting go?" POTUS asked Eleanor crisply, as the two of them sat opposite each other on the cushioned chairs in the Oval Office.

Her deep penetrating brown eyes looked directly into his tired eyes. She noticed that the President looked tired, with specks of dark brown stubble covering his chin and cheeks. And she also noticed his usual sour disposition was present.

He must have had another bad night, she thought to herself. *Poor POTUS.*

"I thought it went fine," she spoke in an even tone, wondering how much of what she really felt she was going to share.

"Did he share anything more than what I thought he would share?" he quizzed nonchalantly, but the sudden droop of his mouth told her there was more to his question than she might be prepared to address.

"Only a quick report on the disappearance of Pitt's mother, which I have here," she replied, noticing that his sullen face became a mixture of irritation and disgust.

"Yes, yes. I know," came his terse knee-jerk reaction. "Agent Cramer made sure I got a copy. Seems we have people who are very interested in what we're doing."

"And according to Agent Cramer, they are very organized and financed."

"And a couple of steps ahead of us," POTUS chimed sourly.

The Deputy Assistant Secretary of Health and Human Services decided to wait the implications of his last comment out, not wanting him to extend his irritation at the ineptness of his crack team in handling the threat to her.

In spite of his vinegary disposition, the President looked at her respectfully.

"That's why I solicited your active support, Eleanor. I know you have as much invested in this enterprise as I do."

She nodded as she placed Agent Cramer's report beside her on the chair, while POTUS continued.

"With my re-election coming up, I'm not going to have the time to devote to this unfortunate glitch in an otherwise smooth-running operation. You have the resources in the health and medical communities to tackle this problem. And you're a person who gets things done," he added to feed her considerably healthy ego.

Her smile told him his praise was a proper inducement, even though he used it quite freely as a corrupting influence.

A knock on the concealed door leading to his personal secretary's desk in the outer office area prompted the two of them to focus their attention there.

"Enter," POTUS ordered wryly and waited for the person brave enough to interrupt their meeting.

His Chief of Staff opened the door and glanced quickly at both of them and then settled her gaze on the President.

"Sir, forgive my interruption, but a Dr. Schönbächler from Geneva is on the phone and has an urgent message for you. I thought you'd want to take the call."

POTUS nodded and rose to take the call on the secure line at his desk.

"Thank you Ginger," he addressed his Chief of Staff. "I'll take it here."

He raised his eyebrows for Eleanor's benefit and motioned for her to stay. Then he headed toward the 'Resolute' desk built from the timbers of the British Arctic exploration ship for which it was named. It was a gift from Queen Victoria to President Rutherford B. Hayes in 1880 and featured solid plantation-grown Honduras mahogany and a real leather top with an authentic Greek Key embossing in gold.

Eleanor remained planted in her chair at the President's invitation, and waited for the call to come through on the speaker phone.

"Yes, Jonas," POTUS extended his greeting. "It's good to hear from you. I have Eleanor Franklin, my Deputy Assistant Secretary of Health and Human Services with us."

"Greetings to you both," he announced, after a slight hesitation. "I have a bit of a concern I felt I must share with you right away."

"Well, Jonas. You can feel free to share it with us now. I have just asked Eleanor to assume more responsibility for our part in the success of the Institute. She will handle the day-to-day logistics and strategic safekeeping protocols of our mutual interests. I hope you will feel free to consult with her as our chief liaison. However, you will have access to me anytime you want."

"I understand ... and I'm counting on that. And I'm counting on you, too, Madame Deputy Assistant Secretary," he recovered, sounding a bit rushed yet cordial.

"Thank you, Dr. Schönbächler," she spoke politely, recognizing he was still processing the change in contact protocols. "I should be able to provide you with whatever resources you need from this end."

"What seems to be the urgency of your call, Jonas?" the President pressed, as he walked to the front of his desk and sat on the front edge to shorten the distance between him and Eleanor.

"We seem to be losing the GPS tracking capabilities of hundreds of our surrogates worldwide."

"What!?" POTUS and the Deputy Assistant Secretary chorused in unison.

"We've notified our local representatives in the affected areas, since we had the surrogates' current or recent addresses, but in many cases the addresses we have are not current. Of course, that's the reason we adopted the GPS system in the first place—to avoid the expense of keeping each surrogate's whereabouts a matter of monitoring their respective brick and mortar home addresses. The boots on the ground logistics for monitoring millions of people day-to-day would have been impossible."

"I'm not liking how this is sounding," POTUS protested rising to his feet.

"Dr. Schönbächler," Eleanor ventured, readying herself to plunge full tilt into the unfolding drama. "Would you describe the current state-of-the-art human GPS tracking devices? I'm not up to speed yet, but I'll get there sooner than later."

"Sure. Years ago we used clothing, watch bands, necklaces and bracelets as GPS devices to monitor and find our surrogates so they would be available for our policy holders' medical needs. Now we use implant devices called RFID transponders. They're encased in silicate glass and can be implanted sub-derminally anywhere on the body. They contain a unique 16 digit ID number that can be linked to information contained in one of the Institute's external databases. It holds information like personal identification, medical history, medications, allergies, and contact information."

She looked at POTUS, who seemed quite pleased at her on-the-spot education.

"And so, it's these implants that have been compromised?" she queried, wanting to amp up her problem-solving skills.

"Yes. Mostly. However, thousands of the surrogates who have been using the old technologies have also gone off our grid," he admitted soberly, pushing his eyeglasses, which had slid down his sweaty nose, up to their normal height at the ridge of his nose.

"Jonas, we're tracking a band of insurgents as we speak," POTUS lied, wincing uncomfortably at Eleanor. "They're evidently friends of the Pitt woman. Remember her?"

"How could I forget? Cecil and I were the best of friends. I've never gotten over her role in his untimely death," the tone and tenor of his voice changed abruptly.

"Well, we have a special ops team of our own working on it and Eleanor's going to make sure the considerable resources of this office are employed to terminate the threat. I'm sure you two will pool your resources very nicely to stop the bleeding," POTUS summarized, the coolness in his tone unmistakable.

"Then I'll be hearing from you, Madame Deputy Assistant Secretary?" Dr. Schönbächler coaxed, realizing the chit chat was coming to a diplomatic close.

"Without a doubt, doctor. You can rest assured we'll keep in constant contact," she verified heartily, returning the smile POTUS had tossed at her from his sitting position on the edge of his desk.

"Jonas. Thanks for calling. We'll keep in touch," POTUS voiced a quick sign-off.

"Auf Wiedersehen."

As the President pushed the off button, he shot a foreboding look at Eleanor, whose face mirrored his concern.

"Looks like they've engineered quite a master plan to shut us down and expose us," he admitted defensively. "Jonas' call has given me the heebie-jeebies!"

"It certainly looks like I've got my work cut out for me," she responded undaunted.

The President walked over to where she was sitting and positioned himself beside her. In an uncharacteristic gesture of vulnerability, his eyes got watery and he looked like he was going to cry.

"Eleanor, I can't tell you how much your support means to me. My wife may need the help of one of her surrogates for a kidney transplant before the year's out. We need … we all need … the Institute to stay viable and profitable for years to come!"

She put her hands on top of his, and leaned closer.

"Raymond, I owe my career to you. I'm going to handle this ... I serve at the pleasure of the President!"

Chapter Eight

Brian, I'll join you and the others in just a minute," Sergio announced, as he parked beside Brian's SUV in the command center's parking lot. "I've got a few things in the back I need to take into the kitchen."

"Need any help?" Brian offered, as he started to walk around the front of his car toward Sergio's SUV.

"No thanks. I can handle it. It's just a couple of bags of sugar and creamers and Keurig cups I picked up my way to lunch with you."

"Okay. I'll see you inside," Brian replied and reversed his steps toward the command center's entrance.

Sergio needed a little more time to collect his thoughts. Their shop talk over tacos was unsettling for two reasons: his best friend, Brian, was having second thoughts about the team's ability to subdue the escalating threat by an unknown rogue entity. And he was losing faith in his lifelong friend who seemed less than enthusiastic about supporting the whole enterprise.

"I'm not going through this again with him," Sergio murmured aloud as he powered the SUV's rear hatch liftgate closed.

Brian even said one of the things we need to fix if we expect to match strength with strength with this unknown group is a talent triage, he complained to himself. *A talent triage? What the hell does he mean? We've got some pretty damn good folks working with us.*

"Brian said we have talent atrophy," Sergio muttered out loud to a robin that had just flown past him and landed on a branch of a dogwood tree a few paces ahead of him.

He stopped to admire the bird's flight trajectory and obvious landing ability.

Realizing it had an audience it wasn't sure it trusted, the robin chirped its next move and flew quickly away.

He's obviously got talent, Sergio announced to himself admiring the bird's innate aeronautics. *And we've got talent, too! I don't know where Brian's coming from. If there's a talent leakage, it's at the top!*

His thoughts had taken him to the center's entrance where he punched in the security code on the panel on the left side of the door. The door buzzed its acceptance and Sergio entered with his arms full.

"Here's the kitchen stuff," he iterated to the receptionist who smiled when she saw him come in.

Nona was a petite brunette in her twenties who was aware of how cute she was. A heavy fringe of bangs settled on her eyebrows, which framed modest eye makeup and facial features that would qualify her for a Miss America contestant. Her narrow ears were punctuated with fragile, but well-proportioned upper edges, like the dainty handles of china cups, but she wasn't fragile at all. She had a black belt in karate and had won her share of interagency hand-to-hand combat competitions.

"Thanks, Agent Rodriguez. I'll take care of those," she responded cheerfully. "We were getting low on Keurig cups."

Sergio handed her the supplies as she stood behind her desk.

Beautiful is too weak a description. Striking is more like it, he thought, *peerless. What a combination of beauty and strength!*

"They're in the conference room," Nona stated warmly, realizing that would be his next stop.

Sergio nodded and a fractured smile crossed his face.

"It looks like it's going to be one of those afternoons, " he confessed wryly, knowing she knew what he meant.

"And, thanks to you, they've got plenty of coffee if you guys need a Keurig moment," she teased glowingly, as she sauntered toward the lounge area on perfectly formed slim stems of legs.

Sergio acknowledged her compliment with a smile and headed toward the conference room.

When he entered, the team was gathered around the custom, U-shaped thirty-two foot, veneered hardwood conference table that had witnessed countless strategic and tactical discussions.

"Sergio, glad you could make," one of the team members welcomed him and pointed to Sergio's usual seat at the table.

Brian was standing behind the podium at the open end of the table. He was on the phone, and the anxious expression painted on his face telegraphed trouble.

As Sergio made his way to his seat, two of the team members high-fived him a 'bro' greeting. Sergio tolerated the customary greeting to fit in, but it was one he would just as soon avoid.

"He's talking to the Deputy Assistant Secretary of Health and Human Services," Agent Cunningham informed him. "She called while we were waiting for you."

Both agents glanced at Brian, who looked as nervous as bushes at a rest stop planted near areas where dogs do their doggy business.

A hush filled the room when Brian took the phone from his ear. His face was a pallet of irritation and nervousness.

"What is it, Brian?" Agent White asked, proxying the apprehension of the group.

Brian let out a lengthy sigh and then looked squarely at the group of agents who lined the U-shaped table.

"Sergio, that was the Deputy Assistant Secretary of Health and Human Services," he addressed Sergio specifically since Sergio was not in the room when she called.

Brian migrated from behind the podium to address his curious colleagues.

"We have a bit of a problem, gentlemen. A serious problem!" he began slowly. "You are all aware of our difficulty this past week in lessening the threats to the Institute's viability. With the exception of one, the good minister, all of the other targets managed to elude us, even the Pitt woman's comatose mother."

The groans from the group confirmed their collective embarrassment.

"The call I just received from the Deputy Assistant Secretary, who, by the way, is now our Capital Hill point person, is a bit disturbing."

In his most official tone, Brian told the group about the conversation between the President, the Deputy Assistant Secretary and Dr. Schönbächler, Director of the Life Extension Institute of Geneva.

"Effective immediately, we're going to work around-the-clock shifts until we get this thing handled once and for all!" Brian decreed. "We've been handpicked by the President. Our counterintelligence capabilities are peerless. We're the best of the best. So, it's time we started acting like it."

Sergio squinted at his friend, studying him, analyzing his facial features, assessing the tone and tenor of Brian's voice.

Looks like we've got the old Brian back, he applauded his friend's apparent about-face silently.

* * * * * * *

They used the Holland Tunnel to get to Newark because there was an accident on 495 tying up traffic in both directions. And because of where they were bivouacked, the I-78 Express was the best route anyway. Their command post was in an old farm house off of Columbia Turnpike between South Mountain Reservation and Seton Hall University.

The old 5,800 square foot retro-fitted farm house was built in the 1960's, but had gone through a number of renovations since it had previously been used as a veterinary clinic and a special education facility for autistic children after the original owners sold it. It sat on eighty secluded acres and the house proper was surrounded by a stately white picket fence once you navigated the half mile cinder driveway to get there.

"This was my uncle's place," Frank boasted, feeling very much at home on the property.

"It's beautiful!" Gabby cooed, as her admiration took her out of the parked SUV.

She was totally enthralled by the sprawling split-level farm house which was screened by tall oak and pine trees bordered by slightly manicured azaleas and rhododendrons that were left alone to grow the way they wanted. Shrubbery and well-organized beds of luxuriant chrysanthemums, dahlias, hyacinths, and pansies lined the walks.

"How did you arrange for us to use this as our command center?" came Andre's follow-up query.

He had joined Gabby outside the vehicle and watched as Rita, Jack, and Hank, three of his team members, appeared through the front and side doors of the farm house, followed closely by Peaches, her mother, and Mrs. Cody.

"It's my brother, Paul's and mine now!" Frank said proudly. We call it Zeus' Den." .

"What?" Andre replied, continuing to be amazed at Frank's business acumen.

"We just had to keep it in the family! It broke our hearts when our uncle sold it, so we decided a year ago to purchase it. We used my brother's disability settlement and what was left of my lottery winnings to buy it outright."

Both Gabby and Andre exchanged astonished looks, but before either could say anything, they joined the huddle at the picket fence gate, who were excitedly waving and cheering their welcomes.

"He's told you, huh?" Rita exclaimed, wearing her military fatigues, but standing on her bare feet. She was the first team member to get to the gate, verifying her claim of being the team member who was in the best physical shape. She had kept her slim figure since college and still ran marathons whenever she could.

"About owning this amazing property!" chorused Jack, who was holding a plastic bowl filled with the remnants of mixed fruit that had miraculously stayed in the bowl after his jaunt to join Andre, Frank, and Gabby.

Even though he was a man of average height, Jack was powerfully built. His black hair was tied back in a short ponytail which exposed his larger than normal-sized ears. Jack was the group's cyber hacker. He used to work in the NSA's cybercrime division and several Silicon Valley firms before he went into business for himself and settled on the counterintelligence route.

"Monica. Monica!" shouted Mrs. Cody and Mrs. Henry breathlessly at the same time.

Frank looked at Gabby, who was already tearing up, and then he made eye contact with Andre.

"We haven't told them about your name change yet, Gabby," Frank whispered. "You said you wanted to tell them!"

Gabby nodded her head.

"You're exactly right!" she verified. "We planned to tell them toni ..."

She was interrupted by consecutive hugs from all three women who lavished her with their collective 'long sought for' reunion.

The four of them huddled in a tight group hug, trying their best to curb their tears, then allowing them to flow freely.

All they could do was share tears of happiness. Letting years of pining for each other, and worrying for each other's welfare, and missing each other's physical presence, gave them permission not to hold anything back.

The group of agents that surrounded them felt the palpable emotion of the reunion. Rita let the tears roll down her face unabated. The guys, including Andre, finally gave up trying to hold their emotions intact, and allowed their tears to flow, without embarrassment.

Gabby was the first of the reunited women to compose herself.

"Sandra. Emma. Peaches. It's so good to see you, to hold you, to know you are all safe!" she let out her adulation for the three of them.

"We've got soooo much to talk about," Emma pressed big-heartedly.

"It's been so long!" Sandra ricocheted her worship for Gabby off of Emma's greeting.

Peaches waited for the older women to voice their praise before she added hers.

"We knew this day would come," she declared softly, reverently.

"I'm so glad we'll be able to do this together … with a little help from our friends," Gabby raised the level of her voice so the others could hear her.

"This must be Andre!" Peaches guessed, looking squarely at him, as he had taken his position next to Gabby.

"Yes! Yes!" Gabby raved. "This is the love of my life!"

"It's nice to have a face!" Emma chorused, smiling at the two of them.

"Back at the three of you," he praised the women. "However, I've seen pictures of all three of you in Gab … Monica's album."

Gabby smiled at Andre's slip.

"You're family," she addressed the three women. "Of course I'm going to have pictures!"

"We'll talk more about us when we get inside," Gabby promised, as she put her arm around Andre's waist.

"And inside it is," cheered Rita. "It's the house that Frank and his brother, Paul, built!"

"He's a wizard," Andre crowed, realizing he didn't have to explore how Frank had acquired the command facilities so quickly.

"And he and Paul are quite the hosts!" Rita chimed, wanting to help both Gabby and Andre get up to speed on the outstanding accommodations.

Frank smiled, appreciating their endorsements.

"You mean your brother is here, too, Frank?" Gabby asked, feeling a bit silly she had asked, since Rita had already announced the brothers were their hosts.

"He's in the kitchen preparing our dinner," Frank added to the surprise.

"And he's a wonderful gourmet cook," Jack reworked Frank's compliment, as he joined the group who were still at the gate, despite the gate having been opened by Frank, who had unlatched it earlier to welcome his guests to enter.

"Well, whaddaya say we go inside?" Frank coaxed. "You guys have got to be tired," he addressed Gabby and Andre.

"Hank and I'll get your bags," Jack volunteered as he made eye contact with the two new arrivals.

Andre nodded his head, acknowledging the collegial hospitality of his subordinates.

The group chatted its way down the sidewalk in twosomes, looking like a crowd of open-house seekers searching for decorating ideas during a Home Builders Association 'Parade of Homes' annual tour.

Rita had corralled Gabby and was pumping her for information.

"Andre adores you, you know. When did you guys meet?"

Gabby laughed good-naturedly while keeping her face pointed toward the front door.

"We met at *de La poste centrale du Louvre* in Paris. I was just learning to speak French and was having trouble figuring out the postage rates and package weights. This absolutely gorgeous French police officer helped me send a package back to Marseille. That police officer was Andre," Gabby recollected cheerfully.

"And the rest, as they say, is history!" Rita chimed in as she glanced at the necklace Gabby was wearing. "That's a beautiful necklace. Did you buy it in Paris?"

Gabby lifted the necklace so Rita could take a closer look.

"It's beautiful," Rita chorused, clasping the diamond-studded Eiffel Tower jewelry piece in her hand.

"Thank you. Andre bought it for me for my birthday."

"So, your history together started in Paris at the post office!" Rita continued.

"Well, we're still making history. If you know what I mean!" Gabby bragged, giving Rita a quick wink. "So, you might say we played post office!"

Rita smiled at Gabby's cleverness and was going to ask her another question, but the group had reached the front door and Frank made a request.

"Jack and Hank, would you see that these folks get to their room? I'm sure they're road-weary!"

Hank, at 54, was the oldest of Andre's elite team. He was slightly over-weight for his size—flesh had been added over the years, and had migrated to the middle of his body, like mud sliding downhill. Nowadays, his idea of exercise was making a refrigerator run during TV commercials and returning to the couch with a beer in one hand and a slice of pizza in the other.

"I want to meet your brother first," Gabby requested, hoping Andre would be okay with that.

"Of course, we want to see the co-owner of this wonderful estate," Andre expressed his agreement.

"Sure," Frank consented. "Jack and Hank will take your luggage up to your room and I'll show you where it is later."

"You've got the only room upstairs with a private bath," Rita chorused. "I'm sure you'll put it to good use!" she winked.

Gabby and Andre purposefully limited their acknowledgement with cordial smiles, not wanting to advertise their intentions for an intimate rendezvous later that night.

The couple waited for Emma, Sandra and Peaches to join them in route to the kitchen.

"I am thrilled we're together!" Gabby said to them, as they walked arm in arm down the wide hallway.

Andre followed dutifully, admiring the foursome.

They've had a rough three years, he thought to himself. *I'm going to see that the rest of their lives are filled with health and happiness.*

* * * * * * *

With growing interest, Jonathan watched an old media news clip about terrorist violence in the streets of a major city.

It was the fifteenth or sixteenth clip he had reviewed. He had decided to use several of the most poignant clips of violence in America and the world to show his congregants as part of his sermon this coming Sunday.

There's just too much violence in the world, he said to himself, as he sat glued to the desk top computer in his office.

"As a minister of the Gospel, I feel compelled to point out the sins of humanity and how a God of justice will make us pay for our indiscretions," Jonathan proselytized out loud to himself.

As shepherd of my flock, it is my God ordained responsibility to help my flock see that their sins contribute to the chaos we're experiencing, he continued his sanctimonious thought diatribe. *They know how I object to their watching violent TV shows and YouTubes.*

He lifted his glass to take a sip of iced tea, but discovered the glass was empty. The temporary shock diverted his attention away from the YouTubes on the screen and prompted him to call for a decaffeinated replacement.

He punched the church secretary's extension on the phone's keypad.

"Mrs. Watson, would you mind coming in here and refilling my iced tea," he summoned expectantly. "I'm right in the middle of an important YouTube sequence and don't want to lose track of where I am ... Oh, would you refill it with ice cold seltzer water instead?"

"Yes, of course, Reverend," Mrs. Watson obeyed dutifully. "I'll be right in!"

He returned his attention to the computer monitor and didn't notice her enter his office to retrieve the empty glass on the coaster at his elbow.

In a few moments she re-entered the office and received the same non-reception she had experienced a minute ago. Wordlessly, she dutifully placed the fresh glass of iced seltzer water on the coaster and quietly retraced her steps, closing his office door as she left.

In a few moments his eyes left the screen as the seltzer water sizzled its readiness.

"Ah, yes," he said out loud, after tasting the cool refreshment. "Good. So good!"

Before he schmoozed with the screen again, he thought of a story he had used years before to illustrate people's Good Samaritan obligation to each other.

Now where did I put that? he quizzed himself, as he pushed the pause icon on the YouTube.

He didn't consult his sermon stories menu folder on his computer because he knew it wasn't there. He hadn't yet asked Mrs. Watson to type the old stories he had collected from *Guideposts, Christianity Today, Simple Grace, Reader's Digest* and other Christian magazines into the online archive.

He left his chair and walked to a pair of four-drawer file cabinets behind him.

I'll find it here before I can think of which sermon it's in, he schooled himself, as he crouched down to the drawer that contained his earlier sermon outlines, sermon notes, and sermon stories.

As he fingered through the alphabetically-arranged files, he thought, *I need to give Mrs. Watson a summer project one file at a time, so we can lighten some of these file drawers.*

"Oh, here it is," he said aloud, as he pulled the huge hanging file out of its nest in the drawer.

He closed the file cabinet drawer with his foot as he stood to plop the file on his desk.

The first thing he did when he planted himself back in his seat was to enjoy another sip of ice cold seltzer water.

"I don't know which I like better," he compared the drinks out loud. "Decaffeinated tea or seltzer water."

Pleased with his aborted comparison, he opened the sermon story file and began looking for the story he wanted to use.

After a half hour's search he found it. It was the true story of a man who sacrificed all he had to save his village from the clutches of fortune hunters who wanted to finance their religious wars cause.

"Yes! This'll be perfect," he applauded himself out loud.

I told this story early on in my ministry, he recollected to himself. *I doubt any long term members remember it, and with so many new members who haven't heard it, I think I'll be fine.*

Satisfied that the story's addition was just what he needed to complement the YouTubes he was going to include, he closed the hanging file and placed it on the edge of his desk.

Renewing his interest in a sparkling refreshment, he took a healthy sip of seltzer water and pushed the pause icon on the YouTube he had deserted over a half hour ago. Suddenly, a particular video clip caught his eye.

Oh, my goodness! Did I see what I think I saw? Let's rewind this thing, he instructed himself, keeping his eyes glued to the news coverage.

As the scene unfolded, he kept rewinding, running it, and then rewinding it again and again, stopping it to get a closer look at what he was seeing.

"Oh, my God!" he shrieked, unable to take his eyes off the screen.

Oh, my God, he repeated wordlessly to himself.

"It's MONICA!"

He restarted the YouTube footage one more time so he could get a clear picture of her and where she was. It was a YouTube of a terrorist shooting in a mall two months ago. People were running out of the mall and one of them was a dead ringer of Monica!

"Paris! She's in Paris!" he shouted, dumbfounded at what he had just seen.

Chapter Nine

"Agent Cramer, thanks for meeting with me again so soon," the Deputy Assistant Secretary greeted him with the customary handshake.

Brian reciprocated, squeezing her hand politely, lightly, and was surprised at the strength of her handshake.

She motioned for him to sit in the chair next to the loveseat adjacent to where she was planning to sit.

"Would you like something to drink?" she asked, as she headed toward the minibar.

"No, Ma'am. I'm fine," he declined cordially.

"Are you sure? I've got coffee, tea, juices, sparkling water," she pressed, insisting on being polite.

"Well. Okay. I'll have some coffee," he surrendered, thinking he'd better drink something.

"Terrific. Decaf or high test, flavored or straight?" she countered.

"Decaf and flavored sounds good. Are you sure you want to go to the troub ... I ... don't want to trouble you."

She looked up from the granite counter top.

"No trouble at all. I was the one who asked you," she propositioned cheerfully.

"Thank you," he said, fully acknowledging her hospitality.

"Decaf hazelnut okay?" she pitched, as she opened the carousel cabinet which contained a wide selection of Keurig coffee cups.

"Absolutely!" chorused Agent Cramer, as he found himself admiring her lavish living quarters.

Her home was an architectural dream. Complete with a vaulted ceiling, that was the focal point of her upscale living room, and an overlook on the second floor made the highly luxurious living room larger than life. Stunning windows added visual interest and plenty of light to the spacious surroundings. A floor-to-ceiling stonework fireplace was the perfect accent to capture the architectural genius of her homespun living quarters.

So, this is how the other half ... the top one percent lives, he kept his thoughts to himself.

"You have a beautiful place," he praised.

"Why, thank you. I like it. I was able to purchase it at a decent price because of the previous owner's unfortunate foreclosure," she admitted. "I know it's quite a house just for two people, but I have made use of all 6,500 square feet."

"Wow! That is quite a house," was the only response Brian could muster.

"It's part of the divorce debris," she confessed, as she made her way over to him with two cups of coffee.

She handed him his cup first and then made sure both of them had coasters before she sat down with her cup.

"It's pretty nice debris, don't you think?" she heckled, feeling quite proud of herself.

"Sounds like you had an amicable settlement," Brian guessed, wanting to appear both sensitive to the emotional upheaval she must have gone through on the one hand and aware of her business savvy on the other.

The Deputy Assistant Secretary exploded in a raucous belly laugh, spilling some of her coffee in the saucer before she could place her cup and saucer on the coaster.

"Oh, it was amicable all right! I took him for all he was worth!" she boasted, as she used her napkin to soak up the spilled coffee.

"I'm sorry. I ..."

"Oh, don't be sorry," she blunted his apology. "He had an affair, and ... deserved what little he got!" she topped off her saucy explanation with a spiteful smile. "I married a billionaire and turned him into a multi-millionaire!" she continued, feeling quite satisfied with herself.

Agent Cramer chuckled, liking her sense of humor.

"I've got this," she acknowledged, extending both arms in a semi-circle to symbolize her ownership of the house. "And the best thing that came out of our marriage, my son!"

Brian threw her a tight, respectful smile, because he wasn't quite sure what to say.

"Dalton is in summer camp," she elaborated, figuring he might be wondering where her son was.

"Oh," Brian responded diplomatically, raising his eyebrows to show his approval.

"He's twelve, and the love of my life. And I would do anything for him!" She took another sip of coffee and fixed her eyes on Brian. "Are you married, Agent Cramer?" she asked rhetorically, noticing he was wearing a wedding ring.

"Yes, Ma'am. Julia and I have a son and a daughter, ages four and six."

She smiled cordially.

"Please call me Eleanor," she urged congenially. "May I call you Brian since it looks like we'll be working together?"

"Yes, Ma'am ... of course ... Eleanor. That would be nice," he agreed, somewhat self-consciously. He took a sip of coffee to settle his nerves. This was the second time he'd met the Deputy Assistant Secretary face-to-face and the first time in her home. So, he was feeling just a bit uncomfortable.

Where is she going with this? he asked himself.

"I suppose you're a policy holder, too?" she pried, studying him.

"Policy holder? Oh, you mean with the Institute?" he reasoned carefully.

She nodded schemingly, enjoying catching him off guard.

"Yes, Brian ... with the Institute. I have one of their Tier 6 insurance policies on my son, as well as myself."

That's a high-end policy, Brian thought to himself. *The Deputy Assistant Secretary has the platinum level coverage. Both*

*her son and her have six surrogates who have been cloned specif-
ically for each of them. Wow!*

"That's really nice," he admired respectfully. "I have Tier
1's on us," he appended, recognizing he didn't need to explain
his first level status.

"It's really a good feeling, isn't it, not to have to worry
about tissue rejection, or waiting lines, or stuffy emergency care
waiting rooms," she chorused jubilantly.

Brian smiled and nodded, apparently giving her the green
light to continue.

"Did you know that the average waiting time to find a deceased donor can be 3-5 years, and in some states, it's closer to
8-10 years? Patients are prioritized by how long they've been on
the waiting list, their blood type, immune system activity, and
other factors. Eighty percent of the people on the waiting list are
on kidney dialysis. Isn't that awful?" she cringed.

Brian just sat there giving her his full attention.

"The organ allocation process is pretty much the same for
all organ donations, except for the differences in waiting time.
That's what I love about the Institute's health insurance policy—
it allows us to by-pass needless hospital regulations and
protocols," she continued, picking up steam.

She's making a whole lot of sense. I'll have to admit, Brian
said to himself. *Someone could die waiting for an organ transplant!*

He nodded again to show his support and agreement.

"We're covered whether it's a heart transplant, or liver, or
lung, or kidney, or pancreas!" she raised her voice, delighting in
retailing the benefits of membership.

With that admission, her entire demeanor changed. A dark
cloud crossed her complexion. Her mouth was arranged in a
smile, but the steel in her eyes spoke differently. Insanely.
Maniacally! Her lunacy was unsettling.

"This is a damnable mess," she cracked, her voice almost
sounding like a growl.

"We are responsible for the safety and smooth-running of the world. We deserve this kind of insurance ... You and your family deserve it! ... POTUS and his family deserve it! We are in positions of power and authority. So, why shouldn't we enjoy certain perks that come with wealth?" she pressed, spraying spittle as she spoke.

He looked at her White House clearance pass lying on the cocktail table near the *Smithsonian Magazine* which was stacked on top of several other magazines next to her coffee cup and saucer—then renewed his eye contact with Eleanor, who looked like a televangelist on steroids.

"Brian, this health insurance perk has never been available to any previous administration or to the shakers and movers in this world. It belongs to the rich and connected! It belongs to the famous and the influencers ... the elite and talented!" she raved and then paused to collect her next thoughts.

They came with such vehemence, demented arrogance, and deranged entitlement that it sent chills up his spine.

"Brian," she bellowed. "The masses have always been here to serve us! To provide us what we need! To die for us, if necessary, so we can live the life of privilege we've earned ... that we deserve!"

The Deputy Assistant Secretary leaned toward him. Her deep, dark eyes were glazed, empty, hollow, maniacal.

"We've got to clean up this damned mess!" she accentuated, building on her previous statements.

This is a woman I don't want to cross, he thought, keeping his eye contact with her.

"You know the mess I'm talking about, don't you, Agent Cramer—Brian?" she queried, sending him her question through narrowed eyes.

"Dr. Schönbächler's report!" he guessed intuitively, wanting to trump his own unsteadiness by demonstrating the second nature of his counterintelligence savvy.

She nodded menacingly.

"They've caused a major breach in our GPS tracking system! Too many donors have gone off grid. And we've got to plug the hole," she fumed, as she looked at the cold coffee in her cup.

"Luckily ... if you can call it lucky," Brian began. "Almost all of the surrogates who've gone off grid are the earlier clones ... donors the Institute created years ago who were supplied clothing, watch bands, necklaces and bracelets with GPS devices in them. We're using the demographics we have on each of them to track them."

"That seems like an awful lot of dots not being connected, Brian!"

"Presently! That's true. But we believe we can connect the dots and terminate the breach."

"I'm counting on it!" Eleanor sputtered, as she picked up her cup and saucer. "I've barely touched this and it's cold," she admitted the obvious. "I'm getting a refill. You want one, too?"

Brian sipped his cup of mud.

"Yes. That sounds good," he agreed, not particularly enjoying cold coffee.

She tilted her head, indicating for him to follow her to the bar.

Brian obeyed without saying a word and joined her at the marble-topped bar.

Before either of them could speak, the phone rang.

"It's the secure line," she announced mechanically. "I'd better get it."

She grabbed her phone and gave a professional greeting.

"Hello, Eleanor," came the reply. "This is Dr. Schönbächler."

Eleanor put the speaker phone on and motioned for Brian to come closer.

"I'm sorry to bother you on a Saturday, but I've got some distressing news again!"

"Oh, Jonas. What is it? Oh, and ... Agent Cramer is here with me. We've been discussing the GPS tracking system issue."

"Hi, Dr. Schönbächler. I'm glad we're connecting!" Brian voiced his presence.

"You may not be so glad, young man," Dr. Schönbächler countered.

Eleanor and Brian shot each other puzzled looks.

"Eleanor … Agent Cramer … The Institute's online cyber security system has been hacked!"

"What?" Eleanor voiced her shock.

Brian raised his eyebrows, but didn't say anything.

"Apparently, they stole cookies, breached a couple of weak passwords and hijacked the second Tier's source code. That puts data for 27,438 surrogate files at risk," Jonas railed contemptuously.

"Have you discovered the source of the hack?" Agent Cramer quizzed.

"We're working on it," Jonas replied sharply. "We don't think it's European or Far East in origin … and we're not suspecting the Russians or Chinese. We're suspecting it may have originated in the States!"

"You're talking about our back yard!" exclaimed Eleanor, looking at her cup of cold coffee that evidently wasn't going to be refilled with a hot cup of Joe any time soon."Do you have any sense about the integrity of your interdepartmental IT trust architectures?" Brian interjected.

"We don't believe they're the cause of the cyber contamination! We're assessing our encryption landscapes and authentication protocols that may have been vulnerable to the outside. We thought we had our management of security configurations down to a science, but obviously, with this latest leak, we don't!"

"Who's in charge of your incident management and cyber recovery over there?" Brian queried, readying a pen and note pad Eleanor had just given him.

"Clément Dubois. He's been with us since the Institute's inception. I'll have him contact you within the hour."

Brian placed the slip of paper with Clément's name printed on it in his jacket lapel pocket.

"Okay. Good. Dr. Schönbächler, you're no doubt resetting passwords on the Tier 2 accounts?" Brian pressed diplomatically.

"Yes, as we speak," Jonas responded.

"Have there been any demands for money?" Brian asked, realizing some hackers install ransomware on their encrypted data.

"No, I ... we ... Do hackers do that sort of thing?" Jonas queried, his voice crackling under the pressure.

"More than you might think," Brian clarified. "If that's what this is about, you'll be getting their demands in a day or so!"

That's the first time I've heard of such a thing, Eleanor thought to herself. She gave Brian an admiring look. *You're definitely the right man for the job. This digital world is getting to be a scary place!*

"What can we do from this end?" Eleanor offered. "Of course, we'll contact our cybercrime people and have them get in touch with you, and Brian and Clément will chat, but are there any other resources we can provide?"

"I can't think of any," Jonas responded, running his nervous fingers through his thinning hair.

"I'll keep POTUS in the loop," she promised mechanically, raising her eyebrows at Brian to acknowledge the importance of keeping the Chief Executive fully informed.

"*Bis später,*" Jonas responded wearily. "You two take care of yourselves."

Eleanor pushed the 'end of call' icon and left the phone on the counter top.

"This isn't good. This isn't good at all," she repeated.

"No it isn't," Brian agreed, resisting the impulse to feel over-concerned.

Eleanor took one more look at her coffee cup and poured the cold coffee down the bar sink.

"I don't know about you, but I could use a drink!" she confessed. Her tone was a mixture of shock and resentment.

It's too early in the day, he thought to himself, *but it was also too early to hear what we've just heard.*

He looked at his digital watch and then at her.

"Yes. Actually, that sounds good."

"Bourbon okay?" she pitched, holding up an opened 750ml bottle of Sazerac's Old Rip Van Winkle, some of Kentucky's finest.

Brian gave her a thumbs up and sat on one of the designer bar chairs which had eluded them during their troublesome conversation with Jonas.

Eleanor pulled two of her personalized whiskey glasses off the overhead hanging glass rack and placed them side-by-side on the counter.

"How's that?" she addressed Brian, as she poured three fingers worth of the distillate into one of the glasses.

He held up three fingers with a smile, indicating he wanted a double.

"Got you covered," she cheered, smiling her appreciation of a man who enjoyed good liquor.

After duplicating his order, she sat in a bar chair across the counter from him and then lowered her gaze to the rich and brilliant amber-colored bourbon with a flame-orange glint. He watched as she placed her nose just above the rim of the glass and savored the aromas. She loved catching the distinctive vanilla and caramel scent of the charred oak barrel it came from. Then she renewed her eye contact with Brian and lifted her glass for a toast.

"To figuring this damn thing out!" she prophesied, wearing her anxiety on her face.

"Amen to that," Brian agreed, and lifted his glass to hers.

Both mirrored each other's enjoyment of the full-bodied whiskey by closing their eyes to savor the soul of the whiskey.

Brian's eyes opened before Eleanor's, who was still letting the savoring taste of good whiskey warm her throat and stomach.

"A key element of data loss prevention centers on restricting inappropriate access through hacking, malicious malware, or seemingly innocent attempts to use data and services by unauthorized users," he rattled off what he had been thinking.

Eleanor looked at him, trying her best to detach herself from the exquisite effects of having just taken one sip of the whiskey.

"The Institute must understand their evolving threat landscapes for enhanced cyber security," he continued, half talking to himself and half talking out loud to her, "because the explosive growth of the 'hacking economy' has made cybercrime a multi-billion dollar business."

Eleanor took another sip before she responded to Brian's forecasting.

"These cyber criminals have to be associated with the Pitt woman," she blasted, as a smothering feeling of dread enveloped her.

"I'm thinking the same thing," Brian agreed. "So, that leaves out ransomware and extortion. These people, whoever they are, intend to shut the Institute down!"

* * * * * * *

"Oh, hi," Paul greeted the entourage as they entered the spacious kitchen.

He was not your stereotypical chef in appearance. He was thin and elegantly postured, and lacked the usual frenzied energy so many chefs seem to radiate.

He and one of the other team members were standing at the large island in the middle of the room, dicing tomatoes and cutting lettuce on their respective cutting boards.

The group parroted their collective greeting at the two cooks and Frank made the official introductions of the newest arrivals.

Paul rinsed and dried his hands off, and then offered both Andre and Gabby handshakes.

"Glad you two could join us," Paul greeted them warmly. "Welcome to our humble home and to the Institute-busting headquarters of North America!"

Everyone's rising decibels of laughter filled the room.

"How was your trip?" Paul extended his greeting.

"Fine," Andre confirmed. "On time flights are always the best flights."

Gabby smiled and nodded her agreement.

"And our wonderful chauffeur gave us door-to-door service!" she praised, referring to Frank, who was peeking at dessert.

"Your wonderful chauffer's going to get into trouble," Rita giggled her announcement, pointing at Frank.

"Get out of there," Paul ordered good-naturedly as Ned, his assistant cook, smacked Franks fingers.

Everyone laughed, including Frank, who held his hands in a prayer position in front of him, pretending to ask for forgiveness.

"You're in for a treat, Monica and Andre," Mrs. Henry addressed Gabby and Andre. "Paul is an exceptional gourmet cook who's very good at helping you add a few more pounds."

The others agreed, mirroring each other's "Ahhhhhh" and rubbing their hands on their stomachs.

Mrs. Cody called the couple's attention to Paul's gourmet world by praising the state-of-the-art surroundings.

"Monica and Andre, just look at these beautiful granite countertops. And his custom kitchen cabinets extend to the ceiling. The tile floor you're standing on is easy to clean. I know..." she caught herself in mid-sentence. "I know because I've cleaned it!"

Everyone joined in the laughfest again.

"Look at the back-splashes," she continued. "Aren't they gorgeous! And look, he has stainless steel appliances throughout the entire kitchen. And double-sized refrigerators."

"And two ovens. And ... I want some of these myself ... glass-faced cupboards!" Peaches added her kitcheny praise.

I want some of those myself, Gabby agreed silently. *I want my life back so Andre and I can have nice things like that.*

"And his pantry area is as big as a normal-sized room," Mrs. Cody bubbled, pointing to the sliding glass doors at the far end of the kitchen. "The light comes on when you open the doors, and goes off when you ..."

"CLOSE THEM!" the group shouted in unison, cutting into what would be her final touches of the spontaneous kitchen tour.

"Okay! Okay! My brother's going to think we came to see the kitchen instead of him!" Frank announced jubilantly.

"Well, didn't you?" came Ned's sly retort, as he gave his best QVC rendition of a kitchen redecorator showing off a model kitchen on the air.

"Cute, Ned. Real cute!" Frank joked, as he threw a hand towel at Ned.

"How do you look so fit and trim?" Gabby asked Paul, wanting to bring the conversation back to him.

"Don't get him started on that," teased Frank. "He thinks he's the chef version of Dr. Oz now. So, don't encourage him!"

"No, seriously. You look different than most chefs," Gabby pressed exuberantly, walking closer to their co-host.

Paul shot the group an embarrassed smile and self-consciously wiped his apron.

"Please tell us," chimed Peaches, who had wanted to ask him that herself.

"Okay. Okay. If you really want to know ..." Paul stalled.

The women nodded their heads.

"I generally eat a little at a time. I hardly sit down for a meal and ..."

"He's got that right," Frank interjected, seeming quite pleased with himself for corroborating his brother's story.

"I ... ah ... fiber is my mantra. In addition to the usual veggie and protein suspects, I eat a lot of blueberries and raspberries, broccoli, cooked artichoke heart, and an apple a day because it keeps more than the doctor away—it keeps the pounds away."

"And he cooks gourmet food!" echoed Frank. "Go figure."

"As you can see, we're cutting up the salad," Paul announced. "The lasagnas, one vegetarian and the other meat, are almost ready. So, if we can get the drinks for everyone and the conference table set, dinner will served in ten minutes."

"That gives you two enough time to get settled in your room upstairs and back down here with us," Frank notified Gabby and Andre.

"Hon," Gabby ventured quietly as she grabbed Andre's arm on their way upstairs. "This house is filled with wonderful people. I don't want anything bad to happen to any of them."

"I'm going to do my best to make sure everyone stays safe. Especially you!" he pledged, halting their ascent on the stairway landing.

Gabby looked lovingly into his steady eyes. "Why especially me?"

"Because you're the franchise!" he praised and cupped her face in his hands. "You're the one who's making it possible to save tens of thousands ... millions ... of decent people's lives."

Andre kissed her and pulled back slightly so that their noses were still touching and her angelic face was still cradled in his strong hands.

"Babe, you have met EVIL face-to-face and are turning it around 180 degrees, so that it spells LIVE for millions of people!"

Chapter Ten

The group was seated around the make-shift conference table in what used to be the large meeting room for the autistic children's center.

Paul had made sure there was plenty of coffee, tea, orange juice and tomato juice, not to mention ham and eggs and French toast, since the group was meeting over breakfast.

"I just want to say, it's my distinct pleasure to work with such a fine group of people," Andre began, exchanging glances with everyone present. "We have everyone here, including Mrs. Henry, Mrs. Cody and Peaches. I asked them to be here for to-day's meeting, and to attend any meeting they want. We've got no secrets here!"

The group, including Gabby, rallied their collective support by chorusing 'yesses' and 'you betchas' and 'absolutely' around the table.

"I feel it's important for Sandra, Peaches, and Emma ... and of course, you," he nodded toward Gabby as he spoke, "to be as involved as they want to be in our discussions, because all of our discussions will be held in their behalf."

The group responded with head nods and corroborating smiles.

"We have quite an agenda this morning, so we'd best get started," Andre declared, as he lowered himself into his seat.

He glanced to his left at Gabby who was seated in the chair next to him, and nodded so that she would be prepared to speak.

"We want to start with an announcement that will come as a shock to you three."

He made eye contact with Sandra, Emma, and Peaches, who shared the same look of surprise across all of their faces.

Gabby rose from her seat and prepared to address the three women directly, knowing that everyone else knew what she was going to say. Andre had told them in his communiqués from France.

"Okay …" Gabby paused to take a breath, and then looked directly at three confused women, who seemed to suspect the others knew something they didn't. "I have changed my name!"

Their faces were commercials of surprise, stupefaction, and utter amazement respectively, from the oldest to the youngest.

"I've changed it to … Gabby Garceau!" Gabby confessed, realizing she didn't have the history with them she did with her mother and ex-husband, but also recognizing the inseparable bond she had established with the three of them over the last three years.

"Gabby Garceau!" Peaches blurted out, smiling her approval. "I like it!"

Both the older women's facial geography showed they were still sorting through their thoughts, while at the same time waiting for their emotions to catch up.

"Mom," Peaches addressed her mother. "Don't you just love it!"

Mrs. Henry gulped her surprise and tossed Peaches and Gabby identical looks of wonderment.

"You've certainly caught us off guard, my dear," Mrs. Cody conceded, and found herself cracking a smile. "But it makes perfect sense …"

"Yes, of course it does," trumpeted Mrs. Henry. "You've had to outrun their henchmen for three years!"

A broad smile made its way across Gabby's face, and she sighed the kind of sigh that releases years of concern.

"I'm so glad you're okay with it!" Gabby whispered out loud. "I didn't know how to tell you during our burner phone contacts and then decided I couldn't tell you for your own safety!"

The three women nodded their understanding, with Peaches seeming the most gleeful.

"When we heard you were flying here from France ... Well, that surprised us," Mrs. Cody spoke for the threesome.

"And now we know why, including a certain young man on your calls this past week! Now it all makes sense!" Peaches attested, winking at Gabby and Andre.

Gabby and Andre pretended to be more embarrassed than they really were by bowing their heads and then smiling at the group.

Members of the group, who had remained silent during the women's love fest, began speaking up.

"You've got yourself a good one there, girl," Rita chimed, feeling quite the after-the-fact matchmaker.

"Gabby asked us not to tell you about the name change," Frank confessed. "Because she wanted to tell you herself. And, well ...."

"She just did!" Hank cut into Frank's explanation.

Jack, Ned, and Paul decided to remain quiet when they noticed Andre growing a bit impatient. He had just adopted his business face, and though his eyes still beamed warmth and enjoyment, it was obvious he wanted to discuss the group's expanding role in staying a couple steps ahead of the Institute's goons.

"I've been living in France for two years," Gabby declared. "And living with Andre for eighteen months of those two years."

"And we'll tell you all about it later," Andre asserted good-naturedly, as he stood to move the meeting along.

Those who wanted to refill their drinks did so and Paul excused himself to refill the pair of Keurig coffee makers with water and to prepare lunch.

"I want to thank Jack and Hank on the fine hack job they've done on the Institute's data bases!" Andre began, leading the applause for the extraordinary cyber attack the two launched a week ago.

Both operatives accepted the applause, with Jack gesturing for more kudos from the group.

"Jack, do you want to say anything?" Andre gave him an opening.

Jack stood, showing his bashfulness, by smiling from side-to-side before he made eye contact with the group.

"We've stolen and encrypted digital data for over 127,000 surrogates thus far," he boasted. "Most of them look like they were earlier files, because the GPS data was associated with their Neanderthal tracking system, dated before 2005," Jack explained, glancing at Gabby, who knew exactly what he meant.

"Almost a third of the files," he continued, "are records based on newer, more state-of-the-art sub-derminal implant technology which, as all of you know, has made our jobs a lot harder, because we have to track each surrogate down by last known address."

The operatives sitting around the table nodded their heads.

Peaches looked at her mother and started to tear up, realizing how lucky she and her mother were to have been sought out and found by Gabby years before.

Jack looked at Gabby and the three women, thinking he should explain how the new technology was complicating the team's mission. He knew Andre had told Gabby, but the other three women must be made aware.

"And here's something none of you, except Andre, knows! We've encrypted two more data bases in addition to the ones we've hacked. That's why Hank and I were up most of the night last night."

Hank rolled his eyes and sighed his nocturnal collaboration.

"We're guessing that means we've downloaded another hundred thousand or so digital files," Hank added.

"Wow!" came Peaches' astonishment, as she grabbed Gabby's arm, unconsciously emphasizing their shared xerographic heritage.

This latest update sent the entire operations group into celebratory jubilation on the one hand and a mild conniption on the other, because they knew what it meant.

Seeing how the group went from awe to lunacy, Gabby decided to expose the elephant in the room.

"What's going on here?" Mrs. Cody asked at the same time Gabby rose to her feet.

Gabby stood at her place at the table and gave the time out sign with her hands.

"Time out! Time out!" she yelled, adding oomph to her time out signal.

Andre stood as well and asked for order.

Their dual abruptness calmed the group, as they all settled back in their seats.

"I believe Gabby has a question," he schooled the group.

"It's more of an observation," Gabby began. "I think what's caused all the ruckus is the elephant in the room!"

Having made the obvious obvious, she sat in her chair to give Andre the floor.

Andre looked at her and then at Jack, realizing there was very definitely an elephant in the room.

"A hundred to two hundred thousand or so digital files means we've got to personally contact two hundred thousand or so surrogates before the Institute's goons figure out who they are!"

"We can locate them," Jack caboosed Andre's revelation. "But we've also got to explain how they got the implants and what the sub-derminal devices mean!"

"And who put the devices in them!" Peaches blasted.

"And how they were born!" Gabby shouted, making her addendum heard too. "Remember, they don't even know they are clones!"

"So, you see, ladies and gentlemen," Andre summarized. "We've got our work cut out for us!"

"And it's going to come to a head," Frank added, "when the *New York Times* investigative reporter meets with Gabby and Andre."

"In the meantime," Andre reminded the group, stepping between Gabby and Peaches and holding their arms up in a victory pose. "We've got to see that the implants are removed in as many people as we can before the news breaks, because those who will run the defunct Institute will want to keep as many surrogates as they can in the cue, and possibly in captivity, to insure their 'insurance policies' remain in effect and valid when the policy holders go into hiding!"

"We can't let that happen," Gabby responded solemnly.

"Two hundred thousand people are depending on us!" Peaches added her sober acknowledgement.

"We will free as many of them as we can, maybe even all of them," Andre promised, "from their genetic concentration camps!"

* * * * * * *

Jonathan dialed the number Mr. Schmidt gave him and got the message cue.

"Hello, Mr. Schmidt. This is Reverend Pitt," Jonathan began. "I think I know where Monica Pitt, my ex-wife is!"

He paused for just a second and continued, "I think she's in Paris! Call me!"

Jonathan had the YouTube news clip pulled up on his computer for reference, and when he was only able to leave a message, he decided to watch the YouTube coverage again.

That's got to be her, he tutored himself. He replayed the clip one more time before he busied himself with Sunday's bulletin announcement.

"Reverend, there's a Mr. Schmidt on the phone for you," his dutiful receptionist, Mrs. Watson, noted on the church office's intercom.

Jonathan looked up from his perusal of the church bulletin and grabbed the phone.

"Hello, Mr. Schm..."

"How do you know she's in Paris?" came the snide response from Agent Rodriguez, who cut into Jonathan's greeting.

"I saw her on the BBC's coverage of a terrorist attack in Paris," Jonathan exclaimed nervously, as he tried to hold back an anxious dry cough.

"When?" Sergio pressed sharply.

"This morning. I was preparing for my sermon and ..."

Sergio blunted Jonathan's explanation again, "What was the date of the YouTube?"

"Oh," Jonathan tried to recover. "Let's see ... It ... It was the attack at the ... Carrousel du Louvre Mall ... two months ago!" he stammered.

"What's the link, Reverend?" the disingenuous mercenary asked.

"The link. Oh, the link!" Jonathan stumbled.

Rodriguez huffed his impatience, which was audible over the phone.

Jonathan glanced up to the YouTube's url address on the navigation tool bar and gave it to the indignant caller.

"Are you sure it was her?" came Rodriguez's crisp response.

Jonathan glanced at the YouTube piece one more time.

"Well, are you?" Rodriguez snapped.

"Yes, yes. I'm sure!" Jonathan cowered.

"Are you absolutely sure, Reverend Pitt? I'm not sending federal agents across the pond on a wild goose chase!"

"I'm positive, Mr. Schmidt. It's definitely her. I was married to her. She always wanted to go to Paris. It's definitely her," he repeated anxiously, telegraphing the nervousness in his speech.

"Okay. I'm holding you to that, Reverend," Rodriguez barked. "Thank you, Reverend Pitt. We'll be back in touch. You've been a great help!"

"I'm glad I was able to ..."

The abrupt click told Jonathan the call had ended.

Well, I didn't expect that, he thought, feeling unsettled and a little bruised.

"I hope I've done the right thing," he second-guessed himself.

He vacated the YouTube site and sat with his elbows on the top of his desk, and put his chin on his thumbs with his fingers steeped in a prayer position.

"Oh, Lord. What have I done?" He whispered softly to the framed Sallman's Head of Christ picture which sat on his desk.

His nervousness brought him to his feet and he started to his office door.

"I feel like Judas Iscariot!"

He opened the door and addressed Mrs. Watson, who had just gotten herself a pastry and a cup of tea.

"Mildred, if Mr. Schmidt calls again, take a message," he instructed her wearily, sighing his decision.

"Is everything all right?" Mildred replied sympathetically, recognizing his mood when he was upset.

"Yes ... No ... It's probably not all right ... Let's hope I've done the right thing," he responded softly, as he retreated back into his office and closed the door.

* * * * * * *

"I'm making a run to the Gateway Center off Shore Parkway," Frank announced to the women. "I'd be happy to take you to see your mother, Gabby. Emma, Sandra, and Peaches, you can come along, too, if you want."

The four of them jumped at the chance.

"Yes, thank you," Gabby said expectantly, speaking for all of them.

"This'll be the first time we've seen her," Sandra confessed.

"Will they actually let us see Marge?" Emma asked, realizing the three of them weren't related to her.

Frank smiled his assurance.

"Yes, you all can see her. Gabby's her daughter, of course, but my father has arranged for you three to see her, too," Frank was happy to report. "But, I'm guessing only two of you can see her at a time."

"Great! I'm soooo looking forward to seeing her," Peaches chorused, as she started to her room.

"Can you give us a few minutes to freshen up?" Gabby spoke for all of them, realizing that was why Peaches was headed to her room.

"Yes, of course," he agreed teasingly, licking his fingers and pasting back the hair on his receding hairline. "I need a little time for my beauty treatment, too!"

"You stinker," Emma mocked, smiling at his antics.

"It's going to take more than getting your hair slicked back to make you presentable," came Andre's quick humor from the living room. He had heard Frank's offer and thought it was a nice gesture, but didn't want to miss an opportunity to have a little fun.

"Oh, ho … ho! Is that what you think, Mr. Muscles?" Frank bantered, throwing Andre a comical look.

"Too bad you don't have one of these," Jack teased, flicking his ponytail. He had just entered the living room from the computer-friendly atmosphere of the downstairs library which was dedicated as the cyber virtual office.

"Not my style," Frank countered, smoothing his hair back again.

"Anything I can bring you two back?" Frank asked the two playful snipers.

"No thanks," Andre conceded. "Just drive carefully."

Jack shook his head.

"Nope! Nothing for me either."

The four women reappeared almost at the same time, with Gabby motioning for Andre to come to her.

"Hon, Caleb called and wants to meet us next Tuesday instead of Wednesday. Is that going to be all right with you? I know you want to move as fast as you can on the implant removals, so how is our meeting with him going to square with that?"

"If early Tuesday morning's okay with him, we can do it. Our initial meet is for stage-setting, so we'll still have a head start before the media blows this whole thing open," Andre assured her.

"Okay. Good. I'll call him on our way to the hospital," Gabby corroborated. "You said we have to go slow to go fast, so I don't want to mess things up with premature news coverage."

Andre nodded his agreement and then gave her an affectionate JFK run kiss.

"Luv you," Gabby said softly as she made her way over to join Frank and the other women, who were waiting for her at the front door.

"Luv you, too," Andre schmoozed. "Give Marge a hug and kiss for me."

"I will," she smiled, as she followed the carpoolers out the front door.

No deflecting wind, Gabby thought. *Mother Nature isn't going to mess with our dos.*

Sunlight slanted down through the trees that lined the walk, and the sky was a flawless canopy of Tar Heel blue. Skies, wherever they were, were always a Tar Heel blue. The last two years in France hadn't dulled her allegiance to her alma mater.

The group was followed by the songs of birds as the women made their way to the black SUV Frank had pulled closer to the sidewalk.

"How nice of you, Frank," Sandra complimented him for shortening their walk.

"I aim to please," he gloated. "I'm going to shorten your walk to the ICU, too!"

"Well, now aren't you the gentleman!" Emma joined the compliment parade.

Frank helped the older two women board the vehicle while the two younger women helped themselves to their seats, with Gabby grabbing the front passenger seat.

"I can't wait to see her," Emma forecasted from her position in the back seat.

"Dad said she's looking much better when I talked to him this morning," Frank reported. "She has more color and her vitals are fine."

"She's a tough old gal," Sandra added. "Monic ... Gabby," she caught herself. "We're going to find out which of the goons did this. Right?"

Gabby tightened her lips and turned toward the trio in the backseat.

"We may never find out who actually caused the accident, but I'm sure their paths will cross with us before this thing's over," she predicted, trying her best to remain objective.

"And when they do, I hope Marge is well enough to pop them over the head with a Dr. Pepper. That's her drink of choice, isn't it?" Peaches crowed, having fun making fun at the heartless goons who put Marge in the hospital.

Gabby smiled along with the other women, appreciating Peaches' sensitivity in recognizing her mother's three years of sobriety.

"Traffic isn't bad today," Frank interjected, intent on changing the subject.

"Route 9's pretty clear so far, but I-78 through the Holland Tunnel will probably be backed up. We'll have plenty of company on FDR Drive up to the hospital, so that's why I'm going to drop you pretty ladies off at the front entrance."

"To shorten our walk, right?" Sandra clarified, elated that he was going to keep his promise.

"Absolutely," Frank chorused, as Emma patted him on the back.

Gabby shot her eyes toward the entrance as Frank fell in line behind several cars chauffeuring family and friends to the main entrance.

"Oh, Gabby, there's an envelop with your name on it at the front desk with passes for Emma, Sandra, and Peaches."

"That's right. We'll need those," Sandra confirmed, appreciating Frank's thoroughness.

"Here we are," Frank announced, as he stopped the SUV at the main entrance. "It's ten fifteen. I'll pick you back up at eleven forty-five-ish. Gabby, call me when you start toward the main entrance. That'll help me gauge the time I need to pick you up."

"Roger that," Gabby spoofed, licking her fingers and pasting her hair back.

Chapter Eleven

As Rodriguez pulled their rental car into one of the underground Carrousel du Louvre Mall's parking lots, Cunningham was studying the notes they had made on the plane on the flight over.

Sergio killed the ignition and waited for Lantz to finish his quick perusal of their location on the map of the immediate area surrounding the mall. They had brought the map with them from D.C. and had already sectioned it off with different colored markers.

"There are two metro stops nearby," Lantz reported, pointing to each of them.

"One is at the Louvre/Rivoli entrance and the other is at the Louvre/Palais Royale just down the street."

"According to the intel, it looks like most people use the metro to get here," Sergio reminded Lantz, who was comparing their notes to the map.

"Yeah, it looks like the main mall entrance is on Rue de Rivoli," Lantz confirmed.

"The thing is," Sergio contemplated. "If she lives close to the mall, she probably frequents the Tuileries Gardens, the Comédie-Française, the Musée d'Orsay, and the Louvre. They're all close by."

Lantz smiled, appreciating where his thoughts were taking him.

"We'll circulate her picture around those tourist areas. Perhaps a local has seen her, or even knows her!"

"We'll also interview the manager and employees of the Meltem Mediterranean Restaurant. The YouTube captured the shooting taking place just outside of it," Sergio followed his own instincts.

"Look," Lantz pointed at the map. "There's also an arts museum, the Musée Des Arts Décoratifs; a performing arts theater, the La Comédie Française; and plenty of above-ground restaurants like Le Fumoir, that may be some of her favorites."

"The Reverend said her favorite restaurants in Raleigh were all French: the Coquette in North Hills, Saint Jacques on Falls of Neuse, and Margaux's on Creedmoor Road," Sergio added, remembering he had eaten at the Coquette a few times himself.

"Okay," Lantz asserted, holding up one of the most highlighted pages of their notes. "It's 1630 hours here," he pointed to the map of Paris, "and 1030 hours here" he grabbed his shirt, which indicated their bodies were still on Eastern Standard Time. "They're six hours ahead of us. That leaves us plenty of time this afternoon and tonight. So, why don't we grab a bite to eat at the Meltem and interview the employees there while we're at it?"

"I agree, partner. Then we can get an early start tomorrow, too."

"Amen to that, as the good reverend would say," Lantz mocked.

"When we find her here, the good reverend will have outlived his usefulness!" Sergio put into words what both of them were thinking.

* * * * * * *

"How was your visit?" Frank asked, as he stood by the doors he had opened for them.

"Good. It was good," Gabby affirmed, hesitating before she got into the front seat, so Frank could help Sandra get into the backseat. "Mother's hanging in there. Dr. Ori was there and told us her over-all responsiveness is predictably negligible at this point, but her vitals are improving."

"He's encouraged by what he's seeing though," Peaches added, as she made sure she was positioned comfortably between Emma and her mother.

"Yes, that's right," Emma cheered.

Gabby planted herself in her seat and waited for Frank to close the rear passenger door on his side and enter the vehicle.

"Detecting definitive behavioral signs of consciousness is currently really difficult, Dr. Ori told us. An error in diagnosis can lead to inadequate care management, especially pain management," Gabby informed him.

"He said many severely brain injured patients recover from coma within the first two-to-three weeks, but others take more time before fully or partially recovering," Peaches volunteered her understanding.

"It's been a little over two weeks now," Frank stated the obvious. "Does the doc have any idea of how long Marge will remain unconscious?"

The women looked at Gabby.

"No, not that he would say," Gabby responded. "One of the distinguishing features of a deep coma is the continuous absence of eye-opening, on the patient's own or following stimulation. So far mother's not shown any evidence of visual fixation or pursuit, even after manual eye-openings by Dr. Ori."

"Consciousness is a continuum, Dr. Ori told us. He assures us that his bedside assessment protocols are state-of-the-art, so to speak, and that her cognitive functions and arousal statuses are well-monitored," Gabby interjected, calming herself with a couple of slow meditational breaths.

"Did you hug her for Andre?" Frank asked, remembering Andre's request.

"Yes," exclaimed Peaches. "And Gabby kissed her for him, too!"

Her announcement brought a smile to Gabby's lips, puncturing her melancholy.

"We should be able to beat the work traffic home," Frank assured them. "Say, who wants ice-cream or frozen yogurt?" he suggested, hoping he could tempt them with a little spontaneity.

The women remained silent, trying to catch up to Frank's invitation.

"Well, I'm going to stop!" he announced. "Anyone wanting a pause that refreshes can join me. There's a nice little ice-cream stop on the way, called Itizy Ice Cream on Carmine Street, just this side of the tunnel."

"I'm good for it!" Peaches was the first to climb out of her melancholy.

"Me, too!" agreed Gabby, motioning for Emma and Sandra to follow suit.

"Emma, let's do it," Sandra propositioned. "The ice-cream's calorie-free there," she fibbed good-naturedly.

"Oh. All right!" Emma surrendered. "But I'll probably get some yogurt!"

"Yogurt's good," Frank chimed. "And a little carpool karaoke to go along with it is even better," he added, smiling in the rearview mirror at the backseat drivers and winking at Gabby in the front passenger's seat before he started his solo, which he hoped would be joined by the rest of the carpool.

"I got this feeling ... inside my bones ... It goes electric, wavey ... when I turn it on ..." Frank's uncultured, but melodious voice rang out, as he began singing the lyrics to Justin Timberlake's, *Can't Stop the Feeling.*

Peaches jumped in right away with her beautiful soprano voice, and she was followed closely by Gabby, who motioned for Sandra and Emma to join in.

Before the karaoke-inspired group got to Itizy's Ice Cream, they had added the lyrics to Calvin Harris' *This Is What You Came For,* sung by Rihanna, and Meghan Trainor's *Me Too* to their spontaneous song pool.

* * * * * * *

"No one ever heard of a Monica Pitt," Agent Cunningham told Brian, who groaned his disappointment.

"Sorry, boss," Agent Cunningham concurred. "I honestly believe there isn't an investigative reporter, or private eye, or criminal investigator, or forensic specialist, or criminologist, or counter-terrorism analyst anywhere on the planet that could have done more than Sergio and I did in the three weeks we were there!"

Lantz had always been good at tucking his security footage expertise boastfulness behind a façade of humility. When he uttered his assertions with such assurance and emotional energy, he was believable. Credible. Trustworthy. Those are three of the reasons he had advanced so quickly in the President's covert ops organization.

The look on both Sergio's and Brian's faces retailed their mutual, positive regard for Lantz's emotional proclamation.

"I don't doubt that for one moment," Brian agreed. "That's why we sent both of you to Paris. And by 'we' I mean the Deputy Assistant Secretary and the President of the United States!"

"We appreciate that, sir," Sergio spoke for both of them.

"I must say one thing about our trip before we leave it altogether," Lantz speculated, glancing at Sergio. "And it's something Sergio and I talked about on our return flight. We have the feeling that the managers and several of the employees of a couple of the restaurants at the Louvre Mall, particularly the Meltem and Le Comptoir du Louvre beneath the Pyramid recognized Pitt's picture, but pretended they didn't."

"Our instincts tell us she's there, or was there up until a month or so ago!" Sergio endorsed his colleague. "As you know, we found six more video conformations that confirmed she frequents, or frequented, the mall area. They all came from security video footage from local restaurants. We believe there's more footage, but small businesses generally tape over footage after a month. We checked to see if she had used credit cards at any of the restaurants, but evidently, she used cash."

"So, before we left ..." Lantz added, "we met with the Institute's security division based in Paris and are going to work with them as they continue the investigation there."

"If she's still there, we'll find her," Sergio predicted, not allowing the tuggable edges of his legendary composure to show.

"I agree," Brian said without hesitation. "I've worked with Antion before and he's quite the junk yard dog when it comes to protecting his territory. The Paris division is lucky to have him. If she's there, or has been there, I believe you're right, Sergio. He'll find her."

"Any intel on the whereabouts of Pitt's cronies?" Sergio changed the subject, wanting to amp up the apprehension of those closest to Monica Stateside.

"Yes, several things," Brian replied, thinking he should update the two of them as quickly as he could without sounding redundant.

Both agents' eyes settled on him.

"You may already know ... tell me if you do ... The burner phone you found, Sergio, at her mother's hairdresser's salon was compromised."

"No, we didn't know," Sergio spoke for both of them.

"The Pitt woman, we're finding, is a lot more resourceful— and lucky—than we originally thought," Brian confessed.

I'm actually impressed with her, Brian gave her a mental thumbs up to himself.

"She appears to have paid someone in Olympia, Washington to activate the phone for her. So, she effectively removed herself from the activation process completely. She, no doubt, found a burner trading site on the deep web. And before you ask who that someone is, we haven't been able to find them."

"No security camera footage?" Sergio posited.

"None that helped. The person who bought the phone knew where the store cameras were and concealed his or her face!"

The other two smiled their admiration for her, too. But it was the type of praise you gave to a snake that was coiled and ready to strike.

"She must have filled her mother's phone with fake contacts before she gave it to her, which made Pitt's whereabouts inaccessible to carriers on the burners SIM," Brian continued, raising his brown brows at her telecommunications technology acumen.

"Looks like we've awoken a sleeping tigress!" Lantz interjected, trying his best not to grant her more praise than he felt she deserved.

"There's more," Brian continued, secretly enjoying the cleverness of her evasive moves.

"Of course!" Lantz joked, realizing her covert savvy was making one of the most, if not the most powerful, covert operations in the world look amateurish.

"Her mother's extraction from the Raleigh hospital by unknown operatives was clean and extremely well-timed and executed!" Brian announced, realizing Sergio was still miffed at being upstaged.

Sergio huffed his irritation and narrowed his eyes at Brian, who held his hand up, with his palm facing his annoyed colleague, much like policemen do to stop traffic.

"Her patient transfer papers were forged and the transfer vehicle hasn't been located. Whoever set this up knew what they were doing."

"Then she may, or may not have been transferred to a hospital," Lantz guessed, mimicking Brian's traffic control gesture to blunt his derogatory comeback. Brian launched an obliging laugh, enjoying Lantz's investigative banter.

"You're right," Brian admitted. "The stealth of their extraction probably means they had their own medical facilities … which have to be state-of-the-art, since her mother was still in a coma and in critical condition."

"The two from Atlanta still missing?" Rodriguez queried, suspecting they were.

"Yes, and the Cody woman is, too," Brian admitted, realizing his men had gotten to her house too late.

"Any more intel from the detail watching the Henry residence in Atlanta?" Lantz asked.

"Nothing useable yet," Brian answered quickly. "They don't believe the steward or the housekeeper know anything. Both of them seem quite happy taking care of her place, waiting for them to return."

"That's if they return," Sergio countered, showing his demonic streak.

* * * * * * *

They met in Caleb's office, Room 304. It was a 3rd floor corner office facing the Newark Bay in a multi-storied office building in Lower Manhattan. It was a typical working class, under-decorated office space that was a perfect, off the main drag setting for their meeting. The chairs were the usual armed leather chairs and the desk was a standard Castle Pines computer desk with a pullout keyboard shelf.

"Caleb, it's nice seeing you again," Andre greeted, as he started out with a handshake which morphed into a bear hug.

"Good to see you, too," Caleb grunted the greeting as he fielded Andre's bear hug.

Gabby watched the two friends exchange greetings and re-membered they hadn't seen each other in four years. They had met in Botswana seven years ago when Caleb was covering the spread of HIV AIDS and a government-wide program to solve the problem of the overexploitation of resources.

"You must be Monica!" Caleb smiled as he stuck his hand out.

Gabby smiled and completed the warm handshake.

"Ever since that James Bond of yours told me about you, I've wanted to meet you face-to-face," he exclaimed, referring to his friend Andre.

"And I, you," Gabby responded. "It's nice to get a face with a voice."

"Yes, and both your face and your voice capture how beau-tiful you are," Caleb complimented her, knowing he would get a cagey smile from Andre, which came with a warning for Gabby.

"Caleb's a flirt, Gab ... Monica," Andre cautioned charitably. "But he's absolutely harmless."

"Well, not absolutely harmless," Caleb bantered. "Mike ..., my significant other," he paused for Gabby's benefit, "says I have a David and Goliath quality that hits the bad guys between the eyes and protects the good guys.

"And that you do," Andre agreed, high-fiving Caleb.

"And this powerful woman here," Caleb was referring to Gabby, "is going to help me bring another behemoth bully down!"

Gabby smiled graciously and was enjoying how the two friends were fussing over her.

"Let's sit," Andre suggested, as the trio took seats at the round meeting table near one of the floor-to-ceiling office windows.

"I can't tell you how privileged I am to meet you, Monica" Caleb revisited his initial greeting.

"I'm glad we could meet you today," she affirmed, reaching for Andre's hand.

"Caleb, before we start," Andre asserted, throwing his friend a disquieting look. "We've got to tell you how much danger you'll be in, if you agree to cover this!"

Gabby leaned toward him and reached for Caleb's wrist with her free hand.

"There have been two brave reporters that tried to help me three years ago who were killed. One worked for your paper, the *New York Times* and the other for *The Atlanta-Journal Constitution!*" she grieved, squeezing his wrist for emphasis.

Caleb slanted his gaze at Gabby and placed his hand over her hand.

"You're talking about Barak Stensen?" he quizzed, thinking about the *New York Times* investigative reporter found at the bottom of Baltimore Harbor.

Gabby bowed her head and held it there, feeling her eyes moisten.

"Babe," Andre extended his concern to her.

Gabby pulled her hand from Caleb's grasp and lifted it, her palm facing him, to signal her needing a moment to compose herself.

"It's amazing how something like this ... affects you so deeply ... years after ... it happens," she sniffled, tightening her grip on Andre's hand.

Andre scooted his chair closer to her and switched hands, releasing one hand to place it around Gabby's shoulders and using the other to hold her hand that he had liberated just a few moments before.

Monica, I'm sorry," Caleb apologized, "I didn't ..."

She looked up, letting a single tear flow unabated down her cheek and onto her blouse.

"It's okay. It's not you, Caleb," she atoned softly. "I guess I'm still not over your colleague's death."

Andre grabbed a couple of tissues from her purse and watched as she did a proper job on her face.

"For months following Barak's death I blamed myself. I've gone over it a thousand times in my mind ..." she stopped to blow her nose. "I was devastated by it! I didn't fully realize what I had gotten him into. How dangerous it was. How awful it was going to be."

Andre fetched several more tissues from her purse and handed them to her.

"Caleb, I had given him eleven files, so he would see that I wasn't making this up! Many of them were current files, because some of them were less than a week old at the time. Others were spaced out over months and years, so he could see how long the Institute had been cloning surrogates. He had their addresses and contact information."

"Monica, you don't have to ..."

Gabby cut into Caleb's penance, "No, I want to. I ... I want to get this guilt out of my ... conscience... Out of its outpost in my mind. Barak died because of me!"

"We never knew who killed him," Caleb acknowledged. "He was working on several stories, but none of them were the kind of news stories that would have gotten him killed. We figured he was the victim of drug addicts or robbers, looking for a quick score."

"We had only met four times, " Gabby said. "And we were supposed to meet the night he was killed. We were going to meet with the Editor in Chief the next day to get his okay to cover the story, but ..." Gabby sighed heavily.

"So, his death is tied to the worldwide human xerography operation we talked about several weeks ago?" Caleb verified, taking out his Zoom H2n recording device. "Is it okay if I record our sessions?"

"Not yet," Andre interjected, looking squarely at his friend.

Caleb shot him a surprised look.

"I'm waiting for you to put the H2n back in your satchel," Andre said firmly, waiting for Caleb to comply.

Gabby watched, unsure of what to do.

Hesitation on the part of his friend prompted Andre to lift the recorder from the desktop and make sure it was off.

"Here, "Andre announced, handing the device to Caleb. "Put it in the bag!"

"I don't get it, Andre," Caleb countered, obliging his friend and stuffing the H2n back in his backpack. "Part of this whole enterprise will be recording the sessions."

"That's fine, but not today!"

"Okay, then. Do you mind explaining?" he asked Andre, who had stood facing him.

"There are ground rules as to how we will proceed," Andre declared, glancing at Gabby before returning his gaze at his be-fuddled friend.

Caleb's face was a commercial of confusion.

"And they'll be our rules, Monica's and my rules! That's how it's got to be, because, if you decide to cover this story, we'll be taking you into hell's kitchen!"

Caleb turned white as a sheet and leaned back in his chair.

"I'm not kidding, partner," Andre raised his voice. "This could be the story of the century, but it could also get us all killed!"

"You're ... You're serious, aren't you?" the seasoned newsman voiced his trepidation.

"As serious as the Zika virus on steroids!" Andre countered. "Look. I asked Gab ... Monica to call you because you've been exposed to twinship yourself! You've investigated the Twin Strangers Studies around the world and you told me you found your identical twin in South Africa."

Caleb nodded. "In Cape Town!"

"Have you kept in touch?" Gabby ventured, realizing she was going to tell him something that would rock his world.

"No, actually I haven't been able to reach him. His phone connection's dead and his roommate said Josh hadn't been home since Easter. The Cape Town police haven't found him either. Josh has vanished!"

Gabby and Andre exchanged knowing looks.

"Caleb," Gabby blushed fretfully, not wanting to tell him what Andre and she knew they had to tell him. "Your friend, your twin, is not coming back!"

What?" Caleb asked, feeling more apprehensive with each breath. "How do you know?"

"His lungs were used for a double lung transplant!"

Caleb sunk into his chair and opened his mouth to speak, but no words came out.

"Josh was cloned so he could be a donor for body parts! He was killed, Caleb, and his lungs were donated to a patient in Dallas, Texas!"

"Oh, my God!" Caleb screamed. "Oh, my God!"

"We told you this," Andre squeezed in what he was going to say, "because we wanted you to know the full ramifications of what you're getting into!"

"I'm a clone," Gabby said softly, "and you're a clone!"

Caleb shot them a glazed look, and tried to pull himself up in his chair, but couldn't. So, he remained slouched and quiet.

"If the Institute gets their way, we could suffer the same fate as Josh!" Gabby hinted, and joined Andre as they each made their way around the round table and hugged Caleb.

"Sorry we had to lay this on you, good buddy," Andre consoled his disheveled friend.

"But you need to know what you're up against!" Gabby added soulfully.

"You're one of six clones!" Andre announced sympathetically, seeing his friend's eyes widen.

"And I'm one of two," Gabby revealed soberly. "So, you see why we've got to stop them!"

"Take all the time you need, Bro," Andre urged his friend. "We've knocked the props out from under you this morning."

"And we're not leaving here until we're sure you're all right! Until we're sure you can drive home safely!" Gabby promised.

"How many more twin brothers do I have left?" Caleb asked weakly, sitting up straighter and wiping his tears and snot away with the back of his hand.

Gabby frowned her sympathy.

"Three, counting you!" Gabby replied sorrowfully.

"So, three of us have been killed for body parts!" he confirmed, closing his eyes to absorb the full impact of what he had just heard.

Both Gabby and Andre nodded in response to his reopening his eyes.

"And we're guessing there's at least two hundred thousand more out there, Caleb, who are unaware they're walking organ donors ... Who don't know that they're expendable. That they are sacrificial lambs waiting to be discarded on the altar of aggrandizement by the heartless rich," Andre prophesied.

Gabby caught herself on her own emotional rollercoaster, fully realizing the truth of Andre's words.

Sandra said she had discovered some more files in Carlton's home office, Gabby thought to herself. *She said they were Monica Proxmire's health records. That means they're my health records! I've got the flash drive they sent me. Why haven't I looked at it?*

"I'm in!" Caleb announced emphatically.

Both Gabby and Andre trained their combined gaze on him, watching his tension and grief morph into anger and resoluteness.

"Are you sure?" Andre pressed.

"I'm in … I'm in. Monica. Andre. I'm in! I want to cover the story!"

Chapter Twelve

As soon as Gabby and Andre pulled into the parking area on the north side of the white picket fence, they saw Sandra waving at them. She was wearing gardener's gloves and had a spade in her hand.

"I was wondering how long it would take her to get her hands dirty," Gabby joked, as she watched Sandra walk toward the yard gate to meet them.

"Well, actually, Frank told me she has been helping Paul in the flower gardens ever since she got here," Andre replied. "And Emma's been out there, too!"

"Wow! Okay then," she showed her surprise, by giving Sandra a smile and a thumbs up through the windshield.

They both stepped out of the SUV and headed toward the front gate.

"I can see you're keeping busy," Gabby addressed Sandra happily.

"Yes, I am. I came out shortly after you two left this morning. It rained last night and I always like to pull weeds after a rain. The ground's softer and it just feels good to be out."

"It is good to smell the fragrance of fresh flowers and breathe the fresh air," Andre agreed, taking a deep breath and exhaling it fully.

Gabby nodded and glanced quickly at the yard and the cloudless sky.

Sandra seemed pleased with their mutual appreciation for the out-of-doors by putting on a smile herself.

Gabby preceded Andre through the gate entrance and a peculiar arrangement of clay pots caught her eye.

"I've never seen that before," she addressed Sandra, pointing to scattered clusters of clay pots that lined the mulched areas along the house and sidewalks.

"Oh, Paul and I did that earlier this morning," Sandra announced proudly. "My landscaper in Atlanta ..." she hesitated, catching herself pining, just for a moment, over her beautifully manicured lawn in Georgia. "We ... used small clay pots like these as hose guides. All you have to do is hammer a foot-and-a-half piece of rebar into the ground near the edging and slip two pots over it—one pot facing down, the other facing up. The guides prevent damage to your plants as you drag the hose along the beds."

"That's quite clever," Andre praised her ingenuity.

"There are other, more decorative guides you can use," she informed them. "There are ones that look like gnomes, or cherubs, or farm animals, or even bouquets. But I prefer clay pots, because you buy them anyway when you purchase potted plants. Oh, and little clay pots make great cloches for protecting young plants from sudden, overnight frosts and freezes. So, using small clay pots is using resources you already have!"

Andre was being polite, but he was thinking: *TMI. Mrs. Henry is a lovely lady, but she's telling us more than I want to know about lawn care.*

"Sandra, you know a lot about gardening, don't you?" Gabby encouraged her as Sandra took off her glove and transferred it to her other hand along with the spade.

"Well, you learn a little something when you want to get out of the house in the fresh air—and when you need some alone time," she summarized.

Gabby looked at her long fingernails polished in lavender Zoya Naked Manicure nail polish.

"I'm afraid these wouldn't last very long out here!' Gabby vouched, flicking her fingers so her nails glistened in the sun.

Sandra's demure laugh was echoed by Andre's nonchalant smile as they approached the front door.

"They're beautiful, dear, but a little long," Sandra agreed, brandishing her own age-spotted hands and short nails. "I generally wear gloves, but you can't keep dirt from under your fingernails unless you know the secret!"

Andre raised his eyebrows and said a quick lip-synced 'Bye' to Gabby when the women stopped just short of the front door.

Her wink gave him permission to leave the women alone before his impatience became obvious.

"I'll see you both inside," he whispered, and bolted for freedom inside.

Oblivious to the couple's leave-taking quirkiness, Sandra didn't notice his having left. She was intent on telling Gabby her secret.

"My dear, to prevent accumulating dirt under your fingernails while you work in the garden, draw your fingernails across a bar of soap," she instructed, by moving her finger tips across an invisible bar of soap. "You'll seal the undersides of your nails so dirt can't collect beneath them. Then, after you've finished in the garden, you can use a nailbrush to remove the soap, and your nails will be sparkling clean. Isn't that amazing?"

"Yes, that is amazing," Gabby agreed, wishing she had followed Andre into the house.

Gabby started toward the door, but Sandra held back.

"You go on in, dear. I'm not quite finished yet with my rural rapture!" she announced, feeling teacher-like at having schooled Gabby on outdoors nail care.

"Okay. I'll see you inside!"

"Oh, wait, Honey," Sandra petitioned soberly. "I want to be sure to talk to you and Peaches tonight about the second set of Monica Proxmire's files. They're the files I mentioned to you on the phone. Remember?"

"Yes, of course. I remember. In fact, I was just thinking about them earlier. Okay if Andre comes too?"

Sandra threw Gabby an uneasy look.

"I guess ... he ... Well, I suppose ... he should know, since you two are an item."

"Sandra, is it something all of us need to look at now?" Gabby pressed, showing some concern on the one hand, yet feeling she'd looked through all of the files about her, Peaches, and their Proxmire twin three years ago.

"It can wait, dear. I'd rather not be rushed when I share it with the three of you."

"Does Peaches know?" Gabby hazarded a guess.

"No. Not yet, dear. I wanted you to be there when I shared it."

"After dinner then?" Gabby forecasted, realizing she hadn't looked at the flash drives yet.

"That would be perfect!" Sandra agreed, biting her lips slightly to hide her tension.

Suddenly the front door burst open. It was Andre, followed closely by Emma, Peaches, Frank, and Rita.

"Gabby! Your mother's regained consciousness!" Andre bellowed joyfully.

* * * * * *

When he knew there would be a group of them wanting to see Mrs. Henry, Dr. Ori instructed one of the nurses to intercept them and escort them into a private meeting room adjacent to the normal family waiting area.

By the time Gabby and Andre and the women made their way to the ICU area, nurse Amelia was waiting for them. She knew what they looked like, because she had seen Gabby and Andre on their previous visits.

"Monica," she addressed Gabby who was setting the group's pace down the hallway. "Hello!" she greeted them cordially, and waited for their full attention. "Dr. Ori asked me to escort all of you to Room 270, so he can speak with you before you see your mother."

"Is anything wrong?" Gabby launched a quick question.

"No, not at all! Dr. Ori wants you to know what to expect when a person comes out of a coma. Your mother is doing fine,"

Amelia assured, catching the worried look that covered Gabby's face. "Really, she's responsive and her vitals are very much improved. Would you follow me, please?"

Gabby nodded and reached for Andre's hand without looking.

They followed the nurse through several double doors which sectioned off the hallway to Room 270.

Amelia smiled and invited them to enter the room.

"I'll let Dr. Ori know you're here. Please make yourselves comfortable."

When Amelia left, Gabby's nervousness ignited her emotions.

"There's something wrong!" she howled, refusing to take the seat Emma and Andre offered. "He wanted to meet us here to give the bad news! That's what they do when there's really bad news! I've got to see her!" Gabby rattled off her anxiety, translating it into rapid-fire sentences.

"Babe, you've got to settle down. Breathe! The nurse said your mother's okay," Andre said softly, pulling her to him to keep her from pacing the floor.

"I can't settle down!" Gabby blasted, pulling away from him and then realizing she was dissing his affection. "I'm sorry, Hon. You're right. I can choose to keep my composure!" she confessed, stepping back into his embrace.

Andre kissed her forehead and smiled his understanding, as he brushed her hair back from her eyes and led her to a vacant chair.

The other women had remained silent, not knowing what to say. But Mrs. Cody used this opportunity to console her.

"Gabby ...." She started slowly to gage Gabby's level of comfort. "I believe with all of my heart that Marge is going to be fine. She's a tough old bird. If she wasn't tough, they would have never gotten her here from Raleigh or New York Presbyterian!"

From her chair next to Gabby, Emma reached for Gabby's hand.

Gabby reciprocated by clasping Mrs. Cody's hand and squeezing it tightly.

Gabby's evolving composure prompted Andre to check on the other two women.

"Sandra, Peaches. You two okay?"

Both nodded from the other side of the room, but showed their visible discomfort at having witnessed Gabby's uncharacteristic meltdown.

"Okay, everyone," Andre announced. "We've all been under a lot of pressure these past few weeks ... and the four of you have lived day-to-day, minute-by-minute, in a sort of pressurized limbo these past three years, wondering when the hammer would fall!"

They trained their collective eyes on him.

"We're the hammer now! It's our turn to go on the offensive!" Andre announced resolutely. "We're going to help nurse Gabby's mother back to health, so she can join in our celebration in getting all of your lives back to a new normal!"

"I would like that," Gabby spoke softly, nodding her head to accent her heartfelt desire.

"Me, too!" Peaches agreed.

Emma and Sandra nodded their agreement.

"Then, let's affirm it!" Andre rallied. "The chances of getting what we want are greater when we affirm it, individually and collectively! So, let's all affirm it out loud. Are you ready?"

"Ready," the women spoke in unison.

"Okay, repeat after me. We affirm that ..."

Andre's rally affirmation was interrupted when the doctor knocked and stepped into the room.

All of them got up from their chairs and circled around Dr. Ori.

"Monica ..." Dr. Ori began, nodding at Andre and the other three women to include him in the report. "Your mother is conscious and responsive. I told her you were here and she wants to see all of you. There are a few things I want you to know before you go in."

Gabby sighed her impatience, but decided to consent to his wishes.

The others were feeling the same urgency to see Marge, but decided to wait Dr. Ori out, too!

"Your mother is stabilized and has been taken off the critical list," he paused, picking up on their collective sense of relief. "Her pupillary responses to light, eye movements, verbal responses, and facial symmetry placed her GCS score over thirteen on the Glasgow Coma Scale. That means her over-all chances of recovery and living a normal life are excellent."

Gabby and the other women sighed, and then smiled their elation. Andre added his jubilation by whispering a resounding 'Yes' as their unofficial spokesperson.

"The ventriculostomy drain the Raleigh neurosurgeon had attached had adequately relieved the pressure inside her skull, and the bone implantation we performed on the left side of her head has healed nicely. We nullified the swelling soon enough which meant there was no ischemia—that means there was no blockage to the blood supply to your mother's brain. So, I don't believe there will be any foreseeable complications."

Once again the group showed their satisfaction with his prognosis.

"Fortunately, she has entered the nonsurgical management of her recovery, which involves close monitoring, administering the appropriate medications, and rest."

"Ladies. Do you hear that?" Andre interjected with a smile. "That means rest. Plenty of rest!"

The women threw him mildly disdainful stares that turned into automatic smiles.

"Over the next few weeks your mother may have difficulty keeping up with conversations. That means she'll probably have trouble finding the right words to say, because her ability to process information has slowed. So, slow down when you speak with her and be patient," Dr. Ori conjectured.

Sometimes I have trouble finding the right words to say, Emma said to herself.

That pretty much happens to me a lot, Sandra silently bookmarked her opinion of herself.

"One more thing before you see her," Dr. Ori cautioned. "I mentioned the Glasgow Coma Scale. The healthcare industry uses several scales to describe the level of response in people like your mother who have had brain injuries. In acute care, the Glasgow Coma Scale is generally used. It rates eye opening, motor move-ment—movement of the arms and legs—and verbal responses that are monitored as soon as possible after the injury."

The consternation in each of their faces told him to use as many non-medical terms as possible.

"Each response has a score. Total scores range from a low of 3 to a high of 15," he continued slowly. "As I said, your mother's GCS score was thirteen. The lower the score, the more complicated or severe the brain injury is. Factors like drug use, shock, low blood oxygen and alcohol consumption can affect the GCS score …" Dr. Ori hesitated, picking up on Gabby's agitated change in demeanor. "We have talked before on the alcohol-related issue, Monica, and I am well aware of your mother's situation. You said she didn't drink—and I believe you! I only mention it now to ap-prise you of the factors that can affect the GCS rating."

"You are familiar with the exigent circumstances surrounding Mrs. Henry's accident, aren't you Doctor?" Andre pressed, want-ing to assure Gabby that he wanted to make sure the doctor was aware of her mother's absolute, unquestioned sobriety.

Dr. Ori scanned the group quickly to determine their emo-tional receptivity.

"Yes, of course! Monica, I've had several discussions with Dr. Marino, who has outlined the witness protection protocols of your mother's on-going care—and the harsh circumstances leading to her accident, including the forced alcohol to impair her driving ability. However, because there was a considerable amount of alcohol in her system, it was a factor we had to consider in determining her Glasgow score … I hope you under-stand. I did not mean anything disparaging or disrespectful!"

"Thank you so much. Thank you for recognizing that, Dr. Ori. We felt you did. We just wanted to make sure," Gabby as-sured him.

"You're quite welcome. I can appreciate the stress you've been under—you all have been under. We're taking good care of your mother. She's still mildly sedated and may not recognize you at first, but that's quite normal, and as the sedatives wear off she'll become less confused and more aware. Also, we plan to move her as soon as possible to our HDU. That's a High Dependency Unit. It's sometimes called a step-down, progressive or intermediate care unit. The HDU is for patients who may need more intensive observation, treatment, and nursing care than is possible in a general ward, but slightly less than that given in ICU. The HDU is a good acute care step for your mother, since she's already been transferred quite a distance this early in her intensive care...Well, that's about it."

Their smiles prerequisited his next announcement.

"Well ... Monica. Speaking of that lovely mother of yours, who is off the ventilator, by the way. How would you all like to see her?" Dr. Ori teased, offering the obvious.

"Yes," Gabby and Peaches sounded off before the others voiced their hurrahs.

"I'm going to allow you to break protocols," Dr. Ori announced. "You can all see her at the same time. HOWEVER, we'll have to make your first visit short, because we don't want to tire her or overwhelm her for the reasons I mentioned a few moments ago. If you all are amenable to that, we can get started."

They followed the doctor down the hallway, although Gabby had to bridle herself to keep from bolting past Dr. Ori.

When they arrived at her room door, a nurse had just checked Marge's vitals and smiled at Dr. Ori's entourage on her way out.

"Mother!" Gabby cried out, letting the tears that started on her way down the hallway to the room flow unabated down her face.

Marge blinked several times before she recognized her daughter, who was at her side in a matter of seconds.

"Monica ... Moni ... ca!" Marge exclaimed, realizing her daughter's voice was coming from the young auburn-haired woman who had just embraced her. "It's you. It's really you!"

"Yes, yes, and you're okay. You're really okay!" Gabby said, as she kissed her mother on the forehead. "Look! Emma and Sandra and Peaches are here to see you, too! I'll explain who that nice looking man is over there in just a little bit."

All of the women were teary-eyed, and resembled the life-like teary-eyed dolls of Marina Bychkova's Enchanted Dolls.

Marge looked weakly at the four of them and then focused her attention on the other three women who had moved up to the side of her bed.

"Mother, remember them?" Gabby exclaimed, pulling Peaches closer to the head of the bed and inviting Emma and Sandra to improve their positions on the other side of the bed.

Marge smiled and squinted at the other women and tried her best to feign recognition to be polite, but showed that she was unable to lift their faces out of her memory bank.

"Marge, Peaches and I love you … We all love you and are so glad you're all right," Sandra declared, recognizing her friend's temporary memory dilemma.

"And Marge," Emma added. "We're all praying for you … We've been praying for you. You're going to be all right!"

Andre stayed at the foot of the bed and waved to get Gabby's attention. Once he got her attention he shook his head and mouthed a '*You don't have to intro me*,' pointing to himself.

She nodded, realizing he didn't want to confuse her mother or tire her unnecessarily, especially since she had never seen him.

"Mother, we're going to go now," Gabby announced softly, as she caught Dr. Ori enter the room out of the corner of her eye. "We'll see you again tomorrow, okay?"

Marge smiled and tried to keep her eyes open.

When the other three women stepped back from her bedside, Dr. Ori realized they had initiated their leave-taking, which didn't necessitate his reminding them to keep their visit short.

Gabby stopped at the foot of the bed next to Andre and took several envelopes out of her purse to leave for her mother. One had pictures of just herself, herself and Andre, and all four women, with notes from each of them on the back. The others contained cards were from Emma, Sandra, and Peaches.

"Dr. Ori, I'd like to stay tonight, if I can," Gabby ventured, searching Andre's eyes for his okay, which she got.

"Give her one more night," Dr. Ori petitioned. "We're thinking about moving her to HDU and will probably up her sedation so she doesn't get confused or upset. You can come as early as you want tomorrow. I'll be here again tomorrow. I'll see that you know where the HDU ward is. I hope that's okay!"

Gabby threw him a frown, but followed it up with an approving smile.

"I understand. Thank you Doctor. I'll see you ... We'll see you tomorrow!" Gabby obliged, getting nods from the other women.

She stepped into Andre's waist hug as they left the room and followed the other three women down the hallway.

"Hon, I want to get here as soon as we can tomorrow. Is getting there by 0800 okay?" she asked coyly, pleased with herself that she referred to the time in his language—military time.

"That'll be fine, Babe. Except that Frank will have to chauffeur you. The rest of the team and I are starting the next phase of our human trafficking-busting. It's got to be done if we're going to stay ahead of the goons! Oh, and by the way, I'll reschedule our meet with Caleb. He's still wading through the files we sent him, so I'm sure he'll be okay with the postponement."

"Oh, okay. Thanks for taking care of that. You're sure Frank won't mind."

"He'll be an easy mark if you bribe him with an Itizy Ice-Cream stop."

"An Itizy fix, huh? I think I can handle that," Gabby chorused, smiling her delight.

* * * * * * *

After making his mid-morning hospital rounds, Jonathan decided to grab a quick bite to eat in the Courtyard Café on the first floor. He'd made hospital rounds each year of his ministry and considered this dimension of his pastoral care one of his most important responsibilities.

As he entered the main dining room, he thought to himself, *Man, this is busy for a Tuesday morning. It's amazing. It's mid-morning, for heaven's sake!*

He bought an egg and cheese croissant and a cup of coffee, figuring he'd eat a more substantial lunch in a couple of hours.

As he was eating his sandwich, he over-heard the conversation of several hospital employees sitting in a couple of chairs from him, discussing an odd patient transfer. The mention of an older woman undergoing an ICU transfer caught his attention.

"Aw, come on David, you're always talkin' conspiracy this, conspiracy that!" a young man who was apparently an ambulance driver was chiding another driver.

"Look, knucklehead, I know what I saw. In all of my years as an ambulance driver I never saw nothin' like it. I'm telling you, protocols were lifted and standard operating procedures were compromised!" the experienced driver bellowed.

"You're talking about the alcoholic woman who totalled her car, right?"

"Yeah. She was in critical condition and in a coma. She's lucky she even survived the crash!"

"David, you're always comin' up with somethin' like this. What makes this such a bizarre transfer?"

Jonathan leaned toward them and tilted his head in their direction, forgetting all about his coffee and the rest of his sandwich.

I wonder if they're talking about Monica's mother, he said to himself. *It sounds an awful lot like they might be describing her quick transfer to somewhere unknown.*

"Dirt ball, I was in the army medical corps in Baghdad, Kuwait, and Qatar in the Mid-East. Well, I saw someone I knew ... Well, knew of, talking to Dr. Taif in the ICU the same night that lady was transferred."

"So, what's so mysterious about that?" his suspicious colleague pressed, laughing at David's cloak and dagger antics.

"What's so mysterious? I'll tell you what's so mysterious. What's a retired army colonel doing in our emergency room late at night brokering a speedy patient transfer?"

"There are a lot of retired army medical personnel working in hospitals. Hell, you're one of them!"

David looked at his friend with a face painted with irritation.

"Maybe so, but it seems strange that this particular army colonel would be the point man for a patient transfer unless the patient was a high value asset for somebody. I'm just sayin'!"

"You're talkin' like you know this colonel."

"Well, I don't know him, but I sure as hell know about him. He's one of the most decorated Combat Support Hospital officers in American history. His name is Colonel Michael Marino."

"Where is he now?" the spellbound driver asked David.

"I have no idea," David responded. "But I know he had something to do with that transfer."

Jonathan stuffed what was left of his croissant in his mouth and gulped his remaining coffee, then he pitched his cup into one of the trash receptacles on his way out of the café.

"I've got to call Mr. Schmidt," he said to himself out loud. "If they find out where the colonel is, they'll find out where her mother is!"

On his way to the hospital parking lot, Jonathan's mind was filled with paparazzi-like thoughts that chased him to his parked car. His feelings of being rejected by Monica were colliding with the self-interest of his revenge. His ethical standards for protecting family and friends were careening into his misplaced allegiance to suspicious people he didn't even know. It was beginning to appear that Jonathan Pitt doesn't like Reverend Jonathan Pitt!

Chapter Thirteen

Agent Cramer had just finished his call updating POTUS and the Deputy Assistant Secretary on the Paris division's discovery of Pitt's shopping habits at the Louvre Mall in downtown Paris. Agent Antion's operatives had found that several of the store managers recognized her in the pictures Agent Antion had brandished in front of their faces. So, it seems she had definitely been, or was still, living in Paris.

"Antion's still looking for her in Paris, but I think she's State side," Agent Cramer gave Sergio and Lantz a sour look.

"Our Commander in Chief and Deputy Assistant Secretary aren't pleased with our progress," Brian announced, as he accepted a cup of coffee from Nona, who looked especially provocative in her low cut blouse and short skirt.

"Thanks, Nona," he extended his cordiality, trying his best not to be too obvious with his appreciation for her seductiveness.

She smiled and gave each of them a flirtatious smile as she left the conference room.

Sergio looked mockingly at his colleagues.

"I know you're thinking the same thing I am," he teased, tilting his head toward the retreating brunette.

Brian raised his eyebrows and Lantz blew out a puff of air to accent their collective arousal.

"You're both married," Sergio reminded them, smiling at the lustful thoughts he knew they must be having.

"It's okay to look, but not touch," Lantz theorized, boyishly protecting his lapse in maintaining a clear conscience. "Besides, what's stopping you, Sergio?"

The three of them laughed, realizing they had all been seduced by her charms.

"She just broke up with her boyfriend," Brian announced. "So, what's any young lady to do when she's on the rebound?"

"Dress provocatively," Sergio predicted, feeling quite proud of himself for his quick-witted banter.

"It could just be she wants to reinforce her self-worth and value as a person. You know, feel good about herself," Brian countered, wanting to give Nona the benefit of a doubt.

Sergio waved his hand, fanlike, back and forth in front of his own face as if to cool himself off.

"Well, she's a hottie. She doesn't need to feel bad about herself or diminished in any way," Sergio admired, putting his hand-fan on idle.

"You may want to check her out," suggested Lantz, winking at Sergio.

"Or give her time to get over her ex boyfriend," Brian corrected, trying to reel both of them in and back to the business at hand.

As they stood there trying to mentally recalibrate the last few minutes of their meeting time, Rodriguez's cell phone rang.

"Hello, Mr. Schmidt. This is Reverend Pitt."

"Yes. Hello, Reverend. I didn't expect to get a call from you," Sergio answered, shushing the other two surprised agents, then putting Jonathan on speaker phone.

Jonathan explained over-hearing the ambulance drivers' discussion about what he believed to be Marge's patient transfer during his brunch at the hospital earlier that morning.

"The reason I think it was Monica's mother's transfer is that one of my church members has a CB and monitors all fire and accident calls. He wasn't friends with Marge, but he said the police description of the car and the driver involved in the accident sounded an awful lot like Monica's mother. So, the next morning I went to the emergency room to find out if the accident victim was her mother and was told she was in critical condition in ICU ...," Jonathan paused. "I was able to get the information, because

I'm a minister. They've seen me many times at UNC Rex and know me quite well."

Sergio's eyebrows rose just a fraction, as he fielded Jonathan's report and made eye contact with his two colleagues.

"You said this David, an ambulance driver, mentioned a Colonel Michael Marino," Sergio pressed. "Do you know David? Have you seen him before?"

"No, but I'm sure I'd recognize him if I saw him again," Jonathan responded.

"That's okay," Sergio replied mechanically, "we'll get in touch with him. You also mentioned David knew the colonel."

"Yes, from what I overheard, he had served in the Mid-East with Colonel Marino. It seemed like he was pretty sure it was the colonel he saw at the hospital that night."

"Any idea where the colonel is?" Sergio asked pre-emptorily, already knowing what their next steps would be.

Brian rose and back-peddled slowly, quietly, gesturing that he would be right back.

"No, the drivers had to leave on an ambulance call before I could explain my eavesdropping and engage in a conversation with them," he apologized, feeling grossly inadequate and inept in this sort of thing.

"Anything else we should know?" Sergio countered, growing impatient with Jonathan's lack of investigative ability.

Brian re-entered and reoccupied his seat next to Sergio.

Jonathan thought for just a moment as an uneasy blush settled on his face.

"That's all I know, Mr. Schmidt, but I thought I'd better tell you. I figured Monica might hear about her mother's accident and want to see her."

"Good thinking, Reverend," Sergio patronized him. "We appreciate your continued support. We'll take it from here. If you hear anything else, call me."

Nona appeared in the doorway and walked quietly to where Brian was sitting. She handed him a note and then left as stealthily as she had entered.

"Okay. I'm going to call Mrs. Cody and Mrs. Henry to see if they've heard from Monica," Jonathan volunteered. "They haven't returned any of my calls lately. I think it's because they're probably busy ... and I'm not exactly on good speaking terms with any of them. But I'll try."

"Fine. That's fine. Let me know what they say," Sergio placated predictably, knowing full well the good reverend would not be able to contact the women.

"Okay, is there a good time to try to reach you?" Jonathan ventured coyly.

"No, you can call anytime."

After the two had said their perfunctory goodbyes, Sergio's lips tightened obstinately and his dark eyes penetrated the looks of his two companions.

"Just when I thought the good reverend was a candidate for the pearly gates, he gives us an interesting piece of information."

Brian's smile was followed by Lantz's raised eyebrows.

"Looks like we'll need to find this colonel," Sergio pitched the obvious.

"Already did!" Brian announced smoothly, brandishing the note Nona had given him.

His two compatriots mirrored each other's surprise.

"He's the Director of Emergency Services at New York-Presbyterian Hospital. If the good doctor is involved in this, we'll need to chat with him as soon as possible," Brian announced, suppressing the grin he had felt coming. "You two and Agent White get on a red eye to New York. Dr. Marino is off today, but he's working tomorrow. Plan to get there around 0800. Find out if he is, in fact, involved and where Pitt's mother is. I'll have a chat with David, the ambulance driver, and see how much he knows."

* * * * * * *

"Mr. President, we have a credible lead on the whereabouts of the Pitt woman's mother," Eleanor reported confidently. "We believe she may be at New York-Presbyterian Hospital, in the ICU there. Agent Cramer's intel has just discovered that Dr. Michael Marino, the Director of Emergency Services there may have been involved in her mother's extraction."

"Any intel on the Pitt woman's whereabouts?" POTUS asked, wearing an agitated look that wasn't obvious on the phone, especially since he was well-practiced in covering his deceit.

Eleanor tightened the lip stick on her tense lips.

"Nothing else since the sightings in Paris I told you about. If she's still there, we'll find her. Our team in Paris is working on that now, but, sir, we're beginning to think she may be closer that we originally thought."

The President, still holding the phone, put both of his elbows on his desk to rest his weariness.

"Closer how?" came his abbreviated response.

Eleanor motioned for Agent Cramer, who had just stepped into her office, to grab a seat, without mentioning to POTUS that Brian was there.

"We believe she may have heard about her mother's accident and is making plans, or has made plans to see her. We feel pretty confident she has communicated with her mother. And we have little doubt she's involved in the disappearance of the other three women. She's obviously getting professional help, and it's just a matter of time before we find out who they are," Eleanor summarized, holding her hand up to her mouth pretending to drink an imaginary cup of coffee and gesturing for Brian to get two cups, one for him and the other for her.

Brian took the hint and retreated quietly to find her administrative assistant to procure the coffee.

"But they're suppositions and not facts," POTUS leveled at her, letting his impatience show.

Oh, boy, she thought to herself, *I should have had Brian get us scotch and sodas, instead of coffee!*

"They're what the secret service calls 'probability of presence,' Mr. President," she fired back as diplomatically as she could. "Sooner or later probabilities either become, or lead to actualities! That's one of the outcomes of relentless monitoring and covert surveillance, sir."

POTUS paused agitatedly before he spoke, thinking to himself, *I'm wondering if I've assigned the right person for this task?* The mismatch in her skills and counterintelligence knowledge hadn't occurred to him before.

"Eleanor, I'm well aware of covert protocols and surveillance tactics. What I'm growing more aware of is whoever the Pitt woman's covert team is has continued to outmaneuver us for the past two months!"

"Perhaps that's about to change, sir," Eleanor countered, throwing Brian a weak smile as she accepted the coffee he handed her. "We believe the Marino encounter will give us the leverage we need to find the Pitt woman."

"I hope so ... For all of our sakes!" POTUS answered, his tone undeniably cynical. "Oh, one more thing. How's the implant tracking going?"

"We've got seven teams, of twenty-five contractors each, scheduled to be briefed next Thursday. Three teams here in D.C., one in London, one in Paris, another in Germany, and the seventh team in the Netherlands. Each team is being assigned 25,000 surrogates. We should have three more teams selected and trained within three weeks to track the remaining 75,000 surrogates," Eleanor elaborated, feeling as if she wanted that scotch and soda after all.

"How will we keep our secret?" POTUS asked, his voice sheathed in roughness.

Eleanor caught his maniacal drift.

"Each team is composed of medical students who need the money for their tuitions. They're being told the implants are defective and being recalled. The new subderminal devices, which the teams can implant in an outpatient setting, are encrypted and will prevent our adversaries from accessing the demographics they need to locate the surrogates."

"Okay, but I don't see how that can authenticate each satellite's direct sequence spread spectrum timing code. At least that's my understanding," POTUS admitted.

Eleanor smiled, realizing he hadn't been briefed on this type of encryption's state-of-the-art availability.

"We have an encrypted, anti-spoofed signal known as the P(Y) code. It's transmitted both on the L1 civilian frequency (1575.42 MHz) and the military-only L2 frequency (1227.60 MHz)," Eleanor informed him.

"How did you…"

"I know people!" she interrupted. "That's why you assigned me this task, Raymond. I intend to tighten our cyber security using encryption technology the world has never seen—with a little help from some very bright people."

POTUS wiped the sweat from his brow and leaned back in his chair, thinking to himself, *I may have underestimated Eleanor.*

"Receivers need the appropriate decryption key," she continued, "and every receiver must have, absolutely must have, the same key at the same time. This makes it difficult to control access to the keys. So they must be periodically changed and distributed only to 'authorized' receivers with physical protection against key extraction."

"I must say, I'm quite impressed with what you've been able to accomplish so far," he admitted.

"You need to talk to retired Lt. Colonel Sayid. I'll give you his contact information. But for now just know that ordinary GPS signals, like the ones that guide your smartphone's mapping apps and location services, come from satellites orbiting the earth. Most techies already know that. But it's possible to create a fake GPS signal here on dry land. And that's how GPS spoofers can trick a navigation system by feeding it counterfeit signals. The counterfeit signal only has to be slightly stronger than the real GPS signal. When we get that operational, the Institute's safe and we're safe."

"And our families and careers!" POTUS added.

"And the world, since all of us policy holders are essential for the political, cultural and financial stability of the planet," crowed Eleanor, who seemed quite pleased with herself for gaining POTUS's confidence.

How 'bout the safety and security and pursuit of happiness for the surrogates who don't know they're being grown as body parts! Brian reminded himself, as he watched the gleefulness wash over Eleanor's flushed face.

"What happens in the meantime?" POTUS queried nervously, referring to the current Pitt threat.

"Pitt's team, our adversaries, cannot possibly be equipped to handle the implant extractions on a global scale. They may have hacked the Institute two weeks ago, but they have to be able to do something with the information in a short period of time to hurt us. Most of the information they have is on our pre-implant, GPS activated donors, which are in the process of being spoofed."

She got up out of her expensive, brown leather, Hooker executive chair and sat on the edge of her desk, so that her legs were more exposed than what Brian felt comfortable with, especially since the Deputy Assistant Secretary knew he was married.

"Raymond, just so you know, we're also looking at jamming GPS systems. Jamming is unlawful, of course. But that hasn't stopped us before. Right?" she teased, winking at Brian, who was growing increasingly uncomfortable with her fanaticism.

Yeah, tell me about it, POTUS thought to himself. *The Iranian government had successfully taken down a highly classified U. S. military drone using GPS spoofing in 2011.*

"We can electronically ambush Pitt's people, just like we're going to ambush the colonel in New York tomorrow morning. Agent Cramer's people are on their way to the hospital now," she forecasted, pulling her skirt up slightly to entice Brian.

Brian smiled at her, but thought to himself, *Boy, she's feeling a bit smug—and a little too flirtatious. Debriefing this call should be quite interesting.*

"Let me know how that goes, and Eleanor, make sure I'm not tied to this in any way."

"Of course, Mr. President. That goes without saying."

"I'm so glad we see eye-to-eye on that. Call me when you know something."

"Yes, sir. I serve at the pleasure of the President."

Eleanor hung up the phone and threw Brian the most twisted look. A disquieting look washed across her face, almost as if she had experienced an unexpected setback in what appeared to have been a glowing conversation.

"Eleanor, what's going on? You look like you're upset!"

She eased herself off her desk and moved, trancelike, over to Brian, who stood to field her melancholy.

"Brian," she said, cupping his right cheek in her left hand, "hold me!"

Not knowing how to refuse her obvious plea, he held her as ordered.

"Brian," she murmured, without taking her head off his chest or her arms from around his waist.

Their embrace was lengthy and Brian was unprepared for such unabashed intimacy from a superior.

Where is she going with this? Brian asked himself, feeling as if her forwardness was a primer for intimacy.

Slowing, she pulled herself away slightly, so that their faces were inches apart and the rhythm of their breaths the same.

"Brian, I'm going to need your help," she cooed softly, as she reached up around his neck and pulled him to her. Their lips collided and her self-absorbed moan accentuated her desire, as she fed on his non-resistance.

He felt the warmth of her breasts through her red silk blouse, and her solicitous hands on the back of his neck and top of his head, tussling his hair as she locked him in their embrace.

"Brian ... I'm ... so sorry. I ... I ... don't know what got into me," she pretended innocently, releasing him completely, and backing up slightly as she straightened her blouse. "I've never ... I've never done that before with a ... work associate.

I'm not that kind of a woman. I ... I ..." she purposefully blunted her own apology.

Brian's thoughts raced so fast that his mouth couldn't catch up. He just stood there, speechless, with his mouth hanging open.

"Please forgive me. I ... I trust you, and I ... feel very comfortable ... and, and safe with you!" she feigned her embarrassment. "I've never felt so ... so vulnerable as I did after that phone call with the President!" she admitted carefully, as she took another step back and leaned against her desk.

Brian narrowed his gaze and tilted his head slightly, trying to grasp what upset her enough to turn her expressed vulnerability into an unsolicited sexual advance.

"I've just had an epiphany," she whispered out loud. "An epiphany that scares the you know what out of me!" she confessed, standing again, and reaching for a tissue in the tissue holder on her desk.

Brian took a step closer to her, but remained an arm's length from her.

"After talking with Raymond just now, I had a distinct impression, an awful foreboding, that I'm being set up to take a fall for him, if this thing goes south!" she theorized, sending her lips quivering slightly as her tears renewed their salty journey down her ashen face.

As he closed the distance between them, intent on shepherding her through her emotional upheaval, he was singularly moved by her.

"Eleanor, I won't let anything happen to you. I ... We ..." he cut himself off, responding to her outstretched arms. His common sense defenses crumbled like a sand castle washed with the tides.

She claimed his lips thoroughly as they embraced, kicking up their passion a few notches.

* * * * * * *

"Dr. Marino, may we speak to you for a minute?" Sergio brandished his bogus Secret Service badge. The other two bogus agents did the same.

Michael assessed the three counterfeit agents, glancing at all three of their badges.

"You caught me on my way out, Agent ..." Dr. Marino purposely blunted his own reply.

"Agent Schmidt," Sergio lied. "This is Agent Weiscoft and Agent Turner," he gestured toward the two accomplices he had just identified with bogus names. "We're federal agents. We promise it won't take long."

"May I ask what this is about?" Michael asked, remembering Frank's warning that he may get some suspicious visitors from time-to-time, asking about Mrs. Henry and Gabby, aka Monica Pitt.

"Could we go somewhere more private?" Lantz interjected, trying to sound like a typical government agent.

Michael nodded, but hesitated slightly, and turned to the rehabilitation specialist he had been talking to before the trio arrived.

"Make sure he doesn't over-do the NuStep. We want his heart to stay healthy," he instructed the intern. "If he's just finishing up tonight, make sure he showers before he goes to his room. He can 'NuStep it' again tomorrow morning."

The intern nodded and turned to walk down the hallway.

Dr. Marino renewed his eye contact with the three scammers.

"Some of my patients are like the intern and I were talking about—motivated, interested in their recovery and easy to work with. Others renege on their exercise and medication, and compromise the quality of their rehab," Michael adlibbed, wanting to give himself enough time to figure out how to lose the three thugs without compromising Mrs. Henry's and Gabby's safety.

Sergio nodded, pretending he was interested in the doctor's chit chat.

"Let's go to my office," Michael suggested, motioning for them to follow him down the main corridor to his office.

On the way to his office Michael thought, *How did they track me so quickly? I thought we did a pretty good job covering all the bases!*

When he invited them into his office, he realized he was short one chair.

"Oh, let me get another chair," he offered, as he started toward his office door.

"We're fine," Sergio halted Michael's advance. "That won't be necessary. As I said, we won't be long."

"Okay. Fine," Michael responded cordially, as he placed himself in the chair behind his desk. "How can I help you?" Looking at his watch, he thought, *It's 2130 hours. It's been a long day. Much too long a day to entertain these clowns!*

"I'll come straight to the point," Sergio began gruffly. "We understand you were involved in a patient transfer between here and UNC Rex hospital in Raleigh, North Carolina last month!"

Michael threw them a surprised look, bringing his fingers into a modified steeple shape and placing his hands on his desk.

"Well, let me see," Michael stonewalled. "I believe I would have remembered something like that. That's quite an operation, requiring inter-hospital protocols and interstate procedures. I…"

"Were you involved in a patient transfer at UNC Rex Hospital anytime last month?" Sergio pressed, watching how the doctor reacted to a frontal verbal assault.

Michael looked at Sergio squarely in the eyes, without blinking or glancing away.

"I don't tend to get involved in over-the-road patient transfers," Michael alibied. "My involvement is usually at the paperwork approval end. I, have a fully competent staff who exercise transportation responsibilities."

Sergio started to launch his objection, "Dr. Marino…"

"I will tell you," he cut Sergio off, "I was at the Raleigh facility last month wrapping up a survey on emergency room procedures sponsored by the American Academy of Emergency Medicine. You can check with the Academy. That's why I was there. Not for the purpose to which you are referring!" Michael stated flatly, hoping to keep them off balance. He also knew that when they checked, they would discover he was chairing the committee that was compiling the survey.

"We will check with the academy, Dr. Marino. I can assure you of that!" Sergio responded emphatically, keeping his eyes steeled on Michael.

"Okay," Michael signaled the adjournment. "We're done here!

"I've got one more question," Sergio pressed, wanting to keep the good doctor off balance.

"We're done here!" Michael repeated sternly, rising to his feet.

He walked the three men to the door and watched as they made their way down the corridor. They were engaged in a heated conversation and looked back toward him occasionally as they disappeared through the emergency room exit.

Michael sighed heavily and turned to go back into his office. He picked the Olympus digital recorder out of his pocket and rewound the recording before he picked up his cell phone.

"Hello, Frank. Is Andre there?"

"Yes, he is Dad," Frank responded quickly, motioning for Andre to come to the phone, and wondering why his father was calling so late at night. "Is everything all right?"

"No! That's why I'm calling!"

"Okay, here's Andre," Frank responded, handing the phone to Andre.

"Andre, I don't know how they found out, but three of the Institute's henchmen paid me a visit tonight at work."

"Oh, are you okay?" Andre asked, realizing the seriousness of the call.

"Yes, I'm fine. Before I summarize what happened, I want you to put the speaker phone on and call the others, Okay? We'll talk after you hear what happened."

"Yes, of course. Just a minute."

Andre rounded up the others, who were still up, and asked them to gather around the phone. Several of them, including Andre, pulled up a chair.

"Okay, Dr. Marino. We're all here!" Andre promised, making room for Gabby to sit on his lap.

Her face was flushed with anxiety, and her nervousness caused her fingernails to dig into Andre's biceps.

Michael pushed the play button: *"Dr. Marino, may we speak to you for a minute?"*

Chapter Fourteen

Looks like the doctor was telling the truth about that!" Agent Cramer responded to Sergio's hurried greeting. "I can't speak to your other concerns, but it looks like he is chairing a standards committee on emergency room protocols and procedures for the American Academy of Emergency Medicine."

"That might be the case, Brian," Sergio snapped, trying not to sound too plaintive to his superior, "but my gut tells me Dr. Marino knows more than he's saying."

"I know you well enough to trust your instincts, Sergio," Brian replied matter-of-factly, "and I agree. His being there at that time of night, at the time of the Henry woman's highly suspicious disappearance, seems too coincidental!"

"Hold on, Brian. I'm going to put you on speaker phone. Agent White, ah, Jeffrey, wants to speak to you."

Jeffrey coughed to clear his throat as he stepped closer to the phone.

"Brian, I just want to say that I agree with Sergio. The good doctor is hiding his collusion. Years ago, I was hired not only for my skills as an intelligence officer, but because of my training as a nonverbal communications specialist in the area of detecting deception. I can tell you, without a doubt, that Dr. Marino was lying. His micro-expressions and other conspicuous tells gave him away. He leaked deception all over the place!" Jeffrey summarized, smiling in response to Sergio's and Lantz's thumbs up approval.

"The colonel's a seasoned high-ranking army medic," interjected Sergio, "so, he's not your typical respondent."

Jeffrey nodded. "That's right, and the information obtained by an interrogator to grill a specific, well-trained individual without sufficient onsight documentation can be quickly discounted by an interrogation savvy respondent."

"So, you think the colonel really is involved?" Brian queried, realizing he was probably asking a redundant question.

"Yes," Sergio and Jeffrey concurred in unison.

"Okay, we'll do more at our end," Brian promised, "by finding out all we can about Colonel Michael Marino. His service record. His civilian employment. His connection, if any, with old army buddies. The pull he has with the American Academy of Emergency Medicine. His personal life and interests. Everything!"

"Good," Sergio replied. "We'll stick around here a few more days to see what comes up. It's 0650. We'll use our fake credentials to get us access into the ICU area and other critical care areas. We'll probably pay the good doctor another visit, too!"

"Keep in touch," Brian stipulated, beckoning Nona, who had just walked up to his office door to enter.

"Roger that," Sergio responded. "I promise you the colonel will have plenty of company."

When Brian hung up the phone, he instructed Nona to find out all she could about Colonel Michael Marino.

"Okay, boys," Sergio addressed the other two, "we've got work to do. We all believe the colonel just might be hiding the Henry woman, either at the hospital or nearby."

"Makes sense," Lantz agreed, rebuttoning his shirt collar and tightening his tie. "She's in too critical of a condition to be sequestered too far from acute care help."

"Sorry, guys," Jeffrey apologized, "if I hadda done my job right back in Raleigh that night, you know, driven into her a little faster, we wouldn't be in this position."

A sympathetic smile crossed Sergio's face.

"Don't even go there, Jeffrey. If you'd have driven any faster you may have been killed or seriously injured."

"That's right, man," Lantz insisted, grabbing Jeffrey by the shoulders and shaking him. "Sometimes the best laid plans go wrong."

Their attempts to console him were well-intentioned, but ineffective.

"Yeah, you keep telling me that, but she's seen us… Well, you and me," he looked at Sergio. "And you know how we all don't like loose ends!"

"Looks like we might get another chance to tighten those loose ends," Sergio countered. "If the colonel has a family, we can use them as leverage. And we're not done at the hospital yet. If she is there, they're going to try to move her. And if she's somewhere else, she's probably nearby, like we said before."

"I'd like to finish the job then," Jeffrey appealed to their sense of justice.

"It will be our great pleasure to give you that pleasure, bro," Lantz obliged, without a hint of conscience or reservation.

"Okay," Sergio cautioned, looking at his watch again. "It's 0720. I'd like to get to the hospital by 0800 since we didn't have much time last night to make our hospital rounds!"

They all laughed heartily, enjoying Sergio's sinister hospital analogy.

* * * * * * *

"Frank?" Michael ventured, unsure of who just answered his son's phone.

"No, this is Andre. Frank just handed the phone to me."

"Sounds like you're on speaker phone!"

"Yes, thought it would be best," Andre replied. "We'll keep it on speaker phone unless the traffic noise prevents it!"

"Where are you?" Michael asked, wiping the perspiration off his forehead with his sleeve.

"We're in route. ETA at 0810 or 0820, depending on traffic," Andre apprised, as he glanced at his watch. "Frank and I are here. Rita and Hank are traveling with us. Gabby is here, too."

Andre made eye contact with Gabby, who scowled at him again, showing him how displeased she was at him for even thinking they could leave her behind.

"After your call last night, we decided it would not be safe for the women to come, ah ..." Andre paused, "Emma, Sandra, and Peaches ... As you can imagine, Gabby insisted on coming," he repeated himself, wanting to reiterate her presence.

"You discussed the possible danger, especially since they probably have pictures of her and can identify her?" Michael quizzed rhetorically.

"Yes, Dad," Frank proxied for all of them, raising his eyebrows while keeping his eyes on the road. "I haven't told them about the 'you know what' yet."

"Good. Let me do that! Gabby, I'm glad you're with the group this morning. Just be careful. Having said that—I know you will be careful."

Rita reached over and high-fived Gabby, who felt quite pleased with herself for insisting on coming.

"She's my mother," Gabby announced loud enough for the colonel to hear her over the phone.

The other travelers, including Andre, smiled their collective appreciation for her courage and determination, in spite of the messiness they all believed they were walking into.

"Actually, that's good. You're coming to the hospital this morning is good," the colonel addressed Gabby over the phone. "I'm on the second floor in the security office," he addressed all of them. "I want you to meet me here first. When you get here, take the steps adjacent to the patient billing counters and go to the second floor ..."

"You're wanting them to take the business elevators to the second floor?" Frank guessed.

"Yes, yes. That's right," Michael verified. "If the bogus federal agents come back, they'll probably try to mill around the emergency room area and infiltrate the ICU quarters. So, the business office areas will probably be off their slimy radar."

"Sounds logical," Frank agreed. "How about if I park near the Greenberg Pavilion? It'll give us covert access."

"I agree," Michael thought out loud.

"Look, guys. I'm not going to be a car sitter," Frank announced. "I intend on helping to ensure your mother's safe evacuation," he pressed, relying on the others' agreement.

"Absolutely," Andre agreed, speaking for all of them.

Rita reached up and tapped Frank on the back of his head with her open palm.

"Of course, you're going to the front lines. We don't know how many of them are here. We're going to need all of us," she affirmed, pushing him playfully from behind.

"Gabby, you still there?" Michael asked, wanting to make sure she heard him.

"Yes, Dr. Marino. I'm here."

"I've got security tapes to show you! To show all of you. They show the amateur trio who invaded my emergency room last night. I got some good views of their faces and body types as they walked down the corridors. We've made stills of them, too."

"Dr. Marino, Michael," Andre began, "that's terrific."

"You'll be able to see what they look like. And except for Gabby, they won't recognize the rest of you. So, that'll give you … us, an edge," Michael explained.

"Thanks, Dad. You're getting that footage was brilliant," Frank approved, as he slowed down to prevent hitting a mindless motorist who had just spastically cut into their lane in front them.

What an idiot, Frank thought to himself, as he censored his own impulse to finger the erratic driver. *Rita and Gabby are in the car. They wouldn't appreciate my sacrilegious hand gesture!* He caboosed his internal thought process with a snide smile, relishing his imaginary finger gesture.

What a clown, was Hank's silent reaction to the errant driver, as he mentally praised Frank for avoiding an accident.

"Gabby, I'm in the process of moving your mother to the HDU ward. She's stable enough to handle the move, but I'm not liking the fact that we have to do it. Unfortunately, it's necessary. I was hoping to keep her in ICU for one more day, but, as you no doubt agree, our priorities have changed," Michael explained.

Gabby and the others understood the delicate nature of the move, and knew it was necessary for her mother's safety and to protect her continued incognito status.

"Frank, you and Paul got the room accommodations worked out at the farm?" Michael continued, wanting to eliminate any loose ends.

"All set, Dad!" Frank replied.

"Yes, of course," came her immediate reply.

"Frank, Andre, has Steve Hopkins contacted you yet?" Michael asked, sounding calm, but hurried.

"No, not ..." Andre stopped himself, reacting to Rita holding her phone up and pointing to it. She was lip syncing '*Yes, he's on the phone now!*'

"Oh, wait, Michael. I think he's on the other phone now," Andre corrected himself, realizing he had given Dr. Marino several of their phone numbers.

Frank motioned for Rita to take Hopkins' call since she was in the back seat.

She got his drift and asked the doctor if they could call him back since they were talking to Dr. Marino.

"Good. Andre, Gabby ... Steve's one of the best, if not the best, concierge doctors in the Northeast. He served on my medical team in the Mid-East and when he retired from active duty with the marines he chose the concierge route instead of the traditional health care system. I'd trust him with my life," Michael assured them.

Rita gave Frank a thumbs up and ended her brief call.

Frank passed her thumbs up on to Andre.

"I took the liberty of contacting Steve, on your behalf Gabby, and, well, for the rest of you, too, since you're all on this humanitarian mission together," he told the group.

Gabby wondered what Frank's father was up to, but Andre looked like he had figured things out. He turned toward the back seat and winked at Gabby and the others. He followed that up with a lip synced '*Wow*' as he nodded his head.

"What Steve's going to tell you … Is he on hold, or are you going to call him back?" Michael queried quickly.

"We told him we'll call him back after we talk with you," Frank interjected for the group.

"Okay. Good," Michael acknowledged. "When we transfer your mother to the HDU ward, Gabby, we're going to make sure she's travel-ready. That being said, I called Frank and Paul last night."

Gabby threw Andre a puzzled look and got one back.

Rita and Hank published their own puzzlement with raised eyebrows and hands raised, palms up.

Frank's face beamed with delight. He knew what his father was going to say.

"I've asked Steve for a *semper fi* 'I owe you.' That means I'm depending on his faithfulness to just causes and his loyalty to our friendship," Michael confessed. "I've asked him to help ensure America's, and in this case, the world's safety by protecting those—like all of you—who want to put an end to corruption in high places."

Everyone, except Frank, and possibly Andre, wondered where Dr. Marino was going with his rather eccentric, but laudable, accolades.

"Gabby, I've contracted Dr. Steve Hopkins to serve as your mother's concierge doctor!"

What?" came Gabby's startled reply, as her hand flew to her mouth.

"When we move her from her temporary quarters in the HDU ward," Michael continued, "we're moving her to Zeus' Den, you know, Frank and Paul's farm house! Your group's command center," Michael announced, realizing it was going to catch them off guard.

"You're moving her where?" Gabby gasped, hearing very clearly what Frank's father had just said.

Andre gave Frank a sly smile, realizing that the two brothers had stayed up late the night before, moving furniture and cleaning the unused parlor room in the back of the house.

"We're setting up concierge quarters in the old parlor, so your mother can join us at the farm house," Frank corroborated enthusiastically."

Gabby's eyes widened in a mixture of surprise and gratitude.

"I ... I don't know what to say!" she blurted out, trying her best not to cry.

"Dad and I had it planned from the moment we moved her from Raleigh to dad's ICU," Frank admitted jubilantly, "but we didn't realize it would have to be this soon!"

"I contacted Steve," Michael's voice boomed over the phone Andre was holding, "and we've been working on the logistics these past few days. He was probably calling you to tell you when the acute care equipment is going to be delivered. Fortunately, Marge is off the ventilator and IVs since she's regained consciousness. So, the equipment needs are minimized. All we should need are an EKG machine, pulse oximeter to measure the amount of oxygen in the blood stream, TED stockings to help prevent embolisms—blood clots—from forming and to assist in circulation of blood and fluids in the legs. Steve's bringing the medications she will need, and one of his work associates, a top notch ICU nurse will stay 24/7 to monitor your mother's vitals and help keep Marge comfortable."

"You've got my head spinning," Gabby confessed. "I'm flabbergasted. I don't know what to say!"

"Your head just might spin a little more when you hear what we're going to tell you next!" Frank assessed, anticipating what his father was going to say. "Dad, should I tell her?"

A faint chuckle made its way through the phone connection.

"Yes, Son. I think it's only fitting!" his father conferred immediately, realizing both of them were on the same wave length.

The others in the SUV mirrored each other's narrowed eyes and puzzled looks.

"We are ... Dad, Paul, Steve and I ... are gifting the concierge expenses. Gabby, it isn't going to cost you anything!" Frank announced proudly, on behalf of all of the benefactor's. "And, one more thing," he paused, waiting for the group's deafening merriment in the confines of the vehicle to subside, "I'm sorry we didn't mention it before, your mother's hospital expenses here are taken care of too!"

Gabby sank back in her seat, dumbfounded. Currents of joyousness and disbelief rushed through her at the same time. The gooseflesh that rose on her arms mingled with the astonishment on her face.

"I don't know what to say!" she repeated her prior dilemma. "I can't thank you enough!"

"Thank you for thanking us," Michael voiced his appreciation on behalf of the others, "we are most definitely glad to do it, but we've got to get her safely from here to there!"

"And there are those who want to try to prevent that!" Andre asserted, as they pulled into the pavilion parking lot.

"Dad, we're here," Frank announced as he found an empty parking place closer to the entrance than he expected.

"Be careful, all of you. See you in a few minutes," Michael replied, fielding his son's announcement, while at the same time, directing his attention to one of the security officers who was pointing to a video monitor. "Wait ... Wait a minute," he cautioned Frank, as he watched two of the three bogus government agents enter the emergency room entrance. "Two bogies have just entered the building. My people will detain them. If they don't have a search warrant, they're not getting in. However, that means they can roam the corridors. We'll see how this plays out. You should be okay entering where you are. See you in a few, and be careful!"

"Here, put this on," Rita spoke to Gabby, as she pulled off her scarf and handed it to her.

"Thanks," Gabby responded, covering her head right away.

Andre looked at his team members, who were checking their firearms and walkie talkies. He waited for their mutual eye contact.

"We ready?" Andre checked, airing his 'down to business' face.

Their head nods were all he needed.

"Okay, let's take a look at that security footage," Andre exclaimed, as he exited the SUV and made room for Hank to do the same.

The group kept their eyes open as they entered the business entrance and kept a respectful distance from one another so they could blend in more with the throng of people who filled the concourse.

"There," Hank gestured, pointing to the business elevators.

Gabby squeezed the borrowed scarf at her chin to limit recognition, but not her line of sight as they made their way to the elevators. She trained her eyes straight ahead, depending on the vigilance of the others.

Before stepping into the elevator as the last one in, Andre quickly surveilled the lobby area. Satisfied that there was no suspicious movement in the lobby or concourse area, he joined the group huddled next to the other passengers in the elevator.

None of them said a word as the metal cage groaned its way to the second floor.

"The security office is this way," Frank directed the group. "An occupational hazard, I guess, since I've visited my father many times," he confessed amicably, as he led the way down the corridor and past a group of nurses and doctors who were perched around one of the standing-height computer workstations which dotted the corridor.

On their way to the security office, Andre remembered that he and Gabby needed to reset their appointment with Caleb, so he texted the reporter to explain why the postponement was necessary and promised they'd get back to him with a date.

When they got to the security office door, Frank knocked and waited for the door to open.

One of the security officers opened it and recognized Frank right away. He invited the group in and they gathered around the bank of monitors like precocious school children on a field trip.

Frank's dad introduced everyone and asked the group to gather around one of the playback monitors.

"Here's the footage from last night," Michael began, motioning for the security officer to begin the tape. "Oh, sorry, Lamont," he addressed the officer, "hit the pause for a moment. I want to show them where the counterfeit agents are at the moment."

He directed the group to move to an adjacent monitor.

"See, the two I told you about are still standing just outside the ICU security check point. They haven't been allowed in. It seems the keystone kops came without a warrant," he smiled mischievously, relishing the duos incompetence. "And the third one, see, there with the short blonde hair that's sticking up like unmowed grass, is walking down the jetway between the emergency room and the general hospital area. We'll keep monitoring them so we can make sure they stay out of our way. They've already been up to my office this morning. But it seems I wasn't home," Michael leaked a devilish smile, as he motioned for the group to return to the playback monitor.

Lamont glanced at Dr. Marino to make sure he was ready, and started the tape after Michael's go-ahead nod.

"When we get clear facial shots, I'll stop the tape so you can get a good look," Lamont instructed the group. "We've also got stills of each one of them for you. Also, watch their body movements for nonverbal tells, so you can recognize them from a distance. And one more thing,…" he paused for emphasis, "they're packin,' you can see the holsters under their arms in some of the shots. It'll be obvious when you watch them on video."

After the group watched the footage and made their nonverbal assessments, Michael had them gather in one corner of the office. He smiled his way into his next statement.

"Since the keystone kops are wrapped up in their own confusion, I'm going to ask you to follow me to one of my colleague's office, Dr. Robert Shephard, since my office is on their radar. I want to go over your mother's transfer," he made eye contact with Gabby, "and do our best to minimize interference from the three stooges. We can't stop them from roaming the halls, but if they become more of a nuisance than they already are, we can ask them to leave. We're not pushing it now, because we don't want to encourage them getting a warrant."

"Where are you in the extraction process?" Andre queried, realizing Gabby wanted to see her mother.

"Steve is with your mother now," Michael explained, "and that's our next step. Getting you two together. Gabby, I want you to go with your mother. That'll get both of you out of here, since they know what you two look like. That means you'll ride in the ambulance with her."

"Ambulance?" Frank questioned, throwing his father a confused look.

"Yes, ambulance!" Michael verified, "We thought about Medivacing her, but felt the helicopter would draw too much attention."

Andre tilted his head in agreement, thinking, *Now that's a military man for you, always thinking clearly about logistics!*

Frank glanced at the text he had just gotten from Paul.

"The equipment has arrived!" he announced to the group. "We're all set at the farm."

"Good," Michael confirmed. "Let's make our way back down to the HDU ward. I feel certain Steve will be ready sometime soon to transport your mother. And just so you know, we're transporting your mother through the cancer center exit at the other end of the building to eliminate any confrontation with those goons."

Gabby thought to herself, *Frank, I'm liking your dad even more. He's describing them the same way we do—goons!*

"Okay, gang," Andre addressed his team, "we need to set up a graduated exit route from the HDU ward, through the cancer center, to the waiting ambulance. So, Hank, Rita, I want you to cover our HDU exit. Frank, you cover the cancer center's main corridor. I'll cover the point of extraction."

"I'll have my security guys help," Michael volunteered.

"Thanks, but your uniformed officers will call attention to us," Andre countered. "Hank and Rita, when we move past you toward the cancer center, take Frank's position. Hank, go to the SUV and pull it around to where the ambulance is. When our extraction is complete, you two meet Frank and me at our vehicle so we can follow Gabby and Steve in the ambulance to Zeus' Den. Everybody got that?"

The group's head nods retailed their agreement.

Michael smiled at the group's efficiency.

"Frank, take your position ahead of us. When you're positioned, walkie talkie us and we'll begin our advance," Andre instructed, wanting to make sure their exit route was secure. "Rita and Hank, you hang with us until we get to the HDU ward and then go ahead to the exit and wait for us there."

The group watched Frank leave until he was out of sight.

Andre put his hands on Gabby and Michael's shoulders and nodded to signal their advance.

"Gabby, shall we see your mother?" Michael emphasized, responding to Andre's go ahead nod.

"I'd like that. I'd like that very much," she replied, as she cradled her necklace in her hand and fingered the diamond studs which glistened in the hallway light.

Chapter Fifteen

W hen they got to her mother's HDU room, Marge was asleep and had been moved to an ambulance gurney. Steve was at her side making sure everything was in place.

Hank and Rita made their way toward the door Michael had designated for the exit route.

"Oh, hi," Steve welcomed the pair and Dr. Marino. "Your mother is fine," he assured Gabby, as he extended his hand for a handshake.

Gabby smiled, but her eyes were trained on her mother, who was wrapped in the patient transport equipment. Although she made eye contact with Steve and returned his handshake, her attention remained focused on her mother as she made her way to her mother's bedside.

"She's mildly sedated so the move doesn't upset or confuse her," Steve reported, wanting to minimize any concerns Gabby had about the transfer.

"We can assure you, Gabby, that we've taken all of the precautions necessary to make your mother's ride a comfortable and safe one," Michael interjected, realizing she needed more assurance.

Gabby mouthed a 'thank you' to both men, and then leaned over to kiss her mother on the forehead. She placed her hand on top of the blanket covering her mother's stomach and waited for their signal to evacuate her mother.

Andre walkie talkied Frank, Rita, and Hank to make sure everything was still copacetic at their locations and that he, Gabby and Steve were ready to start the patient transfer.

Steve made sure the orderly who was helping him with the gurney was ready and gave Michael a thumbs up.

"I'm going to accompany you to the extraction point to handle any contingencies," Michael advised the group, "and to satisfy myself that all is well. Looks like we're all ready, so, Gabby, shall we give your wonderful mother a magic carpet ride to Zeus' Den?"

Gabby clapped her hands silently and painted a humongous smile on her face.

Andre made his walkie talkie rounds again as the extraction team escorted Marge down the HDU corridor. He took up the rear, walking behind the orderly who was helping Steve guide the gurney.

"May I stay at Mother's side?" Gabby asked Michael, hoping he would concur with her request.

He smiled and nodded his consent.

"You should have plenty of room. These corridors are a bit wider. We're in the newer section of the hospital."

Gabby walked as close as she comfortably could to the gurney and allowed tears of joy to make their saline journey, unabated, down her cheeks.

She thought to herself, *If only I could wave a magic wand and settle this thing once and for all! I would heal Mother right away and make sure she was in a safe place. Maybe take her to Paris with Andre and me. She has no roots here any more. We could go to Paris and leave all of this behind.*

She shot a quick backward glance at Andre, who had just turned toward her after scouting out the hallway behind them. He was on the walkie talkie with one of the others and was wearing his covert ops face.

I feel so safe with you, she addressed him silently, and then halted her admiration when the gurney came to a stop. She kept her balance in time to see Hank and Rita standing at the exit door at the south end of the HDU ward. *And you two, too,* she announced to herself. *It's no wonder Andre considers you—all of you—his BFFs. You've become my BFFs too!*

Rita and Hank indicated that everything was fine and that they were headed to the cancer center to relieve Frank.

"We'll see you when we get there," Andre instructed, patting his chest twice with his fist to signal their comradeship.

"How's she doing?" Michael asked Steve.

"Fine," Steve assured him. "The sedation is keeping her comfortable and calm. She's doing just fine!"

Gabby's eyes brightened and a relaxed smile slipped across her face.

"Good," Michael confirmed. "Everyone ready to start again?"

Getting the head nods he expected, Michael pushed the stainless steel exit button which unlocked the HDU ward backdoor, and led the group down the corridor toward the cancer center.

The cancer center's hallways were bustling with activity, as visitors and healthcare professionals zigged and zagged past each other to get to their respective rooms.

As they made their way through the maze of people and equipment, Michael got a call on his walkie talkie.

"Doc, this is Lamont."

"Yes, Lamont. Everything okay?"

"Well … yes, and maybe no," came his hurried response.

The group halted their advance through the hallway, and Andre and his team gathered around Michael, who led them into an open office nearby.

"What is it," Michael quizzed, as they stood just inside the unlighted office's doorway.

"Thought I should tell you the keystone kops have just issued a warrant and are asking to see you! There's only two of them at the ICU main entrance with the warrant," Lamont explained, watching their antics closely on the monitor. "John is down there with them waiting for you."

Michael shot an annoyed glance at Andre.

"Okay, I'll be right there," he told Lamont, and then made eye contact with Andre. "Looks like I'll have to entertain these clowns," he said gruffly. "You guys go ahead. Luckily, we started our evac before they got the warrant."

Andre nodded his understanding and motioned for the group to restart their evacuation.

"Oh, Doc, one more thing. The third stooge has left the emergency room and is headed for the parking lot," Lamont voiced another concern. "We'll watch him to see what he's up to, and get back to you."

Michael called for the group to stop and motioned for Andre to join him again at the vacant office.

The look on Gabby's face retailed her growing concern as she stood vigil over her mother.

"Lamont, I'm giving my walkie talkie to Andre, since I'll be with John. Call Andre with your updates. Besides, I don't want to meet 'Curly' and 'Moe' carrying a walkie talkie."

"Roger that. I'll tell John you're on your way."

Michael handed his two-way radio to Andre.

"Move as quickly as you can, my friend. I'll run as much interference as I can without getting arrested. The good news is, they're at the other end of the hospital!" Michael hurried his explanation.

Andre placed his hand on Michael's shoulder as a leave-taking gesture.

"Thank you. Be careful," he told Michael.

Michael tightened his lips and nodded, indicating his desire to sharpen his stall tactics. Then he turned and walked toward the direction they had just come.

"Steve, Gabby. Let's go!" Andre instructed, holding two-way radios in each hand.

They made their way through the gauntlet of hospital activity without incident and turned down the corridor leading to the exit they knew Hank and Rita would be guarding.

"Andre, this is Lamont in the control room."

"Yes, Lamont. This is Andre."

"'Larry … Ahhh… keystone kop number three," Lamont caught himself, "is driving around the parking lot in a white

Ford Explorer. He's stopping periodically, as if he's watching the parking lot, and then starting again to … Oh, wait a minute. Andre, it looks like he's stopping to look at hospital entrances. Oh, man. You're not going to like this. He's headed your way!"

* * * * * * *

Hank and Rita met Frank at the cancer center exit door Michael had directed that they use to extricate Marge safely.

"It'll just take me a few minutes, guys, and I'll bring the G550 closer to this entrance and the ambulance," Frank announced, as he quickly released his exit sentry responsibilities.

He stopped when he heard Andre's voice come through his walkie talkie.

Hank and Rita also pushed their receive buttons.

"Hey, guys. I just got a heads up from Lamont warning us that one of the keystone kops is driving around the hospital parking lot in a white Ford Explorer. And he's headed our way, so be on the lookout."

"Roger that," came all three team members' responses.

"Okay, you two. Keep your eyes peeled," Frank urged, as he quickened his steps toward the group's vehicle.

"He's probably just checking all the bases," Hank guessed.

"Yeah, a recon of the perimeter," Rita added her guesstimate, panning her eyes across the parking area.

Frank threw his hand up and waved at them without turning around as he headed toward their SUV, acknowledging his agreement.

By the time Frank got in the G550 and started the ignition, he saw the white Ford Explorer circling the pavilion area approximately a hundred yards away. He waited until the Explorer turned down one of the aisles, then realized it was heading toward the parked ambulance.

Oh, no you don't, he said to himself, as he steeled his gaze on the intruder. One quick glance in his driver's side mirror at the gurney surrounded by the extraction team parked at the cancer center's exit told Frank what he must do.

"There's no way I'm letting you do this," he spoke to himself out loud, as he cut between two parked cars in the row next to the row the Explorer was in.

His team transporting Gabby's mother on the gurney saw the white Explorer, too, and Andre shouted for Hank and Rita to take defensive positions beside the ambulance.

"Steve, you guys take Marge back inside. Gabby, go with them," Andre ordered as he joined Hank and Rita, with their guns drawn, at the ambulance.

Frank was close enough to see the other driver's actions.

"He's not talking on the phone," Frank schooled himself in a voice filled with a mixture of apprehension and resolve.

He timed the collision perfectly as he waited for the Explorer to move between the two rows of cars. He pulled out just as the Explorer reached the spot he was parked in and slammed into the operative's vehicle.

Both air bags, Frank's and the other driver's, deployed as metal and fiberglass splintered and scraped against each other. The left front of Frank's vehicle hit the right front of the Explorer. He knew the vehicle's new front bumper design and wider fender flares would protect him and the G550 from minor accidents.

Frank jumped out of his G Class Mercedes and headed toward the other driver, who had just exited his vehicle.

"Aw, man. I'm so sorry," Frank lied, "I didn't see you coming!"

"You imbecile!" Jeffrey shouted at Frank. "Where in the hell were you going so fast?"

Out of the corner of his eye, Frank saw Andre and Hank heading toward them.

"I'm sorry, sir," Frank faked his apology, "I've got insurance. I'll pay for damages."

The balding and grossly over-weight driver sent Frank a caustic look which morphed into rage as Jeffrey saw two men with revolvers drawn headed their way.

"You're transporting the Henry woman, aren't you?" he bellowed accusingly at Frank, who had just drawn his firearm.

Before Frank could speak or discharge his weapon, the henchman shot Frank twice in the chest.

Pow! Pow!

"He shot Frank," Hank screamed! "I'm going to kill that SOB!"

"No, Hank!" Andre countered, as they weaved in and out from between parked cars. "We need him alive!"

Pow! Pow! Pow!

Then Jeffrey fired at them as he shortened the distance between the ambulance and himself.

"Cover me Andre," Hank shouted as he dipped behind a parked pickup truck to shield his advance.

Andre dropped to one knee behind a Mitsubishi and used the hood of the car as leverage to steady his aim, but had to get back to his feet when the assailant ran toward the next row of cars.

However, gun fire from Rita drove Jeffrey back toward Andre, who met him face-to-face three rows from the ambulance.

The assailant fired at Andre, point blank range, but his gun was empty.

"Give it up," Andre commanded, as he walked slowly toward the enraged assailant, with his 9mm drawn.

"No, you give it up!" Jeffrey blasted, his unabashed recalcitrance turned up a notch. "We've been chasing her daughter for over three years, and I intend to finish the job I started several weeks ago when I totalled her car!"

"You staged the accident?" Andre queried, as he saw Hank and Rita standing nearby out of the corner of his eye.

Jeffrey's diabolical smile and unrepentant arrogance added an element of combustibility to their standoff, a combustibility that was about to erupt.

"We're only trying to protect her mother," Andre alibied, knowing full well he wasn't going to disclose Gabby's whereabouts. "Why is your organization so bent on harming her?"

"I'm not telling you who my employer is, you piece of shit! You're obviously helping her, so I'm not telling you a thing," Jeffrey growled, as he ejected his spent clip and reached for another clip to feed his 9mm.

"You don't want to do that!" Hank interjected, to show the assailant he was surrounded.

Jeffrey slowly, calculatedly, menacingly moved the clip closer to its home in the gun handle.

"Stop right there ... or ..." Andre fired a round into his chest when Jeffrey pushed the clip home.

Pow!

Jeffrey fell against a parked car and slid down the side of the car into a sitting position, still holding his revolver. He looked up at the three of them who moved cautiously toward him. His breathing was labored and shallow, and his eyes announced that he was close to oblivion.

Just as Andre stepped closer to take the gun from Jeffrey's hand, the wounded assailant raised it.

Pow! Pow!

The three of them jumped back, checking each other to see who had been shot.

"I couldn't let him do that!" Frank crowed, as he sauntered up to them holding his walkie talkie in one hand over his chest and his smoking 9mm in the other.

"Frank, you're alive!" Rita shouted, rushing over to him.

"We thought you were dead," confessed Hank.

Frank lowered the two-way radio and showed it to them.

"He killed my radio," Frank lamented sarcastically, but gratefully. "It was in my lapel pocket and took two bullets for me!"

He turned the phone over to show them the damage the two gun shots had done.

"You've got to be the luckiest dude I know," Hank praised, putting his arm around Frank's neck and squeezing him.

"Thank God for ingrained habits," Rita cheered, remembering Frank's penchant for putting his phone in his lapel pocket.

"Frank, ole boy, you live a charmed life," Andre joined in the celebration.

It suddenly occurred to the group to scan the parking lot for eyewitnesses. Although the entire confrontation had only taken minutes, they wanted to make sure no one else was hurt.

"As luck would have it, it looks like no one saw our mess," Rita acknowledged, still scanning the parking lot.

The others came to the same conclusion after conducting their own impromptu surveillance.

"Frank, see if the G550's still drivable. Hank, check the Explorer out. Hopefully, they're both road worthy. Oh, and Hank, on your way over to the Explorer, let me help you carry his body, so we can dump it later. Keep his wallet, if he's carrying one. And his revolver and phone," Andre directed.

"I'll rejoin the others." Rita announced. "They'll want to know we're all right."

"Good, let them know we'll be there shortly. Tell them to board Marge as soon as possible. We've spent too much time here already ... And tell Gabby I've got some news to tell her!"

Frank started toward their vehicle as Andre and Hank hauled Jeffrey's hefty body over to the Explorer.

Both vehicles started and Frank pulled the G550 closer to the ambulance.

"Hank, dispose of the body and ditch the Explorer. Then call us and we'll come and get you."

"Roger that," Hank confirmed, as he pulled the SUV between two rows of cars on his way out of the parking lot.

By the time Andre joined the others at the ambulance, they were ready to go."

"We could hear the gun fire," Gabby informed Andre. "It sounded like fire crackers. I'm so glad you're all right!"

Andre kissed her and gave her a hug.

"Thanks, Babe. I'm happy you're okay, too! We're following you in the SUV. You ready to move?" he addressed Steve, who gave him a quick thumbs up. "We weren't expecting a shootout in the parking lot. Any word from Micha...?"

Michael's call blunted Andre's concern, stopping Andre just as he opened the driver's side door. They decided he should drive because Frank was still feeling the effects of his close call.

"Andre, the keystone kops have made their rounds. Their search warrants were only valid for the ICU, HDU wards and acute care recovery rooms. They're standing out in front of the emergency room entrance now, evidently calling their associate. How are things going there?"

Andre sat in the driver's seat next to Frank, explained the shootout, reassured Michael that they had cleaned up their mess, and happily reported that they were pulling away from the hospital.

"You handle things okay there?" Andre quizzed Michael, as they pulled onto FDR Drive.

"Yes, things went pretty well. I believe they're still suspicious of me, and don't know whether to believe me or not. But they didn't find anything. All they've got to show for themselves is a morning that came up empty—AND no driver to take them home!" he chorused, sending his smile through the two-way radio connection.

"Indeed! Well, it looks like both of us have had all the excitement we need today, so how 'bout we connect again a little later tonight. We need to get Marge home and settled in. And, oh … Frank wants to talk to you."

Andre handed Frank the walkie talkie.

"Dad, I'll make sure you get your two-way radio back. Oh, and remember when I said I didn't want to car sit. Well, I've changed my mind. I'll tell you why when you call tonight!"

Chapter Sixteen

Babe, your mother looks really good, especially after another patient transfer," Andre assured Gabby when they got to their room upstairs at the farm house.

"She does, doesn't she!" Gabby exclaimed. "And she remembered who Emma, Sandra, and Peaches are. Dr. Hopkins, ah, Steve says her responsiveness and motor skills are improving ahead of expectations."

"Not to mention her memory," Andre was quick to add. "She remembers the night of the car accident, that is, up to the accident."

"She also remembered the scar on the right hand of one of the men who accosted her that night," Gabby noted, recalling that Frank had told them about that same scar on the agent he killed in the hospital parking lot. He noticed it when he buried the body in a secluded area off of Route 9.

"Unfortunately, he wouldn't allow us to take him alive," Andre interjected. "I was hoping we could get some information out of him."

"Well, I can't say I'm sorry he died," she admitted. "He tried to kill my mother!"

Andre nodded his head, agreeing with her sentiments, as he sat on the bed and freed his tired feet from his shoes.

"It's amazing the kind of people a society grows," Andre philosophized. "It seems the more educated and materialistic a society gets, the more educated and greedy its criminals are—and I'm talking about the world's societies and not just the United States."

"I know. It's too bad people want to settle for their egocentric nature," Gabby postured. "Why can't people care for each other and respect one another? The world needs more goodwill than ill will!"

"Roger that," Andre cheered. "Unfortunately, occupations like mine are needed until humankind elevates its consciousness on a global scale."

Gabby acknowledged his visionary perspective with a ratifying smile and head nod.

"And organizations like the Institute don't help matters," she declared, slipping out of her flip flops at the same time Andre slipped out of his khaki military fatigues.

"I agree wholeheartedly, Babe, but, like you, I believe people are basically good."

"And there's more good than bad," she cabeosed his sentiments.

"Absolutely, and when people the world over love and respect each other, and governments cooperate for the common good, that will be the heaven on earth everyone talks about," Andre projected.

"Look at you now," Gabby teased. "You're sounding like the French idealist, Pierre Teilhard de Chardin."

"Yes, yes, I love what he said," Andre admitted. "He said, and I'm paraphrasing, 'Someday, after mastering the winds, the waves, the tides and gravity—and humankind's shadow side—we shall align our imperfect human selves with our perfect Divine Selves with energies of love, compassion, and mutual respect. And when we do that, for a second time in the history of the world, humankind will have discovered fire."

"Andre, that's beautiful!" Gabby sent him an adoring look. "That would be a wonderful world!"

"It's one I'm envisioning," he confessed, "and its one I know we're both working toward!"

Gabby stood and rushed over to him to high-five him and kiss him. As soon as they smothered each other in a kiss, the phone rang.

"I'll get that," she volunteered. "You look like you're headed for the shower—or for something else," she teased, noticing he had taken off his shirt and underwear.

Andre sent her a mischievous grin, but retreated reservedly to the bathroom to wash the grueling morning at the hospital off while Gabby answered the pesky phone.

"Hon, It's Caleb, and he wants to meet as soon as possible," Gabby shouted his message to Andre, who was just getting out of the shower.

"Yeah. Okay. Set it up," he said dismissively, as he began towel-drying his hair.

"Caleb, how soon is soon?" Gabby asked, noticing that she was losing herself in a preoccupied scan of Andre's muscular body. A nude body. A body worth admiring.

"Hey, Monica," came Caleb's slightly impatient summons. "Are you there? Did I lose you?"

"Oh, Caleb ... Yes, of course, I'm here. I was distracted for a moment," she alibied, as she continued to watch Andre towel his shoulders and chest.

"How does tomorrow morning, say around ten, sound?"

"Just a minute. I'll check with Andre," she replied, appreciating the opportunity to shorten the distance between her across-the-room gaze and the inevitable up close and in person contact with the man she had neglected these past few weeks.

"Hon, how does 1000 hours tomorrow sound?" she asked, launching mischief-making fingers on an area of his body that is best done in private.

Andre's widened eyes precipitated his immediate reply.

"Yes ... ahhhhh ... ten tomor ... rowww ... sounds fine," he responded as tactfully as he could under the circumstances. He mouthed a *'you're sooo bad'* as he stepped back to dry his lower torso and thighs.

Gabby shot him a covetous grin before she returned her attention to the caller. She pressed the speaker phone icon on her phone and put it on the master bathroom sink.

"Ten's fine. We meeting at your office?"

"Yes, if that's okay, and the Editor in Chief will be there. He wants to move on the story with what you've got."

Andre's raised eyebrows and head nod told Gabby the meeting location and the Editor in Chief's presence were fine.

"That's great, and we've got more to share," Gabby added, thinking about her mother's extraction and the shootout the day before.

"Good. We want to hear all about it. See you tomorrow."

"Tomorrow then," Gabby confirmed and ended the call.

"Can I help you with anything?" she solicited, following her kittenish giggle with a thorough scan of his towelless body.

He drew an eager look on his face and lowered his eyes to watch her begin peeling off her braless blouse, one flirtatious button at a time.

Keeping her eyes riveted on him, she backed up slowly toward their bed, flitting her long lashes and removing her kneeless jeans one leg at a time.

Magnetized by her beauty and prompted by their mutual hiatus from the intimacy they shared in Paris, he exited the bathroom, forgetting all about his wet hindquarters and feet.

Freed from the restrictions of her clothing, Gabby positioned herself on the soft covers which blanketed the queen-sized bed as a primer for intimacy. She struck such an alluring pose that Andre found himself powerless to resist her siren-like call.

The passion that had been repressed by the gruesome events of the previous weeks erupted into ravaging desire. Frenzied, uncontrolled passion engulfed them. Andre ravaged her mouth passionately, almost savagely, and she did not want him to stop.

He graced her lips and neck with thirsty, but respectful kisses, moving from her lips to her neck to her breasts. Each bodily kiss he planted was punctuated by her gasps of delight and writhing as she gave herself to his rapturous inquisition.

"I ... I ... love you so much," she whispered, as her sensuality, so long held in check, took hold of her completely.

Her arms, automatically solicitous, pulled him closer, as she floated on waves of desire. She moved relentlessly under him, his passion heightening with her constant stirring. There were no protestations, no holding back, only provocative lovemaking.

Andre could feel her breath on his skin as they fed upon each other.

"Babe, we mustn't let anything ... hinder our intimacy ... from now on," he forecasted breathily.

"I ... I know," she agreed, as the soft collision of their flesh increased the intensity of their lovemaking.

"I don't want ... anything to happen ... to you," Andre whispered, feeling her nails dig into his lower back.

"I can ... I can tell ...you one thing that's ... that's going to happen ... to ... meeeee!" she trailed off, feeling the ecstasy of a long, deferred orgasm.

A rapturous smile curved provocatively on her lips as she let out an extended sigh, enjoying the erotic union they had missed since they left Paris.

Andre's passionate release followed, as he succumbed to the aphrodisiac nature of their steamy lovemaking.

Gabby, with her eyes closed and her mouth formed into a slightly open angelic smile, rested on her back with her arms above her head, clasping Andre's hands in her hands.

Impulsively, he leaned down and kissed her forehead softly, and then moved to her parted lips, kissing them softly, respectfully, contentedly. Then he kissed each of her breasts, and tasted her favorite perfume, Quelques Fleurs 'Royale' Extrait, before he straightened, releasing her hands so he could pull them up to his mouth and kiss them too.

"I love you, Gabby," he affirmed, as he placed her hands at her sides.

"I love you, too," she whispered, feeling quite comfortable lying on the bed. Her hair fanned out across the mound of pillows like spangled threads of emerald-colored silk.

She stretched out her arms toward him, still aware of the faint scent of his after shave. Gabby was always able to erase her fears and doubts with the heat of their bodies.

"I guess we'd better get downstairs," Andre suggested, not wanting to break the mood, but sensing their excuse that they needed to freshen up before they joined the others had expired.

"Yeah, I know. We really did freshen up," she teased, scratching his back as he got off the bed.

Gabby followed him to the edge of the bed, but remained seated on the soft folds of the covers.

A slight smile etched on his face as he turned toward her.

She raised her hands and used her nails to make indentions from the top of his chest, across his six-packed stomach, pausing just below his solar plexus, and down to the top of his thighs. Then she leaned forward and kissed his navel.

"You little temptress, you," Andre serenaded cautiously. "You're making it difficult ... to keep our ... promise to the group."

She looked up at him seductively, preferring to break their promise, but knowing they had to keep it.

"I know. You're right," she surrendered, as she placed the side of her head on his stomach and her arms around his lower back for an extended hug.

Andre put his hands on her head and gently eased her reluctantly to her feet.

"I promise we won't let these moments slip away from us again. Life's too short, and I want to spend every minute with you at my side, working together, and in our bed!" he announced, kissing her softly on her warm, moist lips.

"And I, you," Gabby confirmed, cupping his face in her hands for another kiss.

"And the way we do that," Andre hinted, "is to affirm what we want to manifest, and not doubt it."

Gabby nodded and perfunctorily tidied up her hair as she started her short trip to the master bathroom. As she passed the large horizontal wall mirror, she caught a glimpse of Andre following behind her. As he bent over to pick up the towel he had dropped when she seduced him earlier, she turned and tousled his hair.

"Looks good. Just like that," she taunted good-naturedly, enjoying the way his disheveled hair made him look like he'd just stuck his finger in a live light socket.

"Oh, ho, ho," he ribbed. "If you like this," he was referring to his impromptu hairdo, "you'll love this," he mocked, mussing up her long hair.

"You heathen," she kidded, launching a second attack on his thick head of hair.

Andre hung up the towel, kissed her affectionately, and laughed his way out of the bathroom, figuring he'd give Gabby the time a woman needed to freshen up before he made another entrance to comb his hair—and for both of them to hide their "Just Made Love" looks.

Twenty minutes later they were both ready and made their way down the stairs to join the rest of the group.

* * * * * * *

"He's not answering," Lantz informed Sergio.

"He may have stepped out of the vehicle to grab something to eat or take a pee," Sergio guessed, switching from phone contacts to text Jeffrey.

After he texted Jeffrey he called Dr. Marino.

"Yes," Michael answered sternly, realizing Sergio was the caller.

"Dr. Marino, I need to speak to you for just a minute before we leave. We'll need privacy. Can I meet you in your office?"

Michael sighed, telling himself, *I've had just about enough of you today.* But he decided to meet with 'Curly' in case there was something he needed to pass on to Andre.

"I've got a few minutes—just a few minutes. After all, your warrant's still effective. But you'll need to be brief. I've got a staff meeting in fifteen minutes," Michael attested firmly.

"Okay. Thanks. I'll be right there."

Sergio looked at Lantz who was showing the weariness of a frustrated agent.

"You stay here. Jeffrey's expecting to find us here. I'm going to make a quick trip to Marino's office. Let me know when Jeffrey arrives."

As Sergio made his way toward the Director of Emergency Services office, Michael called Lamont.

"Have you erased the shootout and extraction footage yet?"

"Yes, sir. And I made a copy of it for you before I erased it. I can run it down to you now, if you want!"

"No, thanks. Not yet. I'll be in a meeting with 'Curly.' He wants to see me before they leave. I'll pick up the tape later ... Oh, and thanks, Lamont. I owe you one."

"No you don't, Dr. Marino. Those men are up to no good. They're thugs. I don't mind erasing the footage either, because the footage is supposed to protect the hospital. And, in this case, erasing the footage is *definitely* protecting the hospital — and protecting you, Colonel. I'd do anything for you. You saved my son in Kuwait. I'm forever in your debt!"

Dr. Marino smiled his appreciation, knowing that wasn't the first time Lamont had praised him.

"You're a good friend, Lamont. Thanks for all you do."

"I've got your back Colonel. It's my privilege to serve you."

"Thank you, and listen, I suspect one of the agents may want to see the footage of the parking lot. Do your magic on this past hour's parking lot footage so the missing segment isn't obvious."

"Already done," Lamont announced proudly. "And I've arranged the footage he probably wants to see so we'll have to rewind the tape to get to where he wants to begin."

"You continue to amaze me," Michael praised. "I'll probably see you in a few."

"Be careful over there. You want one of the security officers with you?"

"Good idea ... but no. I don't think there'll be any trouble. He doesn't know about the shootout, or the extraction, so I doubt his antenna will be up," Michael rationalized, as he heard a knock at the door. "I think he's here, Lamont. I'll try to let you know if we're heading your way."

"Roger that!"

Michael hung up the phone and moved the open box of disposable Kimberly-Clark purple gloves on his desk to one corner of his desk and stacked a pile of files on top of his desk. Then he stood facing the white board which hung on the wall behind his desk. It contained a list of his employee's work schedules. Michael thought he could use his pretended interest in the gloves and work schedules as camouflage to make the bothersome agent think he was busy with glove invoices and employee work assignments, instead of colluding with the security office before he got there.

"Enter!" Michael raised his voice, wanting to sound official.

Sergio stepped into the office and approached Michael's desk. He extended his hand for a handshake, but the colonel ignored it.

"I can give you fifteen minutes, hopefully less," Michael declared, continuing to show his disdain for Sergio's hostile presence.

"I know our warrant has upset you, Dr. Marino, but I ..."

"What has upset me, really incensed me, are your accusations that I had anything to do with some kind of clandestine patient transfer operation," Michael blasted, knowing he was lying, but also convinced that he was dealing with a snake.

"Dr. Marino, I'm sorry, but ..."

"Sorry! No, I don't believe you're sorry. You three came into my hospital with your suspicions and arrogant attitudes, and made it clear you thought I was a criminal!"

Sergio opened his mouth to say something, but Michael censored him by pointing his index finger at him.

"I'm not finished!" Michael glared at him. "I want your superior's name and contact information, because I'm going to lodge a complaint."

Sergio took a half step back before he spoke.

"Dr. Marino, I ..."

"Your superior's name and contact information first, if you want to continue this meeting!" Michael blunted Sergio's attempt to speak.

"Dr. Marino, I only want ..."

Michael narrowed his eyes contemptuously and placed his forearms on top of the plastic glove box on his desk, indicating he was going to wait Sergio out.

"Okay ... Okay!" he surrendered, penciling one of Cramer's burner phone numbers and Brian's alias on the Post-it® note Michael provided, reminding himself to get in touch with Brian as soon as possible to let him know what's coming.

"Do I need to call now to verify its authenticity?" Michael tested, scowling at Sergio.

"No, sir, he's my superior. But if you want to call now, go ahead," Sergio countered, figuring Brian could field the good doctor's interrogation.

Michael studied Sergio for a moment and then placed the phone number in his scrubs pocket.

"Mind if I call my associate?" Sergio asked. "Just need to check on something."

Michael looked at his watch, making it obvious his unwelcome guest was on the clock.

"Sure, you've got less than ten minutes. You can spend those minutes talking to your associate, or you can let me know how I can help you."

Sergio shot Michael a cynical look and then called Lantz to inquire about Jeffrey's whereabouts. He was told that Jeffrey was still a no show.

"Stay there. I'll be down shortly," Sergio informed Lantz.

Sergio huffed his resentment at how the day was going and made eye contact with Michael again.

"I'd like to see the last hour's parking lot footage," he petitioned Michael.

"That's not something your warrant covers, my good man," came Michael's sarcastic reply.

He reveled as Sergio huffed his contempt and saw the network of veins on his enemy's face bulge across his forehead and temples.

Before Sergio could spew his anger, Michael decided to cut his adversary some slack and consent to his predictable request.

"I've got nothing—and I emphasize nothing—to hide, so I'll consent to your taking a look at the parking lot footage. But, I'm going to tell you what, mister. That's all the time I'm giving you today. Where your associate happens to be is your problem, and not mine. I'm not in the business of helping you keep track of your employees. I've got several hundred of my own to oversee."

Sergio did his best to marshal his composure to cool his rage, but it was evident that they needed the few cubic feet between them to buffer their mutual animosity.

"I appreciate your willingness to give me a look at the footage," Sergio confirmed with a voice still laced with malice.

"Okay. Let's go!" Michael suggested coldly, as he led Sergio out of his office. The two of them didn't speak on the way to the security office.

"Okay, let's see if they can pull the parking lot footage up," Michael announced, knowing full well his adversary was in for a surprise.

When they entered the security office, Lamont feigned surprise.

"Lamont, he's asking to see this past hour's parking lot footage," Michael tilted his head toward Sergio. "Can you pull up that footage?"

"Yeah. Sure. Give me just a minute," Lamont obliged causally. "Come on over here and let's take a look at our beautiful hospital parking lot. Are you interested in a certain area, or do you want a wide sweep?" he asked their repulsive visitor.

"I'm interested in the total circumference of the parking area around the hospital," Sergio proposed, losing some of his caustic tone.

"Okay. Let's take'er back to the front entrance and scan the parking area. You say you wanted the last hour's worth of footage, right?" Lamont verified with Sergio.

"Yes, that's right."

"What are we looking for?" Lamont quizzed.

"My associate. He was driving a white Ford Explorer."

"Okay, listen you two, I can see this is going to take awhile, so I'm going to leave the sightseeing to you," Michael proposed, "and if you need me for anything, Lamont, you know where to find me."

"Yes, sir, I do," Lamont endorsed Michael's exit.

Sergio gave Michael a conciliatory look, feeling confident that the doctor's lack of interest in what they'd see in the footage meant he had nothing to hide.

Michael stopped at the security office door and gave Sergio a stern look.

"I've helped you all I can today. When you finish here, I'm anticipating you'll leave my hospital," he told Sergio.

Sergio nodded and renewed his interest in the replayed footage.

"Are you sure this is today's footage?" Sergio queried after they had looked at forty-five minutes of replay.

"Yes, sir," Lamont replied, as a flicker of annoyance crossed his face. "It's got today's time stamp on it. See!"

Sergio tightened his lips and sighed his disappointment.

After another five minutes of boring footage, Sergio called it quits.

"Thanks, Lamont. Sorry I put you to so much trouble."

"No trouble at all, it's my job. And my name's Officer Morgan to you," Lamont corrected Sergio.

A scowl returned to Sergio's face as he exited the security office on his way down to the emergency room entrance to join Lantz.

"I'm guessing he hasn't contacted you yet?" he concluded, anticipating what Lantz's answer would be.

"No, and he still hasn't answered his phone. I haven't been able to GPS it either."

"Okay, let's see if we can get a taxi, so we can get our asses back to the hotel. It's obvious something's happened to Jeffrey, and we're going to find out what that is before we leave here. We'll give him just another few minutes, then you hail a taxi. I'll call Cramer to give him a head's up. This has been one helluva day."

Chapter Seventeen

After they left Gabby's mother's room, Gabby and Andre refilled their coffee cups left from Paul's delicious breakfast earlier, and headed up the stairs to meet with Sandra and Peaches.

"She really looks good, doesn't she?" Gabby celebrated, referring to her mother, who was very responsive and talkative — considering her series of transfers.

"Yes she does, Babe. And we're very fortunate to have Steve here to concierge her back to health. Frank's father has been truly heroic in taking care of her — and us! Don't you think?"

"Absolutely, I feel like everything is coming together! Thank you for loving me through this," she praised, stopping to kiss him as they made sure neither of them spilled the coffee they were holding.

""I don't know what I'd do without you, Babe. I'm from the City of Lights, but you're the light of my life!"

She halted their progress again to kiss him, making sure once again their liquid mud stayed in their cups.

"Steve says that by the weekend, Marge might be able to get into a wheelchair," Andre reminded Gabby of something they had both learned just a few minutes ago from Steve.

"And we're all going to celebrate her freedom — well, semi-freedom," Gabby added, as they paused at the first stairway step.

"Yep! And then we're going to figure out how we can keep you two together after all of this is over!"

"I'd like that. Mother and I have gotten a lot closer through all of this. Thank you for thinking about that!"

"You're so welcome. I guess we'd better get upstairs or Mrs. Henry will send out the cavalry for us."

When they got to Sandra's room, the door was open so they entered, cradling their cups of coffee.

Sandra motioned for them to sit and seemed satisfied that they brought their caffeinated comfort.

"As you know, I've been wanting to sit down with you two to share what I found in Monica Proxmire's second set of files," Sandra addressed Gabby and Peaches. "I've already told Emma, and she prefers that I be the one to tell you. Thanks for being here, too," she looked at Andre, who had a vested interest in what Mrs. Henry had found.

Gabby grabbed Andre's and Peaches' hands, anticipating the gravity of the news Mrs. Henry was going to share.

The foursome was gathered around an old oak desk in Sandra's room. Gabby and Andre were holding their recently re-filled coffee cups. Peaches still had her unopened second bottle of water, and Sandra's untouched hot tea cup was sitting next to her as she gingerly held the files.

"I wanted to share these with you weeks ago," she began somberly, adjusting her eyeglasses, which kept migrating down her nose. Finally she pulled them off and placed them next to her tea cup. "But as you know we've all been living in the fast lane these past few weeks."

The group nodded their agreement, with both Gabby and Peaches mirroring each other's nervousness by fidgeting in their seats.

Sandra opened the thin royal blue file labeled Proxmire Xerography 2.2 and picked up the set of papers on top.

"I don't know how these got separated from the other files, but Carlton had them stuffed in the bottom drawer of his desk at home," she announced, glancing at the two women and then lowering her gaze at the file.

"I've read them, and …," she stopped to take a sip of tea, "and I haven't even told you," she looked at Peaches.

Peaches took a deep breath and raised her eyebrows at Gabby and Andre, as if to reinforce her unawareness of the existence of the phantom file.

"Have either of you ever had unusual neck, jaw, upper back, or abdominal pain or discomfort?

Peaches squinted as she looked at Gabby and Gabby lowered her eyebrows at Peaches, both wondering where Sandra was going with her health check.

"Of course, I've had some of all of that," replied Gabby cautiously. "I'm thirty-three years old. I've been on the run for three years and under a lot of stress!"

"I've had some of those symptoms, too," Peaches chorused, her face a shifting landscape of confusion and bewilderment.

"I mean unusual pain and discomfort, the kind that seems more chronic than just every once in a while," Sandra responded, "the kind that doesn't seem to have a logical cause."

Both women shook their heads.

"I've had reading problems," Gabby admitted. "Sometimes I think I need reading glasses. But I attribute that to my being thirty-three years old and Monica Proxmire dying thirty years before I was born. My mother told me, at the time, ten years ago, it was probably because I had a fifty-three-year-old set of eyes!"

Peaches face flushed pink.

"You mean the molecules in my eyes are older than me?" Peaches exclaimed.

All of them exchanged uneasy smiles, accented with nervous laughter.

"Sure, it's possible," Andre interjected, his own face a billboard of bewilderment.

"We've got her DNA," chimed Gabby, " so it makes sense, I guess, that at the time they took samples of her DNA, we've got to add our age to her age to see how old we are biologically!"

"Now you're blowing my mind," Peaches speeded up her nervousness.

Sandra sat motionless, the product of her own Pandora's box disclosure.

"It makes sense that because both of you would have inherited Monica Proxmire's DNA, your gene expression and cellular history would be connected to hers through time," Andre thought reflectively, as if summoned by his esoteric nature. "I'm just guessing, of course. I'm certainly not a geneticist."

"My head's spinning too much to comprehend what you've just said, Hon, but I'm thinking you might be onto something," Gabby confessed, forcing her emotions to catch up to her ensemble of rational thoughts.

All Peaches could do was raise her eyebrows and keep her mouth open.

"Sorry guys," Andre apologized to the women, "I'm trying to come up with premature logical solutions to fix this when I just need to say I love both of you, and it's going to be all right!"

Gabby reached over and hugged him, while Peaches got up out of her chair and walked over behind Andre and hugged him around the neck.

"Mother, we sure got off track, didn't we?" Peaches surmised, as she returned to her seat next to Gabby.

"Well, not exactly," Sandra confessed, her own inner narrative racing ahead of her ability to stay calm.

"Why did you ask us about those symptoms?" Gabby quizzed, reinstituting her handholds with Andre and Peaches.

"Before I answer that question, I have a few more," Sandra announced, trying her best to edit her thoughts. "I also want to ask if either of you have ever had unexplained lightheadedness or dizziness, or unusual fatigue, or pain in one or both arms? Have you …"

"Now, wait a minute," Gabby interrupted. "That's sounding like the symptoms of heart problems! Is that where you're going with this?"

The three of them, Gabby, Peaches and Andre, mirrored each other's leaning toward Sandra, who tried valiantly to still the anxiety that seized her, to control the involuntary twitching that pulsated at the corner of her right eye, a telltale sign of her own nervousness.

Sandra closed her eyes and sighed the kind of sigh that characterizes all mothers who have to give their daughters bad news.

"Monica Proxmire had a congenital heart defect!"

Gabby mouthed a '*What*' that never came out.

Peaches steeled her gaze on her mother, but her lips were immovable, the whirr of her battered emotions taking over.

"Carlton had even kept it from all of us, Emma, Marge and me! Monica had a bicuspid aortic valve instead of a normal tricuspid valve."

With the exception of Andre, who stood, the incredulous looks on the two women kept them glued to their seats.

"Mother, I've been perfectly healthy. I am perfectly healthy," Peaches countered, beneath curved eyebrows.

Gabby let out a sigh, accented with her patented elfish smile.

"I've never had any health problems. I've been healthy all of my life. I exercise every day. I eat right. I've been very fatigued at times, but who wouldn't be? I'm being pursued by people who want to kill me!"

"Anything else, Mrs. Henry?" Andre asked, trying to sound semi-official, yet wanting to focus Gabby's and Peaches' attention on what else her mother had to say.

"Just this, my dears," she addressed the young women. "At some point we need to get both of you physicals. If you've got heart valve issues that may be exacerbated over time, you may both need valve replacements in your forties or fifties."

"Well, I wasn't expecting this on top of everything else," Gabby admitted sorrowfully, as she accepted the tissue Andre handed her to curb the flow of tears that had just erupted down her cheeks.

Peaches was adding her own tears to her mother's surprising revelation, but was allowing them to move unabated down her cheeks and onto her T-shirt. She had politely waved off Andre's offer to provide her with tissues, electing instead to wipe her tears away with the back of her hand.

"I'm sorry, Gabby, I hesitated to tell you today, because I know you and Andre are meeting that news reporter in Lower Manhattan. But, I've been putting it off for too long now, and..."

"No need to apologize, Sandra. We needed to know," she spoke for both Peaches and herself.

"There would have been no perfect time, Mother," Peaches agreed, deciding to accept a tissue offer from Andre.

Sandra could do no more than smile her appreciation for both women's poise.

"Okay if I have the file?" Gabby asked, as she began putting on her public face. "No, wait, I have the flash drive. Do you want the file, Peaches?"

"Why ... yes, if it's okay!"

"I forgot about your having the flash drive, too, Gabby. So, yes, Honey, it's yours if you want it," Sandra responded sympathetically, and handed the file to Peaches.

Everyone was standing by this time, but no one had moved more than two feet from the chairs in which they were sitting.

There was a knock at the door which caught all of their attention.

"Come in," Sandra announced, since it was her room.

When the door opened, Rita stepped in, "I'm sorry to interrupt, but I have something important to share with Andre and Gabby before they meet with Caleb."

"I don't know if I can take any more bad news," Gabby half whispered, half spoke.

"Do you need us to leave the room?" Sandra spoke for her daughter and her.

"No, of course not. We're all in this together," Andre looked reassuringly at Sandra. "It's about the meet with Caleb, right?" Andre confirmed, looking at Gabby to catch her reaction.

"If it concerns the reporter, it concerns all of us," Gabby corroborated, nodding her head to punctuate her consent for Sandra and Peaches to be a part of Rita's announcement.

"Andre, you said that Cao Huang, the Editor in Chief, was going to attend the meeting?" Rita asked, brandishing a download she had copied from the printer downstairs.

"Yes, Caleb told us his Editor had consented to publishing the story and was going to meet us at Caleb's office."

The most incredulous expression jumped on Rita's face, forcing her to give the download to Andre.

"Cao Huang is one of them!" she raised her voice, which was sheathed in an unmistakable accusatory tone. "He's one of the insureds! He's a Tier 6 beneficiary!" she blasted.

"Oh, my God," came Gabby's immediate reply.

Andrea divided his attention between Rita's look of impeachment and the report he held in his hand.

Gabby came up beside him and gawked at the file which outlined Huang's involvement in the Geneva Life Extension Institute's human xerography initiative.

"I thought you'd better know before you meet with them," Rita confirmed, recognizing the implications of their meeting with a powerful enemy they wouldn't have known was a threat.

"Excellent catch, Rita," Andre praised his associate. "You may have just saved us from a very awkward situation, to say the least!"

"Ya think!" Gabby agreed, putting on her game face. "Thank you Rita."

"Hank and I caught it," Rita commented proudly, wanting to share the credit.

"You guys are the best," Andre added, high-fiving Rita.

"What are we going to do?" Gabby asked innocently, folding her arms under her breasts. There was an odd inflection in her voice, as if what she was asking was already apparent.

"One thing we're going to do is increase our odds of getting out of there alive," Andre exclaimed, giving Rita a look that telegraphed the art of surprise and the mechanics of stealth-laden action.

"You mean you're still going?" Peaches wondered, hoping she was wrong, but sensing she was right.

"Yes, we're definitely going!" he replied without hesitation. "And by *we* I mean the team."

Andre's demeanor morphed from one of inescapable defensiveness into calculated offensive action.

"Gabby, that means you're staying. I'm not going to take a chance on you're getting hurt or killed."

She shot him a disappointed look, but a capitulative one.

"I know you're right, it looks like we might be walking into a trap," Gabby agreed, recognizing his team were specialists in the unholy art of warfare.

"I don't believe Caleb knows his boss is our mutual adversary. I've known Caleb for a long time and I don't think for a minute he's in on this," Andre surmised, separating his friend's culpability from the possible impropriety of his employer. Andre's bearing looked like a lion readying itself to spring on its prey.

"Are you going to warn him?" Sandra asked, not wanting to see an innocent person hurt.

Andre looked at his watch.

"0840," he said to himself out loud. "No. No, I'm not! Caleb will have to depend on his investigative reporter instincts. He works for Huang, so he may or may not expect something untoward. At any rate, he's a big boy. If he's been honest with Gabby and I, we'll find out when this thing goes down."

"Our meeting with him is at ten o'clock, ah ... 1000 hours," Gabby corrected herself, wanting to sound militarily savvy.

"That gives us time to establish our perimeter," Andre forecasted, looking at Rita, who already had her game face on.

"I'll get Hank and Jack," Rita volunteered. "We'll put our heads together on the way."

Andre nodded his agreement, as he watched her retreat through the doorway and head downstairs.

"Before any of you jump to any conclusions, the meeting today just might be a fact-finding mission by Huang. He may simply anticipate getting more intel from Gabby and me, and doesn't want to blow his cover yet—or he's contacted the Institute who has sent goons to Caleb's office to ambush us."

All three women recoiled at the prospect of a violent confrontation, sharing looks of concern and downright horror.

"Hon, please be careful," Gabby entreated, grabbing Andre's hand with both of her hands, thinking she might not ever see him again.

"We're all going to be careful," he predicted. "Besides, today's visit may be a benign visit. Huang may not have told anyone yet, thinking he'd find out where we are, and how many of us there are, before he rats on us. One thing's for sure, he knows we're close. He knows we're in the area, because Gabby and I have met with Caleb."

He could tell by the looks on the women's faces that they knew today's meet could be a game changer either way.

"There's something you three should know. Gabby, I was going to tell you on our trip to Lower Manhattan this morning," Andre confessed. "The Institute has upped their game. We haven't been able to hack into any more of their servers. The cyber architecture we've run into tells us they've re-encrypted the rest of their digital files."

"You're kidding!" Gabby bellowed, not realizing her mouth was moving before she could organize her thoughts.

"We're guessing the Institute has over a million subscribers and ..."

"Oh, my goodness," Peaches leaked her surprise, before either Gabby or her mother could voice their own astonishment.

"We believe we still have enough to bring down the Institute and expose the major subscribers like the President, some of his cabinet members and congressmen and congresswomen.

"And we've found some foreign dignitaries and heads of state across the pond that could be indicted along with them, but it looks like we may have to find another way besides the traditional newspaper route. Subscribers like Huang, corporate CEO's, bank presidents, university presidents, health insurance company CEO's and COO's, armed forces generals, billionaires and multi-millionaires across the globe are going to make it tough for us. We'll talk about alternative methods of exposure when we get back!"

"So, you mean they've won," Gabby lamented, resisting the impulse to scatter all of the cups and saucers off the desk in Sandra's room.

"Not at all, love," he countered, tightening his lips, but allowing the fire to dance in his eyes. "We live in an Internet age. A social media global society. A Facebook, Twitter, and hashtag economy. We'll get the evidence you've collected, Gabby, the evidence that some wonderful people have given their lives for seven and a half billion people on the planet, who will be very interested in how corrupt people in high places have become."

He walked up to the women and gathered them into a group hug. Before he said anything, Andre looked lovingly at each one of them.

"I'm including Marge, my entire team of selfless humanitarians, and everyone else in this world who has sacrificed, and is sacrificing their freedom and comfort and basic human rights, in this hug," he announced, putting on his philosophical and spiritual hats.

He could tell by the women's mystified expressions that they wondered what had set him off.

"I invite you all to close your eyes as we stand here, arm-in-arm, shoulder-to shoulder, heart-to-heart. Please understand that I am not exaggerating when I say that each one of you is an extraordinarily powerful and courageous woman who has chosen goodwill over ill will, love instead of hate, faith instead of fatalism, peace on earth instead of war on earth!"

Gabby peeked at Andre, admiring the spirituality in a military man.

You are wise beyond your years, she thought to herself as she closed her eyes again. *You are a credit to the human race!*

"In a world where women and children are mowed down in schools, shopping centers, churches, and malls by deranged cowards with assault rifles," he continued, "and where NRA members mindlessly defend the ludicrous sanctity of AK 47's and AR 15's from prohibition; and where groups of fanatics like ISIS, or the Levant, as it's called, the jihadist group called Boko Haram, the

Quds Force of the Islamic Republic, the murderous Haqqani Network, and the Kataib Hezbollah are allowed to thrive—a clandestine human xerography operation seems like a predictable and logical outgrowth of a growing paranoia in the top one percent of the people in the world who want to protect themselves at all costs from extinction."

He sighed heavily, feeling the combined soul energies of the three women who stood in an emotional circle of oneness absorbing his offhand request.

"We forgive you, Life Extension subscribers and terrorists alike. We forgive you for your ill will and inhumanity to humanity. We forgive all of you for not knowing what you are doing to the welfare and well-being of the human race."

"We forgive you!" Gabby whispered.

"We forgive you!" Peaches said softly, as she tried to hold back a cough.

"We forgive you!" Sandra declared in a voice that sounded angelic.

"We forgive you, AND we're going to hold you accountable!" Andre stated flatly and unapologetically.

Chapter Eighteen

I hear you've lost one of our agents," POTUS aimed at her sarcastically, knowing his disparaging overtone would set Eleanor off.

You nasty viper, you! she said to herself, as she sneered at him through the phone.

"How did you find out?" she countered, putting him on speaker phone so Brian could hear the conversation.

"I'm the President. I know everything that's going on!"

Eleanor winked at Brian and put on a face that said, *He doesn't know about us yet! So, he doesn't know everything!*"

"Well, that was one of the things I planned to discuss with you on this call," she alibied, gesturing to Brian to pour her a bourbon.

She held up three fingers in a sideways direction to indicate how much whiskey she wanted in her glass.

"You have any idea what happened?" POTUS pressed.

"Actually, we do. I told you about our having located a retired colonel who is serving as the Director of Emergency Room Services at New York Presbyterian ..." she paused, waiting for an affirmative response that didn't come. "We believe he may have masterminded the patient transfer of Pitt's mother from Raleigh to New York. We're still gathering inculpatory evidence on Colonel Michael Marino, retired, and believe the Pitt woman has to be nearby, for several reasons."

POTUS straightened himself in his chair as he used his feet to push himself back from his desk.

"Tell me more about that," he lowered his voice. "By the way, are we on speaker phone?"

"Oh, yes, sir. I've got Agent Cramer here," she admitted, as she mouthed an *'I'm sorry'* to apologize for the necessary formality. "Part of the intel he's sharing with me this very minute relates to one of the reasons I indicated a few minutes ago."

"Well, put him on!" POTUS urged gruffly, making his irritation with her more obvious.

Brian shot Eleanor a commiserating wink as he handed her a three-fingered glass of courage.

"Mr. President, it's good to speak to you again."

"What do you have for me?" POTUS's vinegary reply relayed his impatience with small talk.

Brian and Eleanor rolled their eyes at each other, sympathizing with each other in their shared incarceration dealing with such a grouchy personality.

"Sir, shortly after we realized that Agent White's disappearance had to be connected with the colonel, we received a phone call from Mr. Huang, Editor in Chief of the *New York Times*. He said he was a Tier 6 subscriber to the Institute's human xerography program, which we have verified. Later on this morning, he's meeting with one of his star reporters, a Caleb Latourelle ..."

"And I should be interested in their meeting because ..." POTUS interrupted, purposely trailing off, ending his sentence with an acrimonious sigh.

Biting her lip and scowling contemptuously at POTUS's pomposity, Eleanor waved Brian off before he could speak, and blurted out her rebuttal.

"Raymond, if you'll give Agent Cramer a chance, he's about to hand the Pitt woman to you on a silver platter!"

The other end of the line was silent—the kind of silence that characterizes what happens when the most powerful government official in the free world is upstaged by an assertive underling.

"Eleanor, I appreciate your enthusiasm, especially since you've got so much invested in this enterprise, but I believe one of the best field agents on my special ops team is very capable of speaking for himself. Isn't that right, Agent Cramer?"

Brian sent her a half amused, half comical look and then closed his eyes to punctuate his bridled irritation with POTUS's bluster.

Eleanor nodded her understanding and lifted her half empty glass of bourbon to toast their mutual presidential dilemma.

"It is the third party involvement in that meeting, Mr. President, that will totally—and I mean totally—capture your considerable interest," Brian announced, participating in Eleanor's impromptu toast by giving her a thumbs up.

She sent Brian a rascally smile that had 'wait 'til he hears who it is' written all over it!

"Monica Pitt is meeting with them, Mr. President!" Brian explained, reveling in the huge development Huang had just handed them.

"Well. I'll be damned!" POTUS confessed, in a tone that belied his bluster.

"Huang's reporter made the initial appointment with the Pitt woman and a male accomplice. Huang didn't know who her male companion was, because the reporter didn't identify him, but Huang said he believed Caleb, that's the reporter, knew her companion."

"You said they're meeting sometime this morning," POTUS clarified.

"Yes, at 1000 hours," Brian verified, looking at his watch. "It's 0855 hours now," he declared, lifting his eyebrows at Eleanor.

"Mr. President." Eleanor interjected, "We're setting a trap for the Pitt woman and her accomplice, as we speak. Huang has not communicated that to the reporter. The reporter thinks his boss wants to publish the story. That's not going to happen, of course, because Mr. Huang, like us, wants to protect our mutual interests. As soon as the Pitt woman is in custody, I'll let you know."

"Make sure you take her alive. She's the only one who knows where the reams of paper files are. Digitally, we've got our servers protected now, but the paper files could still present an ugly problem," POTUS declared, trying his best to keep his blood pressure under control.

"Our plan is to take both of them alive," Brian attested. "We'll have six agents there, including agents Rodriguez and Cunningham, who have a score to settle with the woman who has evaded us for three and a half years."

"You don't need to remind me of that," POTUS said as he pulled the note out of his wallet that Monica had written to him three years ago.

"I know you've waited a long time for this day, Mr. President," Eleanor expounded, feeling her recent involvement had increased the probability of finding the Pitt woman and ending her threat.

"We're not there yet," POTUS grunted, running his thumb and index finger over the folded note from Monica. "I'll feel better about it when she's in custody. I want to be able to look her in the eyes and know she'll no longer be a threat. To see the look of defeat and hopelessness on her face when I tell her that both she and her mother will pay with their lives for the death of my dear friend and patriot Carlton Henry."

"It will be our privilege to make that possible," Eleanor replied, including Brian in her promise.

"You say their meeting is at ten this morning?" POTUS confirmed almost causally, as if his mind were somewhere else.

"Yes, sir, Mr. President," Brian answered quickly, allowing Eleanor to push back a strand of his hair that had fallen across his left eyebrow.

"I'll be in a cabinet meeting then," the tone of his voice changed from a clandestine inflection to a more Chief Executive timbre. "Eleanor, call me about the success of the operation. If it's successful, tell my aide the code word '*Déjà vu Down*' and instruct him to deliver the message to me during the cabinet meeting. If you fail to corral her ..." his deep sigh came through the connection, "don't call during the meeting. I don't want to embarrass myself by throwing a chair across the room."

"I feel certain you'll get that message, Raymond," Eleanor assured him, as she moved behind Brian, who was sitting, and put her arms around his shoulders.

"You're telling me then, that you're not going to disappoint me!"

"I'm telling you we're 99.99% sure you'll receive that call," she reiterated, bringing her hands up and cupping Brian's face in her hands, and kissing the top of his head.

"Okay, 'till then, it is," POTUS signed off causally.

"Until then, Mr. President," she mimicked, kissing Brian on the top of the head again and sighing her relief that the call was over. She turned off the phone and then raised it as if to throw it against the floor, but thought better of it when she saw Brian's look of astonishment.

"Don't let him do that to you!" he advised, holding out his hand to relieve her of the phone.

At his end, POTUS opened the note and read what he had heard over the phone three years ago:

> *... That whenever any form of government be-*
> *comes destructive of these ends, it is the right of*
> *the people to alter or abolish it, and to institute*
> *new Government ...*

"If there is a new government, it will be without you, my dear," he assured himself, keeping his eyes steeled on Monica's blatant reminder that his job, as Chief Executive, was to serve and protect the people.

"Can you hear an undercurrent of animosity in the way he talks to me?" she asked Brian, as she handed him her phone.

"Maybe what you interpret as animosity is the result of the stress he's under," Brian countered charitably, diplomatically. He rose to his feet so that their eyes were more aligned with one another.

"Maybe you're right. Perhaps I'm just over-reacting ... No, that's not true, you stinker," she punched him playfully in the chest. "As I told you before, Raymond's going to use me as a scapegoat if this thing goes south. I feel it in my bones," she predicted, the worry lines on her face corroborating her sentiments.

"And as I told you before, I'm not going to let that happen!" he promised, pulling her to him for a kiss each of them had been waiting for before their chat with POTUS.

"Have you got time for a little …?" she trailed off, allowing the kittenish glimmer in her eyes to telegraph her intentions.

"Intimacy?" he finished her cleverly woven sentence.

Eleanor nodded and loosened the top two buttons on her lace-lined blouse.

"Are you still okay with this arrangement?" she asked him. "The last several times we've met, it seems like there's been three of us. You know, you've mentally brought your wife with you!"

Her words were like a fingernail scratching a slate chalk board, reminding him that he had promised to leave his wife out of the equation.

"Eleanor, I'm so sorry. We're separated now. And as I've told you, we've been estranged for quite some time. The kids are the only thing I want from the marriage," he confessed, kissing her again, his prelude to more than a simple apology.

"Okay then, I expect you to mentally and physically pay much more attention to me," she teased, making sure she had his interest with her mischief-making fingers.

* * * * * * *

They parked their G550's a block and a half from Caleb's office in a parking lot that was already almost full.

"Rita and Jack, join us in our vehicle so we can all review our plan of action," Andre spoke authoritatively into his head set.

"Roger that," Rita capitulated. "We'll be there asap."

Andre peeped at his watch.

"It's 0912," he announced to his team. "I'd rather have gotten here sooner, but we'll have to make do with what we've got."

"You made the right call in not texting Caleb," Hank proffered, giving Andre a quick pat on the back. "We know he's your friend, but we don't know what kind of stress he's under, especially now, since his boss may have threatened him or promised Caleb something in return for betraying you!"

Andre frowned his agreement and turned catty-cornered toward the back seat as Rita and Jack entered the vehicle. That way he would be positioned to include Hank, who had driven, in the group's discussion.

"We know Caleb and his boss will be here, but we don't know how many bogies, if there are bogies, will contaminate the meet," Andre guesstimated. "But we do know one thing for sure. Mr. Huang is a Tier 6 beneficiary and has a vested interest in making sure his policy is a whole life policy! So, he's probably coming here with that agenda in mind."

"There's a possibility that Huang's only agenda this morning is meeting with you and Gabby to see how much you know and find out where you're staying, so he can pass that intel on to his contacts at the Institute," Jack speculated, wanting to cover all of the contingencies.

"No doubt, but I think we all know it's a little more complicated than that," Rita added her seasoned insight. "The fact that the keystone kops were at the hospital and lost 'Larry' probably means the full weight of their clandestine resources are descending—ah, maybe both ascending and descending—since we're in Lower Manhattan—on these premises."

"Rita's right," Andre announced. "We've got to be very careful about what we're walking into this morning."

"And we've got to consider what your friend's walking into, too," Hank added. "If this really is a setup, he could become a casualty in the crossfire!"

Andre sent the group a worried look, recognizing that Hank could be right.

"You're right, Hank, and that's why we've got to make sure we're not jumping the gun on this. We should be here early enough to scan the parking area near his office and assess if we've got company. If we've got company, we'll determine what play we're going to make, depending on how much company we've got! If it looks like Caleb and his boss are alone, Rita, you and I will join them and determine how much a threat Mr. Huang is. You two," Andre addressed Hank and Jack, "stay in your perimeter positions in the parking lot in case the goons join us."

"If the goons arrive, we'll headset you and Rita to let you know they're here and how many there are," Jack proffered.

"At what point do we engage?" Hank queried.

Andre took a quick scan at his team huddled in the SUV. He could tell that all of them were crackling with adrenaline.

"If Rita and I are upstairs in Caleb's office, notify us and then engage them immediately. If we're all in our perimeter positions in the parking lot, we'll engage them immediately, with the proviso that we'll do our best to protect Caleb. I don't like putting him in the line of fire, but, unfortunately, he may find himself in the wrong place at the wrong time."

"Any thought as to which bogies are expendable and which are salvageable?" Jack asked, wanting to verify exigent encounter protocols.

Andre sighed, not wanting to take anything lightly when human lives were at stake.

"Everyone except Caleb and Huang is expendable! If we can, we'd like to take as many alive as we can, but I don't want any of you putting your lives in jeopardy by hesitating to execute a kill if the hesitation puts you at risk. I hope we'll have an opportunity to interrogate a few of them," Andre summarized.

"It's 0922," Rita announced, appearing a little antsy.

"Yeah, we need to go. Everybody got your Kevlars on?" Andre asked, referring to their body armor.

The group's head nods told him they were protected. They also checked their holstered revolvers.

"Anything else?" Andre quizzed.

"What happens if we're appreciably outnumbered?" Rita asked, wanting to sound macho, and not cream puff.

"I can't imagine they'll send a brigade, if they even send anyone at all; but, if we're substantially outnumbered, we'll stand down. It's no use being foolish about this," Andre assured the group. "Okay, let's go!"

The team exited the vehicle and retrieved their AR-18's from their respective vehicles. When they got to their perimeter locations in the parking area adjacent to Caleb's office, they scanned every inch of the parking lot.

At 0950 both Caleb and the Editor in Chief arrived at the same time. Caleb was the first to get out of his SUV, so he waited at the curb for his boss, who parked his SUV in the third row of parked cars, neglecting to park closer in spite of there being empty spaces at the curb.

That's strange, Andre thought, *Huang must be in his sixties. Maybe he's an exerciser... nope,* Andre corrected himself seeing the grossly over-weight editor inch himself out of the driver's seat. *Looks like the only exercise he might get is drawing water in the tub, pulling the plug, and then fighting the current!*

Andre cut his character assessment of Huang short when the editor and Caleb met at the curb and failed to greet each other with a handshake. He also noticed that Huang scanned the parking lot before he allowed Caleb to escort him toward the front door.

"What should we do?" Rita asked through her headset.

"Let's give them time to enter the building," Andre cautioned. "Everyone stay where you are and surveil your area."

Just as Caleb and his boss disappeared through the front door an SUV pulled into one of the curbside parking spaces. A man and a woman got out and headed toward the front entrance.

The auburn-haired young woman was petite, as rail-thin as a model. Her slim stems of legs and thighs looked even slimmer in her black slacks. He, too, looked like he was in shape. He had a full head of blonde hair which fell just short of his shoulders.

As Andre assessed the young man's looks he thought, *Any resemblance between him and a true blonde is probably purely peroxsidental.*

He even found himself judging the young woman's appearance, saying to himself, *If it wasn't for her Adam's apple, she wouldn't have any shape at all.*

Just about the time Andre was going to ask Rita to join him for their trip to Caleb's third floor office, the woman dropped what looked like a stacked file folder. Papers went everywhere, jettisoned by the gentle breeze which had made the team's surveillance in 90 degree weather bearable.

I'll wait 'till they get their act together before I call Rita, he whispered to himself.

All of a sudden, the doors on Caleb's and Huang's SUV's opened and three armed men piled out of each vehicle.

"Holy shit!" came Hank's reaction over their headsets, mirrored by Rita's "Oh, my God!"

"Stand down," Andre ordered. "Let's wait this out. Everybody copy?"

A mixture of 'Copy that' and 'Roger that' came through the headsets as his team nixed their urge to expose their cover.

The men who had exited the two SUVs converged on the unsuspecting—and surprised—couple in seconds, brandishing their weapons and ordering the couple to their knees.

It became very obvious that the frightened couple was not who the operatives thought they were, because two of the men exchanged head shakes and frowns, indicating the couple wasn't the high value targets they were expecting.

Andre's team watched as the apparent leader of the six pack of keystone kops apologized to the couple and helped them gather the rest of the scattered documents that had blown across the lawn and parking area.

As the disheveled couple hurried their awkward pace toward the front entrance door, the collection of operatives were ordered to fan out across the parking area by the leader of the group.

"I recognize that guy!" Rita announced to the others. "He was one of the bogies at the hospital!"

"You're right, Rita," Hank confirmed, referring to Sergio. "He's the one who got the warrant. Andre, don't you recognize him?"

"I do now," Andre replied, improving his line of sight without revealing himself. "And he's not the only one! See the one over there, standing next to the gray Lexus? We've seen him at the hospital, too!" he exclaimed, pointing out Lantz.

"Well, how about that!" Rita replied. "Huang must have contacted them."

"I knew something was up when Huang looked around the parking lot when he got here," Jack shared his observation.

"Yes, I think we all saw it," Andre inserted, watching the movements of the five operatives, who were responding to Sergio's orders to fan out.

"I say we move on them now, before they have a chance to disperse," Andre announced. "Let's hope we can save the two who were at the hospital, because they probably know more than the others. But don't treat them any differently than the others. When I say go, I want you to terminate the threats that stand before us! Ready! Go!"

Each of them moved quickly toward the unsuspecting cluster of operatives who were preoccupied with establishing their own perimeter.

The distinct haunting sound of four explosive semi-automatic AR 18's discharging their rounds caught the six operatives completely off guard. The brass shell casings from each of Andre's team member's automatic weapon of destruction flew past each of their faces as they weaved in-and-out through the parked cars which shielded them. The sickening, pungent smell of sulfur was in the air. The simultaneous nature of so many rounds being discharged sounded like hundreds of bombs going off.

The operatives' attempts to return fire were short lived. All of the operatives had gone down, some motionless and face down, others writhing from the multiple wounds they had experienced.

"Check each one of them," Andre ordered. "Make sure you separate them from their weapons and from any identification they might be carrying. Also check their vehicles for anything we can use. Get the SUV keys from Caleb and Huang. Hank, Rita. See if the two hospital kops are alive. If they are, we're not through with them yet!"

As the four of them checked the wounded and dead bodies that were scattered across the front of the parking lot, Andre reconnoitered the parking area and sidewalks to see if any more hostiles were present, and to see if any innocent passersby had gotten caught in the milieu.

Satisfied that their combat zone had not impacted innocent people, Andre scanned the occupied section of the half-empty office building. People peeking from their own vantage points, including Caleb and Huang who were standing at their third floor window, were totally shaken by what they were witnessing below.

Andre caught Caleb and Huang out of the corner of his eye, and without tipping them off, called to Jack.

"Jack, I need you to come over here, pronto."

Jack made his way over to Andre without asking any questions.

"I don't want you to look, but Caleb and Huang are staring at us from Caleb's third story window. They're in Room 304. Zip-tie them and bring them down to us. We're taking them with us. Hurry, because we've got to get out of here before the police arrive!" Andre instructed Jack, wanting to wrap up their operation as quickly as possible.

Jack kept his eyes straight forward and headed toward the front entrance.

"Andre," Rita called to him, "this one's still alive. I think he's the one who got the warrant and complicated our patient transfer."

Andre joined her and stared at the wounded operative sitting against one of the parked cars.

Sergio's face was a mixture of anger and rage, mingled with the kind of raw vehemence that comes with being militarily bested in combat.

"Yes. That's him," Andre agreed, steeling his gaze on Sergio's bloody face and shoulder. "Zip-tie him and put him in the cargo space in the back of my vehicle. "I'm glad you suggested we bring moving blankets, Rita. Looks like we're going to need the blankets to keep the G550's from getting soiled."

Rita zip-tied Sergio where he sat, making direct eye contact with him before she stood beside him.

"Get up," Rita ordered, showing her big girl moxie.

Andre helped her get Sergio to his feet and watched as she led the wounded operative who limped into the G550. She Zip-tied him to one of the luggage rings in the cargo hold and left the rear door up so Andre could see him.

"Okay, are there any more of them alive?" Andre addressed Rita and Hank as he checked one of the lifeless operatives lying a few feet away.

"No, he's the only one," Hank confirmed.

"Put their weapons and ID's in your vehicle, Rita. Are we sure they're all ID-less?" he asked both of them.

Their head nods confirmed the team's attention to details.

Andre glanced quickly at Caleb's third story office window and then at the front entrance where he saw Jack leading the Zip-tied reporter and his boss out the damaged glass front door, which had been shattered during the mayhem.

"Jack, put them in the back seat of Hank's and my vehicle. Make sure you blindfold all of them. You and Rita meet us at the remote make-shift interrogation chamber we just procured. We're going to wrap this up this afternoon," Andre explained, loud enough for Caleb to hear, as he made eye contact with Caleb who was approaching him, "one way or another!"

"Andre, I'm sorr …!" Caleb tried to excuse his culpability.

Andre glared at Caleb as his one time friend was led past him.

"They ... they forced me to ... I had no choice. They said they'd ..." Caleb stuttered, hoping to exonerate himself.

"Keep moving," Jack interrupted, strong-arming the two of them, with Hank's help, into the back seat of Andre and Hank's vehicle.

"We'd better roll," Andre announced to the group. "The local police will be here any minute."

As the two vehicles wove their way through the parking lot, they passed four police cars with their rotating red and blue lights and blaring horns announcing their arrival.

"That's cutting it close," Hank declared the obvious, raising his eyebrows at Andre.

Andre nodded, acknowledging Hank's observation, while he watched the police cars turn toward the war zone.

"I don't like cutting things that close," Andre replied, looking reproachingly at Caleb, who bowed his head.

"You three have something to think about for a while," Andre addressed the blindfolded trio in the back. "You're going to tell us what we need to know, or this will be your last trip anywhere, except to a body dump. If you think I'm kidding, each of you've got one foot in your grave right now!"

"You, in the cargo hold," Andre was talking to Sergio, "whoever you are. We've seen you before."

Sergio tilted his head toward Andre, grimacing with pain, but not saying a word.

"And I can tell you, you're going to tell us who hired you; or your wife, fiancée, or significant other will be attending your funeral sometime in the next year or two when they find your decomposed body somewhere in New Jersey!" Andre threatened, steeling his gaze on the wounded operative who had given Frank's father such a hard time at the hospital.

Andre thought to himself, *Promise an adversary his life and he will usually cooperate after some mild persuasion. Promise him his life and money, and he will generally surrender easily.*

"Do you know who I am?" Huang spoke up, lifting his chin as high as he could and sneering at his two captors.

Hank and Andre exchanged amused glances.

"Yeah, you're one of the guys who's going to regret ever having met us if you don't tell us what we want to know," Andre countered, without turning his head to look at the arrogant editor.

"I said ... do you know who I am, you piece of shit!"

Andre sighed, realizing Huang's bravado was going to get the editor into trouble.

"It's amazing to me how someone in your position can be so incredibly harebrained, so oblivious to the risks associated with being so flaky," Andre countered, this time unfastening his seatbelt to allow himself to turn to confront the insolent prisoner.

Huang paused before he opened his mouth again.

"I'm Cao Huang, Editor in Chief of the *New York Times!*"

"That doesn't mean anything to us, Mr. Huang," Andre retaliated. His mouth was arranged in a smile, but the intolerance in his eyes spoke differently. "To us, you're subscriber #786, 206 — Tier 6."

Huang's eyes widened under his blindfold and the pink flush on his face turned cerise red.

"How do you know this?"

"You've lost the right to ask questions, Mr. Huang. As a matter of fact, you won't be asking us any questions. None of you will," Andre addressed all three of them. "We'll be asking all of the questions! And if we don't get the answers we want, you'll be of no use to us."

Andre turned, facing the front again and refastened his seat belt.

He picked up his cell phone.

"Hello, Babe. We're all fine! Yes, everyone is safe and sound. The operation went as planned. We've got a short stop to make, but our ETA should be just after lunch ... Roger that!" Andre responded to Gabby's endearment.

Chapter Nineteen

She checked her phone messages as soon as she got out of her staff meeting, but there were no messages from Agent Cramer.

"Helen, I need a few moments before I chat with Julián," she instructed her administrative assistant, referring to the Secretary of Housing and Urban Development, Julián Garcia.

"Yes, ma'am, When you're ready, just buzz, and I'll get him on the line. Oh, Agent Cramer's on line two."

Eleanor gave Helen a perfunctory head nod and retreated behind her closed door. Although dressed in a very stunning and energetic purple two piece skirt suit with a black belt to accent her thin waist, the worried look on Eleanor's face belied her confidence and panache. She picked up the phone and let Brian know she was there.

"Have you heard anything yet from Agent Rodriguez?" Eleanor asked Brian, who had just gotten off the phone himself with Dr. Schönbächler of the Life Extension Institute in Geneva.

"No, unfortunately, I haven't," he huffed his reply. "However, before my call with Dr. Schönbächler, O'Sullivan and Akimoto, the field agents I sent to Lower Manhattan to check on Sergio's team, shared some rather disturbing news. It seems there was a shootout in the parking lot in front of the reporter's office this morning."

"What! A shootout?" came her incredulous reply, as she lowered herself into her chair. Her subsurface pensiveness became evident as a hollow expression crossed her face.

"Yes, it happened shortly after 1000 hours, and it involved our team. The reporters' SUV's were still parked in the yellow taped-off area in the parking lot."

"Oh ... My God! Who is this woman?" Eleanor asked rhetorically. "She must be a witch. And who are her accomplices? It seems every time we get near her, we lose agents!"

Brian sighed his agreement.

"O'Sullivan and Akimoto flashed their government ID's and were allowed to talk to eye witnesses in the office building complex. They also talked to the police and were told there were five casualties. None of the casualties had ID's so Akimoto went with one of the police detectives to identify the deceased."

"Oh, honey ... Brian, I don't know what to say! You knew all of them. That means there's only one that ..." she stopped herself, not wanting to speculate on his whereabouts. "What about the Editor in Chief and the reporter?" she followed up, remembering they were also involved.

"The reporter's office was empty, except for a handwritten note from Cao which read 'They've found us,' that was taped to a water cooler."

"They're certainly very thorough," she admitted, her despondence coming through the phone. "They have to be part of a larger organization, and that's beginning to scare me!"

"I'm beginning to think so myself," Brian agreed, "and how she's been able to pull this off, time and time again, indicates she has access to intel that's quite sophisticated."

"Do you, I mean POTUS's special ops unit, have any idea who she's working with?"

"It's a mystery to all of us, and we've got some incredible people from all over the world working on it!" he assured her, thinking: *Sometimes money and power aren't enough to censor the fighting spirit of a monomaniac on a mission, especially if that calling involves saving the lives of people who have no idea they're being used as body parts for the top 1% of the richest people on the planet.*

"Where are you?" Eleanor asked, coughing her nervousness.

"At the command center on Wisconsin Avenue. Why?" Brian asked, already knowing the answer.

"Can you meet me here on the Hill?"

"Eleanor ... I ..."

"Please, Brian! I need you here when I talk to POTUS," she pressed, knowing she could get him to capitulate if her voice sounded raspy enough.

"Okay. Yes, of course. I ... I'd like to hear from Akimoto and O'Sullivan first, so we have up-to-date intel."

"They can reach you here, can't they?" she urged, amping up her well-practiced mock dismay.

"Yes, I suppose they could, But I won't be able to stay long, Eleanor. I'll need command center resources to help locate the missing agent and the newspaper reporters. I'll also have to speak to the families of the deceased agents, some of whom are from Gold Star parents who have already lost a serviceman or servicewoman in Iraq and Afghanistan."

"I understand. I just need you here when I make the call to POTUS who is expecting a call from me within the hour," she schemed, turning her forged vulnerability up a notch.

"Eleanor, can you hold just for a minute? O'Sullivan is calling and I need to take it. I think you'll want to know what he's found asap. I won't be long. Hold on."

"Okay. Of course," she surrendered, hoping the news wouldn't send her into an unwomanlike tirade.

She kept the phone to her ear, but began to pace the floor agitatedly, since she was not used to subordinating herself to a hireling, who was her current boy toy, but a hireling nevertheless.

"Darcy, what have you got?" Brian snapped, feeling the burn of being outplayed by unknown opponents who were enjoying an upper hand.

"Brian, I've got good news and bad news. Which do you want first?"

Brian exhaled his emotional ferment before he could find the syllables that made sense.

"Let's have the good news!"

"Sergio must be alive! He's not among the dead!"

This time his heavy sigh was one of relief.

"That is good news! That's really good news!" Brian replied heartily. "The rest are dead, then?" he said disconsolately, knowing he had heard Darcy right the first time, but hoping he hadn't.

"I'm afraid so, sir!"

"Then there are five dead in all?" Brian confirmed.

"That's all they've got here. I told the city coroner we'll perform the five autopsies, since this is a federal matter."

"Good. Thanks. Maybe Sergio and the news people are still alive," Brian figured, talking as much to himself as he was to Darcy. "Is Fumio there with you?"

"Yes, we're both here at the morgue. Wasn't much else I could do at the office site. As I said, except for Huang's note in the reporter's office, there wasn't anything else we could do that the local police hadn't already done. The office was clean of fingerprints, except for the reporter's and Huang's. The eye witnesses repeated to Fumio and I what they had told the police. They said the ones who were involved looked like military and had assault weapons. Of course, we didn't need civvies to tell us that, because the parking lot was full of hundreds of AR 18 casings," Darcy summarized, and then paused for a moment before he began again. "It doesn't look like our guys fired many rounds off. They must have been taken by surprise by a team of combatants who knew what they were doing!"

"Anything else I need to know at this point?" Brian asked, trying his best to cool his rage.

"Yeah, Jeffrey, and now Lantz and Carl ... and Sergio is missing ... They were really good friends of mine—and yours, too! I know we're working for the President and why we're working for him, but I've got to tell you, I'm losing a lot of friends over something that I personally disagree with. You know what I mean, Brian? And Fumio feels the same way," Darcy confessed.

Brian let out a corroborative sigh and hesitated before he spoke.

"I know exactly what you mean, Darcy. We've had this talk before! I think it's best we keep our feelings to ourselves. We're working for some very powerful people who wouldn't be at all enamored with this conversation."

"Yeah, I know. But I'm just saying, I don't like it. I hate what I'm doing! And I know you hate it, too!"

"Okay. Look. I've got to go. I've got someone on hold on another line. I'll meet you two back at the command center."

"Okay if Fumio stays here until our guys pick up the bodies?"

"Yes, of course. I'll see both of you later. Oh, and Darcy, I'm serious, now. What we've just discussed here stays here! The three of us will talk about it over a couple of beers. All right?"

Darcy smiled his understanding.

"All right. Yeah. Sure. Fumio says sure, too! Any idea when you'll be at the command center?"

Brian thought for a moment, realizing how difficult it was going to be extracting himself from a woman who was used to getting her way.

"I'll call you, but it's probably going to be around 1600 hours."

"Roger that."

Brian looked at the phone after he ended the call with Darcy and sighed his hesitance before he re-engaged with Eleanor.

He thought to himself, *Our shared roles in our positions with the U.S. government and our marital similarities have connected us in ways that go beyond mere governmental service. But, I've got to tell you, my dear, I do not share your loyalty to the Institute. Too many good people are losing their lives over this elitist human xerography scheme.* He stopped his train of thought, realizing the Deputy Assistant Secretary of Health and Human Services was on hold.

"Eleanor, are you still there?"

"Yessss! I'm still here. And I'm thinking you must have gotten some really bad news, because I've been on a six shot bourbon hold," she responded, allowing her considerable agitation to erupt over the phone connection.

"You have my sincere apologies," he affirmed, realizing that their off-hours relationship was allowing him to keep his job.

"You want to give me the bad news now, or shall we wait until you get here?"

"As it turns out, you're probably going to want me to share the bad news with the President. So, suppose we wait 'till I get there?"

"How bad is it?" she pressed, knowing she wasn't going to like what she heard.

"Catastrophic!" Brian replied, grabbing his jacket and waving at Nona, as he walked out of his office toward the command's center front door.

"Then you'd better be prepared to pour me—and yourself—a glass of bourbon when you get here."

"I think we're both going to need it," he played into her addiction.

"You're on your way then?" she cooed, sounding like she wasn't grasping, or didn't want to face, the full import of his troublesome intel.

"I'm getting in the car now."

* * * * * * *

The sunlight slanting down through the tall trees, which fringed their drive along the partially shaded creek to the make-shift compound, looked like corrugated light streams lining the left side of the road.

Dust from the heavily-cindered road blew left-to-right across their path, saving the second vehicle from being entirely blanketed by an obnoxious cloud of grayish brown sediment.

The forest canopy overhead added to the secluded nature of their 'off-the-beat' compound which prevented the group from having to worry about exposing Zeus' Den to the watchful eyes of their adversaries.

"Which one of these clowns do you want to grill first?" Hank asked Andre, as he headed the G550 around the last curve to the compound.

"I think we'll start with the warrant guy in the cargo hold," Andre responded, referring to Sergio.

The two civvies in the back seat will have more time to think about what a mess they've gotten themselves into, Andre thought to himself. *The more time they spend worrying about their mortality, the easier they'll be to break.*

"He seemed to be the leader of the other two at the hospital, the kind of leader who has a penchant for losing men," Hank tendered, hoping to get a rise out of Sergio.

Sergio stiffened, partly in response to Hank's unkind allegation and partly to straighten his wounded leg which had gotten cramped on their trip to the compound. The wound in his shoulder was also beginning to throb due to his cramped position in the cargo hold of the SUV. But he held his tongue, refusing to give his captors the satisfaction of letting them know the extent of the rage he was feeling inside.

"Okay. We're here," Hank announced, as he pulled the SUV up to the compound entrance. He waited before he got out to allow Jack and Rita to pull their vehicle up along side of their parked vehicle, to let the dust settle.

"Tie these two under that tree over there," Andre addressed Jack, referring to Caleb and Huang.

Jack pulled the newspapermen out of the back seat and hustled them over into sitting positions at the trunk of a huge maple tree that was adjacent to a few stunted evergreens.

Andre nodded to Hank, who intentionally roughhoused Sergio out of the cargo hold, and led him limping into the compound interrogation room to be cross-examined.

"Rita, see what you can do about his wounds," Andre was referring to Sergio's predicament. "Let me know if they're through-and-throughs or lodged."

She nodded and headed toward the interrogation room.

"I'll be in in a moment," Andre told her, expecting that she'd relay his message to Hank.

Before he went inside, Andre walked over to the two blindfolded newspapermen.

Jack had tied the pair to the base of the tree as low as he could to force them to stay seated.

"Huang, we are very familiar with your association with the Life Extension Institute of Geneva. You are one of their major …"

"They made me drive them to my office," Caleb torpedoed Andre's encounter with his boss.

"Shut up, Caleb," Andre blasted, "I'll get to you in a moment."

Andre renewed his cross-check with Huang by kicking the sole of the editor's expensive shoe before he began.

The surprised editor jerked at the unexpected roughness, but kept his mouth shut.

"You and your wife are two of the Institute's Tier 6 subscribers. That means there are six people who live in a geographic area close to you who have no idea they have been cloned for body parts in case you or your wife should need their organs."

Huang huffed his resentment, but remained silent.

"What you're doing is wrong!" Jack interjected, looking at Andre for approval.

Andre nodded and smiled his consent to have both Jack and him pepper Huang with reality checks.

"The thing that really bothers us is that rich and affluent people like you seem to have no scruples whatsoever seeing people less well-off than you as property to be used—and it appears to be ruthlessly discarded—in whatever way it suits your fancy," Andre accused, kicking him in the sole of his left foot to accelerate the editor's growing nervousness.

"Who ... who are you working for?" blurted the terrified editor.

"We told you we're asking the questions!" shouted Jack.

"You've messed with the wrong people," Andre added, raising his voice, but trying to keep his anger in check.

"You mean Monica Pitt?" Huang announced, in a voice close to whispering.

"Monica Pitt?" Andre countered, lowering his voice to curb his growing animosity. "Who is Monica Pitt," he countered, not wanting to blow her cover in spite of Caleb having met her.

Huang remained silent, realizing he may have compromised his freedom.

"There are tens of thousands of other wonderful people like this Monica Pitt you named, that have been marked by people like you as expendable," Andre continued. "But that's changing as we speak, you arrogant piece of shit! It is our intent to close down the Institute! You and the rest of you parasites will lose touch with your unsuspecting donors, because we're destroying their implants!"

Huang showed that he was visibly upset by struggling against the rope that tethered him against the tree. But all the while, he kept his silence.

"What that means, Mr. Editor," Jack cajoled, "is that you and your wife, and thousands of other upper crust parasites all over the world, have lost the benefit of your expensive insurance policy. And we, I'm honored to say, are the ones responsible for that!"

Andre decided to get his once trusted friend involved in the conversation.

"Caleb, what's happened to you? These people have killed your DNA matches, and will not hesitate to kill you when the subscriber who cloned you needs one of your body parts."

"They ... they promised me ... they wouldn't hurt ..." he limped into his excuse, hoping that Andre would buy it.

"Who's they?" Jack asked on Andre's behalf, leaning as close as he could with his face next to Caleb's terrified, blindfolded face, which was becoming more flushed by the minute.

"The people Cao contacted," Caleb blurted out. "The people who showed up at my office this ..."

"Shut up!" Huang shouted, having no trouble breaking his self-imposed silence. "Shut, the hell up!"

"Who's the operative in there?" Andre pried, directing his question at Huang to identify the wounded goon in the interrogation room. "What's his name?"

Huang retreated into his smug silence again.

"Jack, scoot Huang to the back of the tree and tie him up again in a sitting position. Make sure he's facing toward the woods, so he can't identify any of us by turning his head. Tie his neck to the tree, too, so he has to sit upright. And keep his hands Zip-tied."

Andre looked at Caleb, who sat slumped against the tree trunk facing the compound. Then he glanced at his watch: *1200 hours,* he said to himself.

"Turn this traitor around so he's also facing the woods. Restrain him the same way your restraining Huang. Then reach around and take their blindfolds off their right eyes without letting them see what you look like. Give each of them a note pad and a pencil."

"How tight do you want the rope around their necks?" Jack asked, hoping he was reading Andre right.

"A little tighter than snug," Andre responded. "I don't want either of them wiggling free while we're inside. If you tie them too tight, they'll just have to get used to it."

"Roger that."

"The note pads are for your farewell letters to loved ones, gentlemen. You've got five minutes to write them," Andre announced flatly, without an ounce of emotion present. "Jack, I'll see you inside."

Jack nodded and busied himself with carrying out his superior's instructions.

"Andre ... Bro ...you're not serious," Caleb petitioned, as he settled in his relocation.

Huang didn't utter a syllable, making it clear he was resigned to his fate.

Andre ignored Caleb's plea, and quickened his strides to the compound entrance.

Hank and Rita had already started grilling their blindfolded prisoner.

"Have you gotten anything out of him yet?" Andre asked, noticing there was blood issuing from the prisoner's mouth and nose.

"Profanity!" Rita replied. "He's got the mouth of a sailor."

"And threats," Hank added. "He says that if we don't kill him, he's going to kill us!"

Andre walked closer to Sergio and leaned on his wounded leg, causing Sergio to groan his contempt. Then Andre backed up just a bit and assessed the bloodstained adversary who had the demeanor of an alligator at rest—attentive, observant and unbelievably patient, but very, very dangerous.

"We know you've been hired to do a job, a job that involves protecting the selfish and inhuman interests of a privileged few," Andre began slowly, making sure his weight continued to put pressure on Sergio's leg wound. "It seems that you'll stop at nothing in order to fulfill the orders of a monster, a monster who is not only denigrating the office of the President of the United States, but putting himself—and others like you—in league with the shadow side, the dark side, the satanic side of human nature!"

"I don't know what you're talking about!" Sergio hissed.

"Oh, I think you know full well what I'm talking about. I'll bet that one of the reasons you're fighting so hard to stop us is that you and your family are subscribers to one of the tiers the Institute offers its policy holders," Andre speculated, increasing his weight on Sergio's bandaged leg.

Sergio grunted his discomfort, but didn't object to Andre's accusation.

"And I'll tell you what, you misguided soul, we've gotten enough access into the Institute's servers that sooner or later, we're going to come across your file. We're going to know who you are and who your family is. We're going to find out who your surrogates are and delete their files so you—and your family—won't be able to use them for body parts!"

"You son-of-a- ..."

Andre leveled a brutal blow into Sergio's face, sending his head sharply sideways, and opening up a four inch gash across his left cheek bone.

"There's no way you, or the goons you're working for, or POTUS himself, can stop us from leaking the human cloning atrocities to the media. And we're talking days, not weeks or months! You won't be able to stop it!"

Sergio spit blood onto the floor to clear his mouth so he could speak.

"We stopped you today!"

Andre and the others laughed.

"No, *we* stopped *you* today!" Andre asserted, grabbing the prisoner's shoulder. "We bested you today by staying two steps ahead of you. If you're the best the Institute can field, your chances of stopping us are next to impossible. We've proven your intel is insufficient and your response to that intel awkward and slow. We've hacked into the Institute's main servers and are now ready to make that information public. And I predict the people you're working for, the ones you're trying to protect, are going to make you one of their fall guys."

"If you can't see that," Rita chimed in, "you deserve what you get!"

"You got a name? You, the one who just spoke to me?" Sergio asked, referring to Rita.

"Yes, I've got a name," Rita responded, waving off Andre's and Hank's nervous censorship. "I'm a Gold Star Parent who lost a son or daughter who fought and died for what America should stand for and not for what it has become, because of you and others like you! ... I'm a Human Clone Surrogate Parent who lost a daughter who didn't know she was cloned, but who was killed by your Institute for her heart or lungs or kidneys ... I'm a Nobel Prize winning physicist whose life was cut short, because one of your subscribers wanted his kidneys and pancreas! I'm a six-year-old who was killed for her healthy liver, because she was the perfect match for one of your subscriber's children who needed her liver! That's who I am you piece of garbage!" she blasted, spewing spittle from her scornful lips.

The room was quiet for a few moments. Rita's powerful metaphor had penetrated the heart's of everyone present, except for one.

"I can tell you what I can see," Sergio sneered his response. "I can see the Pitt woman begging for her life as we cut her heart out for a more deserving policy holder!"

Andre lunged at him, but was corralled by both Hank and Jack, who had just stepped inside to join them. It was all they could do to bridle Andre, who struggled against their better judgment.

"Okay ... Okay," Andre surrendered, holding both of his hands up, palms out, to indicate having regained his composure. "I'm good. I'm good!"

The icy smile on Sergio's face telegraphed the heartlessness and harshness of a man who had lost his way. It characterized what happens to people who become so influenced by evil that they become the unconscionable and amoral products of evil themselves.

Andre stood directly in front of Sergio and walked as close to him as he could without laying a hand on him.

"I feel sorry for you, whoever and whatever you are. I'd call you an animal, but animals are much more principled and intelligent than you. It wouldn't do animals any justice to call you one of them," Andre leveled his criticism, speaking softly so the substance of his words would ring loud and clear.

All of a sudden Rita moved past Andre, lifted her knee to her chest, and kicked straight ahead, hitting the insolent prisoner squarely in the chest, sending both him and the chair in which he was tied, crashing to the floor. The impact was so great that it broke one of the legs off the upturned chair.

Her three colleagues were wide-eyed and astonished, surprised that she would do something like that.

"I couldn't hold it in any longer," she confessed, "I thought I'd do it before you did," she addressed Andre, raising her eyebrows so that they disappeared under her bangs and giving the men a tight, triumphant smile.

Andre smiled at her and cupped her right cheek affectionately in his left hand.

Hank and Jack busied themselves propping Sergio back up by turning over an old two-shelf bookcase and placing a corner of it where the forth chair leg had been.

Andre walked up to Sergio and kicked the intact chair leg in the front, causing him to flinch.

Andre looked at his three compatriots and mouthed *'If it's okay with you guys, I'm going to let him go, so he can lead us to his superiors!'*

Their head nods confirmed their support. However, Rita mouthed, *'Can I kick him again?'* to the delight of the others.

"We know who your up-lines are and we're going to terminate as many of the hardliners as we can!" Andre threatened. "So, when you tell them that..." Andre paused, catching Sergio's surprise as the prisoner tilted his head back and straightened in the wobbly chair. "Tell them we're coming to get them, one by one, unless they terminate their human xerography program immediately. We're sparing your sorry ass today so you can communicate our threat, but if we see you again, you won't have a chance to insult us. You got that?"

Sergio sat motionless, wondering if they were really going to let him go.

"You got that?" Andre repeated, tapping him on the side of his sweaty head with his knuckles so it would hurt.

"Yeah," Sergio nodded. "I got that!"

"Untie him from the chair," Andre addressed Jack, "and toss him in the cargo hold of your SUV. We'll meet you out front,"

Andre added, motioning for Hank and Rita to follow him outside.

The two newsies were sitting uncomfortably, tied to the tree
trunk. They were talking, but stopped when they realized they
were being approached.

Jack pushed Sergio into the back of his SUV and tied him to
the tie-down loops. Then he locked the compound front door before he joined the others.

"You got your farewell letters written?" Andre teased, although the tone of his voice didn't sound like he was fooling.

Both Caleb and Huang waved their farewell notes as best as
they could with their hands tied.

"Hand them over. We'll see your sister gets yours, Caleb;
and we'll make sure your subscriber wife gets yours Huang!"
Andre promised, knowing they were going to give the frightened
men their farewell notes back.

"Andre, you don't have to do this," Caleb pleaded in a voice
laced with fear.

Huang remained silent, anticipating the worst.

"Put their blindfolds over their right eyes again and untie
them from the tree," Andre addressed Hank and Jack.

"I don't want to die," cried Caleb. "Please don't do this!"

"Lead them over to the edge of the woods there by the
creek," Andre instructed Hank and Jack again. Both of them sent
Andre puzzled looks, wondering what he was up to. Andre and
Rita followed them to the creekside.

"Please don't do this!" Caleb pleaded.

Andre sent Hank a mischievous smile.

"Remember the last thing we told those three Iraqi prisoners
just outside the Kufa gate in Baghdad on our last tour of duty?"
he asked Hank, sending him a comical wink.

Hank thought for a moment, but couldn't quite place Andre's
context.

"They were in the Republican Guard," Andre reminded him.

"Oh," Hank let out a breathy chuckle, "yeah, I remember!"

"Well, I think these two deserve the same consideration. Don't you think?" Andre suggested, showing his amusement at Rita's and Jack's confused expressions.

"Okay you two," Hank addressed Caleb and Huang, "we've got a long drive ahead of us and we're going to give you a chance to relieve your bladders."

If their laughter bothered the two newsies, it wasn't evident as both Caleb and Huang quickly took advantage of the opportunity.

"You're not executing us then?" Huang conceded, feeling relieved both emotionally and bodily.

"You're already committing harikari with your association with the Institute," Rita was quick to point out.

"We're sparing your miserable lives for two reasons," Andre announced, as he motioned for Jack and Hank to turn the two of them around so he could face both of them.

Neither newsie said a word.

"We want to give you the opportunity to do the right thing, Huang, and disassociate yourself and your family from the Institute before it's too late ... And we expect both of you to tell your contacts to give themselves up before they predecease their surrogates. And that's a threat and a promise!" Andre forewarned.

Andre's team threw him confused looks. Their faces were murals of puzzlement.

Rita mouthed, *'Are we really going to do that?'*

Andre shook his head and mouthed his reply, *'I'm using intimidation tactics!'*

The three of them smiled their approval.

"Okay, load them up," Andre instructed Hank and Jack. "Put them with the other sorry excuse for a human!"

When the newsies were securely in the back seat of Jack's SUV, Andre huddled the team.

"You okay to turn those three into hitchhikers?" Andre asked Rita and Jack.

"It would be our pleasure," Rita dittoed.

"Okay then. Let those three sorry asses out in the Hackensack Meadowlands Wildlife Reserve," Andre instructed them. "Leave them zip-tied and blindfolded, and free to move around. I want them found in a reasonable amount of time so they can deliver our message."

Andre checked his watch.

"1340 hours. Hank and I are going to make a quick stop at Caleb's office to see if we can find anything the local police may have overlooked, assuming they've finished their crime scene investigation."

Andre grinned at the three of them.

"We've done a good job today! I'm proud of all of you. It's time we all got back to the farmhouse."

"Okay. We'll see you two in a few," Rita goodbyed as she and Jack made their way over to their vehicle.

"Be careful," Hank advised her and Jack. "See you both at the crib."

Andre and Hank motioned for the other two to drive off first, so each vehicle could share the road dust.

"Babe, Hi," Andre greeted Gabby, as he held the phone to his ear.

"We've been worried about you," she admitted, her cherubic voice brimmed with both eagerness and concern.

"Everyone's fine. We'll be home around 1400 hours, depending on traffic. Ask Paul if he'd mind fixing an early dinner. We're all tired and a little hungry. We sorta worked past lunch."

"Oh, Andre."

"The team says hi! We're looking forward to getting out of this gear and relaxing."

"Good! We're looking forward to relaxing you! Oh, Mother got in her wheelchair today and loved being around us women and having the run of the house."

"That's terrific! She'll be up and about in no time!"

"I think so, too! I'm beginning to see the mother I knew back in her eyes."

"She's been on quite a journey," Andre added, as their vehicle left the gravel road and found purchase on the macadam.

"Yes, and I know we're all looking forward to a more gentler and kinder one."

"Copy that! Love you!"

"Love you, too!"

Chapter Twenty

Well, that went well," Brian spoke softly to Eleanor, intentionally lacing his voice with a sarcastic tone.

A mechanical smile leaked across her face as she toasted him with her almost empty glass of bourbon.

"What did I tell you?" she boasted pensively, wearing her pessimism like a scolded child. "He's going to see that I'm going to take the fall for this!"

Brian expertly procured the bottle of Kentucky's finest bourbon off the corner of her desk and added a couple of shots to her already well-used glass. Then he added a shot in his own glass and sat on the edge of the desk facing her.

"It's obvious POTUS is distancing himself from the Institute's inevitable fallout. The thing that worries me is how far will he go to insulate himself?" Brian asked, pretty sure he knew what the answer would be.

"I'm clear on that," Eleanor countered. "There's something I've got to tell you. He has severed ties with the Institute. He refuses to speak to Dr. Schönbächler or anyone on his staff. He's even made sure his files have been deleted from the Institute's current data base. I've heard he's made sure other policy holders are safe, too! Fortunately, or unfortunately, as the case may be, I want to remain on the rolls!"

Brian leaned toward her and gave her one of his patented piercing looks that telegraphed not only his intensity, but his forward thinking acumen.

"Deputy Assistant Secretary," he began, in a calculatedly businesslike manner, "you've known him for most of your highly successful and illustrious, professional working life. You've seen POTUS at his best—and at his most conniving worst. Do you think, for one moment, he won't throw you under the proverbial bus when it comes to saving his own neck?"

Eleanor closed her eyes and let out a bitter, hollow laugh. A veneer of searing apprehension migrated across her face as the growing reality of her predicament registered in her slumped posture and amped-up alcohol use.

"I thought it, but I didn't want to believe it! And I still don't believe he'd do that to me," she replied softly, trying her best to mute her exasperation without appearing resigned to her fate.

"I've witnessed the kind of posturing we're experiencing with POTUS in the armed services when generals backpedal, trying to save their asses. And I can tell you, the higher up you are in an organization, the more insulated you are from liability and culpability. I've seen it in the service and I'm seeing it now!"

He reached down and gently relieved her of her glass and placed his own untouched glass on her desk. Then he took both of her hands, lifted her from her chair, and led her to the love seat adjacent to her desk. When she was seated comfortably, he sat down beside her. All the while, Eleanor had kept her doleful eyes glued onto him.

"Have you taken any steps to protect yourself?" Brian asked, taking her hands in his and moving them to her lap.

"Well, I'm encrypting my emails and texts. I've been careful not to leave a paper trail. I ..."

"What have you done about your relationship with the Institute?" Brian intercepted her reply.

She gave him the most lachrymose, teary-eyed look.

"Why, nothing. I've paid a substantial amount of money for that policy! I certainly don't intend on cancelling it! If this thing goes where I think it's going, I'll disavow knowing it was for anything else but making sure my son and I are placed at the top of an organ donor list. I've pulled the information off my policy that relates to surrogate clones and had an associate re-authenti-cate my policy. I ... I've told you before that the average waiting time to find a deceased donor can be 3-5 years, and in some states, it's closer to 8-10 years. Patients are prioritized by how long they've been on the waiting list, their blood type, immune system activity and other factors. I'm not willing to put Dalton or myself through that ridiculous waiting process!"

"Then you're still a policy holder?" Brian cut into her explanation.

She nodded without losing eye contact, wanting to catch his expression.

"After all we've discovered about the Life Extension Institute of Geneva, you still want to remain loyal to them?" Brian pressed, releasing her hands.

"I haven't agreed to add any more surrogates. I've turned down the Institute's requests to up my tier level to #7 or #8!" she blasted, removing her hands from his grasp.

Brian tightened his lips, an arrhythmia of intense criticism seesawing inside of him.

"Well, just so you know, I've cancelled my policy, and I'm not making any more payments."

"That was an easy choice for you, Brian," she countered sarcastically. "After all, you're separated," she added, and then thought for a moment. "How about your son and daughter? Are they no longer covered? I figure you'd already dropped your soon-to-be-ex-wife, so dropping her would be no big deal. But your children? How could you do that to them?"

Brian shook his head, unhesitatingly, having anticipated her rebuttal.

"They're covered on my standard issue government policy. But I can't justify the Institute's policy. Ethically, I'm not comfortable keeping it any more! I ..."

"Oh, so, you think I'm being unethical providing health insurance for Dalton and myself?" she blasted, rising defiantly to her feet so she could look down on him.

Brian stood to meet her insolent gaze eye-to-eye.

"That particular kind of insurance? Yes!" he countered emphatically, "Absolutely!"

Realizing he had upset her, he reached out to console her, but she rebuffed his predilection to put her more at ease.

She stared at him for a contemptuous minute, and then re-treated slowly behind her desk, leaving him standing at the loveseat. The Beltline steel had returned to her demeanor.

"When we were reporting to Raymond you explained how Agent Rodriguez, who was almost killed, by the way, had sur-vived the encounter with what we believe to be Pitt's operatives in the parking lot, and how he had led the Editor in Chief and the reporter back to safety ... You remember that part of the conver-sation, right?" she exploded, her toxicity evident.

Brian nodded, and prepared himself for what he knew was coming.

She pre-empted what she was going to say with a look that extinguished any hope of an amicable outcome to the direction their meeting had just taken.

"Even though he is severely wounded, Agent Rodriguez is showing more loyalty to our cause than you!" her voice was dripping with acid. "Brian ... It looks like I've misread you!" she raised her voice and held her hand out, palm up, to stop him from speaking.

Brian moved closer to the front of the desk, but remained calculatedly silent.

"I don't know what's torpedoed our relationship, but some-thing by damn is ruining it! And I think that something is ... your betrayal to me personally ... and your disrespect for the cabinet post I hold ... and your growing—and I'm going to say it—dereliction of duty!"

Brian started to object, but couldn't get his rebuttal in gear fast enough to prevent her contempt to erupt again.

"I thought we had something special. But our rolling in the sheets is not going to help me keep my job! As far as I'm con-cerned, your negative feelings about the Institute have disqualified you for the job ...."

"Eleanor, I ..."

"I'm not finished," she uttered unalloyed contempt at him, as she picked up her office phone. "What's Agent Rodriguez's phone number at the hospital?"

"Eleanor, you don't have to do this!"

"His number," she demanded, placing her finger on the keyboard.

Brian sighed heavily and gave her the number.

"Hello, Agent Rodriguez. This is Eleanor Franklin, Deputy Assistant Secretary of Health and Human Services," she began, looking defiantly at Brian, who had figured out what she was going to do. "I want to thank you for your service to this country … You're welcome … I understand your wounds are healing very nicely … That's fine. I'm glad … How soon do you think you'll be back on your feet? … What do the doctors say? … That's wonderful … Listen, I've just relieved Agent Cramer of his command, and would like you to assume command. Do you think you could handle that? … Excellent! I'll contact POTUS immediately after we hang up … No, Agent Cramer is fine. He's healthy, but, as I said, he's just been relieved of his command. I'll be in touch with you shortly. Continue to heal … Thank you … It's nice of you to say that … Goodbye for now."

She threw a smug, cold-shouldered look at Brian, who returned her surprising arrogance with a respectful and empathetic, but sage-like smile.

"We could have had something really good," she divulged bitingly. "How could you not see the efficacy in a life of privilege? Of a life with me? Brian, damn it … I'm heartbroken!"

She realized he had no intention of answering her venomous assault when he looked her directly in the eyes and mouthed '*Be well.*' He turned to leave without saying a word and headed toward the closed office door.

"You're officially on administrative leave, until further notice," she chirped, as he stopped before he opened the door. His back was still toward her.

"I'm sorry, Brian. I … I wish it could have been different. I really do!"

He opened the door without looking back, and left the office door open as he made his way down the hallway that led to the front entrance.

* * * * * * *

Marge had listened with the love and devotion—and fervid interest—of a mother who hadn't seen her daughter in a very long time. She was very pleased at her daughter having found a good man, a perfect match. She could tell that every crevice of her and Andre's relationship was filled with love, respect, compassion, and a deep and abiding soul connection. They were a well-matched couple, building on each other's strengths and compensating for one another's vulnerabilities.

One member of a couple is usually a social dog and the other an antisocial cat! But this couple complemented each other. How refreshing, how fortunate, how blessed, she thought to herself. She remembered the ogre her daughter had been married to in Raleigh, and was so happy Monica ... Gabby, had found her soulmate!

"So you played post office, did you?" Marge teased, enjoying the story of how they met.

Both Gabby and Andre laughed, skimming each other's glances with light-hearted pokes into each other's ribs.

They told her mother about their favorite Paris haunts: the Musée d'Orsay, with the amazing works of Van Gogh, Monet and Renoir, and the amazing clock, and impressionist and postimpressionist displays; the Basilica du Sacre-Coeur de Montmartre and the artists at its base; the Eiffel Tower, of course; and the Louvre; and Notre Dame Cathedral; the Luxembourg Gardens, with its oasis-like environment of terraces, chestnut groves and lush lawns; the Opera National de Paris; the Arc de Triomphe; the Musee Rodin; the Saint Germain des Pres Quarter; the Musee Jacquemart-Andre; the Lle Saint-Louis; and the Pantheon, with its neoclassical tone.

"Do you have a favorite above and beyond the favorites?" Marge teased.

"Besides your daughter?" Andre countered, smiling broadly at Gabby, who blushed her approval.

Marge waved her index finger at Andre as she made simultaneous eye contact with her daughter, "You've got yourself a good one here, Moni … Gabby," she laughed, enjoying Andre's cleverness.

"I'd love to go to Paris someday," Peaches thought out loud, as she made sure the wheel locks on Marge's wheelchair had been set. "The French excel in adding doses of modernity to a city steeped in history."

"Yes, you're so right Peaches," Gabby added, "Strolling Parisian streets is in itself a walk through the tomes of time as they are the same *rues* and *passerelles*—that is, streets and alleys— where Thomas Jefferson, Benjamin Franklin, and Victor Hugo, Lafayette, Marie Antoinette, General DeGaulle, Napoléon, King Louis XIV, Claude Monet, Maria Callas, and Marie Antoinette each lived and walked and breathed Parisian air. And Sophie Marceau, my favorite actress, lives here!"

"There are so many things to do in my city," Andre added, "it's really hard to narrow your interests, but we've pretty much given you what we consider the crème de la crème of the city. Some places are well known, and others are off the beaten path, but I can assure you, all that you see will be memorable."

"It sounds wonderful," Emma eulogized.

"It sounds like it is a difficult city to leave," interjected Sandra, as she sent Andre a knowing wink.

He smiled graciously and divided his gaze at all of the women present.

"My home is where Gabby is!" he announced soberly. "Paris is the home of my birthplace, but the new me, the Gabbyized me, is content only in her presence!"

"Where did you find him," Marge looked at Gabby. "Oh, I know. You two played post office," she corrected herself, smiling at the group of crusaders who had taken time out of their busy 'save the world' schedule to be with her.

"My soul found him again," Gabby employed an economy of words to describe their having found one another.

Andre kissed her on the side of her head and prepared himself to make an important announcement to the group.

"There's something we all need to discuss, so I must apologize for having to change the subject. Please forgive a Frenchman for changing such a wonderful mood. It's not that we are opposed to change, it's just that any kind of change is unpopular with us, especially when it affects people's happiness and security."

Gabby used Andre's mood adjustment signal as a cue for her to excuse herself.

"I'll be right back. I'm going to get the others so they can join us," she said softly, as she used Andre's shoulder to lift herself to her feet.

"We have updated you on the events in Lower Manhattan and the interrogations at our temporary compound," he addressed those who remained behind, "but now we must discuss the implications of where we stand at this very moment. Thankfully, we are all safe and healthy," he gave Marge a pat on her knee. "But now we must discuss our mutual future. When Gabby returns with the others, I'll outline what I believe we must do. In the meantime, you may want to use this interlude for creature comforts and to stretch. Let's all reconvene in ten minutes."

The group waited patiently for the others to arrive and engaged in the kind of small talk that characterizes people who know each other very well.

Peaches wheeled Marge toward Steve, who had just appeared to check on her, and Emma and Sandra both stood to stretch their cramped legs. Hank began adding more chairs to the sitting area.

Everyone had collected themselves in the sitting area by the agreed-upon time, and had busied themselves with positioning the snacks and coffee, tea, and water Paul had provided. Some sat in the chairs provided and others took positions on the carpeted floor or on cushions.

Andre scanned everyone in the room: Gabby, Marge, Emma, Sandra, Peaches, Rita, Frank, Hank, Jack, Paul, and Steve.

"I am soooo proud of all of you!" he began. "Emma, Marge, and Peaches, you have given up the life you knew to support Gabby in her crusade against a horrible scheme by the rich and powerful. You have left your homes and friends. You have walked away from a lifestyle that 98% of the people in the world will never see. You have been hunted, and almost killed," he looked at Marge, who had tears in her eyes, but sat ramrod straight in her wheelchair. "I love you all for the sacrifices you've made in order to keep my Gabby safe!"

Gabby closed her eyes and posted a thankful smile on her flushed face, as she felt the hands of the women—including Rita—pat her shoulders, back, and hands.

"And the four of you," Andre sent his proud gaze toward his friends and compatriots, "I couldn't ask for a more supportive and professional team of counterintelligence operatives—and friends, dear friends—who have risked their lives for a guy, no questions asked, who called them out of the blue and asked for help! You have outmatched the strength and wit and resources of one of the most powerful governments on the planet. I ... I'm ... I'm just amazed at what you've accomplished! I thank you from the bottom of my heart!" Andre praised, taking his fist and tapping his heart several times as a tribute to the group's deep and abiding camaraderie.

Rita, Frank, Hank and Jack returned his salute.

"Paul and Steve ... you were brave—and crazy enough—to join us, not fully realizing what you had gotten yourselves into ..."

Everyone interrupted Andre's heartfelt adulation by howling their collective praise at the two recruits, who added their own laughter to show their mutual commitment to the grassroots enterprise.

Andre paused and renewed his individual eye contact with those present.

"You, all of you ... are members of a very special, an extraordinary, a ... timeless, heroic fraternity of the best kind of people humankind has to offer humankind. You have joined those who are often imitated, but never duplicated—when it comes to saving humankind from its heinous, destructive tendencies! You are lights in the darkness!"

The room was quiet, the kind of quiet that is produced when reverence, unconditional love, and sacrifice are mentioned.

"Andre, can I say something?" Rita asked, still showing the effects of the praise that had just been lavished on all of them.

"Yes, of course!"

"People step up when a leader they trust, one who is credible and wise, one who has inner strength and authentegrity, one who has shown he can lead, asks them to serve. You, Andre, are such a leader! And I'm sure I'm speaking for everyone present here today when I say, we would follow you to hell and back!"

The group broke out into spontaneous applause. Those who could stand did, and those with tears in their eyes let their salty rivulets flow unabated.

Andre brought his steepled hands up to his face and covered his nose, allowing his own tears to moisten the corners of his eyes.

"There's something all of you non-military folks need to know about us," Andre announced, with measured slowness. "Frank, Rita, Hank, Jack and I are members of the General Directorate for External Security, the *Direction générale de la sécurité extérieure.* You can call it DGSE for short. It's the French equivalent to the United Kingdom's M16 and America's CIA. We work alongside of France's internal security by providing paramilitary and counterintelligence support to safeguard France's national interests."

He waited for his announcement to sink in before he continued.

"We were able to launch this operation, and I was able to hand pick the people in this room, because I'm ... well, I'm fortunate enough to have a little pull in the DGSE."

The four operatives raised their eyebrows as if they were choreographed eyebrow raises to support Andre's last statement.

"You think!" Frank teased.

Andre smiled his collusion.

"The four of them know what I'm talking about!" Andre postured, thinking, *if the others only knew my covert status and divisional responsibilities. Gabby doesn't even know the bandwidth of my influence.*

"What do you mean, *a little pull?*" Emma asked on behalf of the others, knowing the nature of the conversation was leading to Andre's full disclosure.

"Andre is the fourth highest ranking officer in the Directorate," Rita bragged, smiling broadly at Andre to show her pride, and the other three's pride, in their long association with him.

"And he's the youngest operative to have ever held that position," Frank caboosed Rita's praise.

I didn't even know that, Gabby mouthed her surprise, sending her narrowed eyes and playfully tightened lips in Andre's direction.

The group's 'Wows' and 'Well, what do you knows' and 'Oh, mys' filled the room as they reacted to Andre's covert status.

"So, you see, part of our success has been the direct result of our connection with the DGSE," Andre continued modestly. "That's the good news ... Now here's the not so good news!"

He waited for the non-military members of the group to settle into the implications of what he had just shared.

"France has been an ally of the United States of America since February 6, 1778. Your Statue of Liberty in New York Harbor was designed by Frédéric Auguste Bartholdi, a French sculptor. It was built by Gustave Eiffel, of the Eiffel Tower fame, and dedicated on October 28, 1886. It was a gift to the United States from the people of France. So, we have been friends of America for quite some time," he paused to let his unexpected history lesson resonate with their wondering where he was going with his disclosure.

"Because of this valuable, long term relationship with your country, what we are able to do from now on depends on the people in this room, including Frank's father, who knows we are having this heart-to-heart!"

Frank smiled his understanding and knew he must wait to disclose his father's status until the appropriate time.

"The Directorate has instructed us to continue our covert operations against your government and other governments, as well as corporate and private sector entities, and individuals who are linked to the Institute ... However, France cannot be implicated in the exposure of policy holders who number in the millions in every continent across this planet. That means we are on our own—almost!" Andre emphasized, leaking a smile that belied the predicament he had just reported they had inherited.

"What are we going to do?" Marge spoke for the women.

"We've come so far!" Peaches chorused, struggling with the tuggable edges of her composure.

Andre motioned for the group to remain calm.

"The Directorate is not withdrawing its support," he assured them, "it's hiding it! Let me explain. We will continue to covertly receive funding from an offshore account specifically designed for us—and I mean all of us! By that I mean, my team and the rest of you, will continue to receive the funds you need to create the life you want during our xerography-busting operation and beyond. Because of the global nature of our crusade, and our wanting to protect the universal human rights of all human beings, we are seen as promulgating the perennial philosophy of French idealism and enlightenment."

The timeless impact of Andre's tribute to the human spirit started a new river of tears down Gabby's face. And hers wasn't the only facial geography covered with the salty waterworks of deeply felt emotions.

"Those of you who want to continue our crusade will be given benefits similar to what you Americans call a witness protection program!"

The confused looks from the women prompted Andre to elaborate.

"You'll notice I said similar! Your witness protection program in America is designed to protect criminals who agree to testify against criminals. That's not what the Directorate's witness protection is about. It's protecting you from the criminal elements in your own government, no matter how powerful or wealthy they are, and no matter who they are!"

"You mean when this is over, we won't be able to go back to our homes or communities?" Emma asked, thinking about the dream house she built and the life she had established in Baltimore.

"We've got the same question," Sandra added, speaking for both Peaches and herself.

Andre sighed before he nodded his head.

"We'll all have to relocate, if we pursue this! The Directorate will provide each of us with new identities, lifelong stipends to supplement what we earn, and initial start-up money for housing and other expenses that will be eventually phased out after we've have had enough time to find new means of supporting ourselves. We'll have legally sealed name changes, new passports, new social security cards, and birth certificates. Our drivers' licenses will be routinely issued. Also, any medical and school records will be quickly transferred and fake credit and work histories created to seed our establishing credit under our new identities. If you want plastic surgery, you'll be able to get it. If we all want to be geographically close, the Directorate can arrange that, too!"

The long term implications of their mutual commitment threw a blanket of both excitement and melancholy over the entire group.

"The most important requirement of the program is that we must not make contact with former associates or unprotected family members or friends. That means we cannot return to the towns from which we were relocated for our own protection."

That's where I've been for the last three years, Gabby thought to herself. *It's not really so bad! It'll be better when this is done, because I won't have to look over my shoulder every time I step out in public.*

"How do you guys feel about this?" Gabby asked Andre and his team.

"We're all okay with it," Rita spoke for the team.

"That's right," Jack agreed. "We had our meeting before this meeting. We knew you couldn't do this without us."

"And if we weren't all in," Frank chorused, "we'd be having a different conversation!"

Andre punctuated his team's buy-in by standing and putting his hands on his hips, as he faced the group.

"Then ... ah, um ...you're waiting on our enrollment?" Sandra responded, coughing up her nervousness.

"And if we decide not to pursue this, what happens?" Emma queried.

"You'll still get most of the witness protection benefits as far as your new identity, birth certificates, passports, plastic surgery, etcetera. You'll even receive some start-up money, but the ironclad protection won't be there. You'll be more on your own than in the fold, so to speak!"

"If we don't pursue this," Gabby interjected, "the Institute will get away with it! Millions of unsuspecting people will be used for body parts! I don't think I can live with that!"

"Me neither," chimed Peaches, sending a nervous look at her mother. "I don't want to go back to that house anyway. His downstairs office still smells like him!" she stressed, referring to Carlton's old office.

"The people who mean the most to me are here," Marge trumpeted. "Besides, I'd like to see what they can do with this scarred face of mine. I could use a facelift so I won't be reminded of what they did to me every time I look in the mirror!"

"We'll give all of you time to think about it," Andre advised.

"I'm in!" Gabby chorused unhesitatingly, sending her cherubic smile to Andre.

"Me, too!" Peaches made her intentions clear.

"They know where I live, and I'm not particularly interested in having another accident. What I am interested in is correcting the damage they've done to my face, and shutting them down. So, I'm definitely in!" Marge applauded.

"Where my family goes, I go, and you-all are my family. Besides, I've been wanting to get out of that house, too," eulogized Sandra, giving Gabby and then Peaches a high-five.

"I've lived in Baltimore for most of my life," admitted Emma, "so I'm due for a change of scenery. Count me in!"

"Paul, Steve?" Andre proffered, wanting to make sure the group heard from everyone.

Steve gave a thumbs up and put his hand on Paul's shoulder to show his support.

"I'm in, too," Paul announced quickly. "However, Frank and I have found the perfect place for our tastes right here at Zeus' Den. The government goons we're dealing with don't know Frank and me, so with a little identity grooming and paper trail help from the Directorate, I'm opting to stay here!"

Frank nodded in agreement with his brother.

"I agree with Paul. I think we'll be alright here, especially since we won't be the ones making this go viral on the Internet. We'll definitely work behind the scenes to see this through. Our father hasn't been implicated either, so I think he'll be alright. Am I right about that?" he asked Andre.

Andre nodded.

"We want to expose the Institute as much as you do," Frank continued. "If things change, we'll accept all of the Directorate's bells and whistles. Until then, we'll play our cards close to our vests."

"Rita, Hank, Jack ... you still good?" Andre confirmed.

"Roger that."

"Copy that."

"Does a bear do you-know-what in the woods?" Jack joked, wanting to add some levity to a serious enrollment.

"Just so you know," Andre addressed Gabby and the other women, "I, like the rest of my team, was in this thing from the very beginning! We want to make this world a better place, and it's certainly a better place with all of you in it!"

"So, what's next?" Gabby asked rhetorically, because she knew what was next.

Andre grinned from ear-to-ear and held up his laptop.

"We're going to post thousands of policy holder and surrogate files on Facebook, YouTubes, and Instagram via proxy servers through a virtual private network which hides our IP addresses. When this data hits the worldwide web, it'll go viral in minutes."

"Wow!" Peaches exclaimed, appreciating the digital coverage that was about to blanket the Internet.

"We're also sending thousands of flash drives to high value reporters throughout the world, who we've identified as credible reporters through the articles, op eds, and editorials they've written. We figure there's enough on those drives to spur a Pulitzer frenzy."

The smiles in the room mirrored the excitement everyone was feeling.

"Oh, and with Gabby's blessing, we've pulled all of the files she's had in the storage unit in Marietta, Georgia this past three years, and mailed them to each of the surrogates with a cover letter outlining the Institute's culpability."

"How were you able to do that so fast?" Sandra asked, knowing how many thousands of files were involved.

"The Directorate sent a hundred operatives to Marietta last week to make short work of it!" Gabby bragged, her face lighting up with the announcement.

"It's amazing how a few human rights zealots on a mission can change the world!" Rita raved, shaking Gabby gently from behind.

Gabby walked to where Andre was standing and turned to face the group. The wet stains from her tears that had taken up residence on her face were being washed with a new stream of salty deposits.

"Hon," she looked at Andre, and then at his team. "Rita, Hank, Jack, Frank, Paul, Steve, words cannot express how grateful I am! You have saved all of our lives, my mother's, Peaches,' Emma's, Sandra's, mine! You are truly the salt of the earth. I love you all! I ..." she cut herself off when her tears gushed her gratitude.

Andre hugged her and pulled Marge's wheelchair next to Gabby, as the threesome was joined by the others, who surrounded them for a mega group hug.

"This is the calm before the storm, you know!" he addressed the group. "When the Internet lights up, we'll have to stay outside of the light from the lamppost for just a little while. The Directorate will help us do that. As for now, we're all going to just sit tight and realize we are cutting the legs out from under a behemoth."

"And our first 'sitting it out' will be enjoying the four course dinner I've prepared," Paul announced proudly.

"We've certainly got cause for celebration!" Gabby cheered, giving her mother a modified high-five.

"Come over here, young man," Marge solicited Andre. "You've made my daughter very happy!

She motioned for both of them to kneel in front of her, so she could keep her voice low.

"You won't have to worry about any start-up money from the Directorate," she whispered. "I won the Powerball last year and put twenty-six million in my safe deposit box at the bank!"

"Mother!"

"Keep your voice down, you silly thing," her mother shushed. "Come here," she asked them to lean closer. "I buried four million more under my house in Raleigh!"

"Oh, my God!" Gabby whispered.

Andre's raised eyebrows telegraphed his surprise.

"It's all yours. It's for you two! I was saving it for you Gabby, and now you can share it with Andre. And maybe you could take me to Paris with you!" Marge proposed, winking at Andre and raising an eyebrow at Gabby.

"Are you kidding! When you were in a coma, Gabby and I decided you were going with us to Paris when you recovered. So, you're definitely on," Andre promised.

"Mother, are you sure?"

"Didn't someone mention a bear doing you-know-what in the woods a couple of minutes ago?" Marge badgered. "Of course, I'm sure, silly!"

Both Gabby and Andre kissed her on her forehead.

"I love you both!" Marge smiled, as she looked adoringly at the two of them.

Chapter Twenty-One

I must admit, I'm totally amazed with you, Agent Rodriguez. I've sat for the last forty-five minutes, listening to your report," Eleanor admitted, placing her right leg over her left, exposing her thigh. "Not only am I impressed with your obvious counterintelligence skills, but I'm dazzled at your ability to recover so quickly from life-threatening wounds."

"Thank you, Ma'am."

She studied his weathered, but confident facial landscape. His squarish face was built around a prominent nose, notched with scars that attested to the rough-and-tumble of his military service. His short hair was typical of those with career armed services orientations. He had an air of unflappability which had, no doubt, served him well throughout his military career. The webbing of wrinkles, which etched his face, was punctuated by two prominent lines scoring down from the edge of his nostrils to each side of his mouth, making his over-all facial appearance one of no-nonsensical harshness, filtered with an air of uncompromised capability and proficiency.

"I understand you're wanting to be more thorough than Agent Cramer was with protecting our mutual interests. That tells me there may have been unresolved disagreements between you two."

"Yes, Ma'am. Brian—Agent Cramer—was my friend and a good team leader, but we had philosophical differences that became problematic. Quite frankly, I attribute the Lower Manhattan ambush to his vacillation and indecisiveness in the field," Sergio outlined, trying his best to curb his over-sized ego.

"You're saying his hesitance became a liability?" she quizzed, turning ever so slightly to improve their eye contact, and to use her hand to inch her skirt up, exposing more of her thigh.

Her boldness did not go unnoticed; however, Sergio remained focused on the tactical reason behind the scheduled, getting to know each other, perfunctory visit.

"Yes, Ma'am. I believe his missteps were the direct result of his growing estrangement and alienation in regards to the Institute, which were impacting our unit's ability to meet our defined objectives."

"Then, you're okay with your friend's reassignment?"

"He's not my friend anymore, and, yes, I'm perfectly okay with your decision."

"Just so you know, he's been assigned to an analytics position in HUMINT at Langley," Eleanor announced. "We'll leave him there until we decide what to do with him," she added, referring to POTUS's and her intentions.

Sergio repositioned himself to alleviate the pain he was feeling in his shoulder.

"Well, I can't say our loss is their gain," he criticized.

"What do you mean?"

"Ma'am, Deputy Assistant Secretary, Brian told me he was having second thoughts about the ethical nature of the Institute's surrogate policy. I'm a policy holder myself, and I don't want him, or anybody else threatening my whole life health insurance."

Eleanor thought to herself, *I agree, but Agent Rodriguez is still on a need-to-know basis. No need for me to mention my Tier 6 enrollment.*

"I have every confidence in your considerable ability to help us accomplish the closure we need," Eleanor praised, as she stood to end their meeting.

Sergio followed her lead and extended his hand for a handshake. She returned his leave-taking with a firm handshake of her own.

"Thank you, Ma'am. Then it's okay with you if I personally reduce the risks associated with protecting our interests? The previous commander may have reneged on taking care of a few things," he said with a sly smile, implying Brian hadn't been as thorough as he could have.

Eleanor nodded her consent and motioned for him to accompany her to the office door. She stopped as she grasped the doorknob.

"I've got this eerie feeling that we'd better escalate our efforts to find the Pitt woman and the one's who are protecting her," she forecasted soberly. "I haven't had a good feeling about this for some time."

Sergio took a half step to the side so he could clear the door when she opened it.

"My sentiments exactly, Madame Secretary. My instincts tell me that we must be much more proactive in the field than we've been. I promise you aggressiveness will be my prime objective. Pitt's supporters are sitting here in our backyard. It's about time we closed the door!"

Eleanor smiled at his dauntless determination, as she reached up to grab his arm to emphasize her support, but thought better of it since it was his injured arm.

"We'll keep in touch, of course," she advocated from her position next to the door. "You have my home office number as well as this one."

"Yes, Ma'am. I'll contact you when I know something."

She watched, as he walked slowly down the hallway, nursing a slight limp.

He's just the right man to make something happen, she told herself. *He's a rough around the edges, ninja warrior dressed in 21st century military clothing, with a fearless mindset and the physical wherewithal to thoroughly rout and dismantle opponents. I think he'll do nicely.*

She closed the door to her office and walked over to the mini bar behind her desk. Using her fingers to wipe her lipstick off the empty glass which sat next to her laptop, she indulged herself in an afternoon bourbon pick-up.

As Sergio pulled out of the Ellipse parking lot and made his way down 14th Street toward 395 and eventually 95 South on his way to his next appointment, he picked up his phone and called the command center.

"Hello, Nona. This is Sergio. Just finished the brief with the Deputy Assistant Secretary. On my way to the next appointment, and I've got one more after that which will pretty much complete the week. I'll see you in a couple of days. If something comes up, call me."

He pushed the red 'end call' icon and made the phone disappear into his shirt pocket. He thought about his disagreements with Brian and reflected on their friendship. His coagulation of thoughts led him to the conclusion that Brian was an evolving liability. He wondered, with cold, calculated objectivity, what was going to be the best thing to do with his longtime friend who had strayed.

"Brian, ole buddy," he thought out loud. "I wish you hadn't told me how you felt about the Institute."

You're putting me in a position I don't want to be in, he reminded himself. His ensemble of thoughts carried him back to their tours of duty in Iraq and Afghanistan. *We were tight then, dude. You and I. We had each other's back ... Damn it, Brian ... Why does it have to end this way?*

The strobing blue lights of a state trooper's unmarked car, parked behind a motorist who had just been stopped and pulled over, yanked Sergio's attention back to the objective of his upcoming appointment.

He was on 95 South now and knew he had a drive ahead of him. So, he pushed his favorite J. Lo CD, *Como Ama Una Mujer* in the CD port and settled down to listen to her first Spanish album. He had bought it in Germany in 2007, on his return trip to the States from Iraq. In spite of owning all of her CD's, it was his all time favorite. His favorite song, though, was *On the Floor,* which came from her seventh album, *Love?* that turned out to be the most successful single in her career.

"It's amazing how good music can shorten your trip," he whispered to himself, as he pulled onto the 85 South exit in Petersburg.

Flashbacks of his last trip South surfaced as he closed the distance between himself and the eighteen-wheeler a quarter of a mile or so ahead of him. He had travelled under an assumed name, but reminded himself that was par for the course in his business.

When he checked his gas tank gauge, he realized he'd better refuel, so he decided to feed the SUV and himself. He planted the diet drink in the cup bin on the console and downed a sandwich and fries just outside of Henderson.

He averaged 75 mph on U.S 1 and arrived in Raleigh twenty minutes ahead of Garmin's prediction.

He pulled into the church parking lot which was empty, except for two cars, but stayed in his vehicle in order to fasten his tie and attach his fake ID to his suit jacket. When he completed readying himself, he exited the SUV and headed to the church's main entrance.

The foyer was familiar, but he noticed they had downsized the bookstore and added a guest check-in counter, complete with shelves of religious tracts, pamphlets and magazines. He remembered where the church office was and walked toward the reception desk, where he recognized the older woman behind her name plate on her desk: *Mildred Watson.*

"Good afternoon, Mildred," Sergio greeted her cordially, making sure his fake name badge was prominently visible.

She looked up from the stack of bulletins she was folding and smiled at the unexpected guest.

"Is the good reverend in?" Sergio asked, employing the cordiality that had gotten him past many an office gatekeeper.

"Why, yes, he is, Mr. Schmidt," she chorused, transcribing the printed words on his name badge into spoken words. "Is he expecting you?" she asked, glancing at Jonathan's appointment calendar on her desk.

"No, but it's very important I see him," Sergio alibied.

"Just a minute and I'll let him know you're here."

Instead of phoning him, she got up and entered the open door to Jonathan's office.

"Reverend Pitt, Mr. Schmidt is here to see you."

Jonathan looked up from the Power Point presentation on his laptop to see their visitor over Mildred's shoulder.

"Give me just a minute," he replied, renewing his urgency to complete editing the slide he was on.

Mildred turned toward Sergio and motioned for him to sit in the padded chair next to her desk in the outer office area.

Sergio nodded and headed toward the chair, but detoured his retreat toward the bank of framed photos on the wall adjacent to her desk.

"Those are our Board members and service team leads," she announced. "We are very fortunate to have a very high volunteer-to-member ratio in this church. Seventy-three percent of our membership are volunteers."

"That's wonderful. I'm sure you're very proud of them!"

"It's Reverend Pitt's influence. Everybody loves him here."

Sergio smiled and started to return to his seat when Jonathan appeared at his office door.

"Nice to see you again, Mr. Schmidt," Jonathan greeted his guest, extending his hand for a handshake.

"Yes, nice to see you, too!" Sergio mirrored both the greeting and handshake.

"Mildred, if anyone calls, take a message," he announced, making sure his guest was clear of the door before he closed it.

"To what do I owe this visit?" Jonathan wondered as he sat in the chair behind his desk and invited Sergio to sit in the chair facing the desk.

Instead of sitting, Sergio stood at the front of the desk, the amicability and cordiality that had been there earlier turning into a harsh, almost sinister look.

"Is something wrong?" Jonathan asked, feeling a chilling sense of nervousness in the pit of his stomach.

"Nothing's wrong, Reverend. I just want to keep nothing from bifurcating into something!"

"What do you mean?" Jonathan hyperventilated his reply, feeling his apprehension turning into fear.

Sergio pulled out his revolver, which had a suppressor attached, out from under his jacket.

"Oh, no," Jonathan whispered. "You don't want to do that! I've cooperated with the government from day one … I've helped you. I told you she was in Paris! I … why? Why are you doing this?"

"It's not personal!" Sergio said mechanically, emotionlessly. "I'm just tying up loose ends before they unravel!"

"But I'm no threat to you!" Jonathan pleaded, pushing his chair back nervously.

Sergio's roguish smile was sheathed in the insouciance that characterizes an assassin's detachment.

"Please don't! Please! Oh, God, no!"

Sergio leveled the handgun at Jonathan's head and fired twice.

Fffffpt! Fffffpt!

He looked at Jonathan's slumped body in the chair while he unwound the suppressor from the barrel.

Sorry, Reverend. You were a loose end and didn't know it! Sergio justified his brutal action to himself. He stuck the gun in its holster and slipped the suppressor in his jacket pocket as he walked toward the closed office door. He exited the office and closed the door behind him.

"Mrs. Watson, Reverend Pitt doesn't want to be disturbed until he finishes editing his power point presentation. It was nice seeing you again!" Sergio lied, as he left the reception area.

"It was nice seeing you, too, Mr. Schmidt. You have a blessed day!"

Sergio got into the SUV and checked his watch. *1420 hours. I'll head back up north and see if I can get north of Baltimore before I stop,* he reasoned to himself. Satisfied that his first appointment went so well, he split his divided attention between the CD and the road ahead.

* * * * * * *

"Hi, Dad. Just thought you'd want to know the entire group voted to continue shutting down the Institute and accept the Directorate's witness protection offer."

"That's great, Frank. It looks like saving humankind from its dark underbelly is in our group's collective DNA!" Michael touted, looking up from the medical reports he was reviewing.

"We're launching the Internet and flash drive blitzes tomorrow. How is your wrap-up there coming?" Frank asked, wanting to verify his father's progress in leaving the hospital and taking an extended leave from his Director of Emergency Care Services duties.

"I've just been notified my sabbatical request was approved this morning, and am vacating my office as we speak. They're throwing me a 'sabbatical' party at 0930 hours. Everyone's shocked, of course, that it's happening so fast, and that it's going to be an extended sabbatical!"

"I feel guilty pulling you into this. Dad, I …."

"Don't give it another thought, Son. I knew what I was signing up for. It's the kind of thing I do. You know, save people! Besides, it's only a prophylactic move to keep your mother and me safe until this thing blows over."

Frank sighed his appreciation for his father's foresight, but was still concerned for his parent's, and everyone else's safety.

"And that's how I see it, too, Dad. A temporary hiatus until things get back to normal, whatever normal is! Right?"

Michael laughed, enjoying his son's attempt to describe their mutual life changes.

"Has our family ever been normal?" he teased Frank.

"Not that I can remember!" Frank added his levity.

Each of their smiles was felt through the phone connection as father and son exchanged the warmth of their concern for each other.

"Then we'll see you and mom later today?" Frank asked, knowing that was the plan.

"Yes, of course. Your mother is taking care of the vacation protocols, you know, like notifying the post office, forwarding our mail, messing with the thermostat, making sure we'll have plenty of money, packing-up the food that was in the frig and making sure Apollo has plenty of dog food to bring to your place, contacting Pete to make sure he'll take care of the lawn, etcetera, etcetera!"

"Apollo will love the farm's large fenced-in yard. He'll be leash-free," Frank cheered, knowing the quarter acre enclosure would be all the thirteen-year-old beagle could handle.

"Except for our walks, which will require a leash," his father corrected cordially.

"You bringing your heat with you?" Frank queried.

"Yes, of course. I don't want to leave my mini arsenal at the house. Is Zeus' Den still set-up for a little target practice?"

"Absolutely!"

"Good. I just bought a new Glock 43 and want to try it out."

"Looks like you can take the Colonel out of the military, but you can't take the military out of the Colonel," Frank teased.

"Look whose talking!" his father laughed good-naturedly.

"Touché, Colonel! It must be in the Marino blood!"

"And good blood it is!"

"Enjoy the sabbatical party. We'll see you and Mom for dinner."

"Looking forward to it, Son."

* * * * * * *

Sergio got to the hospital a little after 9 am. It had been a day since he had shot Jonathan, and the minister's execution-style death had been covered by all of the major networks. It seems that Mr. Schmidt was not a very nice man. Mrs. Watson's description of him was not as accurate as he thought it would be.

Of course, his fake mustache and blonde hair had concealed his real identity.

His assassin's mindset made it easy for him to carefully surveil the parking lot and locate hospital security. Before he left the car, he affixed the sound suppressor onto the gun barrel and stuck the loaded gun securely under his belt over his left buttock. It would be easy to reach and facilitate the economy of motion for the kill.

He squinted his eyes as he steeled his gaze on the loading dock behind the cancer center.

This wasn't one of the areas the video playback covered, Sergio reflected. *Well, I'll be damned. I bet this was their exit route. They must have transferred her from here!* He raised his gaze to the second story windows. *I'll bet you watched everything from here, you son of a ... This is where they compromised Jeffrey,* he guessed, sensing his friend had been eliminated as a threat. *They spliced the tapes and I didn't catch it! My bad!* He hit the steering wheel with his palm, trying his best to bridal his anger.

"You're going to pay for this, Doc," he promised himself out loud. "I'm going to enjoy prescribing some emergency medicine of my own."

He exited his dusty vehicle and headed toward the entrance. Flashing his fake badge, he entered through the cancer center's delivery door without incident.

His office is on the second floor, he reminded himself, as he sidestepped a couple of nurses. He kept his head tipped forward to avoid being identified by the ceiling cameras and eased himself along the corridors at a normal pace to remain as inconspicuous as possible.

He used the stairwell to the second floor and made his way toward Michael's office. He tried to enter unannounced, but discovered the door was locked.

"I'm here to see Dr. Marino," he said to a pair of nurses who were heading toward him.

"Dr. Marino is on sabbatical. We had his sabbatical party yesterday morning," they announced cheerfully.

"Oh, I see. Then, he's not here today?" Sergio asked, hoping the good doctor was still wrapping things up and came in to the emergency room area today.

"I don't think so," the senior of the two nurses spoke for both of them. "I believe yesterday was his last day."

"Thank you both, I'm sorry I missed him."

I don't believe this, Sergio chastised himself, as he headed toward the stairway exit. *This is unreal!* He seethed angrily.

As he headed down the flight of steps, he passed two security guards who were headed up the steps. He nodded to each of them, who nonchalantly acknowledged his politeness and continued their private conversation between floors.

How can the universe block my need to make things right? Sergio said to himself.

Acting on that heinous thought, he turned around toward the two guards with their backs toward him and addressed them.

"Excuse me," he declared, pointing his revolver at them. "Tell your families goodbye."

By the time the two men could react to what they saw coming, it was too late.

Fffffpt! Fffffpt!

The sound of the muffled gun shots was hardly noticeable as both men tumbled past Sergio. He waited until they each came to rest on the landing beneath him. He glanced quickly toward the second floor and first floor doors, and was satisfied there were no witnesses.

One of the guards was lying face-up with a bullet between his eyes. Sergio used his foot to turn the other guard on his back as well.

Squarely in the forehead, too, Sergio praised his accuracy.

"Wrong place, wrong time!" he told the corpses. "Just like my friends Lantz and Jeffrey and the others. Oh, and this is for the doc not being here," Sergio hissed as he added another round into each of their lifeless bodies.

Fffffpt! Fffffpt!

He stepped over them on his way to the first floor stairwell door, pushing one of their legs out of the way with the door in order to open it.

I'm not done with you yet, Doc, he promised himself as he made his way to his vehicle.

* * * * * * *

The drive to Lower Manhattan was hampered by two accidents, which tied up traffic in both directions.

"How to make a long day longer," Sergio complained out loud to himself. The irritation prompted him to take a sip of Dr. Pepper, which he pulled from one of the drinking cup holders between the front seats.

"Ahhh, so good. Best soda on the market, if you want to take a traffic break from Guinness," he assured himself, as he stutter-stopped his way south on FDR Drive between E. 34th Street and E. 23rd Street. He turned right onto E. Houston Street in order to get off the bothersome FDR Drive.

"Finally," he said triumphantly, "this has taken much too long.

He pulled into the office parking lot and parked next to the curb. It had started to rain, so he delayed exiting the SUV until he checked his weapon.

Ready to go, he assured himself, as he leaned back to one side and shoved the revolver under his belt. Then he glanced up at the third story office window.

The light's on. Looks like he's there, he whispered the obvious.

He got out of his vehicle slowly and paused before he started toward the front entrance. Less than six inches from his right shoe was a dried blood spot that had been missed in the infamous assassination's cleanup by the local police. Sergio looked for more telltale signs of their ambush and found a couple more dried blood blotches on a section of curbing.

"I lost a lot of good men that day," he reminded himself, sighing heavily as he stepped around an empty soda can on the

sidewalk. Another quick look at the third story window accelerated his pace toward the repaired front door.

As he got to the front door, he heard the wail of fire engines
on their way to another nameless fire in a city that seemed to
spawn fires and police interventions everyday.

The lobby was filled with people coming and going, trying
to finish whatever business that brought them, so they could
beat the rush hour traffic home.

Boy, are you in for a surprise, Sergio smiled to himself. *FDR
Drive's backed up. You may want to take a book with you, or something else to keep you busy while you inch your way home.*

He got to one of the elevators just as the elevator door reluctantly scraped open. An older couple got out, and were too
involved in their conversation to notice him as they moved
quickly past him and a young woman who had pushed a stroller
up beside Sergio.

When the elevator emptied, Sergio motioned for the woman
to go first and was rewarded with one of the most beautiful
smiles he had seen in a long time.

They stood quietly as the paneled metal cage vibrated noisily
from its recessed, greasy perch toward the second floor. She
smiled again at Sergio as she exited the steel enclosure, first
going one way and then the other, as she attempted to find the
office she was looking for.

I've done that myself, he said to himself, as he waited for
the lethargic elevator doors to close.

He stood quietly, eying the door as the elevator groaned its
way to the third floor.

Room 304, he reminded himself, as he mimicked the
woman's confused sense of direction on her second floor moves.

He glanced quickly down each end of the hallway, and then
sighed before he entered Caleb's office. Caleb was sitting at his
desk and speaking to someone on the phone, but raised his eyebrows when he saw Sergio. He motioned for Sergio to sit and
pointed to the Keurig coffee pot at the hot drink station, figuring
his guest might want something to drink.

Sergio smiled and shook his head as he found a seat adjacent to Caleb's desk so that he could see both the reporter and the door out of the corners of his eyes.

"Sorry, it was the *Times*," Caleb apologized, and squinted his eyes at Sergio for a better look. "Agent Rodriguez, isn't it?" Caleb greeted the seated visitor who stood and walked over to his desk.

"Yes, I am, Mr. Latourelle. I see you're back at work, too."

"I am. Looks like your wounds are healing nicely. I didn't expect to see you so soon. I want to thank you again for saving the editor and me," Caleb kept rattling off sentences, hoping to interpret Sergio's brutish gaze.

"Have you two found anything more I should know about?" Sergio quizzed, softening his icy tone a bit.

"No, not really. I gave Huang all of the files she and Andre gave me. I think he turned them over to someone in the government."

"That would be me," Sergio answered mechanically.

"Oh, of course. That makes sense."

"Can you tell me any more about Andre Bordeaux than you've told me already?"

Caleb tightened his lips and shook his head.

"Like I said, I didn't know him that well. I've told you all I know. I was surprised he turned on me the way he did."

"Do you think he'll try to contact you again?"

"I doubt it. I think his tying me up around the base of a tree and threatening my life pretty much ended our relationship."

"That's too bad," Sergio replied in a tone of voice that made Caleb's blood run cold.

"What do you mean?" Caleb asked, beginning to wish he were somewhere else.

"It means you're of no further use to us!"

"Wha ...What are you talking about?" Caleb countered, as he stood behind his desk. "Oh, no! You're not going to ...." His horror blunted his reply when he saw Sergio's revolver.

Fffffpt!

Chapter Twenty-Two

To say that news of the Institute's human xerography operation went viral would have been grossly understated! Less than thirty-five minutes after the simultaneous launch of thousands of flash drives to high value reporters; accompanied by thousands of policy holder and surrogate files, via proxy servers through a virtual private network sent to all major news outlets; the only news aired globally was how a certain segment of the rich and powerful were involved in a human cloning scheme that was using unsuspecting people worldwide as body parts so the super-rich policy holders didn't have to wait for a perfect organ match when they faced life-threatening health challenges.

The cover letters outlining the Institute's culpability that were mailed to each of the surrogates Andre's and Gabby's team had contact information for, sent surrogates all over the world to hospitals in their areas to have the subderminal implants removed.

Gabby and Andre made sure that part of the information on the cover letters each surrogate received stressed that when the implant was removed, it was to be given to them to be destroyed, and not left in the possession of hospital personnel. It was also noted that their implant contained a 16 digit ID number that was being used to link demographic information about them and sent to one of the Institute's external databases to be archived so the Institute could find them when the policy holder needed one or more of their organs.

Suffice it to say, wealthy policy holders all over the world panicked at having been exposed on such a pandemic global scale. Heads of state, corporate CEOs and executives, millionaires and billionaires, famous sports and entertainment personalities, university and collegiate presidents, well-known clergy and public service personalities, healthcare industry executives and hospital administrators—anyone who was considered super-rich and had money and power—had taken immediate actions to limit their liability and step up their efforts to ameliorate damage control.

Many claimed they didn't know they had purchased such a controversial 'whole life' health insurance policy. Others, who had already benefitted from organ transplants, claimed they had no idea someone had given his or her life to contribute the life-saving organ.

A majority of the policy holders lawyered-up, of course, in order to weather what they knew would become a lengthy litigation tsunami and stepped-up security nightmare for years to come.

Policy holders and their families received death threats, and law suits sprung up like weeds after a heavy rain. Many, if not most, of the policy holders left their jobs and went into hiding to protect their business interests and families.

Many policy holders who were heads of state, congressmen and congresswomen, cabinet members, legislators, government and state officials, directors of upper echelon military and governmental posts followed the 'stay out of jail' paths of colleagues who had seen the handwriting on the wall before they did.

A large number of the policy holders were assaulted and more than a few were killed by surrogates' angry family members and/or surrogates who were fortunate enough not to have been used for body parts. Dozens of others, like Dr. Schönbächler, had committed suicide.

All of the major news outlets carried the human cloning scandal—CNN, BBC, ABC, MSNBC, CBS, Fox, CTV, Milenio Televisión, NC23, Global News Brazil, France 24, Germany's DW-TV, Italy's Class CNBC, Poland's TVN24, and global newspapers—Japan's *Yomiuri Shimbun* and *Asahi Shimbun*; *The Times of India*; Germany's *Bild*; China's *People's Daily, Guangzhou Daily* and *Global Times*; U.S.A's *Wall Street Journal, USA Today* and *The New York Times*; the United Kingdom's *The Sun* and The *Daily Mail*; and scores of other newspapers and journals.

Gabby and Peaches Skyped their testimonials from protected IP addresses via proxy servers through virtual private networks which hid their IP addresses. Gabby used her married name, Monica Pitt, and Peaches used her birth name, Monica Henry, to share their stories. Peaches had already gotten her mother's approval to use her birth name, because both were in the process of getting their names changed.

Emma had also appeared on Skyped interviews to share her story and her daughter's story. She elaborated on her daughter's death. She explained the extraordinary circumstances leading up to her initial meeting with Monica Pitt. Emma had voluntarily disclosed all of the personal information, because she, too, had decided to change her name and start a new life.

All four women scheduled numerous Skype interviews over a period of a month and then notified the media they would no longer be available for the overdone redundancy that usually accompanies major news stories. They were going to let the indisputable data on the flash drives, xerography files, and the outrage of tens of thousands of angry litigants worldwide determine the extent and depth of the aftermath.

None of the four women participated in attempts by their interviewers to comment on the reasons for supporting human cloning. They declined to engage in discussions whenever the dialogue dipped into cloning as a viable option for infertility; extolling cloning as a means of by-passing a family's genetic illness inheritance; cloning's efficacy in producing super-human beings; therapeutic cloning; or cloning's potential for transplanting human brains from surrogate to policy holder.

Andre's team remained invisible as far as the news media was concerned, preferring instead to protect their identities and keep the Directorate out of the picture. They also knew that Frank, his parents and brother, Paul, were going to stay at Zeus' Den, and needed to remain completely off the grid.

Rita, Hank, Jack, and Steve were in the process of deciding how they were going to protect their identities and understood how important their invisibility was, especially since their team of crusaders had upset so many very rich and powerful people.

Whenever the media asked questions about the people and/or organizations that supported them, the women declined to divulge their benefactors, stating they wanted to protect the brave men and women who helped them.

Whenever an over-zealous interviewer became insistent and obnoxious at procuring who the women's backers were, the women would end the Skype connection, making it clear they were not going to divulge that information.

The women had stressed that only an unprincipled, heartless, ruthless segment of the super-wealthy had been involved in the Life Extension Institute of Geneva's illegal human cloning initiative.

They had urged the billions of listeners not to judge the majority of the mega-rich harshly or to stereotype all people of means as wicked, self-aggrandizing egomaniacs who thought the masses existed to make their lives of privilege disease-free and unencumbered with the daily inconveniences of living in a human body that wears out sooner than you want it to.

One of the main messages the women shared was this: Because there is no even flow or distribution of wealth—in any country—an arrogant, pompous privileged few—in every country—tends to see the ordinary many as chattel, human property to be used, abused, and disposed of as they see fit. It is this conceitedness and cockiness that leads to clandestine enterprises like the human xerography Institute.

Another message the women made sure they made loud and clear was that, contrary to policy holders sickening rhetoric, every one of the cloned surrogates was a human being who had the same right to life, liberty, and the pursuit of happiness as their narcissistic—and unfortunately, criminally-minded policy holders—because each of the innocent surrogates was a human being who had a soul! They were not soulless pieces of property, as the unconscionable policy holders referred to them.

The women usually ended each Skype session with a quote they had found especially meaningful during the three years Monica was missing. It was from a book written by two Unity ministers, a husband and wife team from North Carolina. The wisdom from the ministers' writings had kept all of them emotionally afloat and sane throughout their long ordeal. The book was called, *More Straight Talk About Spiritual Stuff*, and the quote they used to end each session was:

We feel there are fewer worthwhile 'exercises' for the heart than reaching down and helping someone up with your heartfelt compassion, unconditional love, and respect. We also deeply believe that no compassionate act, no matter how small, is ever wasted. Conferring compassion is one of the highest spiritual callings. A Self-realized spiritual consciousness that cultivates thoughts of openness, altruism, inclusiveness, compassion, kindness, and Self-realization as its chief mental 'residents' is the kind of consciousness that can heal our world.

* * * * * * *

Eleanor was one of thousands of underlings who had taken the fall for their respective superiors. Like many of the others, she had relocated her assets, gone into hiding, and dodged criminal indictments, although charges had been filed. Some policy holders, unlike herself, had opted for plea deals and immunity for tattling on their superiors, but she hadn't been able to gather the evidence she needed to implicate any of her superiors, including POTUS.

"Thanks, Fritz, I'm not going to forget this," Eleanor told the lawyer who had been recommended to her by Sergio as the securities crackerjack and 'cleanup virtuoso' for the rich and powerful.

"That's what I'm here for," he replied perfunctorily, realizing she had just paid for his next status symbol, a two million dollar Koenigsegg Regera.

"When can I move back into my old residence, under my new name, with my new face?"

"In a couple of weeks! My suppliers are the best at what they do. In the short time we've had to assist you, I can assure you, we've dotted every 'i' and crossed every 't.' I've made sure no one will ever know that the 'old' you is the buyer. I've hidden your considerable financial assets extremely well, I might add!" he boasted, allowing his own well-monied pomposity to leak out.

A little nip and tuck has done wonders for my complexion, she praised herself, as she admired the plastic surgeon's work in her bedroom mirror.

"I appreciate your attention to detail—and thoughtfulness. Oh, and, Fritz, I love my new name!"

"I'm so pleased to hear that, Dr. Lisa Archibald. It does fit you very well, doesn't it?"

Lisa smiled and plucked a loose eyelash from her newly renovated cheek.

"Lisa is named after my great aunt, and I've always liked the name Archibald since it comes from my Germanic heritage. It means 'genuinely precious' or 'genuinely bold.' It is also related to Archibald Douglas, the 5th Earl of Angus, who was known as 'Bell the Cat.' Is that TMI?" she teased.

"A little, but I have a penchant for TMI. It's what keeps me at the top of my game. Tell me about the nobleman's 'Bell the Cat' nuance."

"Are you sure?" she queried, thinking he was just patronizing her, because she was a new client.

"Yeah, I'm serious. I've got a little Scottish blood in me, and fifteen minutes before my next appointment."

"Okay, well. 'Belling the Cat' is believed to be an Aesop's fable, but is more likely confused with a tale called 'The Cat and the Mice.' The fable is about a group of mice who debate whether or not to nullify the threat of a marauding cat. One of the mice proposes placing a bell around the cat's neck, so that they are warned of the cat's approach. Sounds strange, I know. Mice can't talk!" she excused her interest in such a silly story.

"No, Dr. Archibald, continue. It sounds like a cute story."

She smiled at her image in the mirror and was amused at his pretended interest, as well as his use of her newly-acquired name.

"The plan is applauded by the colony," she continued, "until one mouse asks who's going to volunteer to place the bell around the cat's neck. All of the mice and 'miceses'—is that a word?— make excuses, of course. But here's the thing, the story teaches us the wisdom of evaluating a plan not only on how desirable the outcome could be or would be, but also on how it can be practically and objectively executed."

"It sounds to me," Fritz interjected, "that it provides a practical lesson about the fundamental difference between ideas and their feasibility."

"Yes, and how reasonableness and plausibility can affect the outcome of a given plan—much like the feasibility of the plan we've just concocted!" Lisa replied, extending the analogy to their plan to save her ass and assets.

"Well, it looks like we've 'belled the cat' by making you invisible so you and your son can enjoy the life of privilege you're used to without having to give up any of your holdings or relinquish any of your well-earned financial assets.

"And the credit goes to you," she praised him.

"And to you, for having the courage and foresight to contact me. Looks like I've got to go. I'll call you when the closing's ready. Oh, how does Dalton like his new last name and new prep school?"

"Actually, he likes his new name. Keeping his same first name was a good idea. Neither of us was enamored with my married name. As you know I thought about going back to my maiden name, but that wouldn't have given me, us, the anonymity we needed to weather this storm. And, yes, he likes his new school. A certain young lady has caught his eye!"

"Oh, I see. It seems the two of you are adapting quite well to your new life. Well, I really do have to scoot. Until later!" Fritz cordially goodbyed, excusing himself politely.

Lisa noticed a phone call had come in while she was talking to Fritz, so she called up the number.

It's Agent Rodriguez, she said to herself.

"He probably wants to know how things are going," she followed up out loud.

She started to swipe the missed call message, but hesitated before calling him, thinking, *He's going to want to know if I've heard from Brian, and I don't want to tell him I have.*

She fretfully swabbed the missed call icon and waited for Sergio to pick up.

"Hey, there. I just called," his bristly voice came through the connection. "Has Fritz hooked you up?"

"Yes, as a matter of fact I was talking to him when you called. I want to thank you again for sending him my way," she replied, using her business voice to keep him at a distance.

"No problem. I told you I'd take care of you."

"And you have. You've helped give me and Dalton new lives in old haunts."

"I had no doubt Fritz could keep you invisible inside the Beltline. Say, I just wanted to report that I've taken care of a few more liabilities, and ..."

"Agent Rodriguez," she cut him off, horrified at the emotionless tone he used to 'notch' his kills in their phone conversations. "I'd rather not know your progress in that area."

He laughed maniacally, unsettling her with his much too familiar outburst.

"My promise to you wasn't the only promise I made," he reminded her.

"I know. I know."

"I also promised POTUS I'd make sure any liabilities in his administration were taken care of."

"I know you promised him that," she recoiled, wishing Sergio didn't feel obligated to share his kills with her.

"Well, I know how you don't like hearing about it. I've got two reasons for mentioning it now."

She took a deep mournful breath.

"I'm just about finished the terminations. POTUS thinks eliminating them was a national security issue—not to mention protecting his shameful ass. That's the first thing I wanted to say. The second thing is this. While I've taken care of the President's lengthy list, there's one more on my short list, and I think you know who that is!"

Lisa tried her best to smother her gasp, but it escaped anyway.

Her silence prompted Sergio to remind her.

"Brian Cramer," Sergio snarled. "I know you don't like me going there, but he's responsible for the deaths of some friends of mine. You know what I'm sayin'?"

She let out such a disconsolate sigh that Sergio thought she had fainted.

"Lisa, you all right?"

"Yes ... Yes, I'm okay! I just wish you wouldn't blame Brian for something that was out of his control. He told you and the others everything he knew. You were his right hand man, for heaven's sake! I ..."

"He wasn't one of us. I've told you that before. And right now I'm beginning to question your loyalty," he hissed unapologetically.

"What do you mean?"

"Whenever you mention his name you call him Brian. You always call me Agent Rodriguez! That tells me you've got more of a relationship with him than me ... That tells me you may want to protect him from me! Does that sound about right?" he mocked scornfully, hoping to unnerve her.

She almost hung up on him, but thought better of it.

"I've known him longer than you ..."

"Well, I've known him longer than you! So, that makes us even. Doesn't it?" he scorned, purposefully clipping her response.

She exhaled another labored sigh, one of the multitude of sighs that had punctuated their conversation.

"I fired him and hired you, Sergio!" she raised her voice, disapproving of his sophomoric insinuations.

"So, you do know my first name," he leveled a quick retort, knowing it would rattle her.

"What do you want from me?" she snipped.

"I want to know where Cramer is!"

"I don't know where he is!" came her calm, but tough-veneered reply.

"Okay. Then I guess an apology is in order," he confessed slyly.

"That's the trouble, Sergio. Your apologies are out-of-order!"

"What do you mean?" he asked shrewdly, not really caring what she meant.

"You need to start with an apology and leave it at that. That means apologize and say no more. Be genuinely apologetic and people may be more empathetic!"

"Well, okay then! Goodbye for now, Dr. Archibald."

She let him hang up without a reply.

I feel like taking a shower, she said to herself. *But I don't know if I'll ever be able to wash him off!*

The disquiet she felt with having fielded his call prompted her to swipe through her digital phone rolodex and press one of her phone contacts.

"Hello, Brian. I'm so glad you're there."

She told Brian of her conversation with Sergio and both agreed they should meet at his townhouse in Silver Spring, Maryland. He told Lisa he had moved and would text her his address.

Her jumpiness in full throttle, she almost didn't answer the knock at her second floor apartment door. She placed the phone on the coffee table and walked toward the front door. She peeked through the slot in the door, and to her amazement—and agitation—it was Sergio!

"What are you doing here?" she crowed, placing her foot against the inside of the half-opened door.

"I'm going to start with an apology, and then I'd like to ask if I could use your bathroom."

Her noticeable recoil urged him to plead his case quickly.

"I was sitting in the parking lot, wondering if I should come in, but our strained phone conversation told me to stay put. When we said our goodbyes, the way we said our goodbyes, I thought I could repair our unease with each other with a face-to-face apology. So, here I am!"

She hesitated opening the door any further, just to be obstinate, but finally allowed him to enter.

"Wait just a minute," she cautioned him. "Stay here for just a minute, Sergio. I've got to tidy up the bathroom a bit. Dalton left his bath towels and dirty underwear on the tub. I'll be right back."

"Yes, of course. Thanks," he replied diplomatically, eying her iPhone on the coffee table.

As she hurried down the hallway toward the bathroom, Sergio pulled Brian's address and time the two them would meet off the text he left Lisa.

He smiled his good fortune, and congratulated himself. *I figured she knew where he was.*

Then he covered his intrusion by backing up a few steps to where he was standing when she left him.

After faking a bathroom break and accepting a small bottled water for the road, he quickly negotiated the stairs and settled cozily—and triumphantly—in his SUV. He figured she'd be watching to see him leave, so he pulled out of the parking lot as quickly as he could.

"There'll be a threesome at your place tonight," he promised Brian out loud. "And I can assure you, Miss Lisa, there will be no apology for taking your lover boy out!"

Chapter Twenty-Three

Apollo was loving all of the attention. He had enjoyed the run of both the house and the fenced-in yard for the past six weeks. He had passport-free entry into everyone's sleeping quarters and had adopted Gabby and Andre's room for his afternoon siestas.

The group had gathered in the large atrium foyer which had been turned into the team's conference room. Paul—with Rita's, Emma's, Peaches' and Hank's assistance—had prepared a six course Mediterranean meal to celebrate the group's success in shutting down the human cloning Institute.

The Persian cucumber and tomato salad, salmon cakes; balsamic and parmesan roasted cauliflower cut into thick slices and tossed with extra-virgin olive oil; chicken piccata with pasta and mushrooms; a garlicky, Middle Eastern-inspired yogurt sauce with pasta, shrimp, asparagus, peas and red bell peppers; and gnocchi with zucchini ribbons soaked in parsley brown butter— were all heavy appetizers for a tray of desserts that included sesame-orange almond tuiles; orange-hazelnut olive oil cookies; and apricot and pistachio baklava with orange-cardamom syrup.

Apollo had already gorged himself on the droppings Paul and Rita had 'accidently' remaindered off the counter tops during the food preparation. His Buddha belly was obvious, indeed, as he sat next to Michael and Janet, Frank's parents, who had allowed his people's food foray.

Andre stood at the head of the table, with Gabby at his side, and made eye contact with everyone seated at the table starting with Frank and ending with Gabby.

"We have done something I don't believe any of us thought we could have ever done when we started eight months ago. It has been quite a ride, hasn't it?" he asked rhetorically.

A light-hearted cacophony of laughter, smiles and applause filled the room, punctuated by Apollo's enthusiastic beagle howl: *Arrroooooooo!*

"To say that we have faced incredible odds would be a gross understatement! We have besieged the walled cities of a corrupt and conscienceless segment of the super-rich and affluent all over the world. We have successfully needled the heads of state in our government and the bunkered bureaucrats of governments around the world.

"We have brought down a tentacled human xerography monster that Gabby exposed just shy of four years ago. We have saved nearly a million lives by preventing a privileged and mercenary few from propagating another senseless holocaust."

When Andre paused to collect his thoughts, his soulful entr'acte was met with complete and absolute reverential silence. Even Apollo seemed respectful of Andre's inspiring tribute that had caused both of the dog's masters to sit, spellbound and breathless in their seats.

"Our work is not done here. We can still do a lot individually here in skin school by continuing to help others and grow personally, professionally, and spiritually in the time each of us have left on the planet. We have assumed new identities and most of us have chosen not to go back to the lives we left eight months ago. However, I have a strong feeling that we're going to stay in touch and most likely work together again on some human rights issue in the future."

Head nods from those present told him many of the group members were already thinking the same way.

"I'm going to ask Frank to pre-prayer the wonderful meal that Paul and his volunteer chefs have prepared for us, and then, during dessert, I'd like all of us to share our individual lifestyle decisions with the group. How's that sound?"

The group applauded enthusiastically, indicating they were looking forward to their individual sharing and collectively appreciating Andre's well-thought-out tribute to the group's sacrifices and heroism.

After Frank prayed the group in, Paul and his proud volunteer chefs served their colleagues a meal they would fondly remember.

* * * * * * *

Sergio watched Lisa enter Brian's townhouse, and the ex-commando's quick scan of the parking area did not go unnoticed.

Old habits are good habits, Sergio reminded himself, as he watched Brian close the front door. *Your problem has always been working with inept superiors, Brian. And the skirt you've just invited into your townhouse just complicated your whereabouts.*

"And she's probably just gotten herself killed, too, because I don't think she'll accept my apology for wasting you," he spoke to himself, as he tightened the noise suppressor onto the barrel of his revolver.

Just as he started to vacate his vehicle, he saw a pizza delivery car pull up next to Brian's townhouse. He settled back in his seat to accommodate the unexpected interruption.

The delivery person turned out to be a young, ponytailed pizza delivery girl, who was a leggy colt with beautifully proportioned slim stems for legs.

Brian opened the door for her and had cash ready for the pizza order. Evidently she got a nice tip, because she tossed him a broad, lipsticked smile which remained on her face all the way to her late model beamer.

Her daddy probably bought that for her, Sergio guessed. *She's probably working for pocket change only.* He watched her sway her hips onto the seat and then swing her rail thin legs inside. *Hum ... when I was younger, I'd tap hot little numbers like that in a heartbeat.* He kept his eyes on her as she drove past him and winked at her when she noticed he was in the car. Her smile featured Botox lips which made great landing zones for kisses.

"What am I hesitating for?" he chastised himself. "I've got a couple of loose ends to take care of."

He stood by his SUV for just a moment to scan the parking area before he started for Brian's townhouse. His gun was hidden underneath his shirt, which he was wearing with the shirt tail out.

All of a sudden he stopped again, when he saw a beautiful, red-haired young woman in a figure-flattering purple lycra T-shirt, who was sheathed very nicely in jeans, run across the parking lot and plant herself at Brian's door.

"Aw come on," he whispered to himself, "this is getting ridiculous!"

He waited for just a moment to see if Brian invited her inside or if her visit would simply be a doorstep visit, before he got back into his vehicle.

I didn't see her get out of a car, so she must live nearby, he thought to himself, as she disappeared through the front door.

"Oh, well! I'll wait a few minutes," he announced out loud to himself as he grudgingly ducked into his SUV.

Five minutes morphed into ten minutes, so he lowered the front seat windows to keep the SUV from becoming an oven. No sooner than he lowered the windows, he reversed their directions, sending them firmly into their overhead sockets.

"I'm not waiting any longer. She's going to find herself in the wrong place at the wrong time," he justified her fate to himself as he exited his vehicle.

A knee-jerk look at the parking lot told him it was time to make his unannounced presence known to the three unsuspecting people in the townhouse.

Sergio eased himself quietly up to the front door and slowly rotated the door knob with one hand while he extricated his revolver with the other. To his not so complete surprise, the front door was unlocked.

The heavy traffic to his place this evening has left his door unlocked and compromised his security, he grinned to himself as he turned the door opening into a slit and listened for the telltale signs of conversation and people's movements.

Good. They must be in another room, he guessed, seeing no other lights on except the overhead foyer light and what looked like a light on in the kitchen area that bordered the dining room.

He stepped surreptitiously into the foyer and slowly closed the front door, so it didn't creak his intrusion. He squinted his methodical surveillance around the interior of the house and could hear voices in the kitchen which was positioned to the left, across the living room and adjacent to a small dining area.

Typical of these Silver Spring townhouse designs, Sergio reminded himself, as he slowed his steps across the carpeted living room to get a better view down the hallway to the right, probably the bedrooms, and to improve his entry angle into the kitchen area.

He raised his gun at the ready and headed toward the voices in the kitchen.

Suddenly, he heard Brian's voice emanate from the kitchen area. "Alexa … Light packages A and C, and J!"

The living room lights came on and the kitchen lights and hallway lights went off in response to Brian's Amazon Echo command.

Sergio halted his cautious advance and divided his gun rotation between the kitchen and hallway.

"Sergio, drop your weapon," came Brian's cool, controlled command.

The intruder narrowed his gaze and continued to surveil the interior, with most of his assessment glued to the kitchen. But he remained calculatedly silent.

"You've got three seconds to do what I've asked," Brian stated flatly and calmly from the kitchen.

Sergio lowered his weapon, but still held it with his arms outstretched, waist high, not wanting to surrender completely.

"Come out where I can see you," Sergio bellowed, readying himself for the assault he knew was imminent.

"We can see you just fine. Put down your weapon!"

Sergio knew Brian was referring to Eleanor (A.K.A. Lisa) and the young woman who had just come in, but he wasn't sure who the young woman was, where she was, and how she figured in the predicament he had gotten himself into.

"Lisa tells me POTUS and you want me dead. You ought to know better than to come into my crib and expect to have an advantage. I thought I taught you better than that!"

A surprised look leaked cross Sergio's hardened face.

"You knew I was coming then?"

"Of course. Lisa and I had your arrival—whenever that would occur—planned in advance. We knew you would try to get to me through her, so once you made your intentions clear, she was to contact me, and we'd plan how your visit would look," Brian explained, inserting a little swag to his voice.

"Then her leaving her iPhone on the coffee table was no accident?" he growled, realizing he had been duped.

"And you fell for it!" Lisa spoke for the first time. "The bottle of water I gave you was a metaphor for the bath you are going to take tonight!"

"Why, you little bitc ..."

"Easy, Sergio ..." Brian interrupted. "You're in enough trouble without insulting the women present."

"I believe an apology is in order," chimed Lisa, enjoying her safety in the kitchen.

Brian whispered for Lisa to kneel next to the refrigerator behind him as he kneeled in front of her next to the ceramic-topped electric stove.

"The women are going to wish they weren't present," blurted Sergio, raising his weapon to his shoulder level, but staying were he was.

"Now, that kind of threat is uncalled for," Brian chastised his defunct friend. "You've definitely taken a turn toward the dark side. And that really disappoints me. It disappoints all of us!"

"Brian, I've got a clear shot," Alysha interjected calmly, standing half hidden just inside the hallway guest bathroom doorframe, with her revolver trained on their obstinate guest. "Do you want me to take it?"

Before Brian could speak, Sergio fired three rounds into the thin wall which separated the dining room from the kitchen area. He knew his fire power would cut right through the interior wall and wound, if not kill both occupants in the kitchen.

Ffffffpt! Fffffpt! Fffffffpt!

And then, using the evasive combat tactics he knew so well, he lowered himself and rolled on the floor to get a better shot at the snippy woman in the hallway.

Fffffpt!

He only had time for one shot, because both Brian's and Alysha's well-placed rounds had found their respective marks in Sergio's upper chest, neck and head.

Fffffpt! Fffffpt! Fffffffpt! Fffffpt! Fffffpt!

Alysha walked up to Sergio's lifeless body and kicked his revolver out of his open gun hand, while Brian stood over his disillusioned and embittered lifelong friend.

"Everybody all right?" Brian asked.

Frowning her apprehension and sadness, Lisa emerged from the kitchen and joined the other two standing over Sergio.

"Looks like we survived the scuffle," Lisa voiced the obvious. "And Brian, thanks for realizing that bullets go through walls."

He smiled at both women, acknowledging the subtleties of warfare.

"Thanks, Agent Southerland, for being here," Brian addressed Alysha.

"I just wish it could have been under better circumstances. He was my friend, too, until he went off the deep end!" she replied, as she breathed out a labored sigh.

"Yeah, I know," Brian agreed. "He left us little choice. But I'm glad to see you're bringing a little sanity back into the CIA," he complimented Alysha.

"Well, I've got to tell you, nothing would surprise me anymore. To find out how many of our heads of state were involved in that corrupt cloning operation absolutely amazes me."

Lisa remained diplomatically silent, hoping Brian and Alysha would change the subject.

"Will you rejoin the force now that the reorg is underway?" Alysha asked Brian. "We could use you, especially a man of your experience and integrity."

Brian looked pensively at Lisa, and then at Alysha.

"Naw! I don't think so. I'm enjoying my private eye business, especially the freedom it gives me. Homeland security may be an option in the future, or even an emerging field called concierge security where the rich and powerful employ the protection they need on international trips … or I just might retire all together and play golf the rest of my life!"

Both women showed their amusement at his last statement by pretending they were teeing off with imaginary golf clubs.

"What do you say I help you get this body out of your townhouse!" Alysha volunteered. "Fortunately, all of us used noise suppressors, so I doubt if your neighbors heard anything. I'll get a cleanup team over here pronto."

"That would be wonderful," Brian praised. "Looks like I'll have to get another scatter rug for the living room."

"We can clean that, too!" Alysha countered, trying to be helpful.

"No thanks. Looking at this rug, soiled or clean, would remind me of what happened here."

The three of them agreed by exchanging head nods.

"The two of you take care of yourselves, you hear?" Alysha urged good-naturedly. "I'll see the team gets here within the hour," she promised, as she made her way to the front door with her phone glued to her ear.

After she left, Brian confiscated Sergio's revolver and smart phone.

"I thought she might take those things, so I'm claiming them," he told Lisa, and then noticed there was blood on the back of her collar. "Lisa, you're bleeding!" he exclaimed, as he sat her in one of the dining room chairs.

She wiped her hand across the back of the left side of her neck.

"I am bleeding!" she agreed, "although it doesn't look like much!"

"One of his shots must have grazed your neck," Brian said softly, as he examined her wound. "I'm going to wet this towel to see what we've got."

Lisa sat patiently while Brian attended to her superficial wound.

"Lisa, I'm soooo glad you weren't injured any more seriously than this. I would never have forgiven myself."

"It's okay. I was the one who insisted on coming in spite of your protests. I've been bruised, and cut, and scratched before on some of my overseas exploits," she alibied to make him feel more at ease.

"Maybe so, but you've never been shot!"

"Where's my purple heart then?" she teased, giving him one of her mischievous looks.

"Any lower and you would have had a bleeding heart!" he countered, before he realized how it sounded.

"Wait a damn minute here, buddy! You're the one who suggested we kneel behind the counter."

Brian looked at the two bullet holes, head and shoulder high, in the dining room wall, and pointed them out to her.

"I think kneeling was better than standing! Don't you think?" he amended her doubt.

A quick look at the perforated wall prompted an automatic head nod from her.

"I'm just processing my first shootout," she retaliated amicably, realizing deep down she was in good hands.

Brian leaned down and kissed the bandage on her neck and then fixed his thoughtful gaze on her.

"There's one more thing I've got to do before the cleanup team gets here," he announced as he plucked Sergio's phone off the table.

Brian dialed the special ops number Alysha had given him that connected to POTUS using Sergio's phone.

"What are you doing?" Lisa asked, wondering what he was up to.

Brian motioned for her to be quiet by bringing his index finger up to his lips.

"Yes, Sergio. What is it?" came the gruff voice over the phone each of them knew very well.

"Raymond, this isn't Sergio," Brian clarified in a firm, even voice, showing his disdain for the man who still held the top political office in the land.

"Who is this?" barked POTUS.

"It's the agent you just tried to have killed! I'd let you speak to Sergio, but he's a little incapacitated right now, because he's dead!" Brian snapped, trying his best to cool his rage. "However, don't take my word for it. You might want to speak to a witness," he badgered, handing the phone to Lisa.

"Why, hello, you piece of shit. This is Eleanor. You know, one of the ones you threw under the bus to protect your sorry ass. I witnessed your boy take on a few rounds of metal this evening. You're going to have to find someone else to do your dirty work!"

"The two of you got lucky tonight," came POTUS's brusque reply. "I'm ..."

"You're going to call off your hyenas," Brian interrupted, "and here's why! If anything happens to Eleanor or her son ... or any of the ladies who helped the Pitt woman or their families ... or any members of her team that bested the best you could throw at them ... I'm going to come for you and kill you! And, by the way, I'm taking tonight very personally! You wanted me dead, and you didn't care who else got hurt. Someone I love dearly was injured tonight. You're not going to get that chance again—ever!"

"Are you threatening me?" POTUS exploded.

"I'm serving notice. I'm promising you, and you damn sure know I keep my promises."

"Sounds like a threat to me!"

"Your life, your future is in your hands, Raymond."

"It's Mr. President to you!" POTUS was showing his arrogance.

"It hasn't been Mr. President for quite some time. You don't deserve the title. You never have. You can live tomorrow or die today. Those are the constraints you'll be living under the rest of your pathetic life."

"You think I'm afraid of you?"

"Yes … I know you are. I've just eliminated your number one henchman, your firewall! If any of the people I just named stub their toe the wrong way, or have an unexplained accident, or get threatening phone calls, or sneeze because they got near the stench of one of your goons who got too close—I'm coming for you. So help me God, I'm coming for you."

"You think mighty high of yourself, don't you?"

"We're done here!" Brian countered and hung up.

"Did you mean what you said?" Lisa asked, rising so she stood face-to-face with Brian.

Brian raised one eyebrow and lowered the other, and then he broke their eye contact and smashed Sergio's phone on the hardwood floor, before renewing his eye contact.

"You said someone you love dearly was injured tonight. Were you talking about me?"

He grinned at her hopefulness and cupped her face in both his hands.

"Yes, most definitely … most, most definitely, I was referring to you!" he acquiesced and planted a kiss on her slightly parted lips.

"But I fired you. I sent you to the CIA's version of Siberia. I told you I never wanted to see you again."

"You were a woman caught up in some pretty serious damage control with an ogre for a boss, who met an appealing, covert government operative on the cusp of a divorce, who kissed you a few times and made promises you didn't believe …"

"Well that young government operative and I did more than kiss," she notched his sentence to clarify their tempestuous relationship.

"Both of us are different people now. We've both grown. We've still got a few rough edges, but I think we could create a wonderful life together."

"Me, too!"

A knock at the door told them the cleanup crew had arrived.

"Lisa, go into the bedroom and stay there until they leave. The less people who see you here the better. I probably don't know these guys, so I'm not familiar with their interagency connections."

"Good idea. That's another thing I love about you... can I call you *Mi armor*? I love your thoroughness!"

"Mi armor's fine. I like that. Now scoot!"

Lisa stopped at the hallway entrance before ducking down the hallway.

"I'd like some of your thoroughness in here after they leave," she announced, raising her eyebrows so they disappeared under her bangs.

"You want me to be thorough, huh?" he sent her a quick wink.

"That's my invitation!" she teased as she put her hands on her hips and marched seductively toward the master bedroom.

Wow, Brian thought to himself as he opened the front door to let the cleaning team in, who quickly walked past him. *Wow!* Her invitation popped into his mind again as he watched the thoroughness of Alysha's team.

Chapter Twenty-Four

"Who wants to begin?" Andre asked, as he accepted an after-dinner coffee from Gabby, who looked radiantly luscious with her stylishly-cut, shoulder-length blonde hair that framed her angelic face, and wearing the white blouse buttoned to the throat he had bought her. The only jewelry she wore was the diamond-studded Eiffel Tower necklace that he had bought her for her birthday two years ago.

"I do!" chorused Peaches, who had changed her pre-dessert casual clothing, too. Her eyes were aglow with the anticipation that comes from starting a completely different life. She was wearing a low-cut, ivory-colored silk blouse that was adorned with dozens of appliquéd Eiffel Towers. Gabby had given it to her the week before, and this was the first time she had worn it. Her earrings were also miniature Eiffels and the bracelets that jingled musically on her tanned wrists had also been gifted to her from Gabby. She was wearing tight-fitting jeans though, with the holes in the knees as her trademark frayed accessories.

"Gabby," she began, subconsciously fondling her Parisian earrings, "I am so proud to look like you—well, almost. You're blonde now and I'm a redhead!" she smiled her delight at their choice of hairdos. "Our clone status means we're twin status, and Emma," she looked admiringly—lovingly—at the woman whose daughter's tragedy started Gabby's four-year quest. "I'm just as proud to be Monica Proxmire's twin."

Emma's moist eyes sparkled with compassion and heartfelt fondness for a young lady who had had her youthfulness accelerate into a maturity that belied her age.

"As you know," Peaches addressed the group as a whole. "Mother and I have decided to live in Paris next door to Alex … Is it okay if I say it?" she looked at Gabby, who was beaming.

Gabby nodded her head and chanced a quick glance at Andre, who was also nodding his head.

"We're going to live next door to Alexa—that's Gabby's new name—and Andre. Everyone knows they're going back to Paris, too! Right?"

Getting collusive looks around the table, she continued.

"Thanks to Marge and Alexa and Andre, I've been accepted at the *Université Pierre et Marie Curie* to major in medicine and epigenetics in the Spring. I plan to add a considerable amount of coursework in transpersonal psychology and MetaSpirituality, too. As you know, I'm a fan of two Unity ministers in Durham, North Carolina who coined the term MetaSpirituality, which combines science and spirituality. They assured us …" she paused to gauge Alexa's okay, which came immediately, "They assured us that all of us clones have human souls, that we are spiritual beings who are housed in physical human bodies like everyone else!"

She bit her lips and leaned her head slightly forward to hide her embarrassment for being so vociferous, but was immediately thrilled with the applause she received from everyone gathered at the table.

"Thank you, thank you all," she repeated, as the group applauded her again.

"Well, I'll go next, since Peach … I mean Sophie, started our roundtable sharing," Sandra anted up. "Honey, I'm surprised you didn't tell them the name you chose."

"I forgot," her daughter cracked an embarrassing smile.

"Peaches … Monica Henry ... is now officially Sophie Bardot," Sandra announced, "and I'm Mrs. Simone Bardot."

The group ratified her announcements with raucous table tapping and hoots of *Sophieeee, Simooone .... Sophieeee, Simooone!*

"We're leaving for Paris this weekend with Alexa and Andre Rousseau. I'll let one of them explain about their shared name, and ... no, they're not married yet. They're going to get hitched in Paris!

"Alexa Rousseau ... Andre Rousseau ... Alexa Rousseau ... Andre Rousseau ..." the group chorused in unison. *"Alexa ... Andre ... Alexa ...Andre ..."*

"I'm going to open an exotic and endangered plant shop and spend all of my time saving 125 of the world's weirdest, most stunning, powerfully medicinal, mysterious, and magical plants. It'll be filled with exotic flora like the Rafflesia, Venus Fly Trap, Green Pitcher, Baseball Plant, Tacca Chantrieri, Titan Arum, Marijuana—yes, Marijuana.

"They're very medicinal, you know. And dozens of other plants. My greenhouse will be state-of-the-art and my shop will be the garden center of France! There you have it!" she smiled and listened to the howls and hoots of her supporters.

"I guess I'll go next," Rita volunteered, glancing at the other end of the table where a cadre of her colleagues were sitting. "Okay if I speak for us?" she asked.

"Yes, of course," they chorused, thrilled at having a spokesperson.

"Frank and his parents, Michael and Janet, his brother Paul, Jack, Hank, Steve and I have decided to stay on at Zeus' Den."

The rest of the group looked like they thought that might happen, especially since both of Frank's parents—and Apollo, of course—had taken up residence there.

"We talked about this again last night when the rest of you were asleep. We'd like to found a healing center for war vets and their families that will fill in the gaps left by our broken Veterans Affairs system, and that includes homeless veterans and women and minority veterans.

"We're going to make sure veterans don't have to wait for care. The men and women who serve our country shouldn't have to go without the medical treatment and medicines they need ..." she paused to compose herself. "We've already got a mascot," she nodded in Apollo's direction, "and Michael has been courting billionaire donors to get us started. And as you know, the Marinos have 80 acres here to build on."

She paused to wipe her forehead with her dinner napkin and looked at her co-founders.

"Do you-all have anything to add?"

"Yes," Frank spoke up. "The Colonel is going to become the Hospital Administrator and my mother has agreed to serve as Director of Nursing until we can find someone to fill the position permanently … Steve, you want to tell them about your position?"

Steve finished taking a swallow of his unsweetened tea and placed the glass on the table.

"I plan to open an onsite medical concierge service to work in conjunction with the hospital's emergency care services. We'll service the upper class, who will finance the concierge services, but we'll offer concierge medicine to vets cost-free!"

As if on cue, everyone at the table stood to applaud the team's dedication to service men and women.

"Dad. Mom. Paul. Hank. You have anything to say?" Frank continued, wanting to include anyone who had something to say.

"Just that we're proud to have raised two sons who have hearts of gold and nerves of steel," Janet eulogized, reaching for Michael's hand. "We always felt you boys would make a major contribution to the world. And you have already! You've also surrounded yourselves with some very extraordinary people. Michael and I feel honored to be in your presence," she finished, letting the joy and admiration she felt for everyone present lower her back into her chair.

The tumultuous applause caught her by surprise, even though she had participated in the previous adulations that had marked the group's appreciation for each other's aspirations.

The extra-volumed round of applause got Apollo standing on his hind legs with his front paws on Michael's lap.

"Oh, do you have something to say, old fella?" Michael teased.

ARRROOOOOOO! came Apollo's vintage beagle yelp.

"Looks like he wants to add a comment," Rita acknowledged light-heartedly.

"No, I think he wants to pee," Michael said, getting up to let Apollo out into the fenced-in yard.

The group laughed at Michael's levity and at Apollo's disciplined predicament.

Michael opened the door for his appreciative canine and returned to his seat at the table.

Marge remembered the border collie Monica had grown up with and how she had always wanted to take Tippy for walks. Even as young as four years old Monica made sure Tippy was fed and watered. Marge smiled her remembrance of Monica's penchant for taking care of others.

"I'll go next, if it's okay with you two?" she asked, gesturing toward the Rousseaus.

Her daughter nodded, giving her mother the floor.

Marge got up from her seat, a little wobbly at first, but up nonetheless.

"I came in here this evening without a wheelchair," she began, feeling very proud of herself, and stood there as the applause filled the room. "And, as life-threatening as the accident was that put me in three hospitals ..." she blunted her own explanation and made eye contact with Steve, "I'm counting what you've done here, at Zeus' Den, as one of those hospitals," she smiled.

"And I want to say that the love you've all shown me has helped me heal much faster ... And I've survived another, more self-imposed, life-threatening illness. I was an alcoholic for fifty years. I attribute that alcoholism to the depression I experienced —and my not wanting to get help for it—from a gut-wrenching, abusive marriage ... Emma, Sandr ... I mean Simone, you two know who I'm referring to!"

Marge motioned for her daughter Alexa to help her return to her seat.

"Are you okay, Mother?"

Marge nodded. "I just need to sit."

She took a sip of water before she continued her personal testimony.

"As I was saying, I *was* an alcoholic. I emphasize *was* because the two Unity ministers Sophie pointed out earlier this evening told her—and she told me—that what follows 'I am' follows you! So, whenever I say 'I am' I want to make sure that the next word is a positive word, because that's what I want to have—positive, life-enriching things happen to me!"

She paused for a moment, appearing to be in deep thought.

"You know, as a member of Alcoholics Anonymous, I always thought having to say 'I am an alcoholic' was a bit odd. Now, I know why. AA was asking us to affirm we were alcoholics! I refer to myself now as a recovered alcoholic! With the exception of that forced alcohol from those government goons, I'm celebrating almost three years and eight months of sobriety!"

The group applauded her with table taps and foot stomps.

"Am I taking too much time Andre?" she sought his assurance.

"No, you go right ahead," he confirmed, winking at her and smiling at Alexa, who was beaming with admiration for her mother.

"I'm saying all of this to say—I'm going to live in a mother-in-law's suite in Paris with my daughter and her soon-to-be husband ..." she broke into another smile, "and I'm going to finish my psychoanalysis degree so I can help women suffering from depression."

There was more table tapping and foot stomping.

"I'm not too old to complete my degree and set up a clinical practice ... So, *ce n'est jamais trop tard!* That's French for 'It's never too late!' That's what these two have taught me," she looked lovingly at Alexa and Andre.

Alexa interlocked her fingers and brought them up to her own lips, appreciating her mother's praise and her mother's desire to finish what she had started thirty years ago.

Marge, with her daughter's willing assistance, stood up again.

"I'm keeping my first name. I like Marge! But I'm changing my last name to Proxmire, in honor of Emma's daughter, Monica.

The respectful silence in the room and Marge's emotional announcement mirrored the silent tears which welled-up in Emma's eyes.

The group's quiet repose made Apollo's loud scratching at the door obvious.

"Oh, I forgot he was out there," Michael's apology was muted by the group's well-mannered gaiety.

Apollo entered with his tail wagging and his tongue hanging out of his mouth, enjoying his rescue. He made his way over to his water dish and his lapping up the water, accompanied by his dog tag hitting the stainless steel dish, brought smiles from the group.

Sorry, Janet mouthed Michael's and her apology, but the group saw the beagle's antics as the levity they needed to honor the transition from Marge's soulful announcement to the group's continued dialogue.

Marge sat down on her own this time and waved off the tenderhearted stares that wondered if she wanted to continue.

After a tactful pause, Emma rose from her chair.

"I want to say how touched I am by your tribute, Marge … I … I … That means so much to me!"

The women exchanged the respectful looks mothers give to mothers.

"I, too, am keeping my first name. Years ago, I changed my married name to my maiden name, but now I see the need to change it again for my own safety and yours. I'm adopting Carlyle for my last name, because it was the last name of the boy I first fell in love with in kindergarten."

The group hooted and hollered respectfully.

"And a name change is fitting," she continued, "because I'm definitely a different person now! Your influence … All of you, have caused me to take a closer look at who I am and what I want to be … and what I can be! Monica … Gabby … Alexa, when I first met you in Baltimore I felt a connection with you that I had only felt with my Monica. And I think I told you that then."

Alexa nodded in remembrance.

"I've had a chance to see what kind of person my Monica might have been through you! I know the two of you are completely different people, even though you share the same DNA ... And that applies to you, too, Sophie !" Emma smiled.

She paused to make eye contact with everyone in the group.

"That tells me that our DNA—and even the DNA we share—doesn't define, or limit, who we really are. As you all know, I've been thinking about the difference between religion and spirituality a lot lately. Religion, in my opinion, focuses on a God 'out there' and spirituality recognizes the God in here, our Divine Nature," she put her hand over her heart. "So, I want to teach that! And I think the route I'm going to take is the New Thought route.

"*Ce n'est jamais trop tard!* It's not too late for me either!" she waved off their applause. "I want to become an ordained minister and renew my oil painting talent. I want to paint angels, you know, our spirit sponsors! I'll probably start ministerial school online, because I'm not sure where I want to live."

She reached for a glass of water, but settled for the unsweetened tea Hank handed her.

"I know it isn't Baltimore. I was alone there, until Monic ... Alexa changed my life," she confessed, smiling at Alexa. "And I want to be near you. You're my family ..."

"Live with us," Rita redirected Emma's thought process. "Be our chaplain!"

"Yes! Stay at the Den with us," Frank dittoed.

"It's an invitation from all of us," Paul agreed. "Besides, I've ... we've grown accustomed to your fantastic cheese and chocolate soufflés!"

ARRROOOO voted Apollo, as he moved up beside her and licked her fingers.

"That does it!" agreed Janet. "If you'll have us, we'd love to have you! You're being here would simplify the yearly ... quarterly visits with our Paris contingent. None of us would have to run around the country to see each other—just here to Paris and Paris to here!"

Emma's tears told them she needed a group hug, so the table cleared, and everyone gathered around her to do a proper, expanded bear hug.

"You staying?" Janet pitched.

Emma nodded and sighed her consent, prompting another rendition of a huge group hug. Everyone returned to their seats except Apollo, who decided to camp out under the table in front of Emma's seat.

"Looks like you two are up," Frank announced to Alexa and Andre.

"You want to go first?" Alexa asked Andre.

Andre shook his head, "No, you go," and smiled as his fiancée stood, placing her long red fingertips on the table.

"I love you guys! I continue to be amazed that there are spiritual beings like you who come into skin school to help humanity live up to its potential. It is my privilege to be a part of your family. I like my new name change. Alexa, which is short for Alexandra, means 'protector of humankind.' That's one reason why I chose it. The other reason is, it's the sobriquet for Alexandra, which is the Greek Goddess Hera's cosmic genealogy," she explained, hoping they wouldn't think she was too far out.

Andre placed his hand over her hand and squeezed it softly, assuring her what she was saying was important.

"Andre will say a little more about it, but we've co-founded The Global Center for Human Rights. Our motto will be 'Justice Delayed is Justice Denied.' There are hundreds of civil rights and human rights organizations worldwide, but our focus will be on the disenfranchised.

"We will represent those who have suffered grave abuses to their basic human rights, and demand justice for those who have been marginalized by society's rich and powerful, but also mistreated by the general populace in every country who blindly perpetuate the disenfranchisement, because of their disinterest and lack of compassion for those who are disabled, differently-abled, or just plain different ..." she stopped herself, realizing she was talking to the choir.

Andre pointed at her from his sitting position, indicating his pride in her unbridled enthusiasm.

"We want to mobilize worldwide public opinion and public conscience!" she continued. "We'll speak out against and expose those who traffic in child abuse, in all of it's forms; genocide; polygamy; slavery; unconscionable medical experimentation like human cloning; war crimes; hate groups; rape; early marriage …" she stopped to take a breath.

"We're going to stop the barbaric acts of sexual exploitation and harassment; dowry abuse that leads to killing brides to get their dowries; intentional poverty; oppressive political regimes; black market organ trading; torture; imprisonment without due process; deprivation of medical care…" she took Andre up on his offer to wet her whistle.

"The pharmaceutical monopolizing of prescription drugs that leads to cost-prohibiting drug prices; enforced sterilization; and discrimination against gay and lesbian groups, and gender preferences has got to stop!"

She shot Andre a facial expression that said: *Oops, I'm talking too long, aren't I?*

He simply smiled and mouthed, *I'm proud of you, Babe,* and encouraged her to continue.

"The magnitude of these horrific violations demands drastic measures and concrete actions by people of conscience who refuse to allow the abuses to continue! Credible efforts are being made to stop these abuses, but progress is slow, excruciatingly slow, mind-blowingly slow! Why? Because not enough people want to step up—like you-all have—risking life and limb, and comfortable lifestyle."

She tossed Andre another embarrassing look and started to sit, but he put his hand on her buttock, insisting that she continue.

"I know I'm talking to the choir, but despite the presence of, and heroic efforts of, international watchdogs, basic human rights continue to be taken away, or not even given, in the name of preposterous communal discrimination, religious fundamentalism, and outrageous racial discrimination!"

One of her patented smiles migrated across her angelic face. She had spent herself! Her enthusiastic delivery had taken its course. Whatever she was going to say next, didn't make it from her gray matter to her speaking voice.

She steepled her hands in front of her nose, lowered herself in her chair, and sighed a sigh of contentment.

The group table-tapped her passionate human rights pitch and waited for Andre to sum up the evening.

Andre got up and positioned himself behind his fiancée, placing his hands on her shoulders.

"It's been important for all of us to share with one another how we're going to use what has happened to us for our own growth, and for the betterment of humankind. I know we've all heard bits and pieces of each other's plans during the last couple of weeks, but it was nice to hear those decisions and plans in a concise evening setting."

He gently squeezed Alexa's shoulders and then kissed the top of her head.

"I don't know what I'd do without this lady," he squeezed her shoulders again, prompting her to cover both of his hands with hers, "but I know what I'm going to do with her!" he confessed, kissing the top of her head again. "I'm going to make sure we live happily and healthily ever after together, and make the world a better place for our having met here."

He showered his gaze over the entire group.

"Il est jamais trop tard pour bein faire!" he rattled off in French. "It's never too late to do good!"

He waited while Apollo, who had freed himself from under the table, lapped up some more water.

"Suppose we make this Christmas our first reunion?" he proposed.

"Joyeux noël, il est! Merry Christmas, it is!" Andre followed up his proposal.

ARRROOOOO! Apollo voiced his opinion.

"That's dog talk for *Joyeux noël, il est!"* Alexa confirmed!

About the Author

Bil Holton is not just a novelist! He has been writing, speaking, teaching, and publishing for over 30 years, and brings quite a background of experience and depth of knowledge to his work.

In 1984, he and his wife, Cher, founded The Holton Consulting Group, Inc., which is still alive and well today! They work with clients in the U.S., Canada, Germany, England, and South America, with a mission of creating extraordinary leaders and engaged employees. Their impressive client list includes Fortune 100 companies, healthcare facilities, universities, associations, and government agencies.

In addition to Bil's novels, Bil and Cher have authored and co-co-authored over 50 titles, including business books such as *The Manager's Short Course to a Long Career*, which was selected by SoundView Executive Summaries as one of their Top 30 Business Books, and spiritual books including *New Metaphysical Versions of Matthew, Mark, Luke, John,* and *Revelation*—the first ever verse-by-verse metaphysical interpretations of these books.

When he isn't involved in work and research, Bil enjoys golf, travel, jigsaw puzzles, the theatre, and landscaping. The Holtons like to push the envelop and maintain their zest for life by taking what they call "Indiana Jones Adventures," such as white-water rafting, sky diving, and fire walking. American-style ballroom dancing is also in their DNA. Although they have retired their competitive dance shoes, Bil and Cher love to perform ballroom showcases and exhibitions. Their two sons, beautiful daughters-in-law, and incredible grandchildren all live nearby. Their visits are always joyful.

To learn more about Bil, order books, and contact him for
speaking appearances and book signings,
visit Bil's novelist site: BilHolton.com
Like his Facebook Fan Page at

Other novels by Bil Holton

Silent Echoes

Ultimate Betrayal

Twist of Fate

www.ingramcontent.com/pod-product-compliance
Lightning Source LLC
Chambersburg PA
CBHW071055250626
47159CB00002B/473